SHATTERED VEIL

A CALLUM MACLEOD ADVENTURE

I0590395

K. A. BEAULIEU

A HIGHLANDER FICTION

PORTHOS PRESS
© 2025

PORTHOS
PRESS
Since 2023

Shattered Veil

Published by **Porthos Press**.
Porthos Press is an independent publishing imprint dedicated to original works of
science fiction, fantasy, adventure, and non-fiction.

For information regarding permissions, licensing, or bulk orders, please contact
Porthos Press at:

PORTHOS
PRESS

Porthos Press
www.porthospress.com

ISBN:
Paperback: 9798994047750
Hardcover: 979-8-9940477-0-5

Cover Design: *K.A.Beaulieu*
Photographs: Adobe Stock

First Edition: **2025**

10 9 8 7 6 5 4 3 2 1

1

AI DISCLOSURE STATEMENT

Portions of the preliminary **outlining and structural development** of this work were assisted by artificial intelligence tools. These tools were used **only in a support capacity**, specifically for brainstorming, organizing narrative beats, and refining the broad conceptual framework prior to drafting.

All prose, characters, worldbuilding, dialogue, thematic development, and creative storytelling presented in this novel are the sole work of the author.

Every chapter, scene, description, emotional arc, and narrative element was written, revised, and crafted by hand. No generative AI systems were used to produce the text of the novel itself.

This is a work of fiction.

Names, characters, places, and events are products of the author's imagination, and any resemblance to actual persons, living or dead, is purely coincidental. This story exists within a fictional mythos and draws from longstanding fantasy traditions while presenting fully original interpretations, plotlines, and characters.

AI was not used to:

- generate character identities or personal histories
- write chapters, dialogue, or narrative prose
- create emotional arcs or relationship dynamics
- design unique mythological elements or fictional technologies
- produce àny of the creative content within the final manuscript

Any suggestions or brainstorming support generated during the initial outlining phase were substantially transformed, expanded, or reinterpreted by the author and do not represent AI-authored content.

The finished novel reflects the **creative vision, interpretation, craftsmanship, and originality of K. A. Beaulieu**, supported by traditional drafting, revision, and editorial techniques.

ACKNOWLEDGEMENTS

Shattered Veil, Book One

Every story stands on the shoulders of the ones that came before it, and this one owes its very breath to the world first imagined by **Gregory Widen**. His vision of Immortals walking among us struggling, fighting, loving, and losing across centuries sparked a mythology that has endured for decades. I am deeply grateful for the universe he created, and for the countless storytellers who expanded it with heart, passion, and unbreakable creativity. Without their work, there would be no world to explore, reinterpret, or honor. To the actors, writers, directors, stunt teams, musicians, and creators behind every Highlander film and series: thank you. Your characters lived with such charisma and conviction that generations of fans, myself included, carried them forward in our imaginations. The echoes of your artistry shaped the foundations of this book.

To the long-standing **Highlander fandom**, the dreamers, theorists, collectors, and sword-wielding convention-goers who kept the flame alive, your enthusiasm proves that myth never dies. You are living proof that a good story doesn't age; it evolves.

To the writers, editors, and friends who read early pages, endured late-night brainstorming sessions, and gently reminded me that mortals eventually need sleep: your support kept these chapters alive. Your honesty sharpened every scene. Your encouragement pulled me across every finish line.

To those closest to me, family, friends, mentors, thank you for your patience as I disappeared into Callum MacLeod's world for hours, days, and sometimes entire weekends. Creating this book meant wandering through centuries, sword in hand, heart occasionally in pieces. Thank you for understanding the pull of that journey.

To the real-world professionals who unknowingly shaped certain scenes, pilots, surgeons, researchers, engineers, and history enthusiasts, your expertise grounded this story's wildest moments, giving it weight where it needed it most.

And finally, to *you*, the reader.

Thank you for stepping into this world with me.

Thank you for trusting these characters enough to follow them through storms, secrets, betrayals, and battles both ancient and modern.

Thank you for believing that new stories can still be written in old worlds, so long as they are crafted with respect, imagination, and a little bit of lightning.

No matter how far this series goes, this book, the first spark, exists because of your willingness to turn the page.

There are more stories ahead.
More Immortals.
More mysteries.
More battles worthy of the Quickening.

Until then, thank you, truly.

K. A. Beaulieu

Dedication

For my wife —

thank you for loving me through every quirk, every late-night writing session, and every moment when my reclusive nature made life a little stranger.

Your patience, humor, and constant support made this book possible.

I love you more than words on any page could ever say.

Prologue

The Highlands wore the storm like an ancient cloak, heavy, battered, and humming with quiet anger.

Wind screamed across the ridgelines, dragging sheets of rain sideways as if trying to flay the land itself. The night sky was a boiling bruise of cloud and lightning, crackling above the solitary military outpost perched on the shoulder of Ben Craeg. The mountain had endured centuries of winter wars, clan feuds, forgotten rebellions, and storms that crushed entire ships along the coast. But tonight's tempest felt different. The old mountain seemed to *listen*.

Inside the primary operations cabin, Staff Sergeant John Drummond rubbed his temples, blinking at the terminal screens that had begun to flicker again.

The outpost wasn't much to look at: chipped gray walls, a humming rack of classified resonance monitors, battered desks, and a heater that wheezed more than it warmed. The Scottish Ministry of Defense referred to the assignment as "electromagnetic vigilance duty." John called it purgatory.

A fresh gust rattled the cabin door.

John muttered, "Place feels like it'll slide off the mountain before Christmas."

He took a sip of lukewarm tea and leaned back in his chair. The

1

internal clock above the doorway blinked past 2200 hours, though the storm made it feel much later.

He checked the perimeter camera feeds, grainy, black-and-white images of empty hills and rock faces. Nothing moved beyond the dancing static of rainfall.

He was alone for the night shift; the two other enlisted staff had rotated out for satellite relay diagnostics in the lower chamber. He would be relieved in four hours. Until then, it would be tea, boredom, and praying the generator didn't die.

He reached for a biscuit.

The console chirped.

John blinked.

Another chirp. Sharper this time. Urgent.

He set the biscuit down and leaned forward.

On the main screen, a resonance waveform was rising, slow at first, then climbing sharply like a needle hitting the red on an old radio dial.

"Now then," he murmured, "what's roused your interest?"

He straightened.

"Control, this is Craeg Outpost Two. I'm seeing a deviation on channel four. Please confirm."

Static replied.

John frowned. He tapped the comm again.

"Control, respond."

Nothing.

The hairs on his forearms lifted.

A low vibration crawled through the floor. Not enough to topple anything, just a pulse, subtle but unmistakable, like the mountain inhaling.

Lightning rippled across the sky.

The waveform surged.

A klaxon blared, a sharp, metallic cry he'd never heard in his three months stationed here.

ANOMALY LEVEL: SEVERE.
FREQUENCY: UNKNOWN ORIGIN.
SOURCE VECTOR: INTERNAL TO REGION.
AMPLIFICATION RATE: ACCELERATING.

The waveform peaked, stalled,
, and then rose again, twice as fast.

John typed commands, but the screens struggled to keep up. "Jesus... c'mon, give me something."

Another pulse shivered through the cabin. The lights dimmed, brightened, then dimmed again.

His stomach knotted.

It wasn't an earthquake. He had lived through plenty of those back home near Stirling. This was measured, rhythmic. Almost like -

THRUM.

- something *alive.*

John swallowed hard, "Right, definitely not normal."

He reached for the emergency comm unit. It crackled, spat static, then died in his hand.

The main lights flickered once more, then failed altogether. Darkness swallowed the operations cabin.

The only illumination came from the storm outside and the dying glow of the consoles. In that brief flicker of light, John saw his breath.

The temperature had dropped ten degrees in seconds.

He backed away from the console, bumping into his chair.

A pressure built behind his eyes, subtle at first, then forming a tight band across his skull. He felt something brushing against his awareness, a presence that did not belong in the realm of physics he understood. Something ancient, vast, and impatient.

The mountain seemed to whisper around him.

Another pulse ripped through the cabin.

THRUMMMM.

Every window shattered inward.

John ducked instinctively as the storm's roar burst into the room. Papers and glass whipped through the air. Wind clawed at every loose object. The vibrations knocked him onto one knee.

And then, just as suddenly, Silence.

A suffocating silence.

John rose slowly, staring at the empty window frames. The storm continued outside, but its sound no longer reached him. It was as if the cabin sat in a bubble of muted air.

He took one step toward the doorway, when he heard it.

A footstep behind him.

John turned toward the door.

The reinforced steel door was opening. The locking mechanism didn't groan or resist; it simply yielded, as though the forces holding it shut had decided, quietly, to step aside.

A figure stepped inside.

Tall. Broad-shouldered. Wearing a black coat that should have been soaked through from the storm, yet sat on him as if untouched by weather. His hair, dark, shoulder length, rain-matted, framed a face carved with austere precision. A face that should have been ordinary but was unmistakably wrong in some deep, instinctive way.

His eyes were the most unsettling part. Pale gray. Focused. Too focused. The eyes of someone who had long ago stopped being surprised by anything this world could offer.

He looked around the cabin, taking in the shattered glass, the dead monitors, the spiral-etched waveform still fading across the central screen.

Then he spoke.

"Impressive," he said softly. "Your primitive instruments felt the echo."

John lifted his chin.

"This is a restricted installation. State your name."

The stranger's gaze settled on him, calm, deliberate, and somehow final.

"You may call me Renwick," he said.

The name meant nothing to John. Yet something about the way the man said it carried the gravity of a storm front.

John tried to keep his voice firm. "You're trespassing on Ministry grounds. I need you to step outside and wait while I, "

Renwick took one step forward.

John fell silent.

The man's presence pressed against him like a gale. It wasn't hostility. It wasn't aggression. It was inevitability.

Renwick's eyes drifted toward the central console. "You recorded the pulse. Good." His tone suggested the equipment had only one possible purpose: to serve him.

4

John's heartbeat hammered in his ears. "What pulse?"

Renwick ignored the question.

He reached out and brushed his fingertips along the shattered monitor, almost affectionately. The edges of the glass trembled under his touch.

"The Veil stirs," Renwick murmured. "After so long lying dormant. A wound has begun to open."

He turned toward John. "And the world will feel its pain."

John stepped sideways, placing a hand subtly near the emergency lockbox where a sidearm was secured.

"Hear me clearly," John said, trying to anchor himself with procedure and training. "You need to stand down and wait for security personnel."

Renwick's lips curled upward, not quite a smile, more a faint acknowledgment of futility.

"You believe you have security."

John's hand tightened on the lockbox latch. "I do."

"No," Renwick said gently. "You don't."

The lockbox clicked open. John gripped the sidearm.

But he never drew it.

Renwick was beside him, movement faster than John's eye could track or his mind could process. A single smooth motion. A hand closing over John's wrist, disarming him with the ease of plucking a leaf from a branch.

"How, ?" The question barely left his throat.

"There are forces older than your governments," Renwick said. "Older than your wars. Older than your science."

He placed the sidearm on the table as though returning a borrowed tool.

"Tonight marks the end of their slumber."

John backed away. His pulse raced. His mind fought to rationalize the impossible speed he had just witnessed.

"You...you're Enhanced? Special forces?" He searched for something to anchor his terror. "Augmented? Something?"

Renwick's expression softened, not with warmth, but with pity.

"No. I am not *augmented.* I am not *modified.* I simply am." He tilted his head. "You humans have so many words to avoid the truth."

K. A. Beaulieu

He moved closer. John stumbled until his back hit the console.

"What truth?" John asked in an inaudible tone.

Renwick leaned forward, eyes gleaming with old fire.

"That you are temporary."

John's breath caught.

"And I," Renwick said, "am not."

He placed two fingers against John's forehead.

Electric blue energy crackled at the touch, thin, jagged tendrils of power that danced across Renwick's skin like living lightning.

John screamed.

Memories tore loose. Visual impressions flashed, screens, numbers, geographic overlays. Renwick sifted through them with surgical precision, peeling back moments until he found what he wanted.

The waveform. The timestamp. The exact direction of the pulse.

Renwick's eyelids fluttered.

"There," he whispered to himself. "So it begins."

John's legs gave out. Renwick let him fall with casual detachment.

John lay gasping on the floor, clutching his head, vision spinning. He managed one question.

"What... are you...?"

Renwick considered him thoughtfully.

"A harbinger," he said. "And soon, something more."

The cabin lights flickered weakly. Sparks trailed from the ceiling panel. Renwick walked to the broken window, lifting his face toward the storm.

Across the highlands, the clouds swirled around a point of light flickering behind the stormfront, something invisible to ordinary eyes, yet bright as a beacon to him.

"The Veil weakens," he said. "The Game awakens. And the next age begins."

He stepped out through the shattered frame, descending into the storm without hesitation.

The moment his figure disappeared into the rain, sound returned, wind screaming, thunder rolling, the world's noise flooding violently back in.

Inside the cabin, John Drummond tried to draw breath.

He would not get another.

The final pulse shook the outpost.

THRUMMMMMMMMM,

The entire structure trembled. Lights burst. Steel groaned.

Then came silence.

A silence so complete that even the mountain held its breath.

The storm swallowed Renwick's silhouette almost immediately, but the disturbance he left behind lingered like static caught in the air. The shattered cabin crackled with fading energy. A faint ozone scent rolled through the room, mingling with the cold breath of the highland wind.

For several long moments after Renwick vanished over the ridge, the only sound was John Drummond's labored breathing. He lay half-curled against the broken console, his body trembling with the aftershock of what had torn through him. The air felt heavy, as if pressure from some great unseen ocean pressed down on the mountain.

Then the world snapped back.

Rain slammed against the broken windows. Wind roared in like a vengeful spirit. The lights flickered once. Twice.

And went dead.

John managed to lift his head. His vision swam. Every nerve in his body screamed, but something inside whispered for him to *hold on*. He didn't know why. Instinct, maybe. Training. Or perhaps something older, some ancestral survival impulse born from centuries of Highlanders refusing to die easily.

His hand inched toward the emergency beacon again. Maybe it would work now.

He never reached it.

A final wave of resonance rolled through the cabin.

Not a pulse.

A *collapse.*

The floor buckled. The remaining lights exploded. A reinforcing beam snapped, sending a cascade of metal and insulation crashing down.

John Drummond never had the chance to scream.

The mountain took him.

London, Thames House, MI5 Headquarters

The storm was a distant thing here. London's night was wet but calm, a typical slate-gray drizzle coating the windows of Thames House. Inside, the atmosphere was its usual blend of caffeine, interdepartmental tension, and the faint hum of servers that never slept.

Evelyn Shaw tapped at her keyboard; her brow furrowed beneath a curtain of dark hair pulled into a loose twist. She was an analyst in the "Unusual Resonance Task Group", a division so small and obscure most of MI5 didn't realize it existed. They handled fringe anomalies that didn't belong to any other unit: odd atmospheric echoes, satellite blips, unexplained energy bursts. Usually, it amounted to miscalibrated equipment or distant nuclear tests.

Tonight was different.

She zoomed in on the data streaming across her screen.

"What in God's name…"

A sharp spectral spike had erupted over the Scottish Highlands. Not like the usual lightning interference. It carried a pattern, almost fractal in its complexity, rippling in concentric rings.

She flagged it, pulling cross-sensor feeds.

The seismic monitors at Ben Craeg outpost had gone offline.

She typed into her mic.

"Outpost Two isn't responding. Are we in contact with them?"

A voice crackled through the line.

"Negative, Evelyn. Last ping was ninety seconds ago."

She ran a diagnostic.

"Then something tripped their surge defense remotely."

"Storm interference?" the voice offered weakly.

"Storms don't create recursive signal architecture." Her chair rolled back slightly as she leaned away from the screen. "This looks… intentional."

She paused.

"Patch into the satellite thermal feed."

A new window loaded.

The mountain ridge glowed.

Not from fire. Not from heat signatures she recognized.

8

It glowed with something pulsing beneath the infrared detection threshold, shifting rhythmically, like breath.

Her pulse quickened.

"Run a pattern match on all atmospheric resonance logs from the last decade."

She expected nothing.

The computer chirped.

MATCH FOUND: 1610 – ANOMALOUS PRE-INDUSTRIAL RECORD.

Evelyn stared.

"Impossible…"

Only one such record existed in the database, unearthed years ago by a historian who'd stumbled across a translated entry in a monk's chronicle, a bizarre account that described "a great trembling beneath the highlands, as if the sky wished to be born anew."

"Crossmatch it with all modern data sources," she said in a hushed voice.

Another chirp.

MATCH CONFIRMED, 98% CORRELATION.

Evelyn closed her eyes.

Something ancient had stirred again.

And nothing in MI5's protocols covered "ancestral sky-birth tremors."

She reached for the secure hotline.

"Director? Shaw here. We have a situation."

The storm bent around him.

Rain parted in sheets, avoiding his path. Thunder softened overhead, almost deferential. Renwick walked with the unhurried stride of someone who did not consider nature an obstacle.

The Pulse still hummed faintly through his veins, residual energy from a source older than civilization. Even he, with nearly nine centuries of accumulated Quickening within him, felt its vibration in his bones.

It was exhilarating.

He paused on a rocky outcrop overlooking the valley. The storm clouds churned like a cauldron, pulled toward a point of invisible tension.

"Your slumber is over," he whispered to the sky. "The Veil cannot remain closed."

He traced a gloved hand across the air, as though feeling the edge of a curtain only he could see. The world felt thin here... the boundary stretched, warped.

And the Pulse had widened it.

He allowed himself a rare moment of anticipation, something he hadn't felt since the Crusades, when the world felt vast and teeming with possibility. His voice was barely audible above the wind.

"The others will have felt it. Even the reclusive ones. He will feel it."

A flicker of disdain crossed his face.

Callum.

Always Callum.

Always the ghost of the Highlands, the man who refused power, refused leadership, refused destiny. The one who walked through centuries trying not to leave footprints.

Renwick's lip curled.

"Well," he murmured, "let him try to hide now."

He turned his face toward the night horizon.

"The Game is no longer merely survival. Evolution demands more."

Lightning flashed behind him, illuminating the scar beneath his coat, an old wound that had never fully healed, even with centuries of Quickening. He touched it absently.

"It begins," he whispered.

Somewhere in the North Atlantic, Aboard a Cargo Vessel
The ship rocked gently over dark waves. Below deck, a young Filipino deckhand named Mateo Santiago sat on a crate, tightening

the straps on a pallet. His other hand clutched a rosary.

The storm outside had been mild when he came on duty.

Then the Pulse hit.

It arrived as a pressure wave, silent and invisible, rolling across the sea like a tide of ghosts.

Mateo jerked upright, gripping the rosary tight enough to hurt.

The lights flickered. Metal creaked. A low hum vibrated through the hull.

He heard whispers.

Not from the crew.

Not from any radio.

From *inside* the metal around him, as if the ship's rivets had begun speaking in a language older than steel.

His throat tightened.

"Dios mio…"

He wasn't religious enough to hallucinate. Not that sort of man.

Yet something brushed against his consciousness, something vast, like a colossal shadow drifting beneath the surface of awareness. It felt like a presence searching. Reaching.

And then,

It *found* someone.

Mateo flinched violently. A searing sensation shot through his mind, like a string pulled taut.

He saw a flash, someone far away jolting awake in a dark room, gasping as if drowning. A man. Tall. Hair darkened by sweat. A katana case near the bed. A heartbeat drumming with the same rhythm as the Pulse itself.

The vision vanished as quickly as it came.

Mateo collapsed to his knees, panting.

"What… what was that?"

He looked around, terrified.

No one else seemed to have felt anything.

But deep ocean swells rocked the ship more violently now, as if the sea itself had been disturbed by something rising far beneath it.

Mateo made the sign of the cross, whispering, "Whatever that was… it wasn't meant for me."

He didn't know it yet, but he had witnessed the first ripple of the coming storm, an Immortal resonance traveling across oceans to the one destined to answer it.

A Remote Temple, Sister Maeve D'Arcy

Candles guttered in the dim stone chamber. Manuscripts lay spread across an ancient table, bound in leather, inked in languages the world had forgotten.

Sister Maeve D'Arcy, nearly six centuries old and long retired from the violence of Immortal duels, paused mid-step. Her fingers hovered above a parchment.

The Pulse slammed through her sanctuary like a phantom hammer.

Candles extinguished in unison. Dust spiraled upward, as if gravity momentarily loosened. Her heart hammered with the strength of ten mortal pulses.

"No..." she murmured.

The Veil screamed in her ears, silent, but unmistakable.

She steadied herself against the stone wall. The air carried the metallic taste of Immortal energy. She hadn't felt anything this powerful since the Siege of Rouen. And this was far worse.

She whispered a prayer for strength.

"For all our sakes, let this not be the beginning."

She reached for a hidden drawer beneath her desk and pulled out a weathered parchment, one she had hoped never to reference again.

A prophecy inked during a time when Immortals still believed their existence followed rules.

The last line glowed faintly with new resonance:

"When the mountain breathes lightning and the sky calls thrice, the Old Strategist rises, and the Veil shall open."

Maeve closed her eyes.

"It's happening," she uttered.

And somewhere in the storm-lashed Highlands, Renwick smiled without knowing why.

The Highlands

The storm finally began to ease, as though exhausted by its own violence. But the mountain was changed. The night was changed. Something had taken root in the world, an energy echoing across continents, threading through the ancient invisible web that bound Immortals to one another.

Far below the ridge, hidden by cliffs and mist, a faint tremor rolled through a cavern carved by centuries of wind. Moss shivered. Pebbles rattled down old stone. A forgotten sword hilt, buried in rubble, glowed faintly for a moment, its dormant resonance stirred from profound sleep.

The age of secrecy was ending.

And in another part of the world, far away, asleep in a bed overlooking a stormy coastline, a man who had avoided destiny for three centuries bolted upright with a gasp.

The Pulse had reached him.

Chapter 1

On clear days, you could stand on the bluff and watch the rockets rise. They clawed upward from the Vandenberg Space Force Base just south along the coast, bright scars against the California sky, trAilíng fire and ambition. The sound took longer to arrive, rolling up the shoreline as a low, patient growl that shook windows and rattled the bones of anyone who had not lived through artillery.

Callum MacLeod usually watched them from the balcony with a glass of water rather than whiskey. After three centuries, even spectacle had to justify its place in his routine.

Tonight, the sky held no rockets. Only clouds and the faint smear of city glow far to the north.

His estate crouched on the cliffs just beyond the base perimeter, where the coastline kinked into a series of broken, jagged teeth. From the water it appeared as a scattered collection of low-slung structures and terraced concrete, softened by coastal scrub and native grasses. From above, viewed by the satellites he quietly owned, it resembled a geometric spiral burrowed into the rock. Most of it was underground. Callum had always preferred stone and earth between him and the rest of the world.

Salt wind rushed up the cliff face and tugged at the edge of his sweatshirt. Below, the Pacific folded over itself in dark, heavy bands. White foam flashed against the rocks when the swell broke, then dissolved into blackness again.

He listened.

There was a different silence here than in the Highlands. The North Sea's sharp, cold bite had been traded for the Pacific's heavier, slower breath. But the deep rhythm was the same. Water, wind, and time, grinding away at anything that believed itself permanent.

He understood the lesson.

"Helios report," he said quietly.

A soft tone answered from the brass speaker mounted above the balcony doors. The voice that followed was clear and unobtrusive, shaped to sound neutral and a little dry.

"Good evening, Callum," it said. "Helios orbital assets are nominal. No launch activity from Vandenberg scheduled for the next twelve hours. Coastal airspace restricted to routine military traffic and commercial corridors."

Callum nodded once. The AI did not need to see the gesture to interpret it; thousands of hours of biometrics and acoustic data had taught THOTH when silence meant satisfaction.

He let his eyes move inland.

The main house was a low rectangle of dark metal and glass that hugged the bluff line rather than dominating it. Light from within was tightly controlled. A few warm rectangles glowed: the kitchen at the far end, the landing above the main stairwell, a sliver of illumination from the gym level below. Beyond that, to the north, a separate pad jutted out from the rock. A single aircraft rested there under the floodlights.

From a distance, it could have been a relic from the eighties. Sleek, predatory, with a pointed nose and distinctive tall fin. Its black paint drank in the light rather than reflecting it. The silhouette was unmistakable to anyone who had grown up with old action shows of the 1980s.

An exact replica of the Airwolf helicopter.

Callum had never bothered to correct Graham's description of it as a "midlife crisis made of carbon fiber and nostalgia." It was, strictly speaking, neither. The airframe was modeled on a Bell 222 helicopter that had never technically entered production in this configuration. The systems under its skin belonged more to Helios Dynamics patents than to any known military catalog. To the handful of engineers who had worked on it, the craft was listed only as *Project FENRIR.*

To Callum, it was simply the fastest way to get from his cliff to his jet when things went wrong.

He watched the helicopter for a long heartbeat, letting the wind sting his eyes. The aircraft sat motionless, yet it always looked ready to leap off the pad, as if bored with waiting. Out of all his toys, the FENRIR held a special place in his heart. He even added more modifications after the project had ended. The FENRIR and THOTH were his closest confidants these days. Yes, he owed Helios, but Graham ran the day-to-day organization. He mostly was a silent partner now, although he was included in every major R&D project that Helios was involved in, on and off the books. Callum prided himself in his anonymity.

"Anything else?" he asked.

"Persistent anomalies in low-frequency magnetic resonance," THOTH replied. "Currently within acceptable variance for this coastline. Do you wish a full report?"

"Not yet." He turned toward the open balcony doors. "Flag anything that climbs above three standard deviations from local baseline."

"Understood."

He stepped back into the house. The glass doors slid shut behind him with a muted hiss, muting the wind but not the distant voice of the surf. Inside, the air carried faint hints of coffee, machine oil, and the clean, sterile undertone of filtered ventilation.

The main living space was open and spare. A long sectional faced a wall of bookshelves and an embedded screen that usually showed satellite tracks or weather rather than entertainment. The shelves held physical books rather than trophies. Scottish history. Engineering manuals. Poets from nations that no longer existed. A battered leather-bound volume of clan records that might have been valuable to museums if anyone realized it was not a reproduction.

No family photos.

He crossed the hardwood floor, barefoot and silent, and paused at the far wall. A collection of blades hung there in an almost museum-like arrangement: a seventeenth-century basket-hilt broadsword, a French smallsword with worn gilding, a naval cutlass, a Japanese tachi. Each carried a quiet weight of memory.

His eyes lingered for a moment on a blank space between the tachi and the broadsword. An empty mount. Waiting.

He looked away before memory could follow.

"Time?" he asked.

"Local time is 22:47," THOTH replied.

Too late for visitors. Too early for old ghosts.

Callum moved to the stairs and descended toward the lower levels. The house perched on the bluff, but its true heart lay beneath it, carved into the rock like a bunker that had decided to reinvent itself as a research facility.

Halfway down, he passed a landing where framed photographs of aircraft lined the wall. An early British biplane, its fabric skin sagging with age. A long, sleek airship with "USS Shenandoah" stenciled on its side. A hulking World War II bomber that seemed to fill the frame. An experimental jet with classified numbers on its tail.

The photos were not labeled. He did not need labels.

In one of them, if you knew exactly where to look, a much younger Callum stood at the edge of a group of pilots, head turned away from the camera as if in mid-conversation. The date on the bottom corner had long since faded.

The stairs ended at a reinforced door scarred with subtle striations. A curved sensor strip traced the frame.

"Open lab access," he said.

"Identity confirmed," THOTH replied. The locks disengaged. "Welcome back."

The lab sprawled across what would have been three generous basements in a normal house. Here, it was a single open volume with workstations along the walls, a central cluster of freestanding consoles, and a far wall of transparent reinforced composite that looked into a smaller chamber lined with equipment racks.

Soft white light flowed across everything, tuned to something that suited his aging yet ageless eyes. The space smelled faintly of solder, plastic, and the faint copper tang of high-voltage electronics.

This was where most of Helios Dynamics' more speculative projects began. At least the ones he trusted with proximity to his living quarters. Everything else lived in anonymous office parks and leased labs across three continents, staffed by people who believed Graham Slate was the visionary behind it all.

Callum stepped up to the nearest console. As he approached, THOTH's primary interface unfolded on the main display. Not a face. Just a rotating geometric pattern that shifted based on function. Tonight it resembled an intricate Egyptian cartouche, lines and arcs intersecting in precise, evolving configurations.

"When are you going to admit you themed the UI after your namesake?" Graham had asked once, with a grin.

Callum had merely shrugged. THOTH as an acronym had been a little forced. Tactical Heuristic Omni-Threshold Hub. THOTH was the adaptive intelligence he'd built over decades. The Egyptian god of writing, knowledge, and measurement had attached itself afterward like a barnacle of meaning. Immortals tended to accumulate those.

The interface rippled. "Primary operational summary?"

"Later," he said. "I want a status check on the resonance mapping project. The global overlay, not just our local grid."

"Understood." A pause. Data flowed across the side screens. "Baseline mapping is ninety-two percent complete for all monitored zones. Remaining blind spots are either low-value regions or areas with limited sensor coverage."

He watched lines of color unfurl on a map of the world. Helios satellites. Government feeds quietly leased or borrowed from agencies that had no idea where the requests ultimately led. A mesh of sensor data superimposed across continents and oceans, each node pulsing at its own steady rhythm.

Resonance mapping had been his answer to a question no one in the modern world had formally asked: what happens at a planetary scale when one Immortal kills another, and the Quickening releases its energy?

For centuries, the answer had been "lightning, property damage, and the occasional terrified bystander." Now, with orbital platforms and sensitive instruments, the answer could be quantified.

Helios called it transient atmospheric energy events in the internal white papers. Callum and the few Immortals who knew what he was doing called it what it had always been.

Quickenings.

"What is our current detection threshold?" he asked.

"We are capable of identifying any Quickening equivalent to or greater than the average energy release of a one kiloton nuclear detonation," THOTH said calmly. "Pattern recognition has reduced false positives by seventy-three percent since last quarter."

He nodded slowly.

When he had pitched the project to himself, it had seemed like paranoia disguised as science. But the world had changed. Immortals could no longer pretend that what they did in remote ruins and alleyways disappeared without a trace. The planet was laced with sensors and eyes. If an Immortal ever decided to weaponize the Game, Callum wanted advance notice.

And tonight, while he had watched an empty sky over the Pacific, something had happened in the Highlands.

He did not know that yet.

He leaned on the console, fingertips resting on the edge. "Run a retrospective sweep for the last six hours. I want to see anything above baseline, even if it was filtered out as noise."

"That will require full stack processing," THOTH replied. "Estimated completion time, three minutes."

"Start it."

The geometric pattern folded inward, then expanded again as the system diverted power. Cooling fans deep in the racks whispered a little louder.

"And set an alert for Graham," he added. "Flag the output to his secure channel."

"Graham Slate is currently airborne," THOTH said. "Private flight from Geneva to London on Helios Nine. Do you wish to wake him?"

Callum considered it.

Graham hated being woken by AI. He complained that it set a precedent. "First it calls me at three in the morning, then it decides what kind of coffee I drink, then one day I wake up and Helios is a sentient hedge fund that has fired both of us." He had said it with a laugh, but the concern beneath it was sincere.

"Not yet," Callum said. "Queue the summary for when he lands."

"Understood."

The lab settled into a low hum of focused computation. On one of the side screens, faint bands of color began to spike and flatten as the system replayed the world's invisible tremors.

Callum stepped back from the console and rolled his shoulders. The weight there was more psychological than physical. His body felt as it had for the last two hundred years: somewhere in his mid-thirties, strong but carrying an exhaustion that no sleep could erase.

He moved to a side rack and opened a drawer, revealing rows of neatly organized equipment. Small tools, circuit testers, specialized optical gear. He checked a few pieces by habit more than necessity.

Some men paced when they were anxious. He maintained his tools.

Above him, Vandenberg's airfield lights threw a faint glow into the low clouds. Somewhere down there, human crews were cycling through checklists, calibrating systems, preparing for launches that would never know what truly moved in the sky with them.

He wondered, not for the first time, how long the illusion could last. How long Immortals could pretend they were still playing by rules written when the most advanced sensor on Earth was a watchful priest.

Behind him, THOTH chimed softly.

"Retrospective sweep complete," it said. "An anomaly has been identified."

Callum turned back toward the screens.

"What kind of anomaly?"

"Not a Quickening," THOTH replied. "Magnitude is significantly higher than any recorded event in your archived data. Pattern is non-random and exhibits recursive framing. Source vector appears to originate from the Scottish Highlands."

20

He went very still.

The Scottish Highlands.

For a heartbeat, the lab fell away. The years fell away. The smell of solder and filtered air was replaced by the memory of peat smoke, wet stone, and blood.

"Show me," he said.

The main screen shifted to a geographical projection. Europe, then the United Kingdom, then Scotland, zooming in until mountain ranges and lochs took shape. A blinking mark appeared in the northwest.

"Overlay the event profile."

Energy signatures cascaded across the display. Not a single spike, but a series of pulses, each larger than the last, like the echo of a vast hammer striking something deep and unseen.

"How long ago?" His voice had gone quieter without his intending it.

"Two hours and seventeen minutes," THOTH said. "Simultaneous partial sensor blackout in the immediate region. One military monitoring outpost went offline at the precise peak of the event."

"Cause?"

"Unknown."

The room felt smaller.

He knew that landscape. He had died there once. He had been born there before that. He had taken his first head there, and his first Quickening, centuries before anyone had thought to measure such things.

"Compare pattern to all stored Immortal signatures," he said. "Looking for correlation."

"Working."

Lines of correlation coefficients began to update. Callum watched the numbers scroll without really seeing them. Something else had his attention.

A faint buzzing at the base of his skull. A pressure behind his eyes. The echo of what had jolted him awake hours earlier, before he had come downstairs.

He had not wanted to name it then.

THOTH chimed again. "Correlation found."

"To what?" he asked.

"One archived Quickening profile from 1639," THOTH said. "Eastern France. Probability match, eighty-one percent. The duel is labeled in your private log as 'Château Graisseux.'"

He remembered the rain on that rooftop. The slate tiles slick under his boots. The other Immortal's last words, half curse and half prayer.

"That Quickening belonged to an Immortal identified as Alastor Renwick," THOTH said.

The name fell into the lab like a stone into still water.

Callum's fingers tightened on the console edge.

"Renwick," he said quietly.

"Is this designation significant?" THOTH asked.

Callum exhaled slowly.

"Yes."

He had not heard that name in centuries. He had hoped he never would again.

"Begin a deep analysis," he said. "I want every detail of the Highlands event broken down. Harmonics, substructures, unknown variables. Everything."

"That will require extended processing," THOTH replied. "Preliminary estimate, nineteen minutes for a high-confidence model."

"Do it."

The geometric pattern on the main display tightened, lines rearranging as THOTH opened additional computation threads. The air temperature dipped a fraction as cooling systems compensated.

Callum stepped away and walked to the transparent wall overlooking the smaller equipment chamber. Racks of hardware blinked softly in the dim light. Somewhere inside all that machinery, the world was being dissected and turned into numbers.

He stared at his reflection in the glass. To anyone else, he would have looked like a man in his thirties who had not slept enough. Dark hair a little disordered, stubble shading his jaw, gray T-shirt under a worn hoodie. Nothing about him said "over three hundred years old."

He murmured, almost to himself, "What are you playing at, Alastor?"

There was only one reason Renwick would surface after so long. Only one reason a man who treated Immortals as pieces on a cosmic board would shake the world hard enough for even mortals to notice.

He wanted to change the rules.

And when Alastor Renwick wanted to change the rules, people died in large numbers.

Callum closed his eyes and listened to the distant thrum of waves against rock.

For decades he had told himself that retreat was the only sane move. The world had become too crowded, too loud, too wired. Better to move from behind the scenes, to guide technology and infrastructure, to prepare quietly for the possibility that the Game might spill into public view. Helios Dynamics gave him reach without visibility. Graham gave the company a face. THOTH gave him eyes.

Now something in the Highlands had torn through all that preparation like it was mist.

He opened his eyes.

"THOTH," he said, "as soon as Graham's wheels touch down, I want him patched to me. Priority one."

"Understood."

"And start updating the long-range jet. We may need to leave California sooner than I planned."

"Destination?"

"New York first," Callum said. "There are some loose ends there I do not want Renwick touching. Then we will see."

"Shall I inform the flight crew?"

"Not yet. Just prepare the aircraft."

He stood in the lab for a long moment, then turned toward the stairs.

On his way up, he passed the empty mount on the wall again. This time his eyes did not linger.

There would be time enough to open that case.

For the moment, he needed to prepare for the one thing Immortals were never truly ready for.

Being pulled back into the center of the board.

Callum emerged from the stairwell into the main living area just as the house lighting shifted subtly, THOTH lowering illumination levels in anticipation of late-night cycle. It was a small thing, but one of thousands of micro-adjustments the system made every day to mimic the predictability humans found comforting.

Callum did not need comfort.

He needed clarity.

He crossed the room, glancing once more toward the blade wall. The empty mount felt heavier now, as if the absence itself radiated weight. A quiet reminder of promises made and debts carried for centuries.

THOTH spoke as he reached the hallway.

"Long-range jet has been placed into warm standby. All diagnostics nominal."

"Fuel load?" he asked.

"Full military-grade Jet A-1. Weather conditions along the transcontinental corridor are stable for the next six hours."

"Good."

He stepped into the narrower hallway leading toward the airfield side of the estate. The walls here were lined with framed topographical maps—regions of the world marked not by political borders but by terrain he knew intimately. Battlefields. Sanctuaries. Places where Immortals had fought, hidden, or died so often the ground seemed to remember.

He paused beside a map of the Scottish Highlands.

His eyes hovered over the region near Ben Craeg.

A part of him thought that he should have gone back years ago. But memory was a blade that cut both ways. There were ghosts in those hills that he wasn't ready to face—until now.

A discreet tone chimed.

"Callum," THOTH said, "incoming transmission from Graham Slate. He has landed at Heathrow and is requesting immediate contact."

Callum exhaled. "Patch him through."

A holo-window blossomed on the wall—faint blue light shaping into the tired, irritated face of Graham Slate. His hair was flattened on one side from the flight, his collar open, his suit rumpled in ways that betrayed a long day of arguing with Europeans about aerospace regulations.

"For the love of God, Callum," Graham said without greeting, "if your AI wakes me one second earlier, I'm going to delete it personally."

"THOTH didn't wake you," Callum replied. "You asked to be notified the moment you were on the ground."

"I thought that was the *figurative* moment," Graham muttered. "Not the literal one. I hadn't even stepped off the jetway."

"You're off now."

"Barely."

Graham sighed and rubbed his eyes. "All right. What happened? The alert came through on four separate devices, which is never a good sign."

Callum leaned a shoulder against the wall. "There's been an event in the Highlands."

Graham stilled. "What kind of event?"

"Not seismic," Callum answered. "Not environmental. Something... else."

Graham frowned. "You mean Immortal-related?"

"Yes."

Graham lowered his voice, conscious that he was in a public space even at this late hour. "Is one of you idiots swinging swords near a sensor array again?"

"No."

"Good. Because the last time that happened I spent three weeks explaining to the FAA why their atmospheric lidar suddenly looked like it had been struck by a divine lightning bolt."

"This is worse than that."

Graham blinked. "How much worse?"

Callum's jaw tightened. "Quickenings don't blackout military outposts."

Graham's expression darkened perceptibly. "...which outpost?"

"Craeg Outpost Two."

"Jesus," Graham hissed. "That's not some random monitoring shack. They watch half of northern Scotland from there."

"They watched," Callum corrected. "Past tense."

Graham swore under his breath.

"Do we know if it's... him?"

"We can't confirm," Callum said. "We can only correlate. And the correlation is strong."

Graham's voice dropped.

"Renwick."

Callum didn't answer. He didn't need to.

Graham pinched the bridge of his nose and exhaled hard.

"All right. What's your plan?"

"I'm flying to New York by morning," Callum said. "I want to secure assets there before anything else moves. If Renwick is active again, he'll go after infrastructure and data first."

"Meaning he'll hit Helios?"

"Or try." Callum's tone held no arrogance, just experience. "He won't expect that we've expanded our defensive measures. But I'd rather not test that assumption."

Graham nodded. "What do you need?"

"Coordination. Keep Helios off the financial radar. Move project funds quietly. And check on Rowan."

Graham's eyebrows lifted.

"Rowan? Why him?"

"He flagged abnormal activity from one of our deep-field relay clusters this morning," Callum said. "He doesn't know what he was looking at, but he noticed it."

"Is it related?"

"Possibly."

Graham's mouth tugged into a wry half-smile.

"You know he's going to panic the moment he hears anything remotely dangerous."

"He won't hear anything dangerous," Callum said. "Not from me."

"Then from whom?"

Callum did not answer. His eyes slid unconsciously toward the map of the Highlands again.

Graham sobered.

"You think Renwick is coming to the States."

"I think he's moving," Callum said. "And movement from him is never small."

Graham swallowed.

"All right. Call me when you land in New York. I'll run interference."

"Thank you."

"Don't thank me," Graham said. "Just don't die. I've worked too hard keeping you legally alive."

The holo-window closed.

THOTH spoke immediately.

"Long-range jet will be ready for departure at 06:00 Pacific."

Callum nodded. "Good."

He walked toward the final set of reinforced doors at the end of the hall. They opened with a hydraulic hiss, revealing the estate's private air hangar. Cool night air spilled in from the open pad beyond.

There, under bright halogens, rested the helicopter.

FENRIR.

Up close, it was even more imposing than its silhouette suggested. Matte-black composite surfaces curved into aggressive lines. The cockpit windows were tinted in a way that suggested secrecy rather than style. Along its underside, recessed panels hinted at weaponry that no civilian manufacturer admitted to producing.

THOTH dimmed the hangar lights by a fraction, as though presenting the craft with quiet reverence.

Callum approached it slowly, footsteps soft on the polished concrete.

"Status?" he asked.

"FENRIR is fully flight-ready," THOTH replied. "Primary engines calibrated. Stealth profile optimal. Weapons systems secured. I recommend initiating a systems run before your departure window."

"Later," Callum murmured.

He rested his hand on the cool surface of the fuselage. The aircraft felt alive under his touch, as though the storm beyond the hangar doors pulsed through its skin.

27

He imagined taking it up tonight, sweeping the coastline, slicing through clouds, chasing ghosts. But there was no benefit in acting on impulse. Not anymore.

He withdrew his hand.

Then...

A low harmonic vibration trembled through the floor.

Different from before.

More focused.

An echo, not a blast.

A ripple chasing the original Pulse.

THOTH detected it instantly.

"Callum—resonance anomaly repeating. Very low amplitude. Directionally filtered."

Callum stiffened.

"Source?"

"Scottish Highlands. Same origin vector as the first."

"Show me."

A new display illuminated in the hangar, projecting a holographic curve of energy patterns. This one was subtle... like a whisper following a scream. But unmistakably from the same force.

THOTH continued:

"Intensity is only four percent of the first Pulse. However... there is something else."

"What?"

"There is a signature embedded in the resonance."

Callum took a step closer.

"A signature?"

"Yes. A harmonic mnemonic imprint." THOTH paused. "It resembles a memory echo."

Callum's pulse quickened.

"Whose?"

The system analyzed.

Compared.

Searched centuries of logged signatures.

Then:

"Unknown," THOTH said. "But it is an Immortal."

Callum stared at the air between them.

A memory echo—broadcast across continents—following the Pulse?

That shouldn't be possible.

Unless...

Unless someone triggered it deliberately.

His stomach tightened.

"THOTH," he said, voice low, "store all data. Encrypt it at highest level."

"Done."

"Prepare everything. We leave at dawn."

"Yes, Callum."

He turned away from the helicopter and looked toward the open hangar doors, where the dark Pacific folded endlessly into the horizon.

Something in those distant Highlands had awakened.

And the world—his world—was beginning to stir with it.

He exhaled, a slow, controlled breath that did nothing to ease the tension in his chest.

"I knew you'd return one day, Alastor," he said, "I just hoped it wouldn't be in my lifetime."

For immortals, such wishes never came true.

Callum remained in the hangar a long moment after THOTH finished encrypting the resonance data. The faint echo of the secondary pulse still lingered along the edges of his awareness—a subtle tingling like the aftertaste of lightning. He pressed his hand against the cold rAiling, grounding himself.

He had felt echoes before. Every Immortal had shadows of distant battles, faint tremors in the soul when one of their kind fell somewhere far away. But this was different. This pulse hadn't been the death of an Immortal.

It had felt like the birth of something.

A fragment of memory surged uninvited - Ailsa Strathearn's voice, rough from battle, cutting through centuries of dust.

"The world sings before it bleeds, Callum. If you feel the song, pay heed."

He clenched his jaw and let the memory fade. Not now. Not with Renwick's shadow crawling across the past.

THOTH interrupted softly.

"Callum, additional data is becoming available."

He turned toward the nearest display.

"Show me."

But the system wasn't projecting a resonance map this time; instead it opened a secure Helios relay window.

Callum's eyebrows lifted.

"Rowan?"

"Yes. He initiated a priority request three minutes ago." THOTH paused. "The request is labeled urgent, though he does not appear to realize the true severity of what he discovered."

Callum frowned. "Patch him through."

The screen blinked twice before resolving into Rowan Calder's face, a pale, wide-eyed, hair in disarray, the glow of three monitors illuminating his apartment behind him. He wore a hoodie with a faded Seattle tech conference logo, and his hands fluttered nervously just out of frame, likely gripping a stress ball or fidget cube.

"Mr. MacLeod? Are you awake? I...uh...I'm really sorry it's late, but I think...I think something's wrong with the relay clusters."

Callum softened his posture slightly. Rowan was one of the few humans he trusted, but the young man was wound tighter than a guitar string.

"I'm awake," Callum said. "What happened?"

Rowan pushed his glasses up, eyes darting to the side as if checking whether the building was about to collapse.

"So, um...earlier tonight I was compiling diagnostics for the Atlantic relay network, just routine stuff, and I noticed a timing drift. Like, a weird one. Not clock skew. More like the packets were...hesitating."

"Hesitating?" Callum repeated gently.

"Yeah. Like something delayed them mid-stream." Rowan rubbed the back of his neck. "At first I thought it was packet loss, but the error correction didn't match packet loss. It was more like...like a hiccup."

"What kind of hiccup?"

Rowan swallowed hard.

"The kind of thing that shouldn't be possible unless someone was manipulating the data path in real time."

Callum's eyes narrowed slightly.

"Has anyone accessed your side of the cluster?"

"No. I triple-checked. No breaches. No privilege escalations. No anomalous authentication calls." Rowan paused. "Unless we hired a hacker god when I wasn't looking."

Callum said nothing.

Rowan took this as a cue to panic harder.

"Oh God, did we hire a hacker god? Is someone inside? Because if someone's inside, I need to know, because I'm really not good with conflict and I kind of faint when there's..."

"Rowan."

He froze.

"You're safe," Callum said firmly. "Whatever is happening isn't local to your system."

Rowan deflated with visible relief, then immediately tensed again when his brain caught up.

"Wait, that's worse. That's much worse."

"Tell me exactly what you found."

Rowan turned his camera slightly to show a side monitor covered in lines of cascading code and diagnostics.

"This. That repeating waveform. It shouldn't exist. Our system isn't designed to generate anything like it. And I checked cross-node logs to make sure it wasn't an echo."

"It wasn't?"

"No. This thing came from outside. It originated...somewhere north of the UK and propagated across the Atlantic in under a second."

Callum exhaled slowly.

"What you're seeing is a resonance pulse."

Rowan blinked.

"A what?"

"Nothing to worry about yet," Callum said. "Just keep monitoring. Forward all raw data to THOTH, and don't attempt further analysis without telling me."

"But..."

"Rowan."

The young man swallowed.

"Okay. Yeah. Sure. But, um...Mr. MacLeod?"

"Yes?"

"Whatever that pulse was...it wasn't natural. I know what natural looks like, even when it's weird. This was...this was like someone plucked a string on a guitar the size of the planet."

Callum felt a faint chill.

"You did well to bring this to me," he said. "Rest for a few hours. I'll contact you if I need more."

Rowan nodded nervously. "Okay. Um...goodnight."

The feed shut down.

THOTH waited a beat before speaking.

"He is correct, you know."

Callum turned to the air. "About what?"

"The pulse contained intentional structure. And the embedded signature within the second echo was not random."

Callum walked back toward the helicopter, needing movement to organize the growing pressure behind his ribs.

"What kind of structure?"

"A directional harmonic," THOTH replied. "One that appears to be...seeking."

Callum stiffened.

"Seeking what?"

"You," THOTH said. "It was keyed to your resonance."

Every Immortal had a signature—a unique energetic fingerprint formed from countless cycles of life, death, and Quickening. But signatures behaved like static imprints, present only during combat or in proximity to other Immortals. They were not signals.

They were not messages.

Yet this one had crossed an ocean.

Callum closed his eyes for a moment.

"Ailsa once told me Immortals could call to one another. She said the oldest of us could do it without swords. With will alone."

"Is this true?" THOTH asked.

"It shouldn't be."

Silence fell.

He opened his eyes and exhaled slowly.

"Query the resonance echoes for mnemonic structure."

"Analyzing," THOTH said.

A faint hum filled the hangar as deeper processors engaged.

Callum paced.

The Pacific wind raked across the landing pad outside, carrying the scent of salt and distant kelp. The helicopter's matte-black frame seemed to darken further, absorbed in the shadows of the night.

Then THOTH's lights shifted into a warmer tone.

"Analysis complete."

Callum stopped walking.

"And?"

THOTH displayed a small holo-sphere above the console pulsing softly like a faint heartbeat.

"This structure contains a partial memory lattice."

Callum's pulse quickened.

"A memory...of what?"

"Of you."

He stared at the projection.

Solar flares of emotion, shock, irritation, disbelief - all flared then resolved into something colder and sharper.

"Show it."

The holo-sphere unfolded.

A blurred image formed first.

Then sharpened.

A woman.

Red hair braided tight.

Eyes bright with ferocity.

A broadsword in her right hand, not raised but ready.

A Highland mist swirling behind her.

Her voice; faint and distorted echoed across the hangar like a whisper carried by centuries.

"*Callum.*"

His breath caught in his throat.

Ailsa Strathearn.

His mentor.

His anchor.

His first teacher.

Dead for centuries.

But her memory had just ridden across an ocean to find him.

As the image flickered, the faintest smile touched Ailsa's ghostly face.

"The world sings before it bleeds," she whispered, voice fragmenting with static.

"And you, my stubborn lad...must listen."

The memory collapsed into motes of light.

THOTH spoke.

"This lattice was embedded intentionally. Someone imprinted this echo inside the pulse."

Callum swallowed hard.

"Only one Immortal ever learned how to do that."

THOTH waited.

"Renwick," Callum answered.

He stood motionless, breath coming steady but deep.

Alastor Renwick had not just returned.

He had called to Callum.

Across countries.

Across oceans.

Across centuries.

It was no longer a question of if Renwick was moving.

Only how soon he would reach them.

Callum mouthed, "He's forcing me out of hiding."

And the sky outside the hangar grumbled in answer, as though the world itself agreed.

The image of Ailsa dissolved into the dim hangar light, leaving a charged silence in its wake. Callum remained still, shoulders squared, jaw locked, breathing slow and even - the posture of a man forcing centuries of instinct not to erupt at once.

The memory echo had been impossible.

That alone meant Renwick had rewritten the rules.

He turned toward the night again. Wind raced across the open pad, pulling faint threads of mist from the bluff edge. Below, the Pacific hammered the cliffs like a giant's heartbeat.

Shattered Veil

"THOTH," Callum said, voice quieter than before. "Begin full-suite threat projection. Use Renwick as catalyst variable."

"Understood," the AI replied. "Gathering historical, tactical, and behavioral data."

Lines of text and geometric visualizations filled the nearest holo-plate the system assembling a psychological profile refined through centuries of recorded encounters. Not only Callum's, but those of a dozen Immortals who had crossed Renwick's orbit.

Calculated patterns of violence.

Scenario trees.

Probabilistic outcomes.

Callum scanned them quickly.

Renwick didn't move without purpose. He didn't strike randomly or lash out blindly. His violence was always part of something larger—another step in an intricate gameboard only he seemed able to see.

THOTH spoke carefully.

"Preliminary thesis: Renwick is attempting to provoke you."

Callum snorted. "He already has."

"Yes," THOTH agreed. "But not merely emotionally. Strategically. The embedded memory echo was not a message of sentimentality. It was a lure. A reminder of your past... designed to guide your next move."

Callum frowned. "Guide me where?"

"Toward confrontation," THOTH replied. "Toward him."

He folded his arms across his chest and stared at the pulsing resonance data still hovering like ghost-light above the console.

"And what does he gain from forcing me out?" Callum asked.

"Probability suggests he wants you aware," THOTH responded. "He wants you involved. Renwick rarely executes a plan without selecting an adversary he deems worthy."

Callum's eyes hardened. "He always chooses the same one."

"That is statistically accurate."

Callum turned and walked deeper into the hangar. THOTH adjusted lights to follow him - soft pools of illumination opening like stepping stones across the wide space.

As he walked, a subtle tremor rippled through his muscles—an Immortal's natural response to rising danger. The Pulse had awakened more than memories. It had tugged at something buried, something primal. A reminder that in the end, the Game was not a matter of choice.

A faint beep signaled new activity from the interface.

"Callum," THOTH said, "Rowan is attempting to contact you again."

Callum paused. "Put him through."

Rowan's face reappeared, paler than before, eyes wider, his voice cracking as soon as he spoke.

"Mr. MacLeod? Um. So., I did what you said and sent the data over and tried to rest, but I couldn't sleep because the packet signature kept bothering me, so I checked it again and...and..."

"Rowan," Callum interrupted gently. "Slowly."

"I...okay...yes...right." Rowan took a deep breath, though it did nothing to steady him. "So that signature? The echo pattern? It's... it's repeating."

Callum's eyes lifted.
"How often?"

"Every... I don't know... hour? But it's gradually speeding up. Like it's..." Rowan hesitated, then said, "...looking for something."

Callum exchanged a glance with the holo of the resonance display.
"It's not looking for something," he said quietly.
"It's looking for someone."

Rowan's breath hitched.
"...you?"

Callum didn't answer.

Instead: "Rowan, keep monitoring, but do not interfere. Do not attempt to trace it. Do not route it through any secondary clusters. If it speeds up again, alert me immediately."

"I...I will. But Mr. MacLeod... this is some next-level horror movie stuff. Please tell me it's not dangerous."

Callum softened his voice.
"It's not coming for you, Rowan."

Rowan exhaled shakily.

"I'm not sure that makes me feel better."

The call ended.

Callum stood still for several seconds after the screen darkened. The rhythmic clatter of waves against the cliffs below filled the silence like distant artillery.

Renwick was accelerating his timetable.

Drawing closer.

Constricting the circle.

THOTH chimed again.

"Threat projection updated. Would you like a summary?"

"Go on."

"Renwick's most likely next strike points center around locations tied to either your resources or your history. Manhattan ranks high on both lists."

Callum's brow furrowed.

"Manhattan?"

"Yes. Specifically, your penthouse location and nearby Helios satellite offices. Additionally, urban density provides Renwick with strategic camouflage."

Callum inhaled a slow breath.

"Is Lila in danger?"

A brief pause - THOTH evaluating why the question mattered.

"Dr. Serrano is geographically near one of the potential strike radii."

Callum's jaw tightened imperceptibly.

Callum's thoughts drifted, unbidden, to Dr. Lila Serrano. They had met only a few months earlier at a charity gala for the children's ward of the hospital - an event Callum had attended out of obligation but left remembering only her. She'd stood beneath the amber lights in a simple midnight-blue dress, dark curls falling in soft waves around her shoulders, her eyes a warm, steady brown that missed nothing. There was a confidence in the way she moved through that room of donors and dignitaries, not with arrogance, but with a calm self-assurance that came from years spent fighting for her patients. Callum had spoken to her only briefly that night, yet the conversation lingered—her wit, her warmth, the quiet strength behind every word. They'd gone out a handful of times since then, cautious but curious, two people feeling the spark of something neither of them had expected. Whatever this was between them, it was new. New enough to be uncertain. New enough to matter.

"Update departure window," he said.
"We leave before dawn."

"Understood. Revising to 04:30."

Callum began walking toward the armory panel built discreetly into the hangar's interior wall. His footsteps echoed between steel and concrete, the sound stark and purposeful.

"THOTH," he murmured, "unlock Case Nine."

A magnetic click answered.
The wall slid open.

Inside was a compact weapons suite—modern, lethal, meticulously maintained. Callum ignored the firearms and instead reached for a slim, matte-gray case with a biometric lock.

His thumb brushed the sensor. The case opened with a soft hiss. Inside lay a single-bladed sleeve knife—carbon-fiber sheath, energy-dampening build, designed for close-quarters use where explosive Immortal clashes couldn't risk collateral damage. Modern craftsmanship grafted onto old instincts.

Callum slid it into its forearm mount beneath his sleeve.
The blade sat snug.
Ready.

Not the blade he needed most.
But the one he could allow himself to carry until the time was right.

He closed the armory wall.

As he stepped away, THOTH triggered another alert.

"Callum, new information regarding the secondary resonance echo appears significant."

Callum turned back toward the nearest console.
"What is it?"

"The embedded memory lattice... contains an additional layer."
"Another message?"

"No," THOTH said. "Not a voice. Not an image."

The AI paused—rare for a system capable of processing millions of variables in a heartbeat.

"It contains coordinates."

A cold stillness washed over Callum.

"Coordinates to what?"

THOTH brought up the data on the holo-projector.

And when Callum saw the numbers, every muscle in his body locked.

Latitude.

Longitude.

A point in the Scottish Highlands.

But not where the Pulse had originated.

A place older.

A place deeper.

A place he had sworn he would never return to unless the world forced his hand.

"THOTH," he said, "confirm the precision of this imprint."

"Seven-decimal accuracy," the AI responded. "These coordinates were embedded intentionally."

Callum felt his heartbeat settle into a slow, heavy rhythm.

Ailsa's memory echo had been more than a warning.

It was a summons.

He inhaled deeply, nostrils flaring slightly as the cool Pacific air reached him.

"Prepare an auxiliary flight plan," he said. "New York first. Scotland next."

"Understood."

Thunder muttered on the horizon.

Callum walked toward the open hangar—toward the night, toward the Pacific, toward whatever came next.

The world was moving again.

And he could feel the old gravity of the Game trying to pull him back into its orbit.

He closed his eyes briefly.

"Damn you, Alastor," he murmured.

The name vanished into the wind.

The hangar lights dimmed as THOTH shifted to tactical-alert mode, bathing the space in low amber illumination. Soft, rhythmic pulses lit the floor markers—subtle, precise, guiding Callum toward the pad where FENRIR waited under the open night sky.

The wind had changed.

The Pacific carried a different undertone now—something electric, tense. The world had felt dormant for so long. Too long. And the Pulse had cracked that stillness like a stone through glass.

As Callum approached the helicopter, THOTH spoke again, voice tighter than usual.

"Callum, be advised: a new anomaly has appeared."

He stopped mid-stride.

"Define anomaly."

"A direct intrusion attempt. Digital in origin. Targeting your Manhattan penthouse security grid and the Helios micro-server node linked to it."

Callum's expression hardened to stone.

"Renwick."

"Probability: eighty-nine percent." THOTH paused. "Attack vector is unusually clean. The intruder is not attempting system ownership. He is not stealing data."

"Then what is he doing?"

"He is mapping your movements."

Cold anger flared behind Callum's ribs.

"And he knows I'm coming."

"Yes," THOTH confirmed. "He wants you to."

The wind outside gusted hard, rattling the gantry rails.

Callum forced himself to breathe evenly, his jaw tight.

"Lock down every Helios node in Manhattan. No signals in or out without direct authorization."

"Done."

"And the penthouse?"

"External grid remains intact. However, the intruder was not attempting to breach it. He was merely...knocking."

Callum's fists curled.

"Renwick doesn't knock."

"No. He announces himself."

The implication hung in the air like a blade.

If Renwick was announcing his presence, then Manhattan was already compromised.

He wasn't hiding his attack.

He was inviting Callum into it.

And that meant lives were already in danger.

Callum moved again - faster now - crossing the remaining distance to the helicopter. The matte-black fuselage seemed to vibrate faintly, as if the machine sensed the urgency of what it was being summoned to do.

He reached the cargo compartment first, twisting the latch and lifting it open. Inside were several hard cases—armored, discreet, containing everything from burner comms to compact medical kits to weapons chosen for precision and minimal collateral damage.

He selected a slim carbon case from the back—one marked only with a quiet embossed symbol: a dragon's head, stylized, angular.

Not the Katana.

Not yet.

The dragonhead katana remained sealed beneath the main floor, connected to ancestry and blood far older than this fight.

But he allowed himself one brief moment to touch the case.

To *remember*.

A faint pressure pulsed behind his eyes. A whisper of Duncan MacLeod placing the blade in his hands, not even three decades ago - twenty-seven years, almost to the month. Duncan's expression had carried the weight of far more than time.

"If I fall, keep it in Highland hands - yours."

He exhaled.

Not now.

Not yet.

He secured the case among the others and closed the compartment.

THOTH interrupted again, voice cutting through the moment like a scalpel.

"Callum, updated threat geometry indicates Manhattan's risk index has risen to critical. If you do not depart within the next twenty minutes, you will arrive after the projected strike window."

Callum climbed into the cockpit, settling into the pilot's seat with practiced ease.

Every switch, every lever, every display was exactly where it needed to be - because he had designed it that way.

"Bring engines online," he said.

"Engines spooling."

The rotors began to turn, slow at first, then with increasing force, sending vibrations through the deck. Dust spiraled upward, caught in the vortex forming beneath the blades.

The HUD activated across the cockpit glass, shimmering into view with tactical overlays: flight plan, weather, airspace monitoring, and a glowing alert marker centered on Manhattan.

THOTH spoke again.

"One more thing, Callum."

"Yes?"

"There was a final data fragment embedded in the second resonance echo."

Callum didn't look away from the HUD.

"What kind of fragment?"

"A timestamp."

He stiffened.

"A timestamp for what?"

"The next Pulse."

Callum froze.

"Project it."

A glowing fragment unfolded across the HUD—numbers forming, stabilizing, locking into place.

THOTH translated.

"You have less than forty-eight hours until the next major resonance event."

Callum's heart thudded once, hard.

Renwick wasn't just making moves.

He was setting a schedule.

A timetable for whatever catastrophe he intended to unleash.

"Coordinates?" Callum asked quietly.

"Unknown," THOTH replied. "The timestamp is the only confirmed detail."

The rotors accelerated, the wind churning fiercely.

Callum looked up at the dark sky, jaw set.

Forty-eight hours.

If Renwick tore the Veil again, or controlled it, or weaponized whatever force lay behind it...

The world would not be ready.

He tightened his grip on the controls.

"We're leaving," he said.

"Confirming departure," THOTH replied. "All systems green."

The helicopter lifted, first a hover, then slowly rising above the bluff. Salt spray exploded upward as the downdraft slammed into the rocks below. The estate shrank beneath him—dark metal, glass, stone—all of it soon to be abandoned until whatever this was played out.

As the aircraft climbed, the coastline rolled out beneath him - Vandenberg's runways glowing faintly in the distance, soft latticeworks of blue and white cutting across the night.

He angled the nose east.

"Callum," THOTH said, voice softer than usual, "you understand what this means."

"Yes," he murmured.

"You will not be returning as the same man."

Callum's eyes narrowed at the horizon.

"I haven't been the same man since 1743."

The helicopter surged forward, blades carving through the night air.

The cliffs fell away.

The Pacific vanished behind him.

California's dark spine unfurled beneath the flight path as FENRIR roared toward the edge of the world where destiny awaited.

THOTH dimmed cabin lights.

Ailsa's fading voice ghosted through his mind.

"The world sings before it bleeds."

Callum drew a slow breath.

"Then let's get to the bleeding before Renwick does."

The helicopter knifed east into the dark sky.

Chapter 2

Manhattan at 6:07 a.m. was a contradiction of noise and stillness.

The streets were already rumbling with delivery trucks, early-shift commuters, and the first waves of taxis weaving into Midtown. Steam curled out of the vents along Lexington Avenue, drifting lazily through the faint winter chill. The sky was a muted gray-blue, the color of cold metal, with the slightest suggestion of sunrise hiding behind the skyline.

Above it all, far from the roar of engines and impatient horns, Callum descended toward a private rooftop heliport nestled between two glass towers.

FENRIR cut through the urban wind currents with surgical precision, its engines purring beneath the sensory noise of Manhattan's heartbeat. The stealth profile did its job, no alarms, no radar pings, no curious eyes peering upward. To any observer below, if they caught a shadow at all, it would look like a nondescript corporate aircraft crossing between buildings.

He needed to reach Lila before anything shifted. Renwick's movements across the Highlands Pulse data made her hospital, Saint Vincent's, a potential target, even if she didn't know it yet. Her work in emergency medicine placed her near situations Renwick could exploit.

Glenfinnan, Scotland, 1743

The storm rolled over the moor in a gray sheet, swallowing the horizon. Young Callum MacLeod, barely twenty, ran through the heather, lungs burning, legs numb from cold. The distant cries of his clan echoed behind him. Steel clashed. Men shouted. The sky flashed white with lightning.

He stumbled over a fallen stone and pitched forward into the mud.

When he rolled onto his back, the world spun.

And over him stood the man who would end his first life.

The raider's face was hidden beneath a soaked wool hood. His blade gleamed in the pale stormlight, sharp enough to split bone cleanly. Callum tried to rise, but his legs refused to obey.

"Please, " he choked out.

The man didn't speak.

Didn't hesitate.

The blade drove straight into Callum's heart.

There was no pain at first. Just cold. A crushing cold that buried him in darkness.

Voices faded. The storm muted.

His breath extinguished.

And then, the world snapped back.

Agony.

Fire behind his ribs.

The scream locked in his throat.

Callum gasped as his heart beat again.

He clawed through the mud, trembling, his fingers slick with blood, his blood. His chest burned as if lightning still crackled in his veins.

The raider was gone.

Only Duncan MacLeod remained.

Soaked, sword sheathed, dark hair plastered to his face, Duncan knelt beside him.

"Easy, lad," Duncan said softly. "You're not dreaming."

Callum stared in disbelief.

"Am I... dead?"

Duncan hesitated.

"You were."

The wind howled around them.

"But you're one of us now," Duncan said. "You'll live. Long after all this."

Lightning split the sky behind him, framing Duncan like some ancient figure carved from storm.

Callum whispered, "What am I?"

Duncan looked him in the eyes.

"Immortal."

Callum trembled.

"Why me?"

A faint static pressure behind his eyes, the same sensation the Highlands Pulse had left echoing through him.

"No one chooses this life, Callum.

But we live it anyway."

He extended his hand.

Callum took it.

And in that moment, reborn and shaking, Callum MacLeod stepped into a world he didn't understand, guided only by the man who would shape his future more than any other.

Callum guided the helicopter down gently.

The skids kissed the pad with a soft metallic hiss.

He powered down the engines. The rotors slowed, then stilled. The world's noise seeped in, the hum of HVAC units, distant sirens, the muted chatter of pedestrians thirty floors below.

"THOTH," Callum said, unstrapping harness buckles, "status of the intrusion?"

"Persistent but restrained," the AI replied through the cockpit speakers. "The intrusion originated from a Helios-backdoor sub node meaning Renwick had inside access. That is why building security responded instantly."

He opened the cockpit door. The cold Manhattan air rushed in, thinner and sharper than the coastal wind back home. He stepped down onto the pad, boots landing with controlled weight.

This rooftop was owned by a subsidiary of Helios Dynamics, registered under a shell corporation meant to bury his name behind layers of corporate anonymity. Only three people had access: Callum, Graham, and the building's security director, who believed his invisible employer was some elusive tech billionaire who hated publicity. It was far from the truth, but for different reasons than the usual tech billionaire.

Callum crossed the pad quickly, the city's breath rising up around him like heat from a forge.

He reached the door leading into the penthouse-level corridor and paused.

Something felt wrong.

Not noise. Not movement. A faint irregularity in the air, not the clean, sharp pressure of another Immortal, but the subtle distortion THOTH had flagged earlier.

"Callum, I am detecting a localized electromagnetic distortion thirty meters below this level."

"Define distortion."

"A resonance signature exhibiting the same harmonic profile as the initial Pulse."

Callum's heartbeat slowed into the heavy, steady rhythm of readiness.

"Is it Renwick?"

"Unknown. But the signature is faint. Not a Quickening. Not an energy release." THOTH paused, analyzing. "It is more like...presence."

Callum's fingers curled slightly at his sides.

"Show me interior schematics."

A translucent holo-map appeared beside the stairwell door, floor plans, wiring, occupancy sensors, access points. The penthouse apartment occupied the top two floors, beneath the helipad.

There, on the lower level.

A small red marker blinked.

A single heat signature.

Humanoid.

Standing still. Waiting.

Callum took a slow breath.

He had walked into traps before.

Hundreds of them.

He knew the shape of an ambush long before the first blade was drawn.

He stepped through the door.

The interior stairwell smelled faintly of steel, oil, and recirculated air, cleaner than most Manhattan buildings, but still touched by the city's signature grit. His footsteps echoed softly on the tile as he descended one flight.

He stopped at the doorway to his penthouse.

This floor was quiet. Too quiet. Even in the early morning.

Normally the space would hum with the faint ambient sounds of the smart-environment system adjusting temperature or light. A refrigerator motor cycling. The quiet purr of the HVAC.

But everything was still.

He keyed the door open.

The penthouse lights flicked on one by one, brightening the foyer, then the open concept living room beyond. Glass walls revealed a sweeping view of the Chrysler Building and the river in the distance. The sleek furniture sat undisturbed. The kitchen countertops gleamed.

His footsteps were soundless on the hardwood.

THOTH's voice remained low in his ear.

"The heat signature is in the main gallery."

Callum moved past the living area and into the hallway that led toward the gallery, a long room where he kept artifacts, maps, and items from centuries of life. Few people had ever seen it. Fewer still had been allowed to step inside.

His hand drifted toward the small, concealed sleeve mechanism beneath his jacket. The knife sat ready.

He reached the gallery door.

It was already open.

"Of course it is," he murmured.

He stepped inside.

A man stood near the far end of the room, tall, lean, wearing dark tactical clothing that bore no insignia. His back was to Callum. He was studying a framed map of 18th-century Scotland as if trying to memorize every contour of the Highlands.

Callum recognized him immediately.

Not his face, he hadn't seen it yet.

Not his clothing, it was generic, forgettable.

Not even his stance, professional, practiced, precise.

It was the *resonance*.

Immortal. A fresh one. Not Renwick, but someone trained in Renwick's doctrine.

The man spoke without turning.

"You're early."

Callum's voice was calm. "I prefer early."

"Renwick said you would." The stranger turned slowly. His eyes were pale blue, sharp, and cold. "He also said you wouldn't run."

"I'm not running," Callum replied. "I'm here."

The man smiled faintly.

"He said you'd say that too."

Callum's expression remained impassive.

"What's your name?"

"Names are for after," the man said. "If either of us still needs one."

He reached behind him.

Steel flashed.

Not a gun.

A sword.

A sleek, blackened blade with a segmented design, modern, optimized for speed, coated in a serrated energy-channeling pattern.

Renwick's doctrine. Refined. Weaponized.

Callum exhaled once.

So it would begin here in Manhattan.

At sunrise.

He slid his forearm slightly, feeling the sleeve knife lock into combat position.

The Immortal opposite him raised his sword in a ready stance.

"Renwick told me one thing," he said quietly.

"He said if I could kill you, I'd be worthy of joining him."

"Then he's already lied to you," Callum replied.

The stranger lunged.

Steel sang.

The Immortal charged across the gallery with a ferocity that broke the room's stillness like shattering glass.

His blade cut a black arc through the air, silent, fast, merciless. The segmented grooves along the steel hummed faintly, channeling energy the way Renwick's brutal doctrine demanded: overwhelm, destabilize, finish.

Callum stepped aside, not fast, not frantic, Just *precise*.

The blade missed by inches, carving a line through the air where Callum's neck had been a heartbeat before. The strike carried enough force to cleave through the antique map frame behind him. Wood splintered. Glass fell.

The stranger pivoted instantly, no wasted motion.

Good footwork, better than average.

Renwick had trained him personally or broke him into shape.

Callum used the momentum of his dodge to close the distance. He dipped low, fingers grazing the floor, and the sleeve knife snapped into his hand with a metallic whisper.

Left forearm forward, shoulder tight.

Eyes locked.

The stranger smiled faintly.

"A modernist," he said. "Renwick said you forget your roots."

Callum didn't answer. He struck.

His knife flashed upward in a tight arc aimed at the attacker's ribs. The stranger twisted his torso just enough to avoid the puncture, only just, and countered with a downward chop, blade aimed for Callum's collarbone.

Callum caught the strike on the reinforced bracer under his sleeve.

The blow reverberated up his arm, rattling bone.

The stranger's eyes flickered with surprise.

"You reinforced your guard?"

Callum stepped back.

"You came armed with a modern blade. Why wouldn't I counter it?"

The stranger lunged again, this time with Renwick's signature aggressive pattern:

Cut high.

Cut low.

Stab centerline.

Disrupt stance.

Break rhythm.

Crush.

Callum recognized it instantly.

He had learned the same doctrine centuries ago, before he had rejected Renwick's philosophy in favor of Ailsa's teachings.

Ailsa's voice surged through his mind as he ducked a high swing.

"Strength is nothing without rhythm. Rhythm is nothing without breath."

He moved with breath - he moved with memory.

The stranger's blade carved a vertical slash. Callum stepped inside the strike and hammered an elbow into the attacker's sternum.

The man grunted but kept his footing, a testament to Renwick's brutal conditioning. He responded with a short, vicious headbutt that clipped Callum's cheekbone.

Pain flashed white.

Real.

Grounding.

Callum wiped blood from the corner of his mouth with the back of his hand.

"Good," he said softly.

The stranger frowned.

"Good?"

"You hit harder than he used to."

Anger flared in the man's eyes.

"He told me you'd mock me."

Callum shook his head.

"No. I only mock bad footwork. Yours is excellent."

The stranger roared and rushed him again.

They clashed amid the gallery's artifacts, centuries of Callum's life forced to witness another battle erupt in their silent space.

A Roman gladius rattled off the wall.

A Ming dynasty vase cracked.

A French map from 1752 ripped as the stranger slid past it.

Their blades collided, modern steel against modern carbon, sparks skittering across the hardwood floor.

The stranger pushed forward with raw strength, forcing Callum toward the glass doors leading to the suspended skywalk that connected the penthouse to the adjacent tower.

Callum allowed the backward movement, until the moment the stranger thought he was winning.

Then he changed direction.

He ducked low, swept the attacker's leg, and twisted the man's sword arm in one fluid, Highland-trained motion. The stranger staggered, losing his line of attack.

Callum's knife struck, fast, precise, cutting a shallow slice across the man's hip.

The stranger hissed in pain.
"You bleed first," Callum said. "Always a bad omen."

The man snarled.
"You talk too much."

He tried to bull-rush Callum again, but Callum sidestepped and used the man's momentum to throw him through the open glass double doors.

The attacker skidded across the walkway; a narrow bridge suspended thirty stories above Lexington Avenue. The wind caught him, whipping his coat and sending loose debris scattering across the transparent floor panels.

The city roared below.
Traffic.
Sirens.
Distant horns.

Life went on, oblivious to the clash unfolding above.

The man scrambled to his feet and charged again, blade raised high.

Callum followed onto the walkway, his movements steady despite the vertigo-inducing view beneath his boots.

The stranger swung horizontally.
Callum parried with the reinforced bracer and countered with a kick to the man's knee.

The attacker's leg buckled.
He stumbled toward the guardrail and caught himself at the last moment.

"You're good," the stranger breathed.

"So are you," Callum said. "For someone trained to die for Renwick."

The man's expression darkened.

"He has a purpose. A vision. You never understood that."

"I understood it perfectly," Callum replied. "I simply didn't accept it."

The stranger roared and attacked with reckless fury.

Mistake.

Callum pivoted, letting the man overextend. He grabbed the attacker's wrist and stepped behind him in one fluid motion, Highland claymore footwork adapted for close quarters.

He twisted.

The man screamed as bones snapped.

His blade clattered onto the walkway and slid toward the edge.

Callum kicked it aside, sending it spinning across the glass.

The attacker fell to his knees, clutching his ruined arm.

But he still glared at Callum through clenched teeth.

"Then you understand nothing."

Callum shook his head.

"You've already lost."

"No." The stranger grinned, bloody and unbroken in spirit.

"I've already won. Renwick said if I failed to kill you, I should make sure you understood one message."

Callum's breath stilled.

The stranger leaned close enough to whisper.

"He's in Manhattan. Already."

Callum's heart clenched.

The stranger laughed despite the pain.

"He wanted you to know."

"Why?"

"So you'd hurry."

Callum's blood ran cold.

And then the man grabbed Callum's jacket, one last act of defiance, and hurled himself backward over the rAilíng.

Callum lunged instinctively, fingers brushing fabric,

But he couldn't catch him.

The stranger fell.

His scream was swallowed by the wind.

Thirty stories down, a dull, sickening thud echoed off the street.

Silence followed.

Callum closed his eyes for a heartbeat.

Callum stood still on the walkway, breath steady, expression unreadable as he stared at the empty air where the man had disappeared.

THOTH spoke softly in his ear.

"Callum...Renwick is in Manhattan."

Callum whispered back, "I know."

He turned toward the skyline.

The Game had arrived.

Then he stepped back into the penthouse.

"THOTH," he said quietly, "scramble the building logs. Nobody sees my entry timestamp."

"Done," the AI replied instantly. "I have also triggered a temporary maintenance alert for the rooftop to discourage arrivals."

Callum took one last look toward the walkway.

The wind whipped through the broken doorframe, carrying the faint smell of ozone and city air.

He wiped the blood from his cheek with the back of his hand.

Then he headed for the interior corridor at a brisk, controlled pace.

From behind him, THOTH spoke again.

"Callum, NYPD units are en route. Estimated arrival in ninety seconds. A pedestrian witnessed the fall."

Callum swore under his breath.

It was inevitable.

In Manhattan, nothing went unnoticed, not even at dawn.

"How many witnesses?" he asked.

"Three so far. One taxi driver, one pedestrian, and one building security guard from the adjacent tower."

"Perfect."

He grabbed a cloth from a nearby drawer and quickly wiped the blood from his sleeve and collarbone. He couldn't fix the cheek bruise, but no one would connect it to a falling attacker.

"Police drones?" he asked.

"Two launched from Midtown South. Both will reach your location within three minutes."

"Kill the interior motion sensors on my floor and feed the cameras a loop."

"Already running," THOTH answered.

The AI's voice shifted, tighter, quicker, adapting to crisis mode.

Callum reached the kitchen and retrieved a nondescript gray backpack tucked beneath the counter. Inside: burner phone, spare clothes, a pair of black gloves, and a collapsible mask that could pass for cold-weather gear if needed.

"Callum," THOTH said, "the police perimeter is forming. They are sealing the street below. The body has been located."

He paused.

"And what's their assessment?"

"Initial report states a probable jumper."

Callum exhaled slowly.

That bought him time, barely.

He zipped the backpack closed and slung it over one shoulder.

As he moved toward the private elevator, THOTH spoke again.

"Callum...there is something else."

He stopped.

Waited.

"The intruder's body is being examined," THOTH said. "Police are noting irregularities."

"What kind?"

"Bone density, muscle mass, and unusual scarring. They are discussing whether to notify the medical examiner."

Callum rolled his jaw thoughtfully.

If NYPD treated the body as a normal suicide, it would vanish into the city's noise. If they escalated it, if they examined the man too closely, they would find the signs. Signs that no mortal body should carry.

Signs of the Game.

"Divert them," Callum said. "Make it appear as if the next of kin has already claimed the body."

"I can generate a valid identity," THOTH replied. "However, the police cameras at street level will show the body's fall. They may cross-check angles."

"Then give them exactly what they expect."

"Understood."

Callum stepped into the elevator.

The doors slid shut with a soft whisper, cutting off the world above.

As the lift descended, he closed his eyes and let the events of the morning settle into clarity.

A trained Immortal had attacked him.

Renwick was already in New York.

And the Pulse, the thing that shook the Highlands and the world, was accelerating.

As if summoned by his thoughts, THOTH spoke again.

"I have intercepted a shortwave transmission originating approximately four miles north of your location. High encryption. Extremely unusual signature."

"Renwick?" Callum asked.

"No. Another Immortal."

Callum's eyes sharpened.

"Who?"

"Identifying…"

The elevator reached the lobby level with a soft chime. The doors opened onto a quiet, marble-floored hall normally used only by private tenants. It was empty.

"THOTH?" he prompted again.

"I have…a partial match," the AI said slowly. "As in, the signal bearer does not appear in my known Immortal database."

Callum stepped into the corridor.

"That's not possible. Run it again."

"I have already run it four times."

THOTH paused, a rare hesitation.

"The signature is faint, but it matches tessellations found in one of your old logs."

"Which log?"

"Entry dated 1998," THOTH replied. "Location: Kyoto."

Callum froze mid-step.

The air in the corridor felt suddenly colder.

Kyoto. 1998.

He knew exactly who that entry belonged to.

"Nia..." he whispered.

Nia Tanaka, the elusive information broker of the Immortal world. A shadow among shadows. A woman who traded secrets the way others traded currency, and who never contacted anyone unless the situation was catastrophic.

THOTH confirmed quietly.

"The signature resonates with her mnemonic pattern."

"What does the transmission say?" Callum asked.

"Decrypting now."

Callum waited, heart steady, breath controlled, until THOTH responded.

"I have isolated a single phrase."

The AI's voice lowered.

"It appears...urgent."

"Play it."

A burst of static filled his earpiece.

Then,

A calm, breathless whisper:

"He's not just in Manhattan, Callum."

The elevator lights flickered.

"He's hunting."

The transmission cut.

Callum's jaw tightened.

Nia Tanaka never warned without reason.

If she was reaching out now,

THOTH continued softly.

"I am detecting additional encrypted packets. They are fragmented. Incomplete. Possibly damaged by the Pulse."

"What's the meaning?"

"I cannot parse them. But the tone suggests danger escalating on multiple fronts."

Callum turned toward the exit, his expression sharpening like a drawn blade.

"THOTH," he said, "get me a route to Helios Manhattan. And alert Graham."

"Graham is already awake," THOTH said. "He is in London, reviewing the Highland Pulse data."

"Patch him through on a secure channel."

The AI complied.

A moment later, Graham's voice emerged, groggy but alert.

"Callum? What now?"

"Renwick is here."

Graham groaned.

"You had one job, don't find him."

"He found me first."

"Bloody fantastic."

Callum stepped out onto the quiet private street, blending into the early-morning flow with the efficiency of someone who had made cities his camouflage for centuries.

"Graham," he said quietly, "we don't have long."

"You're telling me," Graham replied.

"I've just found something in the Highlands Pulse mapping...and you're not going to like it."

Callum slowed his stride.

"What did you find?"

A beat of silence.

"Renwick wasn't the only one there."

Callum's expression hardened, "Who else?"

Graham exhaled shakily.

"I think someone, or something, else triggered the Pulse with him."

Callum's heartbeat thudded once.

"Callum," THOTH said, "I've just identified a pattern near Helios Manhattan."

"What pattern?"

"Immortal. Moving fast. Toward your building."

Callum clenched his jaw.

"Is it Renwick?"

THOTH's answer cut through the morning air:

"No, but it's someone he's using."

Callum broke into a run.

The morning crowd thickened as Callum hit Lexington, merging into the surge of commuters with seamless anonymity. Suits, backpacks, coffees in hand, none of them aware that two Immortals had already fought a duel thirty floors above them; none of them aware that the next clash would erupt in their path.

THOTH guided him through the chaos with soft audio cues.

"Right turn in twenty meters," the AI murmured. "Avoid the police perimeter. They are still processing the fall."

Callum's hood was up, hands in his jacket pockets, every motion precise and unhurried. To the outside world, he was just another early commuter shaking off the cold.

But the sensation beneath his sternum, an Immortal's instinct reacting to another nearby, grew sharper with every step.

"Distance to target?" Callum asked under his breath.

"Four blocks and closing fast," THOTH said. "Trajectory suggests they are moving directly toward Helios Manhattan."

That was no coincidence.

Renwick was pushing his pawns forward.

Callum's stride lengthened, slipping between a cluster of pedestrians and emerging on Park Avenue. He turned east, heading toward 53rd, where the Helios Manhattan building rose with its mirrored façade and understated logo, an unassuming presence among steel giants.

Graham's voice crackled in his ear.

"Callum, I've run the Pulse mapping fifteen times. It keeps coming up the same."

"What are you seeing?" Callum asked.

"Something else was there. Something with Renwick, but not an Immortal signature I recognize. Not even close."

Callum frowned.

"Could it have been a sensor ghost?"

"No," Graham snapped. "How many times do I have to tell you? The sensors aren't drunk."

Before Callum could reply, THOTH cut in sharply.

"Callum, your target has accelerated. Estimated intercept: ninety seconds."

Callum crossed into the next block, approaching the Helios building.

His senses sharpened.

His pulse steadied.

THOTH's tone dropped into tactical mode.

"There is more," it said. "The signature is…unstable."

"Unstable how?" Callum asked.

"Like a newly awakened Immortal who has not yet stabilized their resonance."

Callum cursed softly.

"That means they're dangerous."

"Yes," THOTH said. "And reckless."

Pedestrians streamed past him without noticing as he reached the final crosswalk. The Helios tower loomed above, sleek, reflective, belonging to a man who did not officially exist.

He stepped onto the sidewalk.

THOTH warned:

"Callum, thirty meters."

He stopped walking.

Because he saw the figure approaching.

A man in his mid-thirties, tall, chiseled, jaw clenched in the unmistakable tension of someone overwhelmed by a new Immortal awakening.

His eyes, wild, unfocused, flicking from street sign to window reflection, told the rest of the story.

He had died recently, very recently.

And Renwick had found him.

Or worse, Renwick had *made* him.

Callum murmured, "THOTH, assess. Has he killed yet?"

"No Quickening signatures attached," THOTH replied. "He may have only just awakened."

The man staggered once, gripping a lamppost as pedestrians brushed by him. His resonance rippled, loud and discordant, like the first notes of an instrument that had never been tuned.

Then his head snapped up, eyes locking on Callum as if pulled by a magnetic force.

He shoved past two tourists.

Then a delivery worker.

Then broke into a run.

Straight toward Callum.

THOTH's voice sharpened to a blade.

"He sees you."

The man shouted, wordless, primal.

A cry of pain, rage, and confusion all at once.

Callum inhaled slowly.

Under his breath, "Poor bastard."

He stepped into the street, letting the crowd thin around them. Yellow cabs screeched. Someone yelled. A bus horn blared.

The new Immortal swung first., not with technique, but with fear.

A clumsy haymaker delivered with superhuman strength that would have shattered a mortal's jaw.

Callum sidestepped. The attacker was sloppy, the man stumbled past him, crashing into a parked car hard enough to dent the door.

"Stop," Callum said firmly. "You don't want this."

The man roared and charged again.

Callum braced.

Not to kill,

To disarm.

To protect the people around them.

The man swung wildly.

Callum parried with open palms, controlling wrists, pushing momentum aside. But the new Immortal's strength was erratic, surges of energy that made his strikes unpredictable.

Two blows clipped Callum's ribs before he could redirect him into an alley beside the Helios building.

Pedestrians stopped, startled, but none dared intervene. The fight looked like a violent mugging, too dangerous to approach, but in true voyeur nature, pulled out their phones to record the chaos.

Inside the alley, Callum pushed the man away firmly.

"Listen to me," Callum said, voice low, authoritative. "You are newly Immortal. Your mind is fighting your body. You need to stop before you hur...."

The man attacked again, a feral swing.

Callum dodged, and THOTH's voice whispered urgently:

"Callum...

I am detecting another resonance."

Callum's eyes snapped up.

On the rooftop of a building across the street,

A silhouette, too still, too deliberate, watching the alley with the posture of someone who understood exactly what had just happened.

Not Renwick.

But someone trained to move like his lieutenants.

Callum knew instantly:

The new Immortal had not found Callum by accident.

He had been delivered to him, a test, a distraction, a warning, or worse.

The first piece in a larger strategy.

The man lunged again.

Callum drove his knee into the man's stomach, hard enough to knock the wind out of him, and shoved him backward into the brick wall.

"STOP!" Callum shouted.

For one brief second, the man hesitated.

And whispered:

"He said you'd come."

Callum's blood chilled.

"Who?" he demanded.

The man trembled.

"Renwick."

Then he collapsed to his knees, tearing at his shirt, as if something inside him was burning.

Callum knelt beside him, gripping his shoulders.

"What did Renwick do to you?"

The man choked out the answer,

"He...

He woke me...forced it open."

Callum's breath caught.

Woke... not trained....not found.

Woke.

That meant Renwick had discovered a way to trigger Immortality. To create Immortals on purpose.

That was impossible.

Unthinkable.

Forbidden by every law of their existence.

THOTH spoke urgently:

"Callum, the rooftop watcher is withdrawing."

But before Callum could react,

The new Immortal convulsed, eyes rolling back.

Then something worse,

His entire resonance collapsed inward.

Fast and violent, like an implosion.

Callum's eyes widened.

"THOTH, what's happening?"

"His resonance is destabilizing!" the AI said. "I have never seen this before."

Callum grabbed the man.

"Stay with me, "

The man's final whisper cracked through his throat:

"He... he broke something in me..."

In an instant

The new Immortal's Quickening ignited.

Not a duel.

Not a kill.

"No... no, that's not possible..."

Thunder ripped through the alley.

Electric arcs leapt across dumpsters and brick walls.

Glass shattered along the street.

Pedestrians screamed and scattered.

Traffic halted.

Every car alarm in a two-block radius erupted at once.

Callum shielded his face as the violent miniature storm consumed the man, his body collapsing into radiant energy that tore upward toward the sky in a jagged bolt.

The Quickening struck the fire escape ladder overhead, exploding it into twisted metal, and dissipated into the gray Manhattan sky.

Silence followed.

A choking, horrified silence.

Callum rose slowly, chest heaving.

THOTH finally spoke.

"Callum...

Renwick has broken the rules."

Callum whispered back:

"No.

He's rewriting them – to create an army."

Smoke curled upward from the scorched fire escape. The alley was a wreck of twisted metal, broken glass, and steaming asphalt where the Quickening had detonated. A taxi on the street still honked as its alarm refused to behave.

Callum stood amid the aftermath, breathing slowly and deliberate. His coat was singed at the shoulder; his cheek still carried the faint bruise from the earlier fight. But none of it mattered.

Not compared to what he had just witnessed.

A spontaneous Quickening.

No duel. No combat. No sword.

Just a newly awakened Immortal whose body couldn't handle the resonance.

THOTH whispered in his ear, quiet as a confession.

"I am detecting…no precedent for this. Not in any recorded data. Not in your logs. Not in global Immortal history."

"I know," Callum murmured.

It shouldn't be possible.

Immortality awakened at death, violent, sudden, and final. There were no exceptions.

"What Renwick did to him," Callum said quietly, "wasn't training. It wasn't discovery."

"He stimulated the Immortality trigger," THOTH said.

Callum nodded slowly.

"And he did it wrong."

Sirens wailed in the distance, approaching fast, too fast.

Callum touched the scorched wall, feeling the residue of the Quickening. It vibrated faintly against his fingertips.

"THOTH," he said, "scrub every camera in a three-block radius. Traffic cams, street security, building systems."

"It is already done," THOTH replied. "I have also triggered a power fluctuation alert to explain the fire escape explosion."

"Good."

He stepped deeper into the alley, avoiding the lingering sparks. Police would arrive any second; he needed to disappear cleanly.

"Callum," THOTH said, "there is movement on the rooftop again."

Callum froze.

"Is it Renwick?"

"No," THOTH said. "But the watcher has returned. And he's not alone."

Callum looked upward, toward the edge of the opposite building. For a fraction of a second, a silhouette moved, then vanished.

Too far to pursue.

Too many civilians.

Too exposed.

He exhaled sharply.

"This wasn't an attack," he said.

"This was a message."

"Yes," THOTH agreed. "A demonstration."

Callum wiped soot from his jacket sleeve.

"If Renwick can force Immortality to awaken," he said, "he can weaponize it. He can make new Immortals."

"And kill them at will," THOTH added.

A chill ran down Callum's spine, not from fear, but from memory. Renwick had always believed Immortals were tools, not people. Conduits, not lives. He viewed the Game as a puzzle too simple for the potential he saw in their kind.

A spontaneous Immortal detonation?

A forced Awakening that collapsed under its own weight?

These were prototypes.

Experiments.

Callum moved toward the end of the alley.

"THOTH," he said, "track the rooftop watcher."

"Attempting," THOTH said.

Holo-lines flickered in his ear, bracketing the movements.

"Trajectory suggests…southwest. Perhaps toward Midtown West."

"Toward what?"

"I cannot confirm," THOTH replied. "But I detect an encrypted signal originating from that direction."

"Another Immortal?"

"No."

THOTH paused.

"This signal matches the signature from Nia Tanaka."

Callum stopped dead.

The whisper from earlier, the faint Kyoto voice, had been a warning.

This was something more.

If Nia Tanaka was reaching out, the situation was already worse than he'd feared.

"Patch it through."

A burst of static hissed in his ear. For a heartbeat, the city muted around him.

Then Nia's voice, calm, precise, carrying the faintest edge of urgency, cut through.

"Callum, move."

Callum's breath stilled.

"Move where?" he asked quickly.

The transmission crackled, interference, perhaps from the earlier Quickening.

"He's one step ahead of you. Don't go to Helios."

Callum blinked.

"Why not?"

A pause.

Then:

"Because Renwick wants you there."

Callum clenched his jaw.

"He already sent one of his new recruits after me."

"Yes," Nia said, "and that was just to keep your attention fixed on Manhattan."

Callum's pulse tightened.

"Nia, what is Renwick doing?"

Another burst of static.

And then:

"He's testing the world."

The line crackled violently.

"Nia!"

Her voice returned, fainter.

"Callum...Renwick's next move isn't here. He's drawing you into the open."

Callum's eyes narrowed.

"Why?"

Nia whispered:

"Because someone close to you is about to be pulled into this. Someone he wants you to protect."

A cold realization struck him.

"Lila…"

The name left his lips before he could stop it.

THOTH confirmed softly, almost apologetically:

"Callum, Dr. Serrano is at Saint Vincent's Hospital today. And Renwick is moving in that direction. His agents triggered a silent early-warning alarm inside the hospital's restricted wing three minutes ago, Manhattan PD is already en route."

Callum's blood went ice-cold.

He started running, fast, controlled, weaving through foot traffic like smoke.

"THOTH," he snapped, "get me the fastest route. Now."

"I have already plotted it," the AI replied. "And Callum, "

"What?"

The AI's voice dipped lower.

"You are not the only Immortal converging on her location."

Callum sprinted into the street, dodging a taxi by inches.

The chapter tightened around him.

"Nia," he said into the comm, "if you can hear me, stay hidden. I'm going after Lila."

Saint Vincent's was six blocks away, too close to Renwick's path, too vulnerable, and too important to ignore.

Static.

Then a faint whisper:

"Then hurry, Callum. Before he does. And Callum… you're already behind."

The transmission cut.

Chapter 3

Dr. Lila Serrano had been awake for twenty hours, which was somewhere between "functional" and "borderline hallucinating" by trauma-surgeon standards. The fluorescent lights of St. Vincent's Hospital bleached all color from the hallways, giving every surface a washed-out glow that made the world look slightly less alive than it should.

She walked briskly down the corridor, tugging her lead apron loose from her shoulders, the weight slumping off her like a reluctant passenger. Her dark hair, usually neat, had escaped its tie and now framed her face in loose, tired strands.

"Dr. Serrano!" a nurse called from behind. "CT results are uploading. The pelvic bleed looks stable."

Lila nodded without turning. "Good. Prep the patient for transfer to post-op once anesthesia signs off. And remind Dr. Alcott he still owes me coffee."

"You say that to every attending."

"Because every attending owes me coffee."

The nurse laughed and peeled off toward radiology.

Despite the exhaustion, Lila moved with the controlled urgency of someone who had learned long ago that time, not skill, killed patients. She could dash from OR to trauma bay to consult room without losing her stride, an ability that made her both admired and slightly feared.

But beneath the sharp competence lay the quiet ache of someone carrying more than charts and expectations.

Three shootings last night.

A rollover collision at dawn.

Two surgical complications she had to unravel mid-procedure.

And somewhere around hour sixteen, there was a sudden, unshakable sense that something *wasn't right*.

She didn't know why.

Only that the discomfort grew stronger as the morning deepened.

St. Vincent's wasn't a particularly beautiful building, function over form, tile over aesthetics, but she knew every crack in its floor, every scuffed corner, every flickering light that facilities never got around to fixing.

And today, everything felt one millimeter off.

A stretcher wheel squeaked too sharply.

A vital signs monitor beeped in a rhythm that jabbed her nerves.

Even the overhead paging system seemed to echo too long.

Stress, she told herself.

But stress didn't explain the pressure behind her ribs, tight, insistent, as if something unseen was running toward her.

She shook it off and stepped into Trauma 3.

Inside, a teenager sat hunched on a gurney, arm wrapped in gauze, eyes wide with bravado and fear. His mother stood beside him, hands wringing the hem of her sweater.

"You must be Dr. Serrano," the woman said immediately. "He's in pain. They won't give him anything stronger."

Lila approached gently.

"We're avoiding narcotics until I rule out an arterial tear. Strong meds could mask symptoms."

The teenager groaned. "It's literally a cut."

"It's literally seven centimeters near a major vessel," Lila corrected, examining the bandage with a practiced touch. "You're lucky."

"Sure. I feel lucky."

"You will once I repair it properly." She offered a small, genuine smile. "You'll be okay."

He relaxed fractionally.

Lila reached for a pair of gloves,

Her phone buzzed.

She glanced at it with the reflexive worry of any surgeon expecting consults or cancellations.

Unknown Number.

She froze.

Only one person used that kind of encryption for non-work contact. Callum.

Her pulse kicked.

She excused herself from the trauma bay and stepped into the hall, pressing the phone to her ear.

"Hello?"

At first, she heard only wind, and something metallic humming beneath it.

Then Callum's voice, low and tight:

"Lila, you need to leave the hospital. Now."

Her stomach dropped.

"Callum? What, what's going on?"

"I'll explain later. But you have to get out. Renwick is moving."

She blinked, disoriented. "I don't know who that is."

"A threat," Callum said. "Someone dangerous."

"When have you ever used that word lightly?" she whispered.

Never.

Even their brief interactions, strange, intense, unforgettable, had taught her that much.

Callum inhaled into the mic.

"Lila, listen to me. There are people converging on Saint Vincent's. They're not coming for the hospital."

"Then who are they coming for?"

There was a pause.

"You."

A chill crawled up her spine.

"That's not funny."

"It's not meant to be."

Her breath came fast.

"Callum, I'm at work, there are patients, "

"Lila." His voice cut clean through her panic. "You need to trust me. I am almost there."

"I don't even know what's happening. Why would anyone, "

"Because Renwick wants me," Callum said. "And he knows the fastest way to pull me out of hiding is to put you in danger."

Lila leaned against the wall, the cold tile seeping through her scrubs.

She tried to steady herself.

"Callum... are you saying someone is coming to kill me just to get to you?"

"Not someone," he said.

"Immortals."

Her breath caught.

"What, what does that even mean?"

"I'll explain everything," Callum said. "But right now, where are you exactly?"

"Trauma wing. North hallway."

"Are you alone?"

"No. Staff everywhere."

"Then Renwick's people won't strike yet." His tone softened. "They'll wait for you to be isolated. Do not isolate yourself."

Lila swallowed hard.

"Callum... please tell me you're close."

"Two blocks away."

She closed her eyes.

Then a shadow moved at the far end of the corridor.

A man she didn't recognize.

Tall.

Lean.

Eyes locked directly on her.

And he began walking toward her.

Fast.

Her voice trembled.

"Callum..."

"I see him," Callum said sharply, suddenly breathless as if he'd broken into a sprint.

"Lila, move!"

The stranger smiled.

Predatory.

Certain.

The overhead lights flickered.

The stranger's smile widened as he advanced, a predator who had already decided how the next thirty seconds would unfold.

Lila's pulse hammered.

Her grip tightened around her phone.

"Callum," she whispered, "he's coming."

"Stay where people can see you," Callum said. "Stay *visible*. Renwick's men avoid crowds."

But the corridor was emptying, shift change. Staff peeled off into side rooms, toward elevators, to the break room for coffee. The hospital's pulse was shifting, and the stranger timed his approach perfectly.

He walked with unnatural purpose, his eyes fixed on her like a target.

"Lila," Callum said sharply, "move. Now."

Montana Territory, 1884

Snow hammered the windows of the small frontier cabin, wind howling like a living thing across the empty Montana plains. Callum hauled the door shut behind him, boots sinking into the layer of ice forming on the floorboards. The winter storm had come down faster than any settler expected, harsh, white, consuming.

"Evelyn?" he called, breath turning to fog in the frigid air.

A soft cough answered.

Callum rushed across the cabin.

Evelyn lay on the narrow bed, wrapped in every blanket he owned, her skin pale, sweat beading her brow despite the cold. Her breathing came shallow, each inhale sounding like a battle her lungs were losing.

Callum dropped to his knees beside her.

"Eve... love, tell me what hurts."

Her eyes fluttered open, blue, trembling, full of exhaustion she couldn't hide.

"Everything," she whispered. "Callum... I can't... breathe."

He brushed the wet hair from her forehead.

"I'll get the doctor," he said. "Snow be damned, I'll get Dr. Halverson if I have to drag him from town."

Her hand grasped his wrist weakly.

"No... you won't make it in time. Storm's too strong."

"I can survive a damned storm," Callum said fiercely. "I'll carry you into town on my back if I've got to."

She smiled faintly.

"You forget... I'm not like you."

His chest tightened.

Immortality had complicated everything.

He couldn't tell her what he was.

He couldn't explain why he never fell sick, never bled long, never bruised for more than minutes.

He couldn't explain the nightmares he carried from other centuries.

And he couldn't explain why he would outlive her.

He kissed her knuckles, his voice trembling.

"You promised you'd let me take care of you."

"I know," she whispered. "And you have. Better than anyone."

She turned her head and winced, breath catching.

Callum shot to his feet.

"That's it. I'm carrying you to town."

He slid his arms beneath her, but she cried out, sharp and raw, and he froze.

"Callum," she whispered. "Please. Stay."

He sank back down, swallowing the helplessness rising in his chest like a tide.

Outside, the storm screamed across the plains, merciless, endless.

Inside, Evelyn's breaths grew thinner.

He held her hand between both of his, trying to warm her with his own heat, with his presence, with anything he had left to give.

"You'll be alright," he lied. "You will."

She shook her head weakly.

"No... you can't save everyone."

The words hit him harder than any blade ever had.

"I'm not losing you," Callum uttered, desperate. "Not like this. Not to a fever."

Evelyn's eyes softened.

"You'll live long enough to love many times," she murmured. "But you'll never forget this. Or me."

He bowed his head, forehead pressed against her hand.

"I don't want anyone else," he rasped. "Just you."

A soft tear rolled down her cheek.

"That's why this is so hard… for both of us."

Her breathing stuttered.

Callum's heart pounded in his ears.

"Evelyn, stay with me."

She exhaled, eyes half-lidded.

"Promise me something… Callum."

His voice broke.

"Anything."

"When you love again… don't wait. Don't hold back. Mortals don't have centuries. Don't make them wait for your truth."

He tightened his grip on her hand.

"You're going to live," he said, voice cracking.

Evelyn's eyes softened in the way only someone near the end could manage, sad, warm, knowing.

"Not tonight."

Cold swallowed the room.

Her gaze drifted past him, unfocused.

"Callum… I'm tired."

He held her.

"Stay."

She exhaled one last time.

"Thank you… for finding me…"

Her hand went slack in his.

Callum let out a sound he hadn't made in over a hundred years, a raw, hollow cry torn from some cavern deep inside him.

He gathered her into his arms, rocking her as the storm screamed outside.

He stayed that way until dawn.

He never loved anyone the same way for a long, long time.

She broke into motion.

Not running, yet, but walking fast, cutting right into the trauma bay entrance, where the teenager and his mother still waited.

The mother startled. "Doctor? Are you, "

Lila forced a smile. "Everything's fine. Stay here."

She slipped through the side door into a supply corridor.

The stranger followed.

Lila's heart pounded.

Her fingers trembled around the phone.

"Callum, where are you?" she in a hushed voice.

"Lobby," he said. Voices and footsteps rushed behind his words. "Almost to the west elevators."

"He's in the trauma wing," she said. "Tall, mid-thirties, dark coat, intense stare."

"Immortal or human?" Callum asked quickly.

"How would I know?" she hissed.

"Does he move like he owns the air around him?"

"...yes."

"Then Immortal."

Her stomach dropped.

She pushed through another door, emerging into the main staff corridor. Nurses passed by carrying IV poles. A resident yawned into his coffee. The normalcy made her dizzy.

"Lila," Callum said, "I need you to stay *in public spaces.* Do not go anywhere isolated. Not a stairwell. Not a bathroom. Not a supply room."

Too late.

The stranger appeared at the far end of the hallway, eyes locking onto her again.

He walked faster.

Her breath hitched.

"Callum," she whispered, "you need to get here *now.*"

"I'm almost there."

She turned left and burst into the central nurses' station, a circular hub filled with monitors, rolling chairs, and three nurses charting morning medications.

They looked up in surprise.

"Serrano?" one asked. "You okay?"

Lila opened her mouth to answer,

The lights flickered.

Monitors glitched.

Vital signs screens blinked.

A printer whirred and spat out ten blank pages.

Lila's pulse stuttered.

"THOTH?" Callum snapped. "What's happening in the trauma wing?"

"Resonance interference," the AI replied. "An Immortal is very close to Lila."

"Close as in, ?"

"Seventeen meters."

Lila forced herself to breathe.

The stranger entered the nurses' station slowly.

One nurse frowned. "Sir? Can we help you?"

He ignored her.

His gaze was fixed on Lila.

Her heart slammed painfully against her ribs.

"Callum, " she called out.

"I'm here."

She turned,

And saw him.

Callum burst into the trauma wing corridor at a sprint, hood down, coat flaring behind him, eyes sharp and locked onto the threat with lethal precision.

The stranger paused.

Callum didn't.

He closed the distance between them in seven strides.

"Step away from her," Callum said, voice a low warning.

The stranger smiled faintly.

"I wondered how long it would take you."

Lila looked between them, breath catching.

"Callum... what is happening?"

The stranger raised a hand, not in surrender, but in challenge.

"She's not my target," he said. "She's only leverage."

Callum's jaw tightened.

"You mistake me," the stranger added. "I'm not here to kill her."

He stepped closer.

"I'm here to *warn* you."

Callum's muscles went stone-still.

"Warn me of what?" he asked.

The stranger leaned in.

"Renwick is done waiting."

Callum's expression didn't change, but the air seemed to tighten around him.

The stranger's gaze flicked to Lila.

"Tell her," he said. "Tell her what you really are."

Callum's voice dropped. "This isn't your concern."

"Oh, but it is," the stranger replied softly. "Renwick wants her to know. He wants your world and hers to collide. He wants chaos. He wants, "

His words stopped.

His breath hitched.

His eyes widened,

Not at Callum,

But at something behind him.

THOTH's voice shot through Callum's earpiece like a blade:

"Callum, second Immortal inbound. Fast."

The stranger said with certainty, "...too late."

He turned,

Just as the hallway lights exploded.

Lila screamed as glass rained from above.

A figure slammed through the opposite doorway, another Immortal, faster than the first, crashing into the stranger like a human missile. They collided with the wall, metal clanging, tile cracking.

Nurses dove for cover.

The stranger shouted:

"RUN, DOCTOR!"

The second Immortal drew a modern short-saber, serrated with energy grooves like Renwick's other disciples.

Callum's instincts ignited.

He dragged Lila backward, shielding her as the two Immortals crashed across the nurses' station, sending chairs flying and monitors shattering.

"Callum!" Lila yelled, gripping his arm. "We have to, "

"We're leaving," he said, voice hard.

"But, patients, my team, "

"There's nothing you can do for them if you're dead," Callum snapped.

A nurse screamed as one of the Immortals hurled the other across the room. The man hit a crash cart, knocking instruments and oxygen tanks across the floor.

Lila flinched.

Callum pulled her down behind the desk.

"Stay low."

"What, what are they?".

His eyes met hers.

"Immortals."

Her breath caught.

"And they're here because of me."

A crash reverberated through the room, a body slamming into the floor only feet away.

"Callum," THOTH cut in, "you must get Lila out now. The hostile Immortal's weapon has a conductive mesh. If he discharges a Quickening inside this room, the entire hospital floor could ignite."

Lila stared at Callum, terrified.

"What does that mean?"

"It means we run," he said.

He grabbed her hand.

"Come with me."

She hesitated only a heartbeat, then she followed.

Together they sprinted into the corridor while the two Immortals clashed behind them, steel ringing against steel.

Lila's world fractured around her.

"Callum!" she cried. "What are they? What are *you*?"

Callum didn't slow.

"You'll know soon, Lila," he said breathlessly.

"But right now, survival first."

They dashed past a startled orderly, down a corridor toward the emergency stairwell.

Behind them,

A roar.

A crash.

A shock wave.

One of the Immortals was powering up,

Lila screamed, covering her ears.

Callum threw his arms around her as a brick of the hospital wall detonated behind them.

THOTH's voice shouted over the noise:

"Callum, MOVE!"

Callum kicked open the stairwell door.

Lila stumbled through.

And the door slammed behind them,

Just as the trauma wing erupted into a blinding, lightning-blue flare of Immortal energy.

The stairwell thundered from the Immortal clash exploding behind them. Concrete dust drifted from the ceiling. Harsh fluorescent bulbs flickered, buzzing as if the building itself sensed the unnatural energy tearing through its walls.

Lila gripped the handrail with one trembling hand, the other clutching Callum's arm as they descended two steps at a time.

"What is happening?" she gasped, voice cracking. "Callum, what is happening?"

He didn't sugarcoat it.

He didn't have time.

"You're being hunted."

"That's not an explanation!"

"I know," he said. "But I need you alive before I can give you the rest."

They reached the next landing.

Callum paused, just long enough to listen.

Above them, the roar of combat surged again. Heavy impacts shook the stairwell, followed by a deafening metallic screech.

Then:

Footsteps.

Fast.

Unrelenting.

Inhuman.

They were getting closer.

Callum cursed softly and pulled Lila down another flight.

"THOTH," he said under his breath, "give me the building's full sensor layout."

A glowing overlay flickered into his vision through the micro-earpiece, THOTH projecting the floor plan.

The AI's tone sharpened:

"Hostile Immortal descending the primary stairwell. He is moving at double your speed. Minimal obstacles."

"Where's the second one?" Callum asked.

"Neutralized," THOTH said. "The first Immortal killed him. Quickening confirmed."

Lila stumbled mid-step.

"That sound, back there, I felt it. It was like lightning inside my bones."

"You felt the Quickening," Callum said quietly.

"The wha, the what?"

"Later," he said.

"We're not safe."

They reached the third landing when THOTH spoke again.

"Callum, he's accelerating."

Callum muttered, "Of course he is."

Then,

Above them,

A bellowing voice echoed down the stairwell:

"MACLEOD!"

Lila froze.

Callum's posture tightened sharply, like a blade being drawn.

His last name, spoken with familiarity and venom, meant only one thing:

This wasn't just any Immortal.

This was someone Renwick had handpicked.

Callum grabbed Lila's hand again.

"We can't use the stairs. We'll be cornered."

"Then what do we do?"

He scanned the landing.

A fire axe box.

A locked access panel.

A maintenance door.

He chose the door.

He slammed his shoulder into it.

Metal bent slightly.

He hit it again, harder.

Lila stared in disbelief. "How are you, ?"

CRASH.

The door gave way.

He pulled her inside.

It was a narrow maintenance corridor running parallel to the stairwell, filled with conduit pipes, dusty cables, and the oily smell of industrial coolant.

Behind them, the Immortal's boots hammered down the stairs like war drums.

Callum pushed Lila ahead.

"Move."

She obeyed, barely, but her voice cracked as she ran:

"I don't, I don't understand, Callum, are you, are *they*, human?"

He didn't lie.

"No."

Her breath caught.

"But *you*, you look, "

"Human," Callum finished. "Yes. But I'm not."

She stumbled over a cable, bracing herself against the wall.

"Callum... what are you?"

"Later."

"You keep saying that!"

He turned to face her.

Time slowed for a heartbeat.

"Lila," he said, voice quiet but carved in steel, "if I tell you right now, you'll freeze. And if you freeze... you die. I need you to trust me, just a little longer."

Her eyes filled with a dozen emotions, fear, disbelief, betrayal,
But she nodded.

Behind them,

THOOM.

The Immortal hit the landing above the maintenance door.

Concrete cracked.

Lila flinched.

"That sounded, big."

"It is," Callum said.

They ran.

THOTH guided them through the maintenance corridor, mapping every turn, every ladder, every hatch. The fluorescent lights overhead buzzed in staccato bursts.

Then:

"Left turn. Now."

They slid into a narrow side passage just as the Immortal smashed through the door they'd broken earlier.

The wall shook violently.

Pipes rattled.

Dust filled the air.

Lila coughed. "He's going to break through everything, isn't he?"

"Yes."

"Great," she muttered. "Fantastic."

Callum almost smiled. Almost.

They reached the end of the maintenance corridor,

A grated metal door leading into the mechanical sub-level above Radiology.

Callum shoved it open.

Alarms blared above them.

Not from Immortals,

From the hospital staff responding to the chaos.

"Security breach on Trauma Wing!"

"Code Grey, violent person!"

"Repeat, Code Grey, Trauma!"

Lila winced. "God, my colleagues, "

"They're evacuating," Callum said. "THOTH is directing them

away from us."

"Your... what?"

"AI. Long story."

She shook her head, half-laughing, half-panicked.

"Oh sure. Immortals, AI, explosions. Best morning ever."

Callum didn't have time to reassure her.

This was already spiraling beyond anything he wanted her exposed to.

He moved toward the next exit,

When THOTH's voice sliced into the moment:

"Callum. Renwick has sent a message."

Callum froze.

"What message?"

A pause.

Then THOTH spoke slowly:

"He says: 'You're too slow.'"

Callum's breath hitched.

"THOTH, track Renwick's location."

"I am trying," the AI said. "His signature is masked. He is using multiple decoy resonances."

"Try harder."

"I am."

Lila stared at Callum, heart racing.

"What does 'too slow' mean?"

"It means he's not sending people after you because you're bait."

She swallowed.

"Then why, ?"

Callum turned to her.

His eyes were hard.

"He's sending people after you because he needs you alive."

Lila paled.

"Why?"

"I don't know," Callum said.

"But I'm going to find out."

Behind them,

The Immortal roared:

"MACLEOD!"

Callum grabbed Lila's arm.

"We're leaving. Now."

They punched through the door into Radiology,

And stopped.

Just for a second.

Because the lights were off.

The machines were dead.

And a soft blue glow pulsed through the room,

Like the afterburn of a Quickening.

Or something worse.

"Callum... something's in here."

He stepped in front of her as the glow intensified.

THOTH murmured in his ear:

"Callum... I recognize that frequency."

Callum frowned.

"From where?"

THOTH hesitated,

As if it didn't want to say the words.

"From the Pulse in the Highlands."

Callum's entire body went cold.

And in the corner of the darkened Radiology lab, a figure moved.

Lila gasped.

Callum's eyes widened.

Because the figure wasn't Renwick, it wasn't one of his lieutenants,
It was someone Callum had not seen in decades, someone who should
not be here.

Someone whose presence changed everything.

The figure stepped forward into the dim light.

"Hello, Callum."

Chapter 4

For a moment, Lila thought the blue glow in Radiology was just her vision going sideways from adrenaline and sleep debt. The machines were off. The overhead lights were dead. Yet the room pulsed with a soft, steady radiance, as if someone had poured moonlight into the air and given it a heartbeat.

She could feel it on her skin.

On her teeth.

In the ache between her eyes.

The figure standing in the corner stepped closer, and the glow seemed to gather around them.

Female.

Tall, strong-shouldered, wrapped in the outline of a long coat that might have been leather or wool. Details refused to settle; each time Lila's eyes tried to focus, some small feature blurred, as if the woman existed half a second out of sync with the room.

But Callum saw her clearly.

She could tell from his face.

His posture went from battle-ready to something else entirely: shock, grief, and a strange, taut hope.

The woman smiled, a flicker of warmth in the cold blue light.

"Hello, Callum."

Lila's skin prickled. The voice was accented, Highland, older than the clipped modern Scottish she'd heard in movies. It rolled like hills and stone.

Callum's reply came out rough.

"…You're supposed to be dead."

"In your terms, I am," the woman said. "In the Veil's terms, not quite."

Lila swallowed.

"The what?"

Neither of them answered her.

Callum took a single step forward, as if afraid the figure would vanish if he moved too quickly.

"Ailsa."

Lila froze.

This is Ailsa?

The name meant nothing to her, but the weight in his voice did.

The echo of blue light wrapped a little tighter around the woman's form, clarifying her just enough to see weathered features and eyes like flint struck against sky.

"You've grown slow, Callum MacLeod," she said gently. "But not deaf. You heard the world sing."

"The Pulse," he said.

"The first of many," Ailsa replied. "The Veil has been pierced. Renwick dances at the edge of it, and every step shakes the world."

Lila's heart hammered.

She looked from the woman to Callum and back again.

"Callum," she murmured, "who is she?"

He spoke without breaking eye contact with Ailsa.

"My first teacher," he said quietly. "The one who showed me what it means to be Immortal."

Lila's mouth went dry.

"So she's… like you?"

Callum hesitated.

"No," Ailsa answered for him. "I *was* like him. Now I am something the Game never intended."

The word hung there: *Game.*

Lila filed it away without understanding.

Behind them, down the hall, the pursuing Immortal's roar echoed faintly, closer now, reverberating through walls and bone.

"Time is short," THOTH murmured quietly in Callum's ear. "Hostile's closing."

Ailsa's eyes flicked toward the ceiling, toward the pounding footsteps, toward the chaos above.

"I can't hold this echo long," she said. "The Veil's thin, but not yet open. Every second I stand here, Renwick feels me."

"Then why risk it?" Callum asked.

Her gaze shifted to Lila.

"Because of her."

Lila's chest tightened. "Me?"

"Yes, lass," Ailsa said. "You're the tether."

Lila bristled despite the fear. "I'm a trauma surgeon, not a... whatever any of you are."

Ailsa's mouth curved faintly.

"A healer with a stubborn spine," she said. "You anchor him." She nodded toward Callum. "You remind him why he shouldn't let the world burn just to save himself."

Lila glanced at Callum, startled. She'd known him only in snapshots, strange, intense, guarded encounters around the hospital and in Manhattan's odd corners. Enough to know he wasn't normal. Not enough to understand why she kept thinking about him at 3 a.m.

"Renwick is testing the seams now," Ailsa continued. "Pushing power into places it never belonged. Waking Immortals who should have slept centuries more. Breaking them if they do not fit his design."

"The man in the alley," Callum said quietly.

Lila's stomach lurched, remembering the spontaneous lightning, the way the man had come apart in energy and scream.

"Yes," Ailsa said. "Prototype. A crude one. But he will learn. He always does."

Callum's face hardened. "How do we stop him?"

Ailsa shook her head slightly.

"You don't. Not yet. The Veil has rules even Renwick cannot break without cost. All you can do is prepare and keep the conduits he wants intact."

"Conduits," Callum repeated.

Ailsa's gaze moved back to Lila.

Lila folded her arms, partly to steady herself. "Conduit of what?"

"Of choice," Ailsa said simply. "And of consequence. You're a fulcrum, Doctor Serrano. The decisions you force him to make will shape the path ahead."

Lila wanted to laugh, but it came out hollow.

"I'm one overworked surgeon in a city of millions. That's not how the universe works."

Ailsa's eyes softened.

"It is how *stories* work. And the Veil is nothing but the universe remembering all the stories it's ever been told."

The hospital trembled with another distant impact. Someone shouted down the hall. A code alarm blared overhead.

THOTH spoke calmly.

"Callum, we must move. If the hostile discharges another Quickening on this floor, the electrical systems will cascade."

Ailsa's edges started to fray, blue light thinning like steam.

"Back to the Highlands," she said. "The coordinates I sent you. The old stones remember what the world forgot."

"I can't leave New York in this state," Callum said. "Renwick is here. Lila is here."

Ailsa's expression sharpened.

"You can't *fight* him here. Not yet. You're out of position. You're dancing on his board."

She stepped closer, and for a heartbeat her presence felt almost physical.

"Take her," Ailsa said quietly. "Get her away from his reach. He'll follow. He has to. The moment he realized the Veil could use mortals as anchors, he marked every strong one he saw."

Lila stared. "Use us as *what*?"

Callum's gaze flicked to her, apology, worry, calculation all at once.

"Ailsa..." he murmured. "She doesn't even know what I am."

"Then tell her," Ailsa said. "Or don't. But don't lie. You don't have the luxury anymore."

Lila swallowed. "He hasn't lied."

"Not yet," Ailsa said. "Give him time."

Callum almost smiled despite everything.

"Still blunt as ever."

"Still stubborn as ever," she returned.

The glow thinned further.

Her outline began to unravel.

"Back to the coast," Ailsa said. "To your fortress. To your machines. Let the clever mortal and the clever metal brain help you see what pattern Renwick is weaving."

Her eyes locked with Lila's one last time.

"Hold him to the living world, Doctor," she said. "He'll try to drift out of it. Don't let him."

Then she was gone.

The room plunged into ordinary darkness.

The only sound was their breathing and the faint hum of emergency power kicking back in.

Lila leaned against the nearest dead CT scanner, every nerve rattling.

"What," she said finally, "the hell was that?"

"An old ghost," Callum said. "And a not-so-subtle order."

The stairwell door banged somewhere behind them. The pursuing Immortal shouted something wordless and angry.

Lila flinched. "We're not done."

"No," Callum said. "We're changing battlefields."

He stepped to the side wall, pressed his palm against a nondescript panel. THOTH pinged softly in his ear.

"Accessing service exit," the AI said. "Route clear for forty seconds."

A segment of the wall released with a muted sigh, an old fire exit St. Vincent's had sealed years ago and never properly removed from its plans.

Lila stared. "How did you, "

"THOTH has a long memory," Callum said. "Come on."

She hesitated only a moment, then followed him into the narrow shaft, the smell of dust and cold air filling her lungs.

"Where are we going?" she asked.

"Home," he said. "Mine this time."

She almost laughed. "We just met your undead mentor and watched two demigods trash my trauma wing. Maybe I'll stay at my own place tonight."

He looked back at her, eyes serious.

"Lila, Renwick knows your name now. Your hospital. Your patterns. If you stay, you're a lever he can pull any time he wants me on the move."

Her throat tightened.

"You're asking me to abandon my patients."

"I'm asking you to stay alive long enough to help all of them," he said. "Just on a larger board."

The shaft opened onto a back stair that led down toward the ambulance bay. Sirens wailed outside; paramedics shouted. Hospital security scrambled to make sense of alarms that had nothing to do with ordinary violence.

THOTH's voice, "Rear gate clear. I have looped the nearest camera feeds."

Callum held the door halfway open, scanning.

"Choice time, Doctor," he said, not looking back this time. "You stay, I'll do what I can to keep Renwick's eyes off you. You come with me, you step into a war you didn't ask for. But at least you'll understand what you're in the middle of."

Lila's hands curled into fists.

Every instinct screamed for her to stay.

This was her hospital. Her team. Her people.

But the memory of that alley, of a man tearing himself apart in lightning because someone had "woken him up wrong", would not leave her. Neither would the image of Ailsa's impossible eyes. Or the way Callum had thrown his body around her without hesitation when the trauma wing started to explode.

She exhaled slowly.

"Fine," she said, her voice steadying. "You get one kidnapping."

He glanced at her.

"It's not a kidnapping if you choose."

"I'll decide what to call it later."

A faint smile ghosted across his face.

"There's the surgeon I recognize."

"Don't get used to it," she said. "You still owe me an explanation, MacLeod."

"And you still owe me coffee," he answered.

She snorted despite herself. "You sound like my attending."

"Then we'll get coffee on the way to the airport."

"Airport?" she repeated.

He pushed the door open wider.

"Back to the coast."

The cold morning air hit them as they stepped into the ambulance bay, blending into the organized chaos.

Somewhere above, the Immortal in the stairwell finally smashed into Radiology, two floors too late.

They moved through the ambulance bay like ghosts, purposeful, invisible to the chaos, unnoticed among the swirl of paramedics rushing to respond to the trauma wing explosion.

Callum kept Lila close but not shielded. They looked like a pair of exhausted clinicians slipping out for air after a brutal shift. No one questioned them. No one stopped them.

THOTH's voice guided Callum's every step.

"East exit clear. Two security personnel patrolling west corridor. Avoid."

Callum veered right without breaking stride.

Lila kept up, breath controlled now, though the tremor in her hand betrayed the internal storm.

When they reached the parking structure beneath the hospital, the world finally quieted. The alarms grew distant. The bustle thinned into a dim echo. Concrete walls pressed in, offering a strange sense of shelter.

Lila finally spoke, her voice steady despite everything.

"Callum, you have three minutes to explain something to me."

He glanced at her. "Three minutes?"

"Because that's how long it'll take us to reach the car," she said. "And I need answers before I get into a vehicle with you again."

Fair.

He slowed slightly, giving her room to speak.

Lila inhaled deeply, grounding herself the way trauma surgeons do before a high-stakes procedure.

"Start with the basics," she said. "What are you?"

Callum exhaled.

He had avoided this moment for centuries. Revealing himself to mortals was dangerous, for him, for them, for the Game. But Ailsa had been right. There was no time left for secrecy.

"I am Immortal," he said quietly.

Lila blinked.

"Define 'Immortal.'"

"I stopped aging at thirty-five. I can't die unless someone takes my head."

She stared at him like a doctor hearing symptoms she didn't believe but couldn't dismiss.

"Regenerative abilities," she murmured. "Enhanced healing. That explains the injuries I saw on you that... weren't possible."

She lifted her gaze.

"You don't look surprised that I noticed."

"You're a trauma surgeon," he said. "You see the truth under skin before most people do."

A flicker of something moved across her expression, appreciation mixed with something harder, quieter.

"Okay," she said. "Then what was that lightning explosion upstairs?"

"Its called a Quickening," he answered. "When an Immortal dies, their energy, their life, releases. It's violent. Unstable. It seeks another Immortal nearby."

"So that man, he died because of *you*?"

"No," Callum said firmly. "He died because Renwick forced him into Immortality before his body could stabilize."

Lila swallowed.

"That sounds like torture."

"It is."

Another few steps passed in charged silence.

They reached a black SUV tucked into a shadowed corner. Callum unlocked it. Lila hesitated before climbing in.

"You said Renwick forced him," she said. "How? How do you force something like that?"

Callum closed his door but didn't turn the engine on yet.

"Immortality awakens only when someone dies a violent death," he said. "But in rare cases, a resonance event can trigger it prematurely."

"The Pulse?"

Callum nodded.

"Renwick learned how to manipulate the Veil, the barrier between our world and whatever lies underneath it. He pulled on threads no one should touch."

Lila pressed a hand to her forehead.

"You're telling me he can... manufacture Immortals?"

"Yes," Callum said. "And kill them if they don't fit his purpose."

Her voice shook.

"And what's his purpose?"

Callum hesitated, not for ignorance, but grief.

"He wants a Second Quickening," he said quietly. "A global one. And if he succeeds, the world will not survive it."

Lila leaned back in her seat, breath trembling.

"This is insane."

"I know."

"And I'm... somehow important to this?"

He met her eyes.

"You anchor me."

Her breath caught.

"What does that mean?"

Callum looked down briefly, fingers drumming once on the steering wheel.

"Immortals can lose themselves," he said. "In centuries. In battles. In the weight of it all. I've managed to avoid that. But the Pulse is changing everything. And Renwick is manipulating that change."

He met her gaze again.

"When I met you, Lila... the world felt real in a way it hadn't for a long time."

She stared at him, caught between anger and something deeper.

"You hardly know me."

"Time works differently for us."

She shook her head. "Callum, that's not an answer. That's, "

"A truth," he interrupted softly. "One I didn't want to use against you."

"And yet here we are," she said bitterly.

He took the hit. He didn't defend himself.

Instead, he said:

"If you want to walk away after today, you can. I won't stop you. But Renwick won't stop either. And he already sees you as leverage."

Lila's throat tightened.

"You should've told me."

"You're right," he said quietly. "I should have."

Silence stretched in the SUV.

Not hostile silence.

Hurt silence.

Heavy and human.

Finally, Lila looked out the windshield toward the dim garage exit, her voice softer.

"You asked me to trust you," she said. "Now you have to trust me too."

Callum nodded slowly.

"I do."

"Then answer one more question."

He waited.

"Why me?" she asked. "Why pull *me* into this? Why care what happens to me?"

Callum didn't look away.

Not this time.

"Because," he said, voice steady, "you remind me what I'm fighting for."

Lila swallowed hard, caught off guard by the simplicity of it.

She looked at him with baited eyes,

"...Start the car, Callum."

He did.

As the engine hummed to life, THOTH spoke into his ear.

"Callum, air routes are secure. Your jet is fueled and waiting. But I have detected a new resonance anomaly following your path."

Callum's jaw tightened.

"Define 'following.'"

"Shadowing," THOTH said.

"Someone is tracking you. And they're getting closer."

Lila heard the tension in his silence.

"Another Immortal?" she murmured.

"No," Callum said.

"Something worse."

He pulled out of the garage.

The SUV climbed the ramp out of the underground garage and merged into the Manhattan morning traffic. Sirens echoed in the distance, police drones moved in tight, purposeful arcs above the avenues, and the entire trauma wing of St. Vincent's flashed red across every emergency channel.

Lila stared out the window, watching the skyline blur past, her mind racing faster than the city beneath them.

"This feels unreal," she murmured.

Callum glanced at her.

"It will feel more real with time."

"That's the problem, I don't want any of this to feel real."

He tightened his grip on the wheel.

THOTH spoke softly into his ear:

"The pursuer remains three blocks behind. Maintaining a parallel trajectory."

Three blocks.

Close enough.

Too close.

Callum kept his tone measured.

"We'll make it to the airport before they can cut us off."

"How can you be sure?"

"I know Renwick's pacing," Callum said. "He doesn't want to catch us in Manhattan. Too many witnesses. Too many variables he can't control."

"So he waits?" Lila asked.

Callum nodded.

"He always waits."

Lila turned away from the window.

Her hands were folded tightly in her lap, knuckles white. When she spoke next, it was quieter, more fragile.

"You said earlier... that I anchor you."

He nodded once.

"Why? What does that even mean for someone like you?"

He hesitated, not because he didn't know, but because explaining the truth meant stepping closer to her than he had allowed himself in years.

Before he could answer, Lila continued, her voice threading into the silence.

"When I was in med school," she said, "one of my attendings told me the world breaks two kinds of people, those who run from the cracks, and those who climb into them."

Callum listened, letting her lead.

"My mother died when I was eight," she continued. "Aneurysm. Lightning strike in her brain. No warning. No time. My father never recovered. He was a structural engineer, very analytical, very put-together, but losing her… broke something in him."

Her gaze unfocused slightly, looking inward.

"He stopped going to work. Stopped eating. I practically raised myself from ten onward. The only place I ever saw him come alive again was in a hospital, watching surgeons trying to save her."

Callum's chest tightened.

Lila swallowed hard.

"So I became one. Because if I couldn't save her, maybe I could save someone else."

"You do more than save people," Callum said quietly. "You repair the world one wound at a time."

She gave a humorless laugh.

"Yeah? Because today it feels like the world is tearing itself apart faster than I can stitch it."

He met her eyes.

"It always does, right before a shift."

"Is that what this is?" she asked. "A shift?"

"Yes," Callum said. "The world is waking up. And Renwick wants to guide the awakening in the worst way possible."

Lila watched him carefully.

Her voice softened, not fragile this time, but intent.

"And where do *you* fall in all this, Callum? You talk like a soldier. You move like someone who's done this dance too many times. But all I see is a man who walked into my trauma wing like the roof was on fire."

He considered her words.

"I'm not a soldier," he said finally. "Not anymore."

"But you were."

"Once," he admitted. "A long time ago, in different lifetimes. Now I deal with the things most people never see."

"And me?" she asked. "Where do I fall in this story I never asked to be in?"

"Right beside me," Callum said. "Whether you choose to stay there is the part I can't control."

The SUV crossed into Midtown, the traffic thinning as they approached FDR Drive.

THOTH spoke again,

Sharper this time.

"Callum, trajectory update. The pursuer has shifted north. Heading for the 34th Street heliport."

Callum stiffened.

"Why the heliport?" Lila asked.

"They're trying to guess where we're going," Callum said. "And they're not far off."

"How do we beat them there?"

"We don't have to. They don't know which exit we're taking yet."

They merged onto the FDR. The East River glittered beside them, touched by morning light.

Callum's voice softened again.

"You asked what 'anchor' means."

Lila looked at him, wary but listening.

"For Immortals," he said, "time is long. Too long. We see wars, plagues, and empires. We lose people. We outlive everyone who matters. Eventually... most of us drift. We lose our connection to the world that isn't ours anymore."

"And you?" she asked.

"I was drifting," Callum said simply. "Until I met you."

Her breath hitched.

"That's... a lot."

"It's the truth."

Lila looked away quickly, her pulse fluttering in her throat.

"Callum, I don't want to be, "

"A weakness?" he finished. "You aren't."

"You said Renwick sees me as leverage."

"That's different," Callum said. "He sees everyone as leverage. That's how he works."

Lila exhaled slowly, grounding herself again.

"I'm not sure I'm ready for any of this."

"You don't have to be ready," he said. "You just have to stay with me long enough to stay alive."

"Comforting," she said dryly.

He cracked a brief smile.

"That's the best I can do until I get you somewhere safe."

She looked at him, really looked at him.

In the fading adrenaline, she seemed to see the exhaustion behind his eyes, the centuries of weariness, the worry he tried to hide.

"Callum," she said softly, "you look like a man who's been carrying the world alone."

He blinked at that, just once, but she saw it.

"And you look like someone who wants to help even when it terrifies you," he replied. "That's why you anchor me."

The SUV moved smoothly toward the Queens Midtown Tunnel.

They were almost at the private airfield.

Almost safe.

Then THOTH, voice lower than before:

"Callum… the pursuer changed direction again."

Callum's grip tightened.

"How close?"

"Too close.

One block behind you.

On foot."

Lila froze.

"On foot?" she muttered. "No one on foot can keep up with a car."

"Immortals can," Callum said grimly.

And when he glanced in the rear-view mirror,

A figure slipped between two taxis, moving faster than human physics should allow.

Lila's heartbeat spiked.

"Callum, "

"I see him."

The SUV accelerated.

The figure accelerated with it.

Lila clenched her jaw.

"Okay," she said, "I'm officially regretting going with you."

Callum looked at her sideways, tension and affection mixing in his expression.

"No," he said quietly. "You're doing better than most people would."

"You don't know that."

"You're not screaming."

"Not externally."

He almost laughed.

Almost.

THOTH's voice cut sharply:

"Callum, prepare for impact! He's jumping!"

Lila's eyes widened.

"Jumping wh..."

A dark shape arced up from the asphalt like a thrown spear.

Callum swerved,

And the Immortal slammed into the SUV's roof with a metallic crash.

The entire vehicle shuddered.

Lila screamed.

Callum snarled under his breath, fighting the wheel.

"Hold on!"

A fist punched downward,

Metal tearing,

Sunlight flooding the interior,

The roof buckled inward with a shriek of tearing steel.

Lila screamed, covering her head as shards of metal rained down. The windshield spider webbed. Callum fought the fishtAiling SUV with both hands, knuckles white with effort.

A second blow hammered the roof,

Then a third,

The Immortal's fist punched clean through, a hand gripping the ceiling liner and tearing it open like paper.

"CALLUM!" Lila cried.

"I know!"

A snarling face appeared through the torn roof, eyes wild, teeth bared, hair whipping in the wind. He looked feral. Frenzied. Not Renwick's elegance, this was one of the brute disciples, made for pursuit, not strategy.

He reached inside with both hands,

Callum spun the wheel hard.

The SUV veered sharply toward the concrete divider.

The Immortal braced himself but lost footing. His grip slipped. His weight shifted,

Callum slammed the brakes.

The Immortal flipped forward off the roof,

Just in time for Callum to hit the gas again.

WHAM.

The SUV's rear bumper clipped the Immortal mid-roll, sending him smashing into the pavement behind them.

Lila gasped, chest heaving.

"Did... did that kill him?"

"No," Callum said, checking the mirror. "But it slowed him."

Behind them, the Immortal pushed himself upright, bones snapping back into place, muscles reknitting beneath torn clothing. He bellowed, sprinting after the vehicle again, accelerating like a nightmare gaining ground.

"Not human," Lila called out. "God... he's not human."

"Neither am I," Callum said. "Remember?"

Her breath hitched, fear and awe colliding.

The pursuer launched into another sprint, each stride an explosion of power.

Callum yanked the wheel again.

The Immortal leapt,

His hand slammed onto the rear panel instead of the roof.

The entire SUV jolted.

He began hauling himself along the side, fingers digging grooves into metal. His face pressed against the passenger window, contorted with violent hunger.

Lila met his gaze.

And he smiled.

She recoiled.

Callum slammed the brakes again.

The Immortal swung forward, slamming against the hood. He clawed at the glass, cracking it.

"OUT!" Callum shouted. "Go, GO!"

He didn't give Lila time to argue.

He kicked open his door, grabbed her arm, and yanked her out into the cold wind and shrieking traffic.

They stumbled onto the shoulder as a taxi honked and whipped by inches from them.

The Immortal lunged over the hood,

Callum met him halfway.

The two collided with the force of sprinting animals, rolling across the asphalt, fists and elbows hammering in rapid succession.

A car swerved. Another skidded to a halt. Horns blared in panic.

Lila scrambled backward, heart in her throat.

Callum rolled on top and punched the Immortal hard enough to crack cheekbone.

The Immortal retaliated with a headbutt.

SKULL TO SKULL.

The sound echoed.

Callum staggered.

The Immortal tackled him onto the median barrier.

"CALLUM!" Lila screamed.

He couldn't answer, blood in his teeth, fighting for leverage.

The Immortal raised a jagged shard of the SUV roof, lifted as a makeshift blade,

, and swung downward toward Callum's throat.

Reflex screamed through Lila's brain.

Without thinking, she grabbed a fallen length of broken rebar from the divider and swung it with everything she had.

The metal bar slammed into the Immortal's shoulder.

He snarled, stumbling sideways.

Callum seized the opening.

He grabbed the Immortal's wrist, twisted,

CRACK.

The weapon dropped.

Callum shoved the Immortal backward over the barrier.

They both went tumbling down the slope toward the service road.

Lila ran after them, lungs burning.

At the bottom of the slope, Callum pinned the Immortal against the concrete wall. The disciple fought wildly, kicking, clawing, spitting rage.

"Why her?" Callum snarled. "Why target HER?"

The Immortal only laughed,

A choking, mocking sound.

"She's the tether," the disciple hissed. "Renwick wants the tether."

Lila froze.

Callum's face darkened.

"You don't know what that means."

"Oh, I do," the Immortal croaked. "She's what keeps you from drifting. What makes you fight harder. What breaks you when you lose her."

His grin widened.

"And Renwick will make you lose her."

Callum slammed him against the wall hard enough to crack concrete.

The Immortal laughed through blood.

"That's it," he hissed. "Feel it. Feel what he wants you to feel."

Callum's breath shook, rage and something far colder mixing in his chest.

Lila stepped forward, voice trembling.

"Callum... stop."

He didn't move.

"Callum," she said again, stronger this time, stepping closer. "Look at me."

He did.

Not at the disciple.

At her.

She put her hand on his arm.

"Don't give him what he wants."

The Immortal hissed, "Soft. Weak. Pathetic mort... "

Callum hit him once.

Just once.

Enough to drop him unconscious.

Callum wiped blood from his mouth and stood, breathing hard.

"THOTH," he rasped, "route us to the airport. We're done here."

"Route plotted. Two miles north. No immediate threats detected."

No immediate threats.

Lila wasn't sure she believed that anymore.

Callum climbed the slope and held a hand down for her.

She took it.

At the top, she said quietly:

"You didn't kill him."

"I'm trying," Callum said softly, "to be better than Renwick."

The weight of that hung between them.

They got back into the SUV, dented, roof torn, windshield shattered, and pulled back onto the road.

Lila leaned her head against the seat, breathing slow.

"What happens now?"

"We get to the airport," Callum said. "Then we fly west."

"And after that?"

He looked at her with an expression she had never seen from him before, half fear, half resolve.

"Then," he said, "we get you somewhere Renwick can't reach."

Lila's voice was barely audible.

"Is there such a place?"

Callum didn't answer right away.

Then,

"There is," he said. "But it's not easy to return to."

The SUV sped toward the private airfield.

The Immortal behind them did not rise again.

But the Game was moving.

The private airfield sat on the eastern edge of Queens, quiet and gray in the late morning haze. A few hangars stood like steel monoliths against the sky, their doors cracked open for maintenance crews. The runway stretched long and empty, humming with subtle heat as the sun finally broke through the overcast.

Callum guided the battered SUV past the security gate. The guard, accustomed to Helios' black-level clearance protocols, barely glanced at the authorization before raising the barrier.

Lila sat rigid in the passenger seat, staring at the world passing her window with the hollow focus of someone who had endured more in the last hour than in the last decade.

Finally, she broke the silence.

"Callum... that man back there. He said Renwick will make you lose me."

He didn't answer immediately.

Lila continued, voice low but steady.

"Is that why you're running? Is that why we're going to California? Because you think the safest place for me is the farthest place away?"

Callum kept his eyes on the road ahead.

"It's not about distance," he said. "It's about terrain. I know the terrain back home. I know the systems. The defenses. THOTH controls everything. Renwick can't blindside me there."

Lila absorbed this.

"Your fortress," she murmured.

"Your machines. Your... life."

Callum nodded.

"And you," she added quietly. "You're taking me into all of that."

He pulled the SUV to a stop beside a sleek, matte-gray long-range jet. Its engines were already spooling at idle, heat rippling from the exhaust cones. A pilot in Helios flight blacks waited near the stairs, helmet tucked under his arm.

Callum turned to her.

"You can still walk away."

She laughed softly.

It wasn't humor. It was disbelief.

"After all that? After seeing lightning explode a man? After watching you fight a monster on top of a moving car?" She shook her head. "No, Callum. I think the 'walk away' option expired when Ailsa showed up glowing in my radiology suite."

He exhaled a breath he didn't realize he had been holding.

"Are you sure?"

"No," she said honestly. "But I'm going anyway."

He admired her for that, not the bravado, not the recklessness, but the clarity. Trauma surgeons didn't wait for courage. They moved with fear and functioned anyway.

He stepped out of the SUV and opened her door.

She climbed out.

The pilot approached, only to halt when Callum raised a hand.

"Flight plan?" Callum asked.

"Direct to Vandenberg Auxiliary Field," the pilot said. "Weather's clear. No traffic advisories. THOTH uploaded threat markers."

"Any anomalies on the radar sweep?"

"Negative."

Callum nodded.

Lila pulled her coat tighter around herself. The wind smelled faintly of jet fuel and salt.

"Callum," she said, softer now, "you still haven't told me why me."

He didn't meet her eyes at first.

Then he did.

"When Ailsa died," he said quietly, "something in me shut off. I stopped seeing the world in color. It didn't matter whether I lived another year or another century. Everything felt gray."

Lila swallowed.

"And then I met you."

A beat passed.

"Callum… you barely know me."

"It doesn't take centuries to recognize something that anchors you," he said. "Sometimes it takes moments."

A flicker of emotion crossed Lila's face, confusion, warmth, fear, and something dangerously close to longing.

She looked away, throat tight.

Before she could respond, THOTH's voice sliced in:

"Callum, movement on the south perimeter."

Callum's muscles tensed instantly.

"How many?"

"One. Resonance unstable. Unknown affiliation."

Lila stiffened.

"Another Immortal?"

"Maybe," Callum said, scanning the horizon.

"Or something Renwick made."

They moved fast, Callum pulling Lila toward the jet stairs. The pilot barked an order into his comm and sprinted toward the cockpit.

"THOTH," Callum snapped, "visual feed."

A translucent holo shimmered in his peripheral vision, THOTH splicing through the airfield's security cameras.

A figure limped across the southern taxi lane toward the runway.

Lila gasped.

"Callum... he's hurt."

The figure moved unevenly, clutching one arm, head lowered. Blood darkened the side of his shirt. He looked half-dead, but alive enough to drag himself forward.

"Who is he?"

Callum didn't answer at first.

He moved closer to the edge of the tarmac, eyes narrowing.

The figure lifted his head.

Callum froze.

"Graham," he breathed.

Lila blinked. "Graham? As in, your friend Graham?"

The CEO.

The public face of Helios Dynamics.

The mortal who built the infrastructure that allowed Callum to hide in plain sight.

He staggered closer, voice hoarse.

"Callum, "

Callum ran.

He met Graham halfway across the tarmac, catching him before the man collapsed. Lila followed, heart pounding, adrenaline forcing her legs to move.

Graham's face was pale, streaked with soot and blood. His breath came in ragged pulls.

"What happened?" Callum demanded. "Who did this?"

Graham grabbed his coat, fingers trembling.

"He... found me."

Lila felt a chill go through her.

"Renwick?" Callum asked.

Graham shook his head weakly.

"No. Not him. One of his... constructs." He coughed hard, blood flecking his lips. "They hit me in London. Tracked me when I tried to leave for the Highlands. The Pulse drew them."

Callum's blood turned cold.

"Why London?"

Graham swallowed.

"Because I found something. In the Pulse mapping. Something Renwick didn't want seen."

"What did you find?" Callum asked urgently.

Graham's eyes locked onto his.

"A second location."

Callum's breath stilled.

"What location?"

Graham's voice cracked, the words rasping out:

"Renwick wasn't alone at the Highlands, Callum. He wasn't even the one who triggered the Pulse."

Lila's head snapped up.

Callum's entire world tilted.

"Who?"

Graham's answer was barely audible.

"A child."

Lila's breath caught.

"A... child? Callum, what does that mean?"

Callum didn't move.

"Graham," he said, voice razor-thin, "what child?"

"The one with the strongest resonance I've ever seen," Graham gasped. "More powerful than any Immortal alive."

He clutched Callum's coat tighter.

"And Renwick is going to use them to break the Veil."

Callum felt the ground fall away.

THOTH's voice spoke over the comm:

"Multiple signatures approaching. We must depart immediately."

Callum lifted Graham into his arms.

Lila ran ahead to the jet, pulling the door open as the engines surged louder.

Callum climbed the stairs, Graham fading in his arms.

"Callum..." Graham strained.

"You have to find the child before he does."

Callum's jaw clenched.

"I will."

Graham's eyes fluttered closed.

"Don't let the world end," he murmured.

Then he went still.

Lila covered her mouth, horrified. She reacted instinctively and felt for a pulse...nothing.

"Is there a defibrillator on board?" she asked while trying to assess the situation...trauma, crush injuries, internal bleeding.

Lila went into full surgeon mode.

Callum lowered Graham gently into one of the cabin seats, knuckles trembling with held fury.

Lila was ripping his shirt off to start CPR, when Callum put his hand on her shoulder.

"Lila, stop...he's gone."

Words that no surgeon wants to hear.

Lila was on a plane, not in an operating room, there wasn't much she could do.

"Callum," Lila looked up at him and breathed, "I'm so... I'm so sorry."

He didn't answer.

The engines roared.

Outside, dark figures began emerging at the far edge of the runway.

The pilot shouted, "We're rolling!"

Callum strapped Lila in, then himself. The jet surged forward, acceleration slamming them into their seats.

The runway blurred.

The figures behind them sprinted, too fast, too powerful, closing the distance as the jet lifted off.

But too late.

The wheels left the ground.

The jet climbed sharply, leaving Manhattan, and Renwick's hunters, shrinking beneath a gray morning sky.

Beside him, Lila reached shakily for his hand.

Callum took it.

Graham's words echoed in his mind.

A child.

A resonance like nothing before.

And Renwick wants them to break the Veil.

This wasn't the war Callum was expecting.

It was something worse.

And the coast was only the beginning.

Chapter 5

Graham Slate was dead.

The words did not echo in the cabin, because Callum would not let them, but they carved themselves into the quiet like a blade dragged across glass.

The jet cruised smoothly at forty-two thousand feet, engines humming with the dependable confidence of Helios engineering. Beyond the windows, the world lay far below in a quilt of cloud tops and soft, distant curvature.

Inside, the air felt still. It had been that way for the last three hours while they headed west.

Callum sat beside Graham's body, hand resting briefly on the armrest near his friend's still fingers. The CEO's face was gray and slack, his injuries deeper than he had allowed himself to admit while conscious. His clothing was torn, scorched, and mottled with dried blood.

Renwick had done this.

Lila watched from across the aisle, her chest tight with a different sort of pain, less ancient, less cosmic, but deeply human. The kind that came from watching grief slip through someone like Callum; a private grief, an old grief, yet freshly cut.

She didn't speak. She let the moment be.

Finally, Callum stood, lifting a blanket from the overhead storage and draping it carefully over Graham. Lila noticed the way his hands shook.

Then he turned to her, eyes unreadable.

"He shouldn't have come alone."

Lila swallowed. "He came to warn you."

"Yes."

The word held equal parts gratitude and fury.

Lila stepped closer.

"Callum... I didn't know him, but, "

"He was my friend," Callum said quietly. "For thirty years. The longest friendship I've had in a century."

Her breath caught.

In that single sentence, she understood something essential about Immortals, not just their power, not just the Veil or the Game, but the loneliness etched into their bones.

She stepped beside him, close enough that their shoulders nearly touched.

"Then I'm sorry," she said. "For his loss. And for yours."

Callum exhaled, slow and controlled.

But the grief didn't move. It settled deeper.

THOTH broke the silence.

"Callum, I have reconstructed Graham's final data packet."

Callum straightened.

"Show me."

A holographic projection shimmered in the aisle, subtle blue lines forming a map of the Scottish Highlands. The Pulse epicenter glowed like a starburst north of Ben Craeg.

But now,

A second point pulsed brighter.

Smaller. Sharper.

Not where the Pulse originated, but where it had *collided* with something.

Lila leaned in, breath hitching.

"What is that?"

THOTH answered:

"The second resonance Graham detected. The signature he followed. The child."

111

Lila's throat tightened.

Callum felt his blood cool.

"THOTH," Callum said, "define 'child.'"

"Based on the data available: approximate age: eight to ten. Unstable Immortal signature. Stronger amplitude than any recorded Immortal, living or dead."

Lila stepped back.

"How?"

Callum didn't answer.

THOTH continued.

"The child is not yet fully Immortal. Their resonance is... embryonic. Dormant, but awakened by the Pulse."

A jolt passed through Callum, pain, shock, and a deeper fear.

Lila glanced at him, noticing the subtle shift.

"Callum... what does that mean?"

"It means," Callum said slowly, "this child isn't like us. They didn't awaken through death. They awakened through the Veil."

Lila blinked. "Through Ailsa's world?"

"Yes."

"And Renwick wants them."

"Yes," Callum said again. "Because if he gets them, he can tear the Veil open."

Lila's pulse quickened.

"You said the Veil is... what? A barrier?"

Callum nodded.

"Between the mortal world and all the resonance behind it. All the potential. All the stories that create Immortality."

"And this child is connected to it?"

"More than connected," Callum said quietly. "They're attuned to it. They are the Veil's echo made flesh."

Lila stared at him, stunned.

"Callum... that's impossible."

He gave a humorless smile.

"You should stop saying that word."

She looked away, trying to piece together the magnitude of what they'd stumbled into.

THOTH spoke again:

"Graham was right. Renwick did not trigger the Pulse. The pulse came from the child."

Callum closed his eyes.

Ailsa's earlier whisper echoed in his mind:

The world sings before it bleeds.

He opened his eyes.

"THOTH, can you project the waveform of the child's resonance?"

A second hologram appeared,

A looping, spiraling lattice of harmonic energy.

Lila stared at it.

"That looks like... a heartbeat."

"It is," Callum said. "In its own way."

"And that lattice shape..." Lila said, "I've seen it before."

Callum looked at her.

"Where?"

"In the OR," she said. "In aneurysm mapping. In anomalous blood-flow imaging, it's called the Lattice Boltzmann Method. I don't know what it means in this situation, but it doesn't look healthy."

Her eyes widened.

"If I had to guess, that child isn't stable. They're in danger."

"Yes," Callum said softly. "And Renwick wants to use that instability."

Lila's breath trembled.

"What happens if he gets to the child first?"

Callum held her gaze.

"He will kill them. And take their Quickening."

Lila's face went pale.

"Callum... that's a child."

"I know."

The projection dissolved.

The cabin dimmed.

Lila stepped toward him, voice low but fierce.

"Then we get to that child before he does."

Callum nodded.

"We will."

A long silence followed, quiet, heavy, grounding.

THOTH interrupted:

"Callum, we are approaching Vandenberg airspace. Ready for descent."

Lila exhaled. "Back to your fortress."

"Yes," he said. "Where we regroup. Analyze. And prepare."

"For what?" she asked.

He looked at her.

"For the truth," he said. "About Immortality. About Renwick. About the Veil. And about the war he's trying to start."

The jet banked toward the coastline.

The Pacific rolled beneath them like hammered silver.

Lila reached for her seatbelt.

Callum watched her for a long moment.

Then looked back toward the covered form of Graham Slate.

Forgive me, he thought silently.

Your death won't be meaningless.

The jet dipped beneath a thin line of cloud, and the California coastline unfolded beneath them, raw and wind-carved, a magnificent collision of land and sea. The waves hammered the cliffs with ancient rhythm, sending spray high into the air like shattered jewels.

Lila pressed a hand to the window.

"It's beautiful. I've never been to the west coast"

Callum followed her gaze.

"It's home."

The fortress estate appeared a moment later, at first a sliver of steel nestled into the cliffside, nearly invisible from the air. Then the structure revealed itself piece by piece as the jet's angle shifted:

Terraced platforms layered into the rock.

Glass corridors suspended over the ocean.

Gunmetal helipads.

Solar arrays shaped like angled obsidian wings.

It did not look like a house.

It looked like a citadel designed by someone who had lived through civilizations and outlasted them all.

Lila's breath caught.

"This is where you live?"

"Yes."

"It looks like a Bond villain's summer home."

Callum allowed a faint smile.

"Architect's choice, but I've made some modifications over the years."

The jet banked again, aligning with a private landing strip concealed between two stone ridges. As they descended, Lila caught sight of the structures at lower levels, an underground hangar door disguised as rock, a seawater filtration system glowing faintly, and a long, curved exterior balcony that seemed suspended directly above the ocean.

Her voice softened.

"Callum... it's incredible."

"It's secure," he said. "That's what matters."

Beneath its dramatic exterior, the estate was less a home and more a fortified retreat. Callum had constructed it around THOTH long before the system even had a name, integrating sensor conduits, resonance dampeners, and fiber-spine channels directly into the support structure. The outer walls were layered with a composite he'd patented through a shell corporation, capable of disrupting EM signatures and hiding the subtle, instinctive hum Immortals radiated around each other. Every room, hallway, and even the curvature of its windows served a purpose: to keep him invisible in a world that had become too connected, too curious, and too dangerous for someone with his longevity.

Most visitors saw steel, glass, and extravagance. Lila would soon learn that the estate was a fortress shaped by centuries of hard-won caution. Beneath the cliffside façade lay a sealed armory spine, climate-shielded archival chambers, and shock-absorbing pylons designed to withstand the violent discharge of a full Quickening. Callum had designed it with the same care a soldier reserves for a final fallback position—one place on earth where he could not easily be found, tracked, or overwhelmed. Losing it would mean more than property destruction; it would mean the collapse of every safeguard he had built to survive the modern age.

A few moments later, the wheels touched down smoothly.

A convoy of small electric transports rolled from an underground lift as the jet taxied to a halt. One of the rear doors slid open, revealing a sleek receiving bay lined with thick glass and reinforced steel. No staff emerged, only the bay itself, automated and eerily quiet.

The pilot disembarked first, then nodded for Callum and Lila to follow.

Callum lifted Graham's covered form himself, refusing help. Lila walked beside him in quiet solidarity as they made their way down the jet stairs.

Two black SUVs were waiting.

Two men got out and helps Callum put Graham's body in the back of one of the SUVs and Callum motioned for Lila to get into the other one.

The ride back to the estate was quiet…it felt like a wake of its own. Lila was used to delivering bad news and was surrounded by death all the time, but this was different; this felt personal loss. She could feel the emotion coming off of Callum even though was silent, staring out the window.

The SUV pulled into the estate and Callum seemed to come back to reality. The receiving bay doors opened and the SUVs pulled in.

THOTH flooded the interior with soft light.

"Welcome home, Callum and Dr. Serrano."

Lila flinched.

"I keep forgetting your AI talks like a person."

"That's because it's better than most," Callum said, stepping inside.

The bay sealed behind them with a muted hiss.

Lila took a slow breath, letting the sterile, chilled air ground her. The bay had the smell of ozone, steel, and clean circuits, a surgical suite disguised as a hangar.

"THOTH," Callum said quietly, "prepare a chamber in the memorial vault."

Lila blinked.

"A memorial… vault?"

He didn't look at her.

"For Immortals? Those we lose still deserve dignity."

Lila's heart tightened.

The bay lights dimmed in acknowledgement.

Callum laid Graham's body on a levitating stretcher, then stepped back. His hands lingered on the cover a moment too long before he finally released it.

Only then did he turn to THOTH.

"Status report."

"Perimeter stable. Resonance anomalies remain distant, but I am expanding surveillance by one hundred kilometers. No immediate threats approaching the estate."

Lila exhaled, relieved.

Callum wasn't.

He set his jaw.

"Define 'distant.'"

"One anomaly at ninety-two kilometers. Two more at one hundred forty-five. All unstable. Possibly Renwick's constructs."

Lila stiffened.

"Constructs. You make them sound like... prototypes."

"They are," Callum said.

She didn't want to ask what they were made from.

Instead, she followed him deeper into the estate.

The corridor beyond the receiving bay opened into a stunning, angular atrium, sunlight pouring through transparent ceiling panels, illuminating dark metal floors that mimicked black river stone. The entire space hummed with clean, efficient energy.

The ocean roared below the glass underfoot.

Lila paused, awestruck.

"Callum... this place is unreal."

Callum stepped beside her, his gaze drifting across the atrium as if seeing more than the architecture. "It's the third place I've ever called home," he said quietly. "The first was the Highlands... what's left of it. The second was a stone cottage I shared with someone I cared for, long ago." His hand brushed the rAilíng, fingers tracing a faint etching almost invisible in the metal—a crescent knot carved in the style of old clan markings. "This one I built myself. Every inch. Every design choice. After a few centuries of running, it felt time to stop pretending I was only passing through the world."

Lila followed his line of sight and noticed what she'd missed earlier: subtle splashes of legacy woven into the modern geometry. A claymore-shaped beam integrated into a support column, a rough-hewn stone set discreetly into the wall—Highland granite, its weathered surface deliberately untouched. "Ailsa, my mentor, gave me that stone," he said when he caught her studying it. "Told me to put it somewhere I intended to stay." He exhaled softly, a gesture threaded with memories and old ghosts. "So I built a sanctuary around it—something worthy of her, and of the life I never thought I'd have."

"It was also designed to disappear," he said. "To survive centuries, storms, and whatever war comes."

"Why build something like this?"

He didn't answer directly.

Instead:

"When someone has lived as long as I have, they learn to anticipate trouble. Renwick's return confirms everything I built this place for."

Lila swallowed.

"You've been waiting for him?"

"No," Callum said quietly. "I've been preparing to stop him."

A silence settled as they walked.

Lila's voice softened.

"You said earlier that Immortals drift. Lose their connection to the world. Is that why you built this? To anchor yourself?"

Callum considered her, then shook his head slightly.

"No.

This was built for others.

For the people I failed to save before."

Lila froze.

Not from fear, but from recognition.

Because she understood that sentence more than he realized.

Her mother.

Her patients.

Her own failures still haunted the back of her mind when she closed her eyes.

"This fortress," she said, "is your promise to them."

"Yes," Callum admitted quietly. "And to whoever the world still expects me to protect."

She looked away, lost in her own storm.

"And now that includes me," she murmured.

"It always did," Callum said before he could stop himself.

She inhaled sharply, but didn't argue.

They entered the central command chamber.

THOTH brightened the circular room, revealing a massive holographic display of the globe suspended above the centerpiece console. Energy signatures pulsed across continents in intricate lattices, small for ordinary electromagnetic clusters, larger where resonance anomalies appeared.

Lila's eyes widened.

"Callum... this is..."

"A map of every Immortal resonance on the planet," he said. "And a real-time sensor grid tied to THOTH's arrays."

There were thousands of them.

"Is this legal?" she asked.

He shrugged.

"Probably not in the strict sense of the law."

"You don't care."

"I care about the cost of ignorance," he said. "Especially now."

THOTH interrupted:

"Callum, new data from the Pulse. The child's resonance has shifted."

Both turned to the hologram.

A new sphere pulsed, brighter, sharper than before, deep in the Highlands.

Lila stepped closer, her instincts as a surgeon rising to the surface.

"It's stronger," she murmured. "More consistent. Almost like..."

"Like the child is stabilizing," Callum said.

"No," Lila corrected. "It looks like they're... calling."

Callum stared at her.

"Calling what?"

Lila's voice trembled.

"You."

THOTH reinforced her conclusion:

"The waveform has begun to mirror Callum's signature. Very faintly, but with increasing synchronicity."

Callum went still.

Lila swallowed.

"That child... they're reaching for you."

He didn't answer.

Because inside, he felt something he hadn't felt since he was young, since before the Game, before Renwick, before Ailsa.

A tether that didn't belong to Lila. Something else pulling at him.

Something older.

Something raw.

Something that felt like destiny was being carved early.

Lila watched his face tighten.

"Callum... what does that mean?"

"It means," he said, voice low and dark, "that the Veil didn't send Ailsa only to warn me."

"Then why?"

"To summon me."

The hologram flickered.

THOTH delivered the final blow:

"Callum, resonance analysis suggests the child carries not just power, but lineage."

Callum's eyes narrowed.

"Lineage? From who?"

THOTH paused abnormally long, then spoke:

"From you."

Callum's heart stopped.

The chamber felt suddenly smaller, as if the weight of the holographic projection had pressed the air itself into something dense and electric.

Callum stared at the pulsing signature on the world map, small, brilliant, impossibly alive.

A child.

A Veil-born Immortal.

With a resonance that mirrored his.

His own.

Lila stepped forward slowly, eyes darting between Callum and the hologram, her voice caught somewhere between disbelief and a doctor's instinct to decode the impossible.

"How... how is that even possible?" she muttered.

Callum didn't answer.

He couldn't.

His heartbeat thudded like a deafening metronome in his ears. All his centuries of discipline, past battles, betrayals, victories, and losses, none of it had prepared him for a revelation like this.

He wasn't supposed to have lineage.

No Immortal was.

Lila saw the shock on his face.

"Immortals don't have children. That's the rule." Callum struggled to get out.

"Then explain this!" she demanded gently but firmly, gesturing to the glowing signature.

THOTH answered before Callum could.

"Correction: you cannot pass lineage through biology. However,... lineage can be carried through resonance."

Lila blinked. "Through what?"

Callum finally tore his gaze from the hologram.

"Resonance," he said softly. "Immortal energy. Our... essence."

Lila processed that, her medical mind climbing to meet a problem that logic wasn't built for.

"So you're saying... the child didn't inherit anything from your genes."

"No," Callum said.

"They inherited your... what? Your energy? Your spark as you call it?"

"Yes."

Lila stared at him in awe and something like fear trying to reconcile this with her scientific brain.

"That means," she hypothesized, "this child is connected to you in a way deeper than blood."

THOTH agreed.

"The child's signature is an echo of Callum's. The match is above ninety-three percent."

Callum's breath caught.

Immortals didn't leave legacy except through those they trained.

Immortals didn't echo.

And yet... he felt something tugging at him from across the world.

A pull he had felt only once before.

Ailsa.

Her memory echo.

Her warning.

The world sings before it bleeds... and you, my stubborn lad, must listen.

And now the world was singing with his own signature.

Lila's eyes brimmed with questions that wouldn't form words.

THOTH, however, had no such hesitation.

"Callum," THOTH said, "there is additional data."

Callum steadied himself.

"Go on."

"The Pulse awakening the child also awakened... something else."

Lila frowned. "Something like what?"

THOTH zoomed in on the Highlands map.

Two overlapping resonance fields pulsed,

One was the child.

The other...

Callum's breath hitched.

"That's Renwick," he murmured.

"No," THOTH corrected.

"Renwick's signature is the smaller one."

Lila blinked. "Then what is the larger one?"

THOTH highlighted the massive field pulsing just north of the child's location.

It dwarfed the child.

It dwarfed Renwick.

It dwarfed anything Callum had ever seen.

"That," THOTH said, "is the original rupture point in the Veil."

Lila froze.

"No. That's impossible. The Veil hasn't been breached that deeply since, "

He stopped himself.

Lila's gaze sharpened.

"Since when?"

THOTH answered what Callum did not.

"Since the First Gathering, definitely not since I've had the ability to monitor resonances."

Callum closed his eyes.

Lila turned to him.

"What's the First Gathering?"

He opened his eyes slowly.

"It's the oldest Immortal myth," he said. "Older than Scandinavia. Older than Rome. Older than the written word."

"Callum," she said, "explain."

"It was said," he breathed, "that before Immortals wandered the earth, before Quickening became part of our cycle, there was a moment, a single moment, when the Veil opened on its own."

Lila's voice trembled.

"And what came through?"

Callum stared at the hologram.

"Not what," he said quietly.

"Who."

THOTH added:

"Historical resonance fragments imply that a being, not quite mortal, not quite Immortal, stepped into the world during the First Gathering. A child."

Lila's heart lurched.

Ailsa's final words replayed in her head:

Hold him to the living world, Doctor.

He'll try to drift out of it.

Callum said,

"The child in the Highlands... is not the first of their kind."

Lila's throat tightened.

"And Renwick knows this?" she asked.

"Yes."

"And he wants to use this child to, what? Tear open reality?"

Callum nodded grimly.

"If he takes the child's Quickening, it won't just give him power. It will give him *authority* inside the Veil. He'll be able to shape resonance the way the First Gathering figure did."

Lila felt sick.

Her voice was barely audible.

"Callum... what is the Veil?"

He looked at her gravely.

"It's where our Quickening comes from. The source of the Immortal spark. The divide between life and myth. Between mortality and the stories that shaped us."

"And the child?"

"The child," Callum said, "is a doorway."

Lila gripped the console for balance.

"And you, are the key?"

Callum didn't deny it.

For the first time in centuries, he felt the past calling him,

Not through memories, not through battles, but through something alive and waiting.

A child with his resonance.

A child the Veil chose.

Lila stepped closer.

"What do we do?" she asked.

Callum met her gaze.

"We find them," he said.

"And we stop Renwick from rewriting the world."

Callum paced the center of the command chamber, tension radiating from him like heat from a furnace. The hologram of the Highlands pulsed steadily in the air, the child's resonance beating like a distant heartbeat.

Lila watched him with growing worry.

He wasn't angry.

He wasn't panicked.

He was… adrift.

A man suddenly confronted with a truth he wasn't built to accept.

"THOTH," Callum said sharply, "run the lineage analysis again."

"I have run it nine times," the AI replied.

"The conclusion remains unchanged."

Lila crossed her arms, struggling to wrap her head around the concept.

"You said Immortals don't have children," she said softly. "Are there exceptions?"

"No." Callum shook his head. "There have never been exceptions. Not in all recorded history."

"Then how do you explain the resonance match?"

"I can't," he growled.

THOTH interjected:

"If I may clarify: this is not biological lineage. Resonance lineage is a separate phenomenon. It occurs only when the Veil forms a direct, intentional connection."

Lila frowned.

"Intentional? As in... a choice?"

"Correct," THOTH said.

"The Veil chose Callum. And by extension, chose the child."

Lila felt a chill.

"That makes it sound like, "

"A destiny," Callum finished bitterly.

Lila's eyes softened.

"Callum... is that such a terrible thing?"

He stopped pacing, turning toward her.

"You don't understand," he said, voice low. "Immortals don't get destiny. We get survival. We get centuries of loss and the broken pieces of every life we've lived." His jaw tightened. "We don't get chosen."

Lila stepped closer.

"But maybe this child does."

He looked away.

Lila studied him, seeing the cracks beneath the armor.

This wasn't about fear.

It was about responsibility.

A weight so sudden and so massive it threatened to drown him.

"You've spent your whole life saving people you barely knew," she said. "Maybe now you have a chance to save someone who's actually connected to you."

Callum's throat tightened.

"It shouldn't be possible," he muttered. "Why would the Veil give me a child?"

"Maybe it didn't," Lila said gently. "Maybe the child existed. And when the Pulse hit... they reached for someone who could answer."

Callum looked back at the hologram, something softening in his expression.

"THOTH," he said, "explain the nature of resonance lineage."

The AI responded immediately.

"Immortal resonance carries imprintable patterns from

experiences, emotions, and energy accumulated over centuries. Under rare circumstances, these patterns can be mirrored by the Veil when forming a new resonance being."

Lila blinked.

"Are you saying the child is... an echo of Callum's soul?"

"In a manner of speaking," THOTH said.

"The child embodies elements of his essence. Not biologically. But cosmically."

Lila's eyes widened.

"That means, "

"Yes," Callum said quietly. "They share part of my resonance. Like a memory made flesh."

Lila exhaled slowly.

"That makes you responsible for them."

Callum swallowed.

"I know."

He finally moved toward the console again, steadying himself as though bracing against a storm.

"THOTH," he said, "show me Ailsa's signature compared to the child's."

Two patterns appeared, Ailsa's older, weathered, seasoned by time... and the child's small, brilliant, spiraling.

Lila gasped.

"They overlap, not perfectly, but enough that, "

"She knew," Callum finished. "Ailsa knew about the child before she appeared to us."

THOTH confirmed:

"Based on the memory echo she embedded in the Pulse, Ailsa had knowledge of the child's awakening."

Lila bit her lip.

"Callum... that means she sent you a ghost to point you toward them."

"She never does anything without reason," Callum murmured.

But something else hovered beneath the surface.

Something neither of them voiced.

Ailsa didn't just warn Callum.

She set him on a path.

A path that led to the child.

And to the Veil.

Lila stepped closer to the hologram, studying the massive resonance rupture north of the child's location.

"What about that?" she asked. "That enormous signature. It looks… alive."

Callum stiffened.

"That," he said, "is what scares me most."

Lila straightened.

"What is it?"

"The Veil opening," Callum said. "Or trying to."

Lila's breath caught.

"THOTH," Callum said, "is that rupture stable?"

"No," the AI said. "It is growing."

Lila rubbed her arms, chilled.

"Growing how fast?"

"At a rate that will double in four days."

"Four days?" Lila said. "Until what?"

The hologram zoomed out, showing the rupture billowing wider, spreading like a cosmic bruise beneath the Highlands.

Callum's jaw tightened.

"Until it breaches," he said. "Until the Veil tears."

Lila's voice was a whisper.

"And then what?"

Callum didn't answer.

He didn't have to.

The room shook.

Once.

Twice.

A sharp alarm erupted across the command chamber.

Lila spun toward the display.

"What now?"

THOTH's voice sharpened to a blade.

"Callum, multiple resonance signatures detected. Approaching fast."

Callum's eyes flashed with fury.

"Renwick's constructs?"

"Possibly," THOTH said.

"But their profiles don't match any known entity. These are new."

Lila's stomach dropped.

"New? As in, "

"As in something Renwick built after the Pulse," Callum said.

Lights flickered red.

A holographic projection of the coastline formed,

Three dark signatures streaking toward the estate like missiles.

THOTH's tone dropped:

"Callum... they are not constructs. They are Immortals."

Callum's face hardened.

Immortals.

Plural.

Coming straight at them.

Lila's breath trembled.

"Callum... they found us."

He turned toward her, steel in his voice.

"It doesn't matter."

She blinked. "How does it not matter?"

He stepped forward, close enough for her to feel the heat of his resolve.

"Because we're done running."

The fortress trembled again as alarms blared.

Renwick had made his move.

And Callum was finally ready to make his.

The alarms rose in pitch, no longer a warning, but a countdown. The fortress thrummed with internal power, energy conduits brightening beneath the metal floor like veins igniting.

Lila's pulse spiked.

"What does red-zone alert mean?" she asked, voice strained.

THOTH answered before Callum could.

"It means the estate is entering active defense mode."

The room's perimeter walls shifted with a low mechanical growl as armored plates locked into place, sealing off the glass. Discreet weapon systems emerged from hidden cavities, sleek rail emitters and angular drone pods magnetizing to ceiling rails.

Lila took a step back.

"Oh my god... this place is a battleship."

"It's a sanctuary," Callum corrected.

"Built for this exact moment."

But Lila saw through that.

Behind his calm, his eyes carried a storm.

He wasn't just bracing for a fight.

He was bracing for the revelation Graham died trying to deliver.

THOTH drew their attention to the hologram. The three signatures streaked closer, cutting across land like dark comets.

"Estimated contact in seventy-nine seconds," THOTH said.

Lila's instinctive clinical calm kicked in.

"What happens when Immortals fight inside this place?" she asked. "You told me Quickening is destructive. This estate is wired with, God, with everything. Does a Quickening inside these walls overload the systems?"

Callum shook his head.

"No. THOTH redistributes the energy through the cliff structure. But if too many Immortals fight too close together..."

"Then what?" she pressed.

His eyes met hers.

"Then the cliff might fall."

Her throat tightened.

"Great," she muttered. "Perfect."

Callum's gaze sharpened.

"They're not getting inside."

The hologram zoomed in on the signatures.

Fast.

Aggressive.

Coordinated.

Not like Renwick's unstable constructs.

These were trained.

This was a strike team.

Lila asked, "How many Immortals did Renwick turn?"

Callum clenched his jaw.

"If he's doing what I think he's doing... as many as he wants."

She felt her skin crawl.

"Callum, you said Immortals are born through violent death, not factory lines."

"Not anymore," Callum said. "The Pulse let him cheat the rules."

Lila's stomach knotted.

"So he's building an army."

"Yes."

"And he's testing it on you."

Callum didn't deny it.

THOTH's voice dropped to a tactical cadence:

"Contact in thirty seconds."

Callum moved to the weapons alcove and opened a compartment. The interior lights illuminated rows of custom-forged blades and modern hybrid weapons.

Lila spotted the Katana immediately, the dragonhead sword Duncan MacLeod had given him, its hilt gleaming with an ancient quiet authority.

But Callum didn't reach for it.

He chose two tactical short-sabers instead, lighter and faster, designed for close-quarters Immortal combat.

"Why not the sword?" Lila asked quietly.

"Too soon," Callum said. "Renwick wants me to draw it. He's baiting me."

Her eyes widened.

"You mean... the sword itself is a signal?"

"Yes," he said. "A declaration. Using the Katana tells the world I'm stepping fully into the Game."

"And you don't want that?"

"Not before we know what we're dealing with."

THOTH's tone sharpened:

"Five seconds. Impact trajectory confirmed. They are not landing. They are *penetrating*."

"Penetrating what?" Lila demanded.

Callum went cold.

"The outer perimeter."

A thunderclap hit the fortress, shaking the entire structure.

Lila stumbled, Callum caught her arm.

The hologram flared with static.

THOTH spoke rapidly:

"Defensive outer shell breached. Three hostiles inside the cliff tunnels. They are splitting into separate approach vectors."

"That's coordinated," Callum muttered. "Someone's guiding them."

The lights dimmed, then surged.

A nearby display flickered to life, live footage from a cliff tunnel camera.

Lila's breath froze.

Three figures advanced through the tunnel, moving with terrifying speed.

The first was hulking, broad-shouldered, his eyes glowing faintly with unstable resonance, Renwick's handiwork.

The second carried a chain-saber, its edges humming with energy.

The third,

The third made Callum's heart stop.

THOTH, "Signature confirmed. The lead Immortal is Cormac the Red."

Lila turned sharply.

"Who is Cormac the Red?"

Callum's grip tightened around the sabers.

"He was my brother."

Lila reeled.

"What?"

"He trained beside me under Ailsa. We fought together for decades."

"What happened to him?"

Callum's face hardened.

"He died. Two centuries ago. Renwick killed him. I buried him myself."

Lila's stomach turned cold.

"Then how, how is he alive?"

THOTH answered grimly:

"Renwick resurrected him using Pulse interference. He is not fully Cormac. His resonance is corrupted."

"Renwick brought him back to break me."

The screen showed Cormac ripping a reinforced door from its hinges.

His eyes glowed with the same eerie instability as the constructs,
But beneath that... Callum recognized something familiar.
Something agonizing.

Lila covered her mouth.

"Oh, Callum..."

He stepped forward, jaw set, sabers lowering into ready position.

Another explosion rocked the chamber. Concrete dust drifted from
the ceiling.

THOTH declared:

"Breach imminent. Three vectors converging. Prepare for contact."

Lila reached out, grabbing Callum's arm.

"Callum, this is your brother."

He looked at her, anguish flickering behind his eyes.

"No," he said softly.
"He used to be."

And then,

The wall on the far side of the chamber buckled.

Stone fractured.

Lights shattered.

A massive fist punched through the steel plating.

Callum's sabers ignited with a metallic whisper.

Cormac the Red's roar tore through the fortress.

Lila's heart pounded as Callum stepped forward to meet the
impossible.

"Stay behind me," he said.

She nodded.

With the corrupted Immortal ripping open the wall, Callum
whispering the name he once spoke with love:

"...Brother."

Chapter 6

Seconds Ago

The first tremor was subtle, just enough to rattle the glassware on the command chamber shelves and send a low hum through the metal floors. Lila felt it under her shoes before she understood what it meant. Callum felt it in his bones.

THOTH felt it everywhere.

"Structural impact detected on Sub-Level Three," the AI announced, calm but edged with urgency. "Hostile forces breaching the cliff tunnels."

The second tremor was not subtle.

The lights flickered. Dust drifted from the ceiling seams. An alarm blared in sharp, cutting tones as reinforced panels sealed the windows with mechanical finality.

Lila gripped the console.

"What, what does that mean?"

"It means," Callum said, stepping toward the weapons alcove, "Renwick found us."

The calm in his voice unsettled her more than the alarms. He had shifted, subtle, but undeniable, from grief and shock into something colder. Focus that bordered on ruthless.

The fortress sensed it too. Panels slid away in the walls, revealing embedded rails, drone ports, pulse projectors, elements Lila had walked past earlier without seeing the weapons hidden in plain sight. The air filled with the faint ozone scent of systems charging.

She took a shaky step back. "Callum, this place is a war machine."

"It's a sanctuary," he corrected. "Only becomes a war machine when it has to."

"And now it has to?"

He didn't answer, his attention fixed on the hologram of three blinding resonance signatures streaking toward the estate from the north. THOTH magnified the feed, translating energy readings into humanoid silhouettes.

Lila's mouth went dry.

Those weren't constructs.

They weren't even close.

They were Immortals.

Their signatures burned with a heavier weight than Callum's or the ones in the hospital, raw, unstable, pulsing like live wires sparking on wet ground.

THOTH's voice sharpened.

"Impact in ninety seconds. Vectors confirm deliberate targeting of your position."

Lila's pulse spiked. "So they're coming here, right here?"

"Yes." Callum crossed the room in three long strides, grabbing two of his tactical sabers, sheathing them across his back. His movements were efficient, automatic, nearly silent.

She grabbed his arm. "Callum, talk to me. What are we dealing with?"

He paused, looking at her, the gravity of the moment reflected in the soft tightening around his eyes.

"Trained Immortals," he said. "But not the way you think. Renwick's playing with resurrection, forced resonance reconstruction. That creates something faster. Stronger. But unstable."

"Unstable how?"

He hesitated.

"Like a reactor that doesn't know it's going critical."

Lila swallowed.

The tremor returned, harder, followed by the deep metallic groan of the cliffside tunnel supports bowing under an inbound shockwave.

Callum turned on his heel.

"THOTH, seal interior levels two through seven. Reroute power to defense nodes. And lock down every supply corridor."

"Executing."

The fortress responded instantly. Heavy partitions slammed shut throughout the estate. Somewhere deep in the structure, a turbine whirred as backup power engaged.

Lila looked at the sealed exits, then back at Callum.

"We're trapped in here."

"No," he said. "They are."

The third tremor hit, rocking the chamber. Screens glitched. A camera feed showed a blur of red and black streaking past one corridor, then a section of wall imploding.

THOTH identified the signature.

"Primary hostile entering the north tunnel. Callum, brace for impact."

Callum's eyes narrowed as he unsheathed one saber.

"Lila," he said without looking back, "get behind the main console. Keep low. Don't run. No matter what happens."

Another tremor cut him off, then a deep, thunderous boom.

Silence.

A stillness colder than the air before a storm.

"Callum?" Lila whispered.

He raised the sabers slightly… listening.

Another boom.

This one closer.

The floor vibrated under their feet.

The hologram flickered as static interference crawled along its surface.

Then,

A hand punched through the wall.

Stone shattered outward like shrapnel. A cloud of dust and fractured metal filled the chamber in a suffocating burst.

Lila ducked behind the console.

Callum did not move.

A massive figure tore open the remaining structure, stepping through the gap as the dust began to settle.

For a moment, the world slowed.

Lila saw broad shoulders beneath torn, dark armor.

A mane of red hair, wild and matted.

Veins pulsing with resonance beneath gray, scar-scored skin.

Eyes burning, not with Immortal light, but with something fractured, corrupted, almost feral.

He stepped forward.

Lila's breath stopped.

Callum's heart did too.

"...Brother," he whispered.

The man, no, the thing, towered over Callum by several inches. His arms were thicker, heavier, scarred from countless battles. But there was something wrong beyond the horror of resurrection.

His movements were off.

Lagged.

Like the body remembered how to be alive, but the spark inside it didn't match.

The red-haired Immortal tilted his head at Callum.

For a sliver of a moment,

Recognition surfaced.

"Bro...ther..."

The voice cracked like dry earth splitting under heat.

Pain. Memory. Rage.

All tangled together.

Callum's grip tightened around the saber.

"Cormac... if you're in there, listen to me."

Lila watched the exchange with her heartbeat pounding in her ears. She sensed the weight in Callum's voice, not fear, but grief so naked it hurt to witness.

Cormac took one halting step forward.

His eyes flickered, light twisting between familiarity and corruption.

Then,

A roar tore from his throat.

Raw. Animalistic.

A sound of pure pain and fury.

He charged.

Callum moved too,

But not fast enough.

Cormac slammed into him with the force of a battering ram, sending Callum crashing across the chamber, skidding into the hologram console. The display sputtered and flickered.

Lila cried out, half-rising,

But Callum shot her a look, bloody but sharp.

"Stay, down."

Cormac turned toward her.

Callum was on his feet before she could blink.

He intercepted the giant's path, swinging the saber in a clean arc. Sparks exploded as the blade scraped across Cormac's metal-threaded armor.

It did almost nothing.

Cormac grabbed Callum by the throat.

Lila gasped as Callum's boots left the floor.

The resurrected Immortal squeezed.

Callum choked, struggling.

Cormac's face hovered inches away.

And for a heartbeat,

For one fleeting heartbeat,

Callum saw something break through the corruption:

Recognition.

Memory.

Regret.

Cormac's grip loosened, fractionally.

His lips trembled.

"Callum…"

Callum's voice cracked.

"I'm here."

Another flicker in Cormac's eyes,

A war between the man he was and the monster Renwick engineered.

It lasted less than a second.

Rage won.

Cormac hurled Callum across the chamber a second time, this time into a reinforced support beam. The impact shook the entire room.

"Hostiles Two and Three approaching main chamber from lateral corridors. Closing."

Callum staggered to his feet just as the second Immortal burst through the west entrance, a lean, wiry figure with a chain-saber crackling blue in hand. The third dropped from a ceiling vent with a feral hiss.

Lila felt the air thicken with an oppressive resonance, three Immortals, each unstable, each radiating an energy that even her mortal senses found frightening.

Callum now faced all three.

"Callum!" she cried. "You can't fight them alone!"

He didn't look back.

"I don't have a choice."

Cormac roared and charged again. Callum parried a strike from the chain-saber carrier, then ducked a descending blow from the ceiling attacker.

Three against one.

The sound was deafening, steel on steel, resonance discharges crackling like thunder. Sparks danced across the chamber. The fortress groaned under the assault.

Lila watched in terror, yet with awe.

Callum moved with centuries of discipline, footwork smooth, strikes precise, defense fluid.

But he was outnumbered.

And the corrupted strength of the resurrected trio was overwhelming.

Cormac caught Callum by the shoulder,

And slammed him into the floor hard enough to crack the composite surface.

Lila screamed.

She ran forward before she could stop herself.

Callum forced out a rasping, desperate shout:

"Lila, NO!"

A chain-saber streaked toward her, its humming edge bright with lethal resonance.

She froze.

The blow never reached her.

Callum lunged, slamming his broken saber into the attacker's wrist.

138

The weapon spun away, embedding itself into the wall with a violent crackle.

He shoved Lila behind him.

"Stay back!"

"You're going to die!"

Cormac swung for Callum's head.

Callum ducked, rolled, and evaded a second strike, barely.

Lila watched in horror as he fought three Immortals with one functional blade and a body already bruised and bleeding. Every movement had a cost. Every defense left him more vulnerable.

The attackers coordinated.

Renwick had trained them for this.

Callum dodged the chain-saber wielder, blocked the ceiling attacker, but Cormac's fist caught him square in the ribs,

The crack was audible.

Callum staggered, breath collapsing out of him.

Lila's stomach dropped.

Callum could survive blades.

He could survive resonance.

He could even survive death,

But he could not survive being torn apart by three Immortals before he could stand back up.

He fell to one knee.

Cormac loomed over him.

The ceiling Immortal advanced.

The chain-saber wielder ignited his blade.

Three killing blows lined up simultaneously,

Callum lifted his head.

There was no fear in his eyes.

Only devastation.

He muttered something Lila barely heard:

"Ailsa… forgive me."

Then,

He reached behind him.

His fingers closed around the hilt of the Katana.

The dragonhead pommel pulsed,

A dormant heart awakening.

A myth recalling its legend.

The entire chamber seemed to pull taut.

Cormac hesitated.

The other Immortals faltered.

Even Lila felt it,

A hum.

A pressure.

A presence.

The Katana slid free with a sound like metal remembering its purpose.

A deep, resonant *chime* echoed through the fortress, building into a low, vibrating rumble.

THOTH, "The Katana is active."

Callum rose.

Light flared along the blade's length, silver, blue, alive.

Every Immortal in the room took an involuntary step back.

Callum stepped toward Cormac.

The resurrected Immortal let out a broken, pained roar,

And charged.

Light and darkness collided.

Katana's first strike in decades cut the chamber open,

The Katana struck the air with a sound that was not sound,

A low harmonic tremor that vibrated not through the ears, but through the bones.

Lila felt it in her teeth, in her spine, in the space between her heartbeats.

Cormac felt it too.

His charge faltered, ribs expanding in a ragged inhale. His corrupted eyes widened, not in fear, but in something older. Recognition. Memory. Pain.

Callum moved.

Not as the man Lila met in Manhattan.

Not as the surgeon's mysterious protector.

But as a warrior he had been long before either of those lives existed.

The Katana arced, leaving a ribbon of shimmering light in its wake.

Cormac swung at the same moment, bringing down both colossal fists with earth-shattering force,

The impact met the sword.

The sword didn't yield.

Cormac did.

A shockwave ripped outward from the point of contact, blasting dust and loose equipment across the chamber. The two other Immortals staggered back, shielding their faces from the pulse of light.

Lila threw her arms over her head as debris flew past her.

Callum pressed forward.

Cormac, massive as he was, grunted and stepped back, resonance flickering wildly along the red scars patterned across his arms and neck.

Callum attacked again,

Three strikes in rapid succession, each delivered with surgical precision.

Cormac blocked the first.

Barely caught the second.

The third cut deep across his shoulder, spraying corrupted resonance into the air like embers.

Cormac's roar shook the chamber.

He swung in a wide arc, trying to catch Callum off-balance.

Callum ducked.

Rolled.

Came up on one knee and sliced across Cormac's thigh.

Cormac staggered.

The chain-saber wielder recovered first.

He lunged toward Callum's flank.

Callum twisted.

He saw the chain-saber coming too late to dodge fully.

He threw up the Katana.

The chain-saber met it,

And shattered.

A burst of electric resonance exploded backward into its wielder, knocking him off his feet and slamming him into the ceiling. His body dropped like a stone.

The Katana had absorbed the energy.

Consumed it.

And glowed brighter.

Cormac swung again.

Callum blocked.

The force of the impact slid him back across the floor.

Sparks hissed beneath his boots.

The third Immortal,

the one who had descended from the ceiling before,

leapt onto Callum's back, slashing downward with twin daggers pulsing with Quickening-hungry energy.

Callum grimaced, straining under Cormac's assault and now the added weight from behind.

The daggers cut across his shoulder, drawing a line of bright blood.

Lila's breath caught.

"CALLUM!"

He twisted violently, shoulder screaming, but using the pain as leverage. He slammed the attacker against the support pillar, knocking the breath from him. Then he spun, gripping the Immortal by the throat, and hurled him across the room.

Cormac saw the opening.

He lunged.

His corrupted hand closed around Callum's wrist, squeezing until the bones creaked.

Callum gasped,

but didn't drop the sword.

Cormac growled through clenched teeth:

"Bro...ther... stop..."

For a heartbeat, all movement froze.

"I want to," he strained.

Cormac leaned closer.

The light flickered in his eyes, confusion, pain, remnants of the man he was.

"Help... me..."

Callum's resolve trembled.

And that was the moment Renwick's corruption surged.

Cormac's expression twisted into something monstrous.

His muscles bulged.

His grip tightened brutally around Callum's wrist.

The chamber lights flickered.

Energy crackled around them.

Cormac's voice dropped into something hollow and cruel:

"Renwick… commands."

Then he lifted Callum off his feet and hurled him across the chamber.

Callum hit the eastern wall hard enough to leave a dent.

Lila ran to him,

But he was already pushing himself up, coughing, spitting blood, gripping the Katana like the last promise he had left.

THOTH's voice cut through the chaos.

"Callum, his resonance is collapsing. If he releases that energy inside the chamber, the entire foundation will destabilize."

Callum wiped blood from his lip.

"I know."

"Recommend immediate termination."

Callum's jaw clenched.

Cormac charged again.

Callum rose to meet him.

The clash was cataclysmic.

Steel rang.

Energy crackled.

Two Immortals collided with centuries of history between them.

Every strike from Cormac rattled Callum's bones.

Every counter from Callum carved a deeper wound into the corrupted shell Renwick had forced Cormac into.

Lila watched helplessly, tears streaking her face.

Callum pivoted, evaded a crushing blow, and locked swords with Cormac again. His voice broke as he answered:

He pressed his forehead briefly against Cormac's, their breaths intermingling in a moment too small for the violence around them.

"I'm sorry," Callum said, voice thick with grief.

"Oh, brother… I am so, so sorry."

Cormac's corrupted eyes flickered again.

For a moment, Lila saw a man inside the monster.

Cormac's lips formed a single word:

"Home."

Callum's face twisted in silent anguish.

Then,

Cormac raised both fists to kill him.

Callum stepped back.

Lifted the Katana.

And struck.

The blade cut through the neck of the corrupted resonance, through muscle and bone, through Renwick's chains.

Light erupted.

The force of the Quickening slammed into Callum like a tidal wave. The other two Immortals were thrown to the floor, bodies convulsing under the raw discharge.

Lila fell to her knees, shielding her eyes.

The chamber filled with swirling, violent arcs of blue-white energy.

Screens shattered.

Consoles blew sparks.

Walls cracked.

Callum dropped to one knee as Cormac's essence poured into him, rage, grief, memories of Highland winds, the laughter of battles long past, and the unbearable pain of death and resurrection.

Lila watched him convulse, screaming silently as light poured into him.

THOTH rerouted power to prevent the fortress from exploding.

"Quickening containment at seventy percent... sixty... fifty..."

"Callum!" Lila cried.

The storm intensified.

Then,

Silence.

Cormac's body crumbled into dust.

Only Callum remained.

Slumped.

Exhausted.

Breathing in ragged, broken pulls.

Lila ran to him, catching him before he collapsed.

"Callum, Callum, stay with me, "

He leaned into her, trembling, gripping her arm as the last tendrils of energy faded around them.

His voice was a whisper of shattered pieces.

"He's gone."

Lila pressed her forehead to his.

"I know."

He swallowed, tears mixing with sweat and dust.

"He asked… to go home."

Lila's heart broke for him.

"You brought him home, You did."

He closed his eyes.

But the danger wasn't over.

The other two Immortals staggered to their feet.

Callum rose slowly, pain painting his entire posture, but he still put himself between Lila and them.

"Stay behind me," he said.

She knew better than to argue this time.

The two Immortals, now weaponless, disoriented, still shaking from the redirected Quickening, backed away slowly. Their eyes flickered to the Katana and the corpse-ash that had once been Cormac the Red.

Fear.

Real fear.

Then,

A voice echoed through the chamber.

Smooth.

Cold.

Familiar.

"Callum MacLeod."

Lila froze.

"Who, who is that?"

Callum's grip tightened on the sword.

"Renwick."

The voice rolled like a whisper sliding beneath a door.

"You've drawn the Katana.

At last."

The walls vibrated with the resonance of it.

This wasn't Renwick's body.

This was him speaking through the Immortals he had resurrected.

Lila felt a chill crawl up her spine.

Renwick continued:

"Cormac was my gift to you, Callum. A reminder of all the things you've lost... and all the things you will lose."

Callum's teeth clenched.

"Face me yourself, Renwick."

A soft, cruel chuckle.

"Oh, I will.

But only after you find the child."

Lila's breath hitched.

Renwick's tone sharpened.

"Bring them to me, Callum.

Or I'll take your surgeon instead."

Lila's blood ran cold.

Callum's rage ignited.

"Touch her and I will, "

Renwick cut him off with a hiss.

"You will do nothing.

The Veil has already chosen its path.

And you will follow it... just as it has always commanded you to."

The two remaining Immortals collapsed to the floor, unconscious, Renwick's control severed.

Silence filled the chamber.

Callum's shoulders sagged with exhaustion, grief, and a fury so deep it almost eclipsed the Quickening still burning through him.

Lila touched his arm gently.

"Callum... what does he want with the child?"

Callum looked at her with eyes shadowed by centuries of loss and the fresh wound of Cormac's death.

"He wants what the Veil gave them."

"What is that?"

Callum exhaled slowly.

"Power to open worlds."

Lila swallowed hard.

"And you?"

He looked at her, expression softening despite everything.

"I'm supposed to protect them."

"Why?"

His grip tightened on her hand.

"Because they're connected to me.

Because they're the key.

And because Renwick won't stop until he has them."

Lila felt the truth settle in her chest.

The war had begun.

Cormac's resurrection was only the first strike.

The next strike would not be aimed at Callum.

It would be aimed at the child.

At the Veil.

At the world itself.

Callum pulled her gently behind him, toward the interior corridors.

"We need to leave," he said. "Now."

She nodded, voice barely above a whisper.

"Where?"

Callum's eyes hardened.

"The Highlands."

The Katana hummed softly in his hand.

Chapter 7

Callum did not sheathe the Katana even after the last of the corrupted Immortals fell unconscious. The sword hummed faintly in his grip, a living relic that seemed to sense the death it had just consumed. Lila could feel the energy radiating off it, like standing too close to lightning after it struck the earth.

The command chamber glowed in scattered embers and broken light. Sparks still snapped from ruptured consoles; smoke curled in ghostly ribbons toward the ceiling; dust rained down in slow, drifting patterns.

Callum stood at the center of it all, motionless except for the rise and fall of his breath. Not the sharp breath of exertion. The uneven breath of grief barely held together.

Lila approached him cautiously.

"Callum... you're bleeding."

He didn't respond.

She moved closer. Slow and gentle, as if approaching a wounded animal that might lash out from instinct alone.

"Callum."

Her voice cracked, not with fear, but with the weight of everything they had just survived. Everything *he* had survived.

Finally, he spoke.

"He said 'home.'"

She swallowed hard. "I heard."

"He remembered me. For a moment." His voice dropped to a raw, quiet tone. "Cormac remembered."

Lila didn't touch him, not yet. He wasn't ready for touch. Instead, she stood beside him, shoulder to shoulder, sharing the space, sharing the silence.

"It wasn't him who tried to kill me," Callum said. "That wasn't my brother. Renwick... twisted whatever was left."

"And you gave him peace."

Callum closed his eyes, anguish creasing the corners.

"He deserved more."

"He deserved freedom," Lila said. "And you gave him that."

He turned toward her at last, eyes rimmed with pain, but focused.

"You shouldn't be here for any of this."

"Don't say that" she murmured.

"You saw me kill my own brother."

"He wasn't your brother anymore."

"That doesn't make it easier."

"No," she agreed softly. "But it makes it necessary."

Callum stared at her, really stared, and something in his posture eased, if only by a fraction. He let out a shuddering breath, the kind that only escapes when you are too exhausted to hold it in anymore.

The Katana dimmed slightly in response, as if sharing his exhale.

Lila glanced at it. "Callum... why does that sword matter so much? Beyond being legendary, I mean."

He looked down at the blade.

"It's not a weapon," he said. "It's a responsibility."

"And now that you've drawn it... what does that mean?"

Callum hesitated.

Then, quietly:

"It means the world will hear."

She frowned. "Hear what?"

"That I've returned to the Game."

A chill crossed her skin.

"The Game... as in the fight you Immortals spend centuries avoiding unless you have no choice?"

He nodded, "Some avoid it, and some seek it."

"And drawing it signals your... what? Intent to fight?"

"It signals readiness," Callum said. "Resolve. It's a declaration that I've accepted a role I've refused for decades."

"And Renwick wanted that?"

"He's forcing the old rules back into play. He knows the Katana is... symbolic. When I draw it, others feel it. Everywhere."

"So Immortals around the world will know you're involved."

"Yes."

"And Renwick wants them watching?"

"No," Callum said. "He wants them afraid."

The lights flickered again as backup power stabilized the chamber. THOTH reactivated the damaged displays, reconstructing what data it could.

"Callum," the AI said, its tone unusually careful, "we have a problem."

Lila exhaled a weary laugh. "Just one?"

Callum stepped away from the shattered consoles.

"What is it?"

"Two of the Immortals who attacked you are dead. Their signatures collapsed when Renwick severed control."

"What about the third?" Lila asked.

THOTH paused.

That alone made Callum tense.

"The third is alive. But... empty."

Lila frowned. "Empty?"

Callum's face darkened.

"He means resonance empty. The spark extinguished."

"But that means,"

"It means," Callum said grimly, "Renwick drained them before cutting the tether."

Lila's stomach twisted.

"Callum... what happens to an Immortal with no spark?"

He didn't answer.

THOTH did.

They don't survive for long.

A heavy silence fell.

Lila's clinical instincts flickered, guilt, grief, the stubborn sense that a life lost is always a failure, even when rationally unavoidable. But this wasn't a patient she could save. This was something beyond medicine, beyond biology.

Callum moved toward the exit corridor.

"We need to go. Renwick won't stop with this."

Lila followed.

"Where are we going?"

"To prepare," Callum said. "We need supplies. Intel. And the Katana needs to be stabilized, its resonance is, "

THOTH cut in suddenly.

"Callum… there is another matter."

Callum froze.

"What now?"

"Cormac's Quickening."

Lila blinked. "I thought you absorbed it."

Callum clenched his jaw, "I did."

"Not all of it."

That stopped him cold.

"What do you mean?"

"Cormac's Quickening was… incomplete."

"Incomplete how?" Lila asked.

THOTH's voice dropped, as if the AI itself felt unease.

"Part of him resisted you."

Callum's blood ran cold.

"That's impossible."

"Not if Renwick altered the resonance."

Lila looked between them. "What does that mean?"

Callum exhaled slowly.

"It means Cormac's Quickening didn't fully die with him. It means Renwick left part of him… alive."

Lila went pale.

"Callum… what kind of monster is he?"

Callum shook his head.

"He isn't a monster."

He looked toward the damaged wall, where Cormac had first stepped in.

"He's something worse."

Lila's voice trembled.

"What's worse than a monster?"

Callum met her eyes.

"An Immortal who learned how to break the rules."

Another tremor shook the fortress, deeper this time. The cliffs groaned.

THOTH spoke urgently.

"Callum, structural integrity is compromised from the fight. Secondary tunnels have collapsed. We must leave immediately."

Callum nodded.

"THOTH, begin flight prep for FENRIR. Lila, come with me."

She swallowed, gripping the edge of the console.

"Back into a fight?"

"No," Callum said.

He touched her shoulder gently.

"Into the truth."

The corridors leading deeper into the fortress were dim, illuminated only by emergency strips of cold white light lining the floor and ceiling. The automated doors remained locked in their defensive positions, leaving only one viable route open, a narrow passage that angled down toward the sublevel hangar.

Lila followed close behind Callum, her breath quickening in the sterile, metallic air. She kept glancing over her shoulder even though THOTH reported no immediate threats. The fortress felt too quiet now, like the hush after a storm when you're not sure if the worst has passed or is simply circling back.

Callum walked with a slight limp.

She noticed.

He did not acknowledge it.

"You're hurting," she said gently.

He didn't answer.

He didn't have to, she saw the stiff pull in his shoulders, the way his breath faltered with each step. The Quickening had ravaged his nervous system, even if his body hid the wounds.

Lila's voice was soft. "Callum... stop pretending you're fine."

He turned his head slightly; exhaustion shadowed the sharp lines of his face.

"You don't have to worry about me."

"But I do."

He froze for a moment, just long enough for her to see the conflict ripple across his expression before he shut it down again.

"We don't have time for this," he said.

"And we don't have time for you collapsing in the middle of a corridor," she countered.

He kept walking.

She didn't stop following.

Finally, he slowed enough to let her come alongside him.

"You absorbed a Quickening," she said. "Your whole nervous system is overloaded. Even if you heal fast, you heal *painfully*."

He let out a soft breath, a laugh with no humor.

"That's one word for it."

"What's another word?"

His eyes flicked to hers.

"Agony."

Her chest tightened.

He didn't say it for sympathy.

He said it because it was true.

"Callum..." Her voice softened to something gentler. "You did what you had to. Cormac's death wasn't your fault."

"It doesn't matter," he said. "He's still gone."

"But he was already gone," she tried to reason with him. "What died in that chamber... wasn't him."

Callum stopped walking.

For the first time since the fight, he let his pain show, barely, but enough that she saw it.

"I know," he said after a long moment. "But telling myself that doesn't make it easier."

Lila stepped closer.

"You're allowed to grieve."

He held her gaze, the blue of his eyes darkened by sorrow.

"I don't have time to grieve."

"Then let me worry for you," she said quietly. "Just this once."

He blinked... and she saw the faintest crack in his armor; not weakness, but humanity.

He exhaled.

"Lila… you're not supposed to be part of this world."

"But I am now."

He swallowed.

The truth of that weighed heavily on both of them.

She touched his arm, light but steady. "Callum… help me understand. Why would Renwick resurrect your brother like that?"

Callum's voice went low.

"Because he knows me. And he knows what Cormac meant." He paused. "To bring him back like that, to twist him, was Renwick's way of saying: I see your past. And I will use it against you."

Lila shivered.

"That's cruel."

"It's the point," Callum murmured.

She wanted to reach out again, but before she could,

THOTH's voice filled the corridor.

"Callum, approaching the hangar now. Be advised, FENRIR is in pre-flight. I have also scanned an anomaly in the tunnel above you."

Callum instantly stiffened.

"What anomaly?"

"A residual resonance signature. Weak but… familiar."

Lila frowned. "Familiar how?"

Callum's expression darkened.

"Ailsa."

Lila's breath caught. "She was here?"

"No," Callum said. "But an echo of her was."

The AI elaborated:

"Not her presence. A warning. Imprinted into the Pulse residue. She left it for you."

Callum's jaw tightened.

"Ailsa never leaves a warning without purpose."

Lila felt the air shift around him, something colder, sharper.

"What did she warn you about?"

THOTH paused.

"That your next opponent will not be someone sent to kill you."

Lila blinked.

"What does that even mean?"

"...that Renwick is finished testing," Callum said.

The AI continued:

"Ailsa's imprint suggests the next one to come will be someone whose death will break you."

Lila's eyes widened.

"Callum, what does she mean by 'break'?"

He didn't answer.

He couldn't.

They reached the final door before the hangar.

Callum placed his palm on the sensor; the door slid open with a soft pneumatic sigh.

The hangar was huge, hewn directly into the cliffside like a cathedral of steel and stone. The bay doors overlooking the ocean were sealed, but the cavern still smelled faintly of salt air.

And in the center,

FENRIR.

The rotorcraft was perched on its cradle, sleek and predatory even at rest. Black composite hull. Retractable ducted fans. The faintest shimmering texture where adaptive camo plating had engaged during the fight.

Lila stared at it in awe.

"That's... not a helicopter."

Callum gave a faint, tired smile.

"No. It's FENRIR."

"It looks like something DARPA would have nightmares about."

He snorted softly.

"That's because DARPA tried to build one and failed."

THOTH chimed in:

"I can confirm that statement."

The faint humor was welcome.

Needed.

But it didn't last.

Lila shook her head.

"Why FENRIR, what does that mean?" she asked.

Callum paused for a second as if he was trying to remember what the acronym meant, "It technically means, Focused Engagement &

Neutralization Recon-Integrated Rotorcraft."

"Wow, that's a lot of words."

"Aye, typical government nomenclature, but the name FENRIR has another significant meaning in Norse Mythology." He paused briefly to gauge her interest in this impromptu history lesson. She didn't seem to look bored, "Fenrir, in Norse Mythology was a gigantic wolf that Loki created to kill Oden."

"You mean like the Marvel movies?"

A smile could be seen at the edges of Callum's mouth, "something like that...this FENRIR embodies everything that the mythical Fenrir was described to be."

THOTH cut in, "A predator."

"I see." She said, still being impressed by the AI.

Callum walked toward FENRIR with purpose.

"THOTH, double flight speed to the Highlands corridor. We need to get there before Renwick's next move."

"Understood. Fueling boost systems now."

Lila followed him up the loading ramp.

"Callum... are we really going after this child alone?"

"Yes."

"That's insane."

"I know."

"And dangerous."

"I know."

"And exactly what Renwick wants you to do."

Callum turned suddenly.

His face, exhausted and haunted.

But resolute.

"Lila... this child is connected to me. If Renwick gets them, the Veil collapses. The world won't survive it."

She swallowed.

"I'm not arguing that."

"Then why, "

"I want to know where I fit in this. Why I matter." Her voice dropped. "Why Renwick keeps threatening me."

Callum stepped closer.

"You're my anchor," he said softly. "The tether that keeps me in the world. Without you... I drift."

She felt a warmth bloom in her chest, fear and affection colliding.

"That's not fair."

"No," he said. "It isn't."

Silence stretched.

Lila looked down.

"If you lose me... would you lose yourself?"

Callum swallowed hard.

"Yes."

She looked up with wide, unsettled eyes.

"And Renwick knows that."

Callum nodded.

"Yes."

THOTH interrupted gently:

"Fueling complete. Systems ready. Hostile signatures receding. You have a window."

Callum offered his hand.

"Come with me."

Lila stared at it.

Shaking.

She took it.

The two of them boarded FENRIR together.

Lila strapped in behind Callum. The cockpit glowed with soft, holographic displays that unfolded like blooming petals of light.

Callum laid his hand on the throttle.

"THOTH," he murmured, "take us up."

FENRIR's engines roared.

The cliffside doors opened.

Wind surged in, salt and cold and sharp.

The rotorcraft lifted from its cradle like a hunting bird waking from slumber.

Lila gripped her harness.

Callum tightened his grip on the sword's hilt.

Far below, the Pacific churned.

And far away, across the ocean, the Highlands called.

Callum whispered under his breath:

"Hold on, little one. I'm coming."

FENRIR shot into the sky.

Clouds streaked across the cockpit windows as FENRIR cut a knife's path through the upper atmosphere. The rotorcraft's adaptive systems automatically shifted between modes, with its ducted fans retracting as the aircraft transitioned to hypersonic glide. THOTH managed the trajectory with effortless precision.

The world fell away beneath them, oceans turning to shimmering sheets of silver, sunlight scattering off distant cloudbanks like molten glass.

Lila pressed her hand against the side panel, steadying herself as the horizon curved far below.

"This doesn't feel real," she murmured.

Callum adjusted altitude, his eyes pinned forward.
"What part?"

"All of it." She let out a breath she hadn't known she was holding. "The fight. The Immortals. Cormac. Renwick. The sword. This... machine."

Callum didn't answer immediately.

He didn't need to.

The weight of silence between them said enough.

After several seconds, Lila spoke again, this time softer.

"You said I'm your anchor. But what does that actually mean? In practical terms?"

Callum's fingers tightened slightly around the throttle.

"Immortals live a long time," he said. "Longer than anyone should. Sometimes we forget why we're still here. Who we're meant to protect. What we're meant to be."

Lila studied his profile, stone-strong jaw, blue eyes shadowed with exhaustion, centuries of war carved into the lines of his face.

"And I remind you?"

"You remind me what life looks like," Callum replied. "Not just survival."

A quiet fell over them.

The rotors hummed softly, and the Pacific miles slipped beneath their flight path like threads easing from a spool.

THOTH's voice broke the silence gently.

"Callum, approaching geodesic waypoint seven. Estimated time to

Highland corridor: four hours, thirty-one minutes."

"Copy," Callum said.

Lila leaned back.

"You haven't slept."

"Immortals don't need much sleep."

"That's not what I asked."

Callum let out a slow breath. "No. I haven't."

"Callum… you can't go into whatever awaits us in the Highlands half-dead."

He almost smiled.

"You sound like Ailsa."

Lila blinked.

"Is that a good thing?"

"It is," he admitted. "Most days."

Lila considered him.

The exhaustion was showing now, subtle tremors in his fingers, the faint pallor under his skin, the tightness around his mouth every time he inhaled.

"Callum," she said carefully, "you're going to crash."

"No," he murmured.

"I already did."

Her breath caught.

"Is that what losing Cormac did?"

He didn't answer.

"You're not talking," she pressed. "Talk to me."

Callum's jaw flexed.

Finally:

"He and I were supposed to face the world together."

A beat.

"And then I buried him."

Lila's voice softened to a whisper.

"And then Renwick made you do it again."

Callum closed his eyes, a moment of raw pain slipping through.

"Yes."

Lila reached out, resting her hand lightly over his on the throttle.

"And because of that, you think you have to carry this alone."

"I do."

"No," she said firmly. "You don't. You're not the only one with skin in this game now."

He turned toward her, eyes stormed with grief, fire, fear, and something deeper still.

"The Veil is calling me," he said. "It's not calling you."

"So what? I'll go anyway."

"Lila, "

"Callum," she interrupted. "Stop trying to protect me by pushing me away."

He stared at her in stunned silence.

"Protecting me doesn't mean excluding me," she said. "It means letting me stand next to you even when you're terrified."

His breath trembled.

She held his gaze, unwavering.

"You drew that sword for the world, But you also drew it for yourself."

A pause.

"And for Cormac."

Callum swallowed hard.

"And now you're going back to the place where everything started," she concluded. "You shouldn't go alone."

THOTH cut in, gently, as if aware of the emotional strain.

"Callum, Lila is correct. Statistically, your survival probabilities increase by twenty-three percent when she remains within proximity during high-resonance events."

Callum shot the AI a look.

"THOTH, "

Lila laughed despite the tension. "Did your AI just tell you I make you harder to kill?"

"It's an oversimplification," Callum muttered.

"But not wrong," THOTH added.

Lila smirked, folding her arms.

"I knew it."

Another hum of silence filled the cockpit.

Callum finally let out a long, slow breath.

"You're stubborn."

"Yes."

"You're reckless."

"Probably."

"And you're completely untrained."

"Definitely."

Callum shook his head.

"And yet..."

"And yet what?" she asked softly.

His eyes softened, no longer the hardened warrior, but the man beneath the centuries.

"And yet I can't imagine doing this without you."

The air thickened.

Not with danger this time.

With something else entirely.

Lila's breath hitched, warmth blooming behind her ribs.

But before she could speak,

THOTH's tone sharpened.

"Callum, long-range scan picking up a resonance anomaly ahead."

Callum instantly snapped into focus.

"Define anomaly."

"Unstable. Growing. And familiar."

Lila stiffened. "Familiar how?"

THOTH paused.

"It matches Callum's signature."

Callum froze.

Lila's hand went cold.

"That means the child made contact."

Callum stared out into the horizon, his expression shifting from grief to something fierce, determined, and afraid.

"No," he said slowly.

"They're not contacting me."

Silence stretched.

Lila swallowed.

"Then what are they doing?"

He tightened his grip on the sword.

"Calling for help."

The anomaly grew stronger.

Lila watched it rise on the holo-display like a pulse of heat beneath the world map, irregular, bright, almost frantic. The signature trembled at the edges, struggling to stabilize, like a heart under too much strain.

"Callum..." she whispered, "is something wrong with the child?"

"No," Callum said softly.

But the edge in his voice said otherwise.

THOTH expanded the waveform. And for the first time, Lila saw it clearly. The resonance pattern flickered between coherence and collapse, spiraling in strange, unstable harmonics.

She pressed a hand to her lips.

"It's like ventricular fibrillation," she murmured.
"A heart that's beating, but in chaos."

Callum glanced at her, curiosity slicing through his tension.

"Explain."

"This pattern, it's not stable. Something is triggering them repeatedly. Like the child is scared. Or in pain. Or, "

"Trying to survive," Callum finished.

THOTH's tone dropped.

"Callum... additional data suggests the child's resonance is encountering environmental resistance."

"Where?" Callum demanded.

"The Highlands."

Lila frowned. "Environmental resistance? Like... geological interference?"

"No." Callum's expression darkened. "Like the land itself is pushing back."

Lila blinked. "The land?"

"The Highlands are old," Callum said. "Older than most mortal civilizations. Some places remember what the Veil once was."

Lila shivered.
"You make it sound alive."

He didn't deny it.

"It is. At least partially."

The rotorcraft dipped slightly as they rode an airfront. Lila steadied herself, her eyes flicking back to the display.

"Callum," she said, "look."

The child's resonance flared,

Then folded in on itself.

Then flared again, brighter, sharper, more desperate.

"What does that mean?" she asked.

THOTH answered:

"It is a distress signal."

Callum inhaled slowly.

"They know we're coming."

Lila's voice steadied with renewed purpose.

"Then we need to get there faster."

Callum nodded.

"THOTH, engage boost cycle."

"Warning: Boost cycle increases detection probability by ninety-two percent."

"Engage it," Callum repeated, jaw tightening.

"Confirmed."

A deep hum filled the rotorcraft. Lila felt the cabin walls vibrate as the aerospike booster lit, invisible to the naked eye but unmistakable in its acceleration.

Gravity pressed her into her seat.

The horizon blurred.

The Jetstream folded over them in long, streaking ribbons.

FENRIR leapt forward like a spear through the blue.

Through the vibration, Lila murmured:

"Callum... if the child's calling for help, who are they calling *from*?"

Callum didn't answer immediately.

His fingers tightened around the sword.

"The Highlands aren't empty," he said finally. "They haven't been for centuries."

She frowned. "You mean other Immortals?"

"Yes."

"And... Renwick?"

"Not Renwick," Callum said darkly.

"Someone older."

Lila felt her pulse jump.

"Older than Renwick?"

Callum didn't look at her.

"Yes."

THOTH added:

"Historical resonance records indicate two Immortals disappeared three decades ago near the same region where the child's signature now originates."

Lila turned sharply. "Disappeared?"

"As in consumed by the Veil," Callum said.

Lila's breath caught.

"What does that mean?"

He exhaled.

"The Veil doesn't just form Immortals. Sometimes... it takes them back."

She shivered.

"So there are Immortals in the Highlands?"

"Yes," Callum said grimly. "And they'll feel the resonance of the Katana long before we arrive."

Lila stared.

"But if they're like you, "

"They're not."

Callum's voice dropped into something darker.

"They're older than the Game. They don't play by the same rules."

Lila leaned forward, fear sharpening her focus.

"What kind of Immortals don't follow the rules?"

"The kind," Callum said quietly, "that Renwick learned from."

That landed like a blow.

Lila bit her lip. "So we're flying into a nest of unknown Immortals, corrupted constructs, Renwick's schemes, and a child who's connected to the Veil itself."

"Yes."

"And you plan to land in the middle of all that?"

"Yes."

She stared at him.

"You're insane."

He almost smiled.

"Probably."

She shook her head.

"You're also doing it without thinking of yourself."

"For the child," he said. "And for what saving them might stop."

Lila gripped the armrest, knuckles white.

"You keep talking about the child like they're important to you, more than just someone who needs saving."

Callum didn't respond.

"Callum," she said softly, "why does the Veil tie them to you?"

His throat tightened.

"You know why."

"No, I want you to say it."

He hesitated.

Lila held his gaze.

"Say it."

Callum exhaled slowly.

"The child carries my resonance."

Her breath caught.

"You mean... like family?"

"No," Callum said. "Stronger."

He paused.

"Like destiny."

Lila's mind reeled.

Destiny.

Then THOTH interrupted sharply.

"Callum, new anomaly detected."

Both of them snapped toward the display.

A single resonance signature flickered into existence south of the child's position.

Lila gasped.

"What is that?"

THOTH's voice dropped.

"It is neither Renwick... nor the child."

Callum's heartbeat thundered.

Lila's voice shook.

"Then who?"

A pause.

A long, unsettling pause.

Then,

"An Immortal who has not appeared on any grid in over one hundred and fifty years."

Callum muttered the name like a wound reopening.

"...Morrigan."

Lila blinked.

"Who?"

Callum's face hardened into something carved from stone.

"Morrigan.

The Witch of the Veil."

"Of course there is a witch." Lila's skin crawled. "What does she want with the child?"

Callum said nothing.

Because he already knew.

And the truth was worse than anything Lila had imagined.

Her voice trembled.

"Callum... who is she?"

Callum's grip tightened on the Katana.

"Morrigan," he said slowly, "was the first Immortal to ever cross the Veil... and survive."

Lila stared.

"What does that make her?"

Callum looked at her, eyes haunted, voice low.

"Something Renwick fears.

Something the child calls.

Something no Immortal wants to face."

He swallowed.

"Something we are not ready for."

Lila looked at him, "Then why are we going?"

He looked out at the rushing horizon, the sword glowing faintly beside him.

"Because if she reaches the child first, the world ends faster than Renwick can tear it apart."

Silence settled thickly over the cockpit.

Not the peaceful kind.

The kind that follows a revelation so heavy the mind needs a heartbeat, or several, to absorb it.

Morrigan.

The name hung in the air, sharper than the altitude-thin wind, colder than the steel beneath their feet.

Lila found her voice first, though it came out tight and uncertain.

"Callum... who is she really?"

He didn't answer immediately. He kept his eyes on the horizon, jaw clenched, posture coiled like a man bracing for a blow he already knew was coming.

THOTH answered in his place.

"Morrigan was the first Immortal to stand between worlds."

Lila frowned.

"Between worlds?"

"Between the mortal world and the Veil," Callum said quietly.

He didn't look at her.

He didn't need to.

His voice already carried the weight of memories too old and too dark to surface easily.

"She was born before the Game had rules," he continued. "Before Quickenings. Before 'there can be only one.' Before any of the structure we learned to survive by."

Lila listened, heart pounding.

"Before," Callum said, breath slow, "we even understood what Immortality *was*."

THOTH elaborated:

"Historical resonance suggests Morrigan crossed into the Veil itself and returned alive. No other Immortal has done this... except Ailsa."

Lila's eyes widened.

"Ailsa crossed the Veil?"

Callum closed his eyes.

"Yes."

"And that's why she appeared to us in the hospital?"

"Yes."

"And Morrigan can do that too?"

Slowly, Callum shook his head.

"Morrigan doesn't appear with warnings."

A chill crept up Lila's spine.

"What does she do?"

He finally turned toward her, eyes blue and bleak with truth.

"She hunts."

Lila swallowed.

"Hunts... what?"

"Resonance," Callum said. "Power. Souls. Immortal essence. She takes what the Veil offers, twists it, and becomes something more."

THOTH added:

"Her Quickening does not follow the ancient laws. It does not release. It devours."

Lila felt her stomach knot.

"Callum... the child, "

He nodded grimly.

"She senses them."

Lila pressed a hand over her heart. "Why them? Why the child?"

"Because the child is the first new resonance the Veil has created in centuries," Callum said. "Because they are unstable. Vulnerable. And powerful."

"And because they're connected to you."

Callum's eyes flicked away.

Lila leaned forward, urgency creeping into her tone.

"She'll kill the child if she gets there first?"

"No," Callum said. "She'll take them."

"And do what?"

He shook his head slowly.

"There's nothing worse she could do."

Lila sat back, breath shaky.

"I thought Renwick was the worst of it," she murmured. "But this... this sounds bigger."

"It is."

THOTH chimed in.

"Callum, updated trajectory required. The child's resonance is spiking again, stronger. Their distress signal has increased by thirty-seven percent."

Callum gripped the controls, jaw hardening.

"We're coming," he said under his breath.

FENRIR surged forward, skimming the edge of the jetstream. The ocean blurred beneath them, a deep, endless blue stretching into the worlds Callum had lived far too long to trust.

Lila steadied herself, her breathing easing slowly with the rhythmic hum of the engines. After a moment, she turned back to him.

"Callum," she said softly, "what are you afraid of?"

He didn't hesitate.

"Losing you."

Lila froze.

He continued.

"And losing the child.

And losing the Veil.

And losing everything I've been fighting to protect."

He exhaled, shoulders slumping slightly.

"And I'm afraid I won't be strong enough to stop what's coming."

Lila reached over, resting her hand gently on his.

"Callum... you don't have to be strong enough alone."

He looked at her, eyes softening in spite of everything.

"You're mortal, Lila."

"You keep saying that like it's a flaw."

"It's not."

"Then stop treating it like one."

A faint, exhausted smile tugged the corner of his mouth.

The moment held,

brief, fragile, real.

But THOTH broke it.

"Callum, new development."

He straightened.

"What now?"

"The child's resonance is no longer just calling."

Lila's breath caught.

"Then what are they doing?"

A pause,

long, cold, heavy.

Then:

"The child is trying to open the Veil."

Callum's blood ran cold.

THOTH's voice turned urgent.

"Callum, projections indicate the child will attempt Veil breach within the hour."

"Then we need to get there first."

"Warning," THOTH added, "Morrigan is closer."

"How much closer?" Lila queried.

"Thirty miles."

Callum's eyes narrowed.

"And us?"

"Two hundred fifty."

Lila's heart stopped.

"Callum… we're too far."

THOTH interjected:

"Unless you engage the aerospike and burn the reserves."

Lila frowned.

"What does that mean?"

"It means," Callum said, voice grim, "we risk burning out FENRIR's engines."

"And if the engines burn out?"

"We crash."

Lila stared.

"She needs us."

Lila blinked.

"She?"

Callum paused.

He hadn't told her that part yet.

Yes.

He knew.

He felt it.

THOTH confirmed:

"The resonance profile is feminine."

Lila's eyes softened.

"A little girl…"

Callum inhaled slowly.

"Run the aerospike, THOTH."

"Warning, structural stress will exceed ten percent."

"Run it."

"Confirmed."

The engines screamed to life.

FENRIR lanced forward.

Lila gripped her harness, knuckles white.

"Callum…"

He didn't look away from the horizon.

"I won't let Morrigan touch her."

Lila swallowed.

"What about Renwick?"

Callum's jaw clenched.

"If Morrigan reaches the child first, Renwick doesn't matter."

Lila understood.

And hated the truth.

She reached over, took Callum's free hand, and squeezed.

"You'll reach her."

"I know you will."

He squeezed back.

The engine's roar deepened.

The horizon sharpened.

And ahead,

beyond clouds and sea and ancient whispers,

the Highlands waited.

.

Chapter 8

Edinburgh, Scotland, 1995

The candle burned low on the wooden table, casting long shadows across the ancient tomes stacked haphazardly in the Watcher safehouse. Callum paced between them, restless.

"This doesn't feel right," he muttered.

The Watcher assigned to him, Jonas, was young, eager, and entirely too optimistic for his line of work. He adjusted his glasses nervously.

"You asked for information on the Four," Jonas said. "I'm just doing my job."

Callum stopped pacing.

"That's not what worries me," he said quietly. "It's your director."

Jonas swallowed.

"Director Renwick is... intense. But he's committed to keeping records pure."

"No," Callum said. "He's committed to controlling us."

Jonas looked away.

"We're historians."

Callum stepped closer.

"You spy on us. Follow us. Record our lives like we're cataloged beasts."

Jonas opened his mouth to protest, but the door creaked open.

Renwick entered.

Younger, clean-shaven, sharper in the eyes, but unmistakably him. He carried a folder under one arm, posture straight and predatory.

He smiled politely.

"MacLeod."

Callum's gut twisted.

"Renwick."

Renwick set the folder on the table.

"Your lineage fascinates me," he said. "The MacLeods have produced more recorded Immortals than any other clan."

Callum crossed his arms.

"You came all this way to discuss genealogy?"

Renwick's smile didn't reach his eyes.

"No. I came to advise caution."

He slid the folder toward Callum.

Inside: sketches of ancient artifacts. Tablets depicting men with sparks bursting from their chests. Etched symbols matching the resonance of Arkael and Boroun.

"Your bloodline intersects with legends older than history," Renwick said. "If the Four ever return, and some believe they will, Immortals like you could be the key."

Callum felt a chill.

"And what would you do with such a key?"

Renwick took a slow breath.

"Use it wisely."

Callum closed the folder.

"You're not a historian, Renwick," he said quietly. "You're a hunter."

Renwick's jaw tightened.

"Not yet."

He walked out.

Leaving Callum with a folder on the Four, and a certainty that Renwick's ambitions would one day ignite a disaster.

———————◆———————

The Highlands rose like a memory through the clouds. Crags of stone burst through the fogbank in jagged silhouettes, dark and ancient, carved by time into sharp angles that seemed less like geology and more like the ribs of something titanic and buried. FENRIR dipped between the formations with a predator's grace, its adaptive plating shimmering to match the gray sky.

Lila stared out the cockpit window, breath catching at the sight. This land felt older than language. Wind twisted through the valleys like a living force, whistling against the glass in a keening tone that set her nerves on edge.

"Callum," she asked, "why does this place feel… wrong?"

"It's not wrong," he said quietly. "It's awake."

That did nothing to calm her.

Below them, the moorland was soaked in early mist. Sparse trees bent in the wind as though bowing to some unseen pressure. Lochs cut across the landscape like mirrors, their surfaces trembling as if reacting to pulses she could not hear.

Lila tried to steady herself, but an unsettling truth lingered beneath her ribs:

This land feels alive.

And it is watching us.

THOTH chimed softly into the cockpit.

"Callum, the resonance spike has grown. The child is within a ten-mile radius, but the epicenter is fluctuating."

"Fluctuating how?" Lila asked.

"Like an arrhythmia," THOTH said. "Unstable. And worsening."

Callum adjusted the controls, angling FENRIR lower.

"She's trying to open the Veil," he murmured. "Probably without knowing what she's doing."

"Morrigan is close."

Lila's pulse spiked.

"How close?"

THOTH did not sugarcoat it.

"Nine miles. Approaching fast."

Callum's grip tightened on the throttle, the tendons in his forearm straining.

"We're catching a headwind," he said, frustration tightening his voice. "This terrain always fights aircraft."

"Why?" Lila asked.

"Because it isn't just terrain."

THOTH elaborated:

"Certain Highland regions resonate with pre-Immortal energy. It distorts electronics and enhances supernatural signatures."

"In English?" Lila asked.

"It's a magnet for trouble," Callum said.

Something flickered through him, an echo of memory tinged with pain.

"This place," he said softly, "is where I died my first death."

Lila turned sharply.

He kept his eyes on the horizon.

"There's a reason I don't come back here."

FENRIR dropped lower, skimming just above the mist line. Wind battered the hull, making the entire craft shudder.

Lila braced herself.

"THOTH?" Callum said. "Status?"

"Boost reserves at twenty percent. Ducted fans adjusting for crosswinds. Structural stress at nominal levels."

"Good."

Another gust slammed the hull.

Lila gripped her harness. "Callum, are we going to crash?"

"No."

"You don't sound entirely convinced."

He offered a strained half-smile.

"If I thought we were going to crash, I'd tell you to start praying."

"That's comforting," she deadpanned.

Wind howled again, echoing deeper this time, almost like a voice. Lila shivered involuntarily.

"What was that?"

"Wind," Callum said.

"That didn't sound like wind."

Callum's jaw flexed.

THOTH cut in sharply, "Callum, multiple resonance signatures emerging directly ahead."

Callum's posture tensed.

"Morrigan?"

"No. Smaller."

"Corrupted constructs?"

"No. This is... different."

"What kind of 'different'?" she asked.

The AI hesitated.

"They are... echoes."

Callum immediately throttled back. "No. Not here. Not now."

Lila frowned. "Callum, what's an echo?"

But she didn't need THOTH to answer.

The clouds parted, and she saw them - shapes.

Human silhouettes made of pale shimmer and memory, drifting across the moor like ghosts caught in the wind.

Some moved slowly, some fast.

Some flickered out as quickly as they appeared.

But none of them were solid.

Lila felt her throat tighten. "Holy Shit... what are they?"

Callum's voice was tight.

"The Veil remembers everyone who has died here. The echoes are fragments of Immortals long gone."

Lila's eyes widened.

"Are they, dangerous?"

"Yes and no."

He focused on their movements.

"They're not alive, but they're not memories either. They're imprints caught between this world and the Veil."

"Do they hurt people?"

"Only if touched."

She swallowed hard.

"So... avoid touching ghosts."

"That's the general idea."

FENRIR maneuvered carefully, weaving between the drifting silhouettes.

Lila found herself pressing back in her seat, a primitive instinct screaming at her that these weren't spirits meant for mortal eyes.

"How much weirder can this get?" Lila said under her breath, but apparently loud enough for Callum to hear.

"You haven't even scratched the surface yet" he replied.

One of the spirits turned toward them.

A flicker of a face.

A remnant of a scream.

Or a warning.

She looked around,

"Callum... that one is looking at us."

He didn't look away from the controls.

"Don't meet their eyes."

"I didn't know echoes had eyes."

"They don't," he said grimly. "That's why meeting them is worse."

THOTH's voice came low, urgent.

"Callum, the child's resonance is spiking again, severely. We may be seeing sympathetic echo discharge."

"Meaning what?" Lila asked.

"Meaning the child's power is waking the dead," Callum replied.

Lila's breath hitched.

"What will happen if this continues?"

Callum finally met her eyes.

"This entire glen will come alive."

"And that's bad?"

"Very."

FENRIR shuddered as another strong gust buffeted the hull.

Callum cursed under his breath.

THOTH's voice rose with warning:

"Callum, new signature detected."

Lila straightened.

"Is it Morrigan?"

"No," THOTH said.

"And yes."

Callum's eyes narrowed.

"What does that mean?"

"It's her resonance," THOTH explained, "but diffused. Projected-like."

Lila choked out a breath.

"She's sending her voice ahead of her."

Callum's blood ran cold.

"Brace," he said.

"What for, "

The Highland winds suddenly went silent.

Every echo froze.

And a woman's voice, ancient, cold, and impossibly close, filled the cockpit.

"Callum MacLeod."

Lila's heart slammed against her ribs.

Callum gripped the sword.

Her voice seeped through the air like black smoke:

"Come to me."

Lila felt her breath evaporate.

Callum's knuckles whitened around the Katana.

"Morrigan," he mouthed.

The voice answered, "The child is not yours."

Callum's jaw clenched.

"The hell she isn't."

A long, distant laugh echoed through the glen.

Cold and cruel.

"Then come claim her."

Thunder rolled across the moor.

An impossible storm began to form.

And the child's resonance, now frantic, now terrified, spiked to a level that shook the airframe.

FENRIR plunged toward the ancient valley where fate, legend, and death all waited for them.

The storm burst across the Highland valley with unnatural ferocity.

Wind sheared sideways, ripping along the glen in violent currents that snarled through the rocky spires and sent curling mist spiraling upward like torn veils. Lightning flashed, not white, but blue, streaking across the sky in jagged bursts that left a metallic aftertaste in the air.

Lila flinched as one bolt struck a ridge less than thirty meters from the aircraft.

"Callum!" she shouted over the deafening thunder, "are storms like this normal?"

"No," Callum said, his voice grim. "This is Morrigan."

As if summoned by her name, the clouds convulsed, folding into a massive whirl above the valley floor. The rotation deepened into something darker, something that pulled light inward instead of reflecting it.

Lila's stomach twisted.

"Is that... a storm or a portal?"

"Yes," Callum said.

She shot him a horrified look.

He clarified.

"It's a resonance funnel. Something between weather and power. Morrigan's trying to control the Veil from the outside."

Lila felt her heart rattle against her ribs. "Can she do that?"

"In this valley?" Callum's jaw tightened. "Yes."

THOTH's voice came through, strained by interference.

"Callum, structural integrity at ninety-three percent. Environmental interference worsening. Recommend immediate descent."

"We're already descending," Callum snapped. "Give me a path."

"Searching..."

Lila looked out the cockpit window again,

Her breath caught.

Far below, through the swirling mist, a ring of ancient standing stones encircled a small clearing, massive monoliths carved with symbols older than written history. The grass inside the circle glowed faintly, pulsing with blue-white light.

At the center of the stone ring stood a child.

A girl, in a simple wool dress, wild hair whipping in the wind. Barefoot. Alone. Eyes closed, hands raised slightly as if feeling the air. The resonance around her fluttered like a heartbeat under attack, fast, erratic, desperate.

"Callum..." Lila said, "she's so tiny."

The child could not have been older than eight.

Her resonance was luminous, fierce, and completely uncontrolled, flaring outward in bursts that made the standing stones vibrate like

179

tuning forks.

The wind around her wasn't blowing.

It was responding.

"THOTH," Callum said quietly, "confirm identity."

"Resonance match ninety-three percent.
This is the child."

Lila's eyes stung.

"She looks terrified."

Callum nodded once, jaw clenched so tight it trembled.

"We land," he said. "Now."

"Callum," THOTH warned, "Morrigan is approaching from the southern ridge, fast."

Lila craned her neck, looking to the left. Through a break in the clouds, she saw her.

A woman, or something shaped like one, moving across the air as if gravity were an optional formality. Long dark hair trAilíng behind her like ink in water. A long coat or cloak whipping in the wind.
A faint shimmer surrounded her body, and something like shadows curling from her skin.

Even from miles away, Lila felt the wrongness.

This was an Immortal the way a hurricane was "just weather."

Callum's voice dropped to a razor's edge.

"She's closer than I thought."

Thunder cracked so loud Lila flinched.

Callum angled FENRIR sharply, lining up the descent toward the stone circle. Wind buffeted them violently as they dropped, but Callum fought it with precise, harsh manual adjustments.

"Hold on," he said.

Lila grabbed the rail with both hands.

Thunder roared again, this time not from the sky.

From the ground.

The child's resonance discharged in a massive burst,
a shockwave of blue light rippling outward.

It hit FENRIR like a hammer.

The cockpit alarms screamed.
The aircraft lurched sideways.

"THOTH!" Callum shouted. "Stabilize, "

"Attempting! Structural strain seventy-seven percent, "

A second blast erupted from the ground,

Callum swore and jerked controls, fighting the downdraft with everything he had.

The aircraft spun.

The world tilted.

Lila screamed.

The Katana vibrated against its mount, humming in response to the child's energy.

Callum gritted his teeth.

"THOTH, override! Put all power into the forward stabilizers!"

"Warning, overload risks damage to, "

"DO IT!"

"Executing."

FENRIR leveled abruptly, hard enough that Lila nearly blacked out.

They were almost on top of the stone circle now.

The child stood in the center, her eyes wide open and glowing with unspent power.

Lila gasped.

"She sees us."

The girl's gaze locked onto Callum's through the cockpit window,

And the resonance around her snapped into place for one heartbeat.

She lifted one hand toward him.

Lila, voice trembling,

"...she knows you."

Callum swallowed hard.

And for the first time, he felt something pulling him.

Not destiny.

Not duty.

Recognition.

"Callum," THOTH warned sharply, "Morrigan is descending behind us, twenty seconds to intercept."

"Too late," Callum muttered. "We're landing."

He dropped FENRIR into the clearing with a precision born of centuries of flight and desperation.

The landing skids struck earth.

K. A. Beaulieu

Lila immediately unbuckled.

Callum did too.

THOTH screamed through the cabin.

"CALLUM, MORRIGAN HAS ARRIVED!"

The southern ridge exploded in a shower of stone,

And Morrigan stepped into the valley. Her eyes glowed with a sickening, unnatural light. and when she saw Callum, she smiled a slow, terrible smile.

"Ah," she purred, voice curling like smoke.
"MacLeod."

Lila grabbed Callum's arm.

Callum's hand locked around the Katana.

The child's resonance pulsed like a beating heart.

The storm swallowed the valley.

The storm bent around Morrigan as if the wind itself feared touching her.

Mist curled back from her silhouette, peeling away from her form like it was being repelled by something far more ancient than the gale tearing through the valley. The standing stones trembled, not from the child's resonance this time, but from the cold, oppressive presence descending the ridge with predatory calm.

Lila felt her knees weaken.

Callum felt something else entirely.

"Callum, what is she?"

He didn't look away from Morrigan.

He couldn't.

"Something the world forgot on purpose."

The child clutched her arms close to her chest, eyes wide with terror, the glow beneath her skin flickering like a fAilíng lantern. Every time Morrigan took another step, the resonance around the child spasmed.

"She's scared," Lila murmured.

Callum nodded once.

"She should be."

THOTH tried to cut through the tension.

"Callum, detecting a field distortion around Morrigan, unknown composition. Recommend you maintain distance."

Morrigan's lips curled into a knowing smile.

"Your machine is loud," she said, her voice drifting across the clearing like silk dipped in venom. "It speaks too much."

Her gaze shifted to Lila.

"And you bring mortals now? How quaint."

The way she said *mortal* made Lila's blood run cold.

Callum stepped forward.

Sword in hand.

Stance low, grounded.

Every muscle aligned to one truth:

He might die here.

"Stay away from her," Callum said, voice steady despite the storm tearing at his hair and coat. "The child doesn't belong to you."

Morrigan let out a soft, dismissive hum.

"She doesn't belong to you either, MacLeod."

Callum's jaw clenched.

"You don't get to choose what happens next."

Morrigan tilted her head.

"Neither do you."

The wind around her shifted abruptly, spiraling in unnatural patterns.

"What is she doing?"

Callum didn't answer.

He recognized the technique.

Because he had seen Ailsa perform it centuries ago.

Veil-walking.

Lila saw it a second later.

Morrigan was phasing,

not leaving the world entirely,

not entering the Veil completely,

but occupying the thin threshold between both.

She was becoming untouchable.

And unstoppable.

Callum exhaled once, slow and deliberate.

"I'm going to make her come here."

The Katana hummed as if awakened by his resolve.

Morrigan's eyes flicked to it, amusement flickering across her face.

"Ah. Duncan's toy."

Callum tightened his grip around the hilt.

"It's not a toy," he said quietly.

"No," she purred. "It's a chain."

Those words hit him harder than the wind.

She stepped closer, the air distorting around her like heat above a flame.

"Callum MacLeod," she said, "you are tethered to that blade. To the man who carried it. To the world he protected."

She smiled.

"And I?

I am tethered to nothing."

The storm growled overhead like some ancient beast stirring.

Lightning struck one of the standing stones, splitting it down the center. The fracture glowed blue, resonance leaking like electricity.

The child yelped, covering her ears.

That was all the opening Morrigan needed.

She moved, not fast, not slow, but with the terrifying inevitability of something that had mastered time itself.

Callum lunged in front of her.

Morrigan stopped.

Not because she had to.

Because she wanted him to see her smile.

"You are predictable," she murmured.

"You still protect."

Callum's eyes narrowed.

"You still prey on the weak."

Morrigan's smile sharpened.

"Only the valuable ones."

Lila stepped forward instinctively, but Callum shot an arm back without looking.

"Stay behind me."

"No," Lila said, her voice trembling but resolute.

Morrigan arched a brow.

"Oh? You let her speak for herself now?

How modern."

Callum growled, low, animal, barely restrained.

"Back away from the child."

"Or what?" Morrigan asked lightly. "You'll wave your sword at me? Mmm...that worked so well against Renwick's little pets."

She turned her gaze to the girl in the circle.

"And you, little one...look at you. Born from the Veil, wrapped in its light. A newborn star in a dying sky."

The child whimpered.

Callum stepped forward again.

"I said, stay away from her."

Morrigan's eyes snapped back to him.

And for the first time,

they were not amused.

They were hungry.

"You claim resonance ties to a child you did not sire," she said. "You claim kinship to a power you do not understand. You claim protection of a life shaped by the Veil."

Her expression hardened into something colder.

"You have no idea what she is."

Lila stepped closer to Callum, fear and defiance intermingling.

"She's a child."

Morrigan's gaze swept Lila's face, "She is a disaster."

Callum's knuckles turned white around the Katana.

"Then I'll protect her from you."

"Oh, Callum..." Morrigan said dismissively, "You couldn't even protect your brother."

Every breath in Lila's chest froze.

Callum did not move.

Not visibly.

Not outwardly.

But the air around him fractured,

A ripple of grief so violent Lila felt it like a punch to the sternum.

Morrigan's smile returned.

"Yes," she purred. "Feel it. Your wound, your failure. It makes you *delicious.*"

The ground beneath them trembled.

The standing stones hummed.

The child cried out, and the resonance around her burst in a jagged pulse.

Morrigan's eyes widened.

"There," she whispered. "That is the Veil's voice. Calling through her."

She lifted her hand.

The air between her fingers shimmered, a tear forming in reality's surface.

Lila grabbed Callum's arm.

"Callum, she's trying to open it!"

"I see it."

"We can't let her!"

"I know."

"What do we do?"

Callum drew a breath that tasted of dread and inevitability.

"We force the Veil closed."

"How?!"

His eyes softened for half a heartbeat.

"With a sword built to sever destiny."

Morrigan heard it too.

Her smile vanished.

For the first time since stepping into the valley, her expression changed.

Fear.

"You would wield that here?" she breathed.

Callum raised the Katana.

"Yes."

Wind spiraled violently around them. The child screamed.

The Veil began to tear and Callum stepped forward to face a nightmare older than Immortality itself.

The moment Callum raised the Katana, the entire valley reacted.

Wind snapped violently in the opposite direction, as if the storm itself recoiled from the sword's awakening. The standing stones brightened, runes glowing with ancient fire. Grass flattened in a circle around Callum's feet, pulled down by a force older than gravity.

Morrigan's expression, once calm and mocking, shattered into something harsher.

She stepped back, not fast enough to reveal panic, but fast enough to betray concern.

"No," she murmured. "Not that blade. Not here."

Lila confused, "Callum... what is happening?"

But Callum didn't answer.

He couldn't.

The Katana vibrated with a resonance so intense it tremored through his entire arm. His eyes flickered with reflected blue light. The sword hummed as if remembering the countless Immortal souls it had consumed across centuries.

Morrigan lifted her hand sharply.

"MacLeod, stop this! You do not know what you're invoking!"

Callum took another step forward.

"Then enlighten me."

The ground rumbled underfoot, stones shifting as if the earth was trying to pull away.

Morrigan did not advance.

She did not attack.

She *circled*.

Always keeping distance, not from Callum himself, but from the sword.

"Do you know why Duncan carried that blade?" Morrigan asked, her voice slipping into something almost pleading. "Why Methos refuses to touch it? Why even the Veil recoils when its metal wakes?"

Callum raised the blade higher, its glow intensifying.

"I'm listening."

Morrigan's expression twisted.

"Fool."

The shimmering tear she had begun forming in the air collapsed with a sharp crack. She reached up and dragged her fingers along the ruptured space, resealing it with a hiss of displaced air.

Then,

She pointed at the child.

"She is not a doorway, Callum. She is the lock. *That*," Morrigan nodded toward the Katana, "is the key."

Lila felt her breath freeze.

"Oh no..."

Callum's grip tightened.

"You're lying."

"Am I?" Morrigan asked softly. "Do you really think the Veil birthed her to be saved? she is some cosmic gift? A miracle?"

Her eyes gleamed with cruel certainty.

"She was made to open things.

Made to tear the world open."

Lila grabbed Callum's arm.

"No," she breathed, "she's a child."

Morrigan's voice sharpened, not loud, but cutting.

"She is *not* a child. She is the Veil trying again."

Callum's stomach clenched.

"No."

"Oh yes," Morrigan said, stepping closer.

"She is what you were nearly forged into, Callum MacLeod."

Lila's heart slammed.

"What, what does that mean?"

Morrigan's gaze slid to Callum, cold and hungry.

"Tell her, MacLeod."

Callum's voice shook.

"Don't."

Morrigan's smile returned, slow and vicious.

"The Veil chose you once. Centuries ago. It tried to open through you. Ailsa stopped it." She tilted her head. "Ask yourself why your resonance matches the girl's. Why she called *your* name."

Lila stared at him, the truth slamming into place.

"Callum...

you and she..."

He didn't deny it.

Morrigan laughed softly.

"You were meant to be the Veil's emissary. But the Veil made a mistake."She glanced at the trembling girl.

"So it made another."

Callum stepped in front of the child.

"You don't touch her."

Morrigan's eyes narrowed.

"I don't want to touch her. I want to close her."

Lila blinked.

"Close her? What does that even, "

"Kill," Callum growled.

Morrigan didn't argue.

The storm howled.

But the child, the girl whose resonance had torn the land open, stepped forward from behind Callum.

Her voice was small, trembling.

"Please...don't let her take me."

Lila crouched instantly, arms open.

"Sweetheart, come here."

The child rushed into Lila's embrace, clinging to her with desperate strength. Lila felt the tiny body trembling against her, felt the heat of energy that radiated from beneath her skin, a faint hum like static electricity and starlight.

"Callum, she's terrified."

Morrigan hissed.

"Of course she is terrified. She exists in two worlds and belongs in neither. She hears every whisper in the Veil. Every hunger. Every call. And every creature waiting for her to open the door..."

She extended a hand toward the girl.

"And if she opens it, none of us walk away."

Callum moved between them.

"You're not taking her."

"No," Morrigan said, "I'm saving you from her."

Thunder rolled again, this time directly overhead.

The standing stones blazed brighter, their runes surging with life.

The girl whimpered.

"Make it stop...

Please... make it stop..."

Lila held her tighter.

"It's okay, sweetheart, Callum's here."

Morrigan's expression twisted.

"Oh, how sweet. The mortal comforting the apocalypse."

Lila snapped.

"She's not an apocalypse! She's a frightened little girl!"

"AND THAT IS THE PROBLEM!" Morrigan roared, her voice splitting the air like thunder.

Every echo in the valley froze.

Every stone vibrated.

Even the storm paused for a heartbeat.

Morrigan's chest heaved as she regained her composure.

"She is innocent," Morrigan said softly. "But innocence is the most dangerous thing the Veil has ever touched."

Callum raised the blade.

"Then we'll teach her to control it."

Morrigan's eyes hardened.

"You don't have time."

"Watch me."

Morrigan lifted her hand.

Callum braced.

But instead of casting an attack,

Morrigan pointed to the child's chest.

A pulsing glow thrummed beneath the girl's skin, small, bright, fragile.

"That resonance," Morrigan said, "is not yours.

It is not human.

It is not Immortal."

Lila's breath caught.

"Then what is she?"

Morrigan hissed:

"A beginning."

Thunder shattered the silence.

The child screamed,

a sound that tore like a blade through Callum's heart.

Her resonance spiked, blinding, unstable, frantic.

The standing stones cracked.

The air split.

Reality began to thin.

Morrigan snarled:

"See? She is tearing the world open by accident."

Callum lifted the Katana, the only thing in this valley with the authority to cut the Veil.

"Callum!" Lila shouted. "What are you doing?!"

"What I must."

Morrigan hissed in delight.

"Yes. Do it.

Cut the resonance.

Sever the connection.

Before she becomes what she was meant to be."

"No!" Lila screamed. "Don't you dare, "

Callum's voice broke.

"This isn't about killing her."

He raised the sword high as reality twisted around them.

"This is about saving her."

Lightning struck the ground at their feet.

The Veil cracked open.

And Callum brought the Katana down,

Not on the girl.

But on the tear in the air.

The Katana sliced downward in a brilliant arc, and the valley erupted.

Light tore across the glen in a rippling shockwave, blue-white and blinding. The tear in the air crackled like a wounded star. Shredded resonance spilled outward, blowing the grass flat in concentric circles. Thunder detonated overhead, louder than any storm, shaking the ground so hard Lila had to throw herself over the child to protect her.

Callum braced against the force, arms shaking, spine locked, teeth clenched. The sword vibrated violently, as if the Veil itself was trying to yank it from his grip. Waves of power slammed into him, each one threatening to tear him off his feet.

But he didn't fall.

He *held*.

Because she needed him to, because this was the only way.

Morrigan staggered back, eyes flaring with fury.

"NO, MacLeod, STOP! You don't know what you're…"

Callum didn't hear her.

He heard only the child's scream behind him.

The resonance burst again.

So uncontained it felt like a knife made of sound.

The tear widened, jagged edges of reality splitting like torn cloth.

Morrigan lunged.

She moved like wind without resistance, half-phased, half-shadow, her form flickering at the edges. She extended a hand toward the girl, fingers curling with purpose.

"Let me stabilize her, she will tear herself apart, "

"Don't touch her!" Callum roared.

He twisted the Katana mid-swing, shifting its angle in a practiced motion Duncan had taught him decades ago, one designed not to cut flesh but to *splice energy.*

The move tore through the tear, slicing the rift's unstable resonance in half.

Morrigan screamed.

The child didn't.

She collapsed against Lila, exhausted, breathless, trembling, but alive.

Lila clutched her tighter.

The rift surged violently,

Then began to collapse.

The valley shuddered as the tear folded inward, as if the world were inhaling a deep, furious breath. The standing stones pulsed with ancient fire one last time, cracks glowing like molten veins.

Wind spiraled upward.

Mist funneled into the closing seam.

Callum held the blade steady, guiding the contraction with sheer force of will.

His body shook violently, every muscle screaming in protest, but he didn't stop.

He couldn't.

Not when she watched him with terrified, hopeful eyes.

Not when the Veil roared for a doorway and he refused to give it one.

Not when he finally understood what Ailsa had died protecting:

The world was never meant to open again.

Morrigan staggered forward.

"MacLeod, NO, if you force it closed now, "

Her voice was drowned out by the final shudder of the rift collapsing in on itself.

And then,

Silence.

The tear sealed. The storm stilled and dissipated.

The stones dimmed.

And Callum collapsed to one knee, gasping for breath, the Katana dimming in his hand.

He had done it.

He had cut the Veil closed.

Morrigan stared at him in disbelief, then rage.

"You ignorant *child.*"

Her voice dripped venom.

"You have no idea what you've just ruined."

Callum forced himself to his feet.

"I saved her."

"You doomed her," Morrigan hissed.

Lila pulled the child tighter to her chest.

"She's alive."

"For now," Morrigan said coldly. "But the Veil chose her for a reason. It won't stop calling. You closed one tear, but she will make others."

The child whimpered softly, burying her face in Lila's coat.

Morrigan's eyes softened for a fraction of a second, something like pity flickering through her expression before being devoured by fury.

"She cannot help what she is.

And you cannot protect her from what comes next."

Callum raised the blade again.

"Watch me."

Morrigan's gaze snapped to the sword.

A shadow of fear passed through her eyes.

"You wield that blade like you understand it, but you don't. Duncan barely did himself."

Callum tightened his grip.

"Then teach me."

Morrigan laughed, a sharp, bitter sound.

"You wouldn't survive the lesson."

She stepped backward, the mist curling around her legs as though eager to reclaim her.

"MacLeod…"

Her voice darkened.

"Renwick is coming. He will not remain in the shadows much longer."

Callum's jaw hardened.

"Let him come."

Morrigan's smile was thin and cold.

"Oh...he will."

The mist enveloped her.

The shadows swallowed her.

And Morrigan vanished.

The wind died.

Silence returned.

Callum lowered the Katana at last, its glow fading to a low, exhausted hum.

Lila remained kneeling with the girl, who now clung to her with small, shaking hands.

Callum turned to them.

"Is she alright?"

Lila nodded shakily.

"She's scared... and overwhelmed... but she's breathing."

The girl looked up at Callum, eyes huge, luminous, and too knowing.

Her voice was barely more than a whisper.

"Please don't leave me."

Callum's heart cracked.

He sheathed the blade and knelt beside her.

"I'm not leaving you," he said softly. "Not ever."

Lila watched him, realization dawning slowly in her eyes.

This wasn't just a mission or a duty. This was family.

The girl wrapped her tiny fingers around Callum's.

Lila swallowed hard, tears forming.

Callum's voice trembled, barely.

"What's your name?"

The girl blinked.

For a moment, her resonance flickered, gentle, soft, safe.

Then she muttered:

"...Ailín."

Lila felt her pulse stop.

Callum's breath caught.

Ailsa's tongue.

Old Gaelic.

Little Light.

"Ailín," he repeated softly, voice breaking. "I've got you."

The girl leaned into him.

Lila wrapped her arms around them both.

And as Callum held her, this Veil-born child who carried his echo,

Chapter 9

The storm fell away behind them in layers.

First the screaming wind, then the jagged flashes of blue lightning. The roiling Highland clouds, thinning as FENRIR clawed its way higher and finally leveled out into smooth, cold air.

Callum felt the shift in his bones. His muscles, locked in fight-or-die tension since Manhattan, finally registered something new.

Exhaustion.

The cockpit lights glowed soft and steady. Out ahead, the sky stretched wide and pale, the horizon washed in steel gray and faint gold as the day leaned toward evening. From altitude, the clouds looked almost peaceful, a soft blanket wrapped around the brutal land they'd just escaped.

Lila leaned back in her harness and shut her eyes for a moment, the adrenaline ebbing enough for the aches to appear. Her ribs hurt. Her shoulders hurt. Her head pounded.

"How long have we been going?" she asked quietly.

THOTH answered instead of Callum.

"It has been thirty-one hours, seven minutes since you met in Manhattan Presbyterian."

Lila's eyes opened again, heavy.

"Thirty-one hours," she repeated. "

She let out a tired, humorless breath.

"No one's supposed to have that much plot in a day."

A faint smile ghosted across Callum's face.

"Welcome to my life."

She turned her head.

"You look worse than I feel."

"Good," he said. "That means you're still human."

A small shape shifted between them.

Ailín.

The girl was curled in the copilot's seat, legs tucked under her, arms wrapped around herself. The too-large harness almost swallowed her slight frame. At some point in the climb, she'd fallen asleep against Lila's arm, little fingers clenched in the fabric of Lila's sleeve.

Now she stirred, eyelids fluttering.

"Are we... falling?" she mumbled.

"No," Lila said gently. "We're flying."

Ailín shivered.

"I had a dream," she whispered. "There was a lot of light. And a woman with red hair. She was angry."

Lila and Callum exchanged a look.

"Morrigan," Callum said.

Ailín's brow furrowed.

"She said I was... wrong."

Callum's throat tightened.

"You're not wrong," he said, a little more roughly than he intended.

The girl's eyes opened fully at that. They were still faintly luminous, but softer now that the storm was behind them.

"Where are we going?" she asked.

"Somewhere safe," Lila said automatically.

Callum didn't contradict her, but he didn't quite confirm it either.

"Western coast," he said. "Helios maintains a private facility there. A safehouse built into an old estate. Remote and off-book."

Lila blinked.

"You have a secret Scottish ocean lair and you made me sleep in a Manhattan hospital call room?"

"You're here now," Callum said.

She squinted at him, but the comeback lost its edge as the fatigue settled deeper in her bones.

"How long?" she asked. "Until we get there?"

"Two hours," THOTH replied.

Lila groaned softly.

"Two more hours in the air..."

Her stomach rumbled in protest.

"We haven't eaten since, " She paused. "When *did* we last eat?"

Callum thought.

"Airport lounge. Sandwich. Before New York."

"That was yesterday."

"Yes."

"That's not okay," she muttered.

Callum's attention eased from the instruments, just a fraction.

"You can sleep," he said. "THOTH will alert us if anything changes."

"Will *you* sleep?" she asked.

He shook his head.

"Someone has to keep this thing in the air."

"You're Immortal, not made of titanium."

"Close enough."

She gave him a look.

"You can't keep running on rage and Quickening forever."

He didn't answer that.

Ailín yawned, then sagged against Lila again. Lila settled her properly, adjusting the harness, pulling a folded thermal blanket from the compartment overhead and tucking it around the girl.

Callum watched her do it, a strange tightness in his chest.

He hadn't expected this, not a child, not now, not with his past. But the moment Ailín grabbed his hand in the stone circle, something had settled into place inside him he couldn't easily name. He didn't have another name for it, except... responsibility. No, that was too small a word... Family.

The word scared him more than Morrigan.

He pulled the aircraft a little higher, a little faster.

Behind them, the Highlands swallowed by the lingering storm.

Ahead, the western sea and the Helios estate waited.

For the first time in thirty-one hours, the plan did not involve immediate bloodshed. They were finally headed toward rest.

Dusk had fallen by the time the coastline came into view. From the air, it looked like the edge of the world, cliffs carved into sharp, slate-dark teeth where waves crashed and threw up white spray. Patches of green clung stubbornly to the rock. Further inland, hills rose into silhouettes against the darkening sky.

"Approaching perimeter," THOTH announced.

"Engaging stealth profile."

FENRIR's outer skin shimmered, its thermal and radar signatures shifting. Callum dipped the aircraft lower, following the contour of a narrow sea loch that cut into the land like a wound.

"There," he said quietly.

Lila followed his gaze.

Halfway up the cliff, just above where the waves hammered the rock, a stone manor seemed to grow from the land itself. Old, gray, weathered. Warm light burned in only a handful of windows. From above, it was clear the house was larger than the facade suggested, most of it went into the rock, not out from it.

"Is that... all yours?" Lila asked.

"Helios'," Callum said. "On paper."

"And in reality?"

He didn't answer.

Which was answer enough.

FENRIR angled toward a disguised platform cut into the cliff face behind the main house. A disguised hangar door raised open, stone panels retracting like segments of a puzzle.

"Welcome to Helios Black Site Aleph-Seven," THOTH said.

"Catchy name," Lila muttered.

The landing was smooth, the engines' whine echoing in the enclosed space. As the doors to FENRIR opened, cool salt air flowed into the cabin, carrying the smell of the sea and wet rock.

Ailín blinked awake, squinting in confusion.

"Where are we?"

Callum unbuckled, muscles protesting as he stood.

"Somewhere you can sleep without the sky falling on your head."

He offered a hand.

She took it without hesitation.

The hangar lights brightened as they stepped out of FENRIR. The space was cut directly into the cliff, a high-ceilinged cavern reinforced with steel ribs and studded with equipment: maintenance rigs, storage lockers, a row of emergency generators. A single corridor led deeper into the rock, warm light spilling from the far end. It looked like a scene right out of Ian Fleming's James Bond characters

"Environmental systems active," THOTH reported.
"Security grid online. No unauthorized signatures detected."

"That's the first good news I've heard all day," Lila said.

Callum led them down the corridor. The stone gradually gave way to more traditional walls, still solid, but softened by wood paneling and muted light. The air smelled faintly of lemon oil and old paper.

The corridor opened into the back of the manor: a modest but well-appointed kitchen and great room combo overlooking the sea. Dark beams. Stone hearth. Shelves lined with actual books. A long table. A kettle already steaming on the stove.

Lila stopped.

"You have a… cottage."

Callum looked faintly offended.

"It's a fully functional secure facility."

She pointed at the stone fireplace.

"You have a cottage."

THOTH chimed in from a ceiling speaker.

"Callum, I activated the domestic systems when your ID pinged the perimeter. The pantry is stocked. Water heater is at optimal temperature. You should all eat. And bathe. And sleep."

"Are you… scolding us?" Lila asked.

"You have not slept in thirty-one hours," THOTH replied. "You are both operating at a measurable deficit. And the child's system is depleted from her resonance event."

Callum exhaled slowly.

"For once, THOTH is right."

"Hey," Lila said. "I've been right too."

He looked at her.

"Yes," he said. "You have."

The acknowledgment should not have mattered as much as it did.

"Food first," she said quickly. "Then sleep. Then whatever

Immortal disaster-planning session you have in mind."

"Deal," Callum said.

They moved automatically, the way people who have lived long in hospitals and war zones know how to move when rest finally seems allowed: careful, a little cautious, still listening for alarms that might yank them back to work.

Callum pulled together something simple but real from the pantry: bread, cheese, cured meat, tinned soup upgraded with fresh herbs from a small planter by the window. Lila boiled water for tea and tried not to think about how absurdly normal it felt to be stirring a pot while an Immortal with a dragonhead sword checked cabinets for bowls.

Ailín perched on a chair at the end of the table, wrapped in a wool blanket that dragged along the floor. She watched everything with wide, tired eyes.

The first bite of food hit Lila's system like medicine.

"Oh..." she groaned quietly. "I'd forgotten how good hot soup is when you're not eating it out of a paper cup between codes."

Callum ate with slower, more controlled movements, but the way he cleaned the bowl said enough about how long it had been.

They didn't talk much at first. Just the clink of cutlery, the crackle of logs catching fire in the hearth, the distant roar of the sea battering the cliff.

It felt... almost peaceful.

It scared Lila a little.

Because peace never lasted.

Not in stories like this.

Not in lives like his.

Later, with dishes rinsed and stacked, Ailín asleep on a small sofa near the hearth, and the house's quiet warmth seeping into their bones, Callum and Lila finally found themselves alone at the long table.

Lila cupped a mug of tea in both hands, savoring the heat.

"So," she said quietly, "is this the part where you finally tell me what I've stepped into?"

Callum sat opposite her, elbows on the table, fingers loosely laced.

"You've already seen most of it," he said.

"I've seen fragments," she countered. "Pulse events. Quickenings.

A dead man getting back up. Morrigan. Ailín tearing the sky by accident. And you, in the middle of all of it, acting like this is just your Tuesday."

He didn't argue.

"I need to understand," she said. "Not the sci-fi veneer. The real rules. The… Highlander part."

He huffed softly at that.

"Highlander part," he repeated. "That's one way to put it."

"Are there rules?" she pressed. "You keep saying 'the Game.' What is it really?"

Callum stared into the fire for a moment before answering.

"Once," he said, "it was simple. We were told: *There can be only one.* Immortals live, fight, die, and when one of us takes another's head, we take their Quickening, their strength, their knowledge, their power. Eventually, one is meant to stand at the end. That was the story."

"And now?"

"Now the world is more complicated. We don't live on islands and fight with claymores in the rain. We live in boardrooms and warzones, hospitals and data centers. There's still a Game, but there are factions now, technology, agreements, and old grudges that span empires."

He glanced at her.

"Renwick wants to change the Game. Bend it. Use technology and… other things… to control how Quickenings work. To manufacture winners."

"And you?" she asked.

"I just want to stop him."

"And Morrigan?" Lila pushed.

He hesitated.

"She's old," he said. "Older than most. She remembers when the Game wasn't a legend but an active, open hunt. She's seen what happens when Immortals stop hiding."

"And she's afraid of Ailín."

"She's afraid of what Ailín could become if someone like Renwick gets to her first."

Lila looked toward the sofa.

The girl was a small bundle of blanket and tangled hair, curled on her side, breathing softly. In sleep, the faint luminescence under her skin dimmed, but it never vanished entirely.

"She's... pre-Immortal?" Lila asked.

Callum nodded slowly.

"She hasn't died yet. But she carries the spark. And something about her... sings differently. She hears the Veil more clearly than most full Immortals ever will."

"And she called your name."

"Yes."

"Why?"

He exhaled.

"I don't know. Not entirely. It could be something in our resonance. It could be a connection I don't remember forging. It could be the Veil's idea of a joke."

"Is that how you see it," Lila asked quietly, "as a joke?"

His mouth twitched.

"Not a funny one."

Silence settled again, softer this time, heavy but not hostile.

Lila studied him in the firelight: the lines at the corners of his eyes, the scar near his temple, the way he rolled his shoulder as if it still ached from Cormac's blows.

"You carry a lot," she said.

"So do you," he replied.

"Not for three hundred years."

He gave a small, rough laugh.

"No. You've crammed your burdens into fewer."

She held his gaze.

"Tell me about Cormac."

His expression closed, then opened again, just a fraction.

"He was older than me," Callum said. "Not by much. We trained together, fought together, and survived some really stupid decisions together. He was... loud. Reckless. Never knew when to shut up." A ghost of a smile touched his lips. "He called me an old man even when I was young."

"You loved him," Lila said.

He nodded.

"And I failed him."

"No," she said sharply. "Renwick killed him. You didn't."

"I buried him once," Callum said quietly. "That should have been the end. Instead, Renwick dug him up and turned him into a weapon. He twisted what was left."

"And you freed him," Lila insisted. "You didn't fail him, Callum. You saved what you could."

He didn't argue further.

But he didn't agree either.

"You know," she added softly, "if you keep carrying everyone you've lost alone, you're going to break."

"I already did," he murmured.

Something in her chest squeezed.

"Then maybe let someone help glue you back together," she said.

He looked at her. Really looked at her.

"I'm trying," he said.

It was almost an apology.

Almost a promise.

They slept.

It wasn't graceful.

Callum insisted on taking first watch, claiming he was less tired. Lila called him a liar with enough conviction that he almost smiled. In the end, they reached a compromise THOTH approved of, the AI would monitor external signatures and wake them if anything shifted. The manor's security grid put the estate under a silent electric dome.

"Renwick's not here yet," Callum said. "He'll need time to regroup."

"You're sure?" Lila asked.

"No," Callum said. "But it's the best bet we've had in thirty hours."

He gave Ailín the small bedroom nearest the hearth. Lila tucked the girl in, brushed hair from her face, and tried not to think about how surreal it was to be putting a Veil-touched pre-Immortal child to bed in a black-site manor in Scotland.

When she stepped back into the hall, Callum was still standing there.

"I'll be across," he said. "You'll be in the next room. If she wakes…"

"I've got her," Lila said.

He nodded.

The rooms were simple but comfortable: clean linens, heavy duvets, walls thick enough to swallow the sea's roar into a distant murmur.

Lila sank into the mattress and was asleep almost before she realized she'd closed her eyes.

She dreamed of blue light, stone circles, and a sword humming with the weight of too many lives.

When she woke, gray light filtered through the curtains, and her muscles ached in a way that told her the sleep had been deep, heavy, restorative, and too short.

She checked the clock on the bedside table.

They'd been out for six hours.

Not enough , but better than nothing.

She padded into the hallway barefoot.

The house felt different now, less like a set and more like a place people actually lived in. Someone, Callum, she guessed, had added more wood to the fire. The smell of coffee drifted from the kitchen.

Ailín's door was ajar.

Lila peeked in.

The bed was empty.

Her heart lurched,

Then she heard voices from the great room.

"…no, the stove is not a good place for an experiment," Callum was saying.

"But the flame looks like it wants to stretch," Ailín replied.

"It doesn't," Callum said firmly. "I promise you; it's perfectly happy where it is."

Lila stepped into the room.

Ailín was perched on a stool at the counter, hair a wild halo, drowning in one of Callum's old Henley shirts that hung to her knees. Callum stood by the stove, frying something in a pan with practiced motions.

"Please tell me that's actual food and not some Immortal alchemy," Lila said.

Callum glanced over.

"Eggs," he said. "Toast. Tea. Your mortal system is safe."

Ailín twisted on the stool.

"Morning," she said shyly.

Lila smiled.

"Morning, kiddo."

She reached out automatically and tested Ailín's forehead.

Cooler.

Better.

"How do you feel?" Lila asked.

Ailín thought about it.

"Tired-but-less," she decided. "And hungry."

"We can fix the hungry," Callum said.

They ate together at the table, the sea visible through the windows now as a restless sheet of gray-blue. Gulls wheeled overhead. The storm had moved inland, leaving only streaks of cloud and the usual wild Highland wind.

For a brief, fragile moment, life felt almost normal.

A man making breakfast.

A woman with her mug of tea.

A child dunking toast in her egg yolk.

Lila held onto that image, because she knew it wouldn't last.

"Callum," she said eventually, "what's Renwick's next move?"

He didn't answer right away.

He cut a piece of toast, chewed, swallowed.

"He knows we're alive," Callum said. "He knows the Katana's been drawn. He knows Ailín's signature is active."

"And Morrigan?" Lila asked.

"She'll have told him I interfered," Callum said. "But I don't think she'll tell him everything."

"Why not?"

"Because she's playing her own game," he said. "Always has."

THOTH's voice slid into the room from a discreet speaker.

"If I may," it said, "Renwick has already begun moving pieces."

Lila set her mug down.

"What do you mean?"

"I intercepted encrypted Helios traffic an hour ago," THOTH said. "Renwick initiated an 'internal audit' of your European assets, Callum. Several black sites flagged for 'compliance review.' This estate is not listed by name, but its grid segment is included in the sweep radius."

Lila frowned.

"He's hunting your safehouses."

"Yes, he knows that I would use Helios assets, so he's going to take that piece off the map," Callum said. "And trying to make it look like corporate hygiene."

"So he's coming," Lila concluded.

"Eventually," Callum said. "He'll narrow it down and try to box me in, just like you try to box in the king in chess, then he'll send humans first. Then... others...immortals or resurrected ones. Not to mention any other immortals that think they can gain an advantage. The MacLeod lineage is highly sought."

"And we have a child to protect," Lila said.

"And a surgeon who's now very high on his list of leverage targets," Callum added.

She swallowed.

"Lucky me."

Ailín's small voice piped up.

"What about me?"

Callum leaned forward, forearms on the table.

"You," he said, "we keep off every grid we can. Off camera. Off systems. Renwick thinks in networks and matrices. If he can't see you, you're harder to grab."

Ailín considered that.

"Okay," she said. Then, more quietly: "Will he stop if I... if I go away?"

Lila's breath caught.

"No," Callum said gently. "He won't."

"Why?"

"Because men like Renwick don't stop when they get what they want," Callum said. "They stop when someone makes them."

Ailín nodded solemnly, as if that made a terrible kind of sense.

Lila met Callum's gaze over her mug.

"So, we rest today," she said. "And tonight, we start planning how to make him stop."

Callum nodded.

"Agreed."

Chapter 10

Morning broke gently over the western cliffs. A pale gold washed across the sea, illuminating the stone manor in soft light. The storm had moved on hours ago, leaving behind a crisp, quiet world painted in gray-blue calm. Wind rattled the heather on the cliffside but didn't reach the house, tucked safely into its carved ledge above the waves.

Inside, the manor smelled of coffee and woodsmoke.

Callum stood at the kitchen counter, reading a glass-panel display THOTH projected above the stove. He held a mug in one hand but hadn't actually taken a sip yet.

His brow furrowed.

He'd been staring at the same pattern of numbers for too long, encrypted signals bouncing between Helios satellite relays, a change in traffic patterns across their European holdings, and a spike in activity at their Zurich financial node.

Something was wrong.

Footsteps padded softly down the hall.

Lila entered the kitchen barefoot again, hair messy from sleep, wearing one of the Helios sweatshirts Callum swore had been folded in a storage drawer since 2004.

"You're up early," she said, voice still thick with sleep.

"I haven't been to bed yet."

She blinked hard.

"Callum…"

He waved it off gently.

"THOTH and I had things to check."

"Mm-hm," she said, taking a mug from the cabinet. "And is there any reason your 'things to check' sound like they might ruin my attempt at a peaceful morning?"

He hesitated.

"Yes."

Lila sighed deeply and gestured with her mug.

"Alright. Ruin away."

THOTH's voice filled the room, warm but edged with urgency.

"Dr. Serrano… Renwick has resurfaced."

Lila's stomach tightened. "How?"

Callum gestured to the projection.

"He's moving across multiple fronts. Careful. Quiet. But unmistakable if you know how to read the pattern."

"Which you do," she said.

"Unfortunately."

Lila stepped closer, taking in the glowing data. She wasn't a cyber specialist, but she knew enough about how hospitals, corporations, and governments interacted to understand that this wasn't normal corporate noise.

"What exactly am I looking at?" she asked.

Callum pointed to a web of lines branching from a central node.

"Signal intercepts. Encrypted, but not enough. Renwick is accessing Helios black channels."

"I thought you said this estate was off-book."

"It is. But Helios owns a lot of land in Scotland. When he triggers an audit of our regional grid…"

He tapped the air.

"…it brushes against this district."

"So he knows we're here?"

"No," Callum said. "But he knows someone is using a Helios facility."

Lila rubbed her forehead.

"How is he doing all this so fast? We've been here less than half a day."

"Because Renwick has been preparing for centuries – its strategy," Callum murmured.

Lila froze mid-sip.

"Explain."

He finally took a drink, as if bracing himself.

"Nine hundred years gives a man time to learn how the world works. How institutions grow. How power shifts. Renwick understands geopolitics better than most governments. And he's ruthless enough to use that knowledge the instant he needs to."

"So this is... what? Revenge? Punishment for losing Cormac?"

Callum shook his head.

"No. This isn't retaliation. This is strategy."

THOTH elaborated:

"Renwick is not simply reacting. He is orchestrating. His signals reflect long-standing backdoor networks he embedded years ago. Possibly decades."

Lila felt a shiver crawl under her skin.

"He's been planning this since before you fought in Manhattan," she said quietly.

Callum gave a single nod.

"And he's accelerating the timeline," he added.

"Why?"

Callum glanced toward the hallway, toward the sleeping child in the adjacent room.

"Ailín's awakening changed the board."

Lila wrapped her hands tighter around the mug.

"So what's his next move?"

Callum stared out the window at the sea, waves rolling like the breath of some ancient beast.

"He's going after Helios," Callum said. "First through audits. Then with legal pressure. Then with force."

"Force?" Lila asked.

"Not a siege," Callum said. "Assassinations. Data siphons. Targeted attacks. Systematically taking away every advantage and resource I have until I don't have an alternative."

"That sounds like a lot for one man."

"He's not alone," Callum said. "Immortals never are. Renwick has allies. Lieutenants. A small army of people who believe he's the future of our kind, not to mention mortals that just work for the companies and think they are just doing routine work."

"And what about your side?" Lila asked.

Callum looked at her.

"Right now? You, me, Graham, THOTH, and a child who can accidentally break reality."

Lila groaned.

"That's not reassuring."

"No," Callum said. "It's not."

She walked to the far counter, splashed water on her face at the sink, and took a few slow breaths.

"We need help," she said finally.

"Yes," Callum agreed.

"From who?"

Callum's jaw tightened.

"Nia."

Lila turned.

"The information broker? The one in the character file?"

"Yes," Callum said.

"Is she trustworthy?"

"In her own way."

Lila frowned. "What does that mean?"

"She trades in information, not loyalty. But she's never played Renwick's game. She hates men like him."

"And she knows about... all of this?" Lila asked.

"She knows everything," Callum said.

THOTH cut in:

"I can open a secure line at your command."

Lila set her mug down.

"Now?" she asked.

Callum nodded.

"Now."

THOTH dimmed the kitchen lights slightly, shifting the atmosphere from domestic calm to something closer to operational readiness. The air took on a quiet tension, the kind that followed surgeons into a trauma bay or soldiers into a briefing room.

Callum set his mug aside. "THOTH, patch the call through the encrypted dead channel. The one she set up the night she left Berlin."

"Channel is live," the AI replied. "Though I should warn you, Nia has not responded to a Helios-initiated signal in seven years."

Lila frowned. "Why not?"

"Because she doesn't respond to anyone unless she wants to," Callum said. "You don't find Nia. She finds you."

Lila crossed her arms. "Then how will calling her help?"

Callum didn't answer. He simply said: "THOTH. Begin."

A soft hum filled the room. The hanging light fixtures vibrated gently as the encrypted frequency modulated through the manor's internal systems. A thin blue waveform appeared against the far wall, THOTH using the plaster like a display.

Static crackled,

"Callum MacLeod."

The voice cut through the air like the edge of a silk ribbon, smooth, feminine, slightly accented, and carrying the weary amusement of someone who'd seen too much and survived most of it.

Lila straightened.

Callum exhaled slowly.

"Nia," he said. "Thank you for answering."

"I didn't."

Lila blinked.

The waveform shimmered, and gradually resolved into a projected image:

A woman sitting in what looked like a dim lounge or safehouse. Early forties by appearance, though that meant nothing; flawless skin, sharp almond-shaped eyes, hair in long dark braids. She wore a deep green silk blouse and an expression that suggested she was three steps ahead of everyone in the room.

She leaned back, crossing her legs.

"You tripped one of my sleepers," she said. "A failsafe trigger I embedded seven years ago in the Zurich node. Took me a moment to verify it wasn't a ghost."

"Wow."

Nia's eyes flicked to her, keen, curious, amused.

"And you've taken an apprentice since we last spoke," she said to Callum.

Lila choked.

"I'm not his apprentice."

"Not yet," Nia said, sipping a drink that wasn't quite visible. "But you're carrying yourself like someone who intends to survive."

Callum cleared his throat.

"Nia, this is Dr. Lila Serrano."

Nia gave a slow nod.

"The trauma surgeon from Manhattan. Yes. Impressive."

Lila blinked.

"You know who I am?"

"I know everyone," Nia replied smoothly. "Now, why have you stirred every hornet nest in Europe to reach me?"

Callum's posture tightened.

"Renwick is moving."

Nia's expression didn't shift, but something in the air did, just slightly.

"I see," she said. "And the child?"

Lila's pulse spiked. "She knows about Ailín?"

"Of course she does," Callum muttered.

Nia raised a brow.

"Renwick knows she's awake," he said. "He started a quiet sweep of Helios assets this morning. Not loud enough to draw attention. Just enough to tighten the net."

Nia steepled her fingers.

"He's looking for you."

Callum nodded, "And Ailín."

Nia let out a slow sigh.

"This is why I warned you he would eventually make his play. Renwick doesn't tolerate loose variables."

Lila stepped forward.

"If you know so much, then help us. Tell us what he wants. Tell us what he's planning."

Nia's eyes warmed slightly at Lila's directness.

"You're bold," she said. "That's a good trait in your line of work."

"I'm a surgeon," Lila said flatly.

Nia smiled.

"Exactly."

Callum cut in.

"Nia, what can you tell us?"

Nia set her glass down.

"Renwick's network has been quiet for years. Too quiet. He has contacts in the EU Commission, the WEF, and three major private defense contractors. The moment Ailín awakened, his signals changed. He's testing his old channels. Stirring allies. Reawakening dormant cells."

Lila felt cold creep down her spine.

"This is coordinated," she uttered.

Nia nodded.

"He's preparing for something he's been waiting centuries to finish."

Callum leaned forward.

"What is it?"

Nia studied him for a long, measured moment.

Then quietly, she said:

"He wants control of the Awakening Cycle."

Callum's entire body went still.

"…that's impossible."

"Not anymore," Nia said.

"Not with the Katana active."

Lila looked between them, confused.

"Okay, someone explain. What the hell is the Awakening Cycle? And why does Renwick want it?"

Callum rubbed a hand over his face.

"It's an ancient Immortal theory," he said. "One of the oldest. It says the Veil chooses when new Immortals appear, chooses when the Game intensifies, when factions rise, when the balance of power shifts. It's not random. It's cyclical."

"And Renwick wants… what? To predict it?" Lila asked.

"No…to control it," Nia said.

"He believes he can influence when and how Immortals awaken. Who awakens. Who doesn't. And Ailín is proof the Cycle has begun again."

Lila's heartbeat stumbled.

"Because she awakened early."

"Because she awakened loudly," Callum corrected. "Too loudly. Morrigan wasn't the only one who heard her."

Lila tensed.

"Who else?"

Nia held Callum's gaze.

"Old enemies."

Callum swallowed.

"And older friends."

Ailín padded sleepily into the doorway then, rubbing her eyes with a small fist.

"Callum...?"

He immediately stood and crossed the room, crouching so they were eye level.

"I'm here."

She leaned against him.

Nia watched, expression unreadable.

When Callum lifted the girl into his arms, Nia spoke again, voice quiet, almost gentle:

"You don't have much time, MacLeod. But you do have allies... if you're willing to call them."

Callum's jaw clenched.

"I was hoping I wouldn't have to."

"You don't have a choice anymore."

"Who?" Lila asked softly.

Nia's eyes shifted to her.

Then to the child.

Then back to Callum.

"The ones who stood with Duncan."

Silence.

"You mean... other MacLeods?"

Callum shook his head.

"No."

Nia smiled faintly.

"Older."

The projection faded, Nia's image dissolving into a stream of static before THOTH dismissed the channel entirely. The kitchen felt heavier afterward, as if her presence had pulled old memories out of the walls and left them behind like dust.

For a long moment, no one spoke.

Ailín tucked her face into Callum's shoulder, still half-asleep, her small hands clutching at the fabric of his shirt.

Lila watched Callum closely.

He wasn't simply thinking. He was *remembering*.

And whatever memories Nia had just resurrected were ones he'd rather have left buried.

Lila broke the silence first.

"So," she said softly, "who exactly are the 'ones who stood with Duncan'?"

Callum didn't answer immediately.

He set Ailín down gently on the sofa and tucked the blanket around her again. She curled up, soothed by the warmth and the rhythm of the sea outside the window.

Only then did Callum straighten and face Lila.

"There aren't many left," he said quietly. "Most of Duncan's old circle scattered after the last Gathering. Some died. Some disappeared by choice."

"But some didn't?" Lila pressed.

Callum nodded once.

"Some didn't."

THOTH added delicately:

"Your contact list still contains four unarchived Immortal signatures. Only one is currently traceable."

Callum's jaw flexed, a tense muscle jumping near his temple.

Lila stepped closer.

"Callum... talk to me."

He looked at the floor for a moment; hands braced on the edge of the counter.

"When Duncan died," he said, voice low, "everything changed. The alliances he built, the friendships he maintained for centuries, all of them started to fracture. He was the center of a network that shouldn't have existed in the first place. The Game didn't allow alliances. But Duncan had them anyway."

"And you were part of that," Lila said softly.

"For a time," he said. "Until the end."

She frowned. "Why did it end?"

Callum looked away.

"Because Duncan believed... things about destiny that I didn't. He believed the world could be shaped. That Immortals could choose the outcome if they stood together. I thought it was naïve. Too idealistic."

Lila folded her arms.

"You fought beside him for decades."

"And still disagreed with him," Callum said.

"About what?" she pressed.

Callum met her gaze then, something hard and haunted flickering in his eyes.

"He wanted to end the Game."

Lila's breath caught.

"End it? How?"

"He believed the Game only continued because Immortals chose to keep fighting. That if we stopped hunting each other, stopped feeding the cycle, the Veil would stabilize. The Awakening Cycle would slow. And we could... live."

"Was he wrong?" Lila asked.

Callum's silence was answer enough.

He didn't know.

Or didn't want to.

"What does this have to do with calling an ally?" she asked.

Callum exhaled sharply and walked to the window. The sea beyond was gray and restless, waves slamming in rhythmic fury against the cliff below.

"Because the person Nia means," he said, "was one of Duncan's closest confidants. Someone who believed in that idealism even more fiercely than he did."

He paused.

"And someone who thinks I betrayed it."

Lila stared.

"Callum... who is it?"

He closed his eyes.

When he answered, his voice was quiet and heavy.

"Connor's last apprentice."

Lila blinked.

"Connor MacLeod?"

Callum nodded once.

Lila tried to piece the history together, the lineage of Immortals she had only begun to understand. She felt like she was going to need a chart.

Connor. Duncan. The men who had shaped the Game in their eras and whoever Connor's last apprentice was had to be older, trained, and deeply embedded in the old rules.

"Are they dangerous?" she asked.

"Yes," Callum said.

"To us?"

He hesitated.

"...depends."

Lila stepped closer.

"What happened between you two?"

Callum let out a low breath.

"We were on opposite sides of a choice Duncan made near the end. A choice that cost lives. I believed it was the only way. They believed it was a betrayal."

"And you think they're still angry?"

"Immortal grudges don't fade," Callum said quietly. "They calcify."

Lila crossed her arms.

"But Nia said this person might be willing to help."

Callum didn't respond.

He didn't have to.

His silence was enough to tell Lila that the idea terrified him in a way Renwick never had.

After a long moment, she touched his arm gently.

"You don't have to do this," she said.

"Yes," he murmured, "I do."

"Because Nia said so?"

"No," he said, turning to her. "Because Duncan did."

Lila's breath caught.

"What do you mean?"

Callum didn't smile. "He asked me to watch over the next generation if he fell." He glanced toward Ailín sleeping peacefully beside the fire. "And now we have one."

Lila looked between him, the child, and the sea.

The weight of destiny, or something like it, settled into the room.

Callum straightened.

"THOTH," he said quietly. "Find him."

The AI paused.

"Are you certain?"

"No," Callum admitted.

"But do it anyway."

"Locating signature…"

Lila touched his shoulder gently.

"Callum… whoever this is… do you trust them?"

He looked at her, weariness and resolve etched equally in his features.

"No," he said.

"Then why call them?"

Callum's eyes softened just slightly.

"Because they're family."

THOTH worked silently for several seconds, long seconds, the kind where even the fireplace seemed to hush itself so it wouldn't interrupt whatever ancient name was about to be dragged back into the light.

Lila paced slowly across the great room, arms wrapped around herself. She wasn't cold, but the weight of the last thirty hours sat on her shoulders like a lead vest.

Callum stood still by the window, watching waves detonate against the stone a hundred feet below. He looked carved, like one of the cliffs themselves, unmoving, but carrying centuries of erosion in his posture.

Ailín shifted on the sofa, mumbling as she slept, her tiny hand reaching out blindly. Lila moved to tuck the blanket around her again.

Callum watched that small gesture with a gaze Lila couldn't quite read, something halfway between gratitude and fear.

Then THOTH's voice filled the room.

"Callum… I have located him."

Callum closed his eyes.

Lila pressed a hand against the back of the sofa.

"Where?" Callum asked.

"Outer Hebrides. Harris Island. Near the old monastery ruins."

Lila leaned forward.

"That's remote."

"Deliberately," Callum said.

THOTH continued:

"Signal suggests he arrived there forty-eight hours ago. He has not left since. His resonance signature is stable but... elevated."

Callum straightened.

"Elevated how?"

"Heightened in the way Immortals resonate just before or after conflict."

Lila frowned.

"So he fought someone?"

"Or something," Callum said quietly.

Lila stepped closer.

"Callum, what's his name?"

THOTH hesitated.

Even the AI seemed wary about saying it aloud.

"Cadigan."

The word hit the room like a cold gust slipping through a stone crypt.

Lila blinked.

"Cadigan? That's his name?"

Callum nodded slowly.

"Aye."

"Is he older than you?"

"Yes."

"Stronger?"

Callum didn't answer.

THOTH did.

"Statistically speaking... overwhelmingly."

Callum shot THOTH a sharp look.

The AI recalibrated.

"Apologies. I meant: Cadigan's record suggests superior experience in one-on-one Immortal combat."

"That's not better," Lila said.

Callum rubbed the bridge of his nose.

"Cadigan trained under Connor long before I did. He's one of the few who took Duncan's death… personally."

Lila winced.

"And now you're calling him for help."

"Yes."

"Callum, that sounds like a terrible idea."

"You're right," he interrupted. "It is."

"Then why… "

"Because we don't have time," he said sharply. "Renwick won't stop. Morrigan won't stop. And when the Awakening Cycle starts rolling, the others will feel it."

He nodded toward Ailín, sleeping peacefully in the fire's glow.

"And they'll come for her."

Lila looked at the child. Soft hair. Small hands. Breath rising and falling in steady rhythms.

Barely a day ago, she'd been a faint pulse under a cracked ceiling in an overworked trauma bay.

Now she was at the center of the next war between Immortals.

Lila swallowed.

"Do you think Cadigan will help her?"

Callum hesitated.

"…I think he'll help Duncan's legacy."

Lila frowned.

"That's not the same thing."

"No," Callum said. "It isn't."

The fire popped quietly.

Ailín shifted, curling further into her blanket.

Lila took a breath.

"Then let's go."

Callum blinked.

"You're not going."

"Like hell I'm not."

His brow furrowed.

"Lila, "

"You said Renwick is tightening the Helios grid," she said.

"Searching assets. Hitting nodes. If he traces any of those signals out here, this place won't stay safe."

Callum stared at her.

Lila folded her arms.

"And you need someone watching Ailín while you parley with a centuries-old Immortal who might want to kill you on sight."

He tried to argue. He really did. But she was right and he knew it.

"You don't know what Cadigan is capable of."

She stepped closer.

"Neither do you anymore."

Callum exhaled slowly through his nose.

She was right about that too.

THOTH broke the silence.

"Callum, external surveillance sweep indicates no immediate threat. Weather conditions are optimal for departure if you intend to reach Harris before sunrise."

Callum nodded reluctantly.

"Prep FENRIR."

"Already warming the engines."

Lila grabbed a backpack from the coat-hook by the hearth.

"What can I do?" she asked.

Callum tried to smile.

"You're a surgeon," he said softly. "We could use a medic."

Lila nodded.

"And a child psychologist," she added with a grim half-smile.

"That too."

Ailín stirred again and opened her eyes.

"Are we leaving?" she asked sleepily.

Callum knelt beside her.

"Yes, little one. For a bit."

Ailín blinked up at him, then at the window, then back at him.

"Is the bad man coming?"

Callum's heart clenched.

"No," he lied gently. "Not yet."

Ailín nodded, trusting him the way children do, without question, and lifted her arms.

Callum scooped her up easily, and Lila felt something tighten behind her ribs at the sight.

THOTH spoke again, quieter this time.

"FENRIR is ready for departure."

Callum stood, Ailín in his arms.

Lila slung the backpack over her shoulder.

She nodded once.

"Let's go find your old friend," she said.

Callum's jaw tightened.

"'Friend' is stretching it," he murmured.

The sea wind howled softly outside.

The night waited.

And on an island in the Outer Hebrides,

an old Immortal opened his eyes, as if he already sensed Callum coming.

Chapter 11

The night air bit cold as the hangar doors slid open. Salt wind rushed across the landing platform, carrying the roar of the distant sea and the cry of seabirds settling into cliffside crevices. The world beyond was a deep navy blue, the last remnants of twilight bleeding into the horizon. Far below, waves slammed against the rocks with relentless, ancient fury.

Callum stepped onto the platform, Ailín bundled in his arms, her head resting against his shoulder. Lila followed close behind, her own breath forming pale clouds in the frigid air.

FENRIR crouched on the pad like a sleek metal beast, its engines humming low as THOTH completed the flight checks. Blue position lights blinked in slow, steady rhythm, the only soft illumination against the dark.

Lila shivered.

"Does it always feel colder up here at night?"

Callum shook his head.

"That's not the temperature," he said quietly. "It's the wind. It changes when an Immortal is thinking too much."

Lila shot him a look.

"That makes no scientific sense."

"Neither do most of us," he replied.

Callum helped Lila into the aircraft, then secured Ailín into the copilot's seat with a blanket tucked around her. The girl leaned into her seatbelt and was asleep within seconds.

When Callum settled into the pilot's chair, Lila fastened herself beside him.

"Okay," she said, exhaling. "Cadigan. Tell me what I'm walking into."

Callum paused.

"He was Connor's last apprentice," Callum said. "He trained under him longer than Duncan did. Longer than I did."

"So... he's older?"

"Not older than Connor," Callum said. "Not older than Duncan. But older than me."

"And stronger?"

Callum hesitated.

"Stronger in the ways that matter," he admitted. "Cadigan is... disciplined. Cold when he fights, careful when he chooses sides. He doesn't play the Game unless he must. But when he does..."

He didn't finish.

He didn't have to.

Lila studied him.

"And he hates you because of something that happened with Duncan."

Callum stared forward through the windshield, the night reflected in his eyes.

"Yes."

"Callum... if he wants to fight you, "

"He won't." Callum's voice was calmer than she expected. "Cadigan doesn't kill out of anger. Only purpose."

"Does he have a purpose now?"

Callum didn't answer.

THOTH interrupted the tension.

"Flight path is clear. Weather stable.

Destination: Harris Island. Estimated flight time: seventy-three minutes."

Callum nodded.

"Let's go."

FENRIR lifted off smoothly, rotors whispering through the cold air.

The cliff fell away beneath them, replaced by an endless expanse of dark ocean broken only by moonlit swells.

Lila pulled her jacket tighter.

"You're quiet," she murmured.

"So are you."

She huffed softly.

"I'm thinking."

"About what?"

"About how surreal this all is," she said. "Yesterday I was lecturing residents about overusing CT scans. Today I'm flying across the Hebrides with an Immortal, a glowing child, and a sword that scares gods."

Callum gave a soft exhale, not quite laughter.

"Tomorrow could be stranger."

"That wasn't comforting."

"Wasn't meant to be."

She studied him again, the hard line of his jaw, the subtle furrow in his brow.

"Are you afraid?" she asked.

He didn't answer immediately.

Then, quietly:

"Yes."

"Of Cadigan?"

"No."

Lila frowned, "Then what?"

He looked at Ailín, asleep and small beneath her blanket.

"Of fAilíng her," he whispered.

Lila absorbed that.

The vulnerability. The truth.

She lowered her voice.

"You won't."

Callum didn't look at her, but she saw the corner of his mouth soften.

The sea stretched endlessly beneath them.

Ahead, in the distance, a dark shape began to emerge from the fog, the shadowed coastline of Harris Island, windswept and ancient.

THOTH spoke again.

"Callum… we have a resonance match.
Cadigan is awake."

Lila stiffened.

"Does he know we're coming?"

A brief pause.

"Yes."

Callum tightened his grip on the controls.

"Good," he murmured.

"Then he won't be surprised when I ask him for the one thing he swore he'd never give me."

Lila turned slowly.

"And what's that?"

Callum's eyes hardened with something old and painful.

"Forgiveness."

Harris Island appeared through the rolling fog like a memory rising from water.

Like most of the Scottish Highlands - Sharp cliffs and Jagged black rock, and perched on a rise overlooking the sea,
the ruins of an old monastery, its stone ribs jutting skyward like the bones of some ancient beast.

FENRIR slowed as they approached, rotors dipping to counter the fierce coastal gusts. Rain began to spatter the windshield in thin, icy needles.

Lila peered out through the glass, breath catching.

"People actually lived out here?"

"Monks," Callum said. "Before that, clans. Before that, who knows."

"Feels haunted."

"It is."

She swallowed, not sure if he was joking.

He wasn't.

THOTH dimmed the cabin lights.

"Resonance spike detected directly ahead."

Callum exhaled, jaw tightening.

"He's close."

Lila scanned the ruins. "Where?"

"Everywhere," Callum said softly. "Cadigan always chooses the high ground."

The aircraft descended between two broken stone walls, blades stirring centuries of dust and sea spray. The landing skids touched wet earth with a muted thump.

Ailín stirred awake at the movement, blinking groggily.

"Is... is this where the man lives?" she asked.

"For now," Callum answered.

She rubbed her eyes.

"Is he nice?"

Silence.

Then Lila spoke instead.

"He's someone we need to talk to."

Ailín seemed to accept that, pulling her blanket around herself like armor.

Callum powered down the engines and unbuckled, the tension in his shoulders unmistakable.

They stepped out onto the uneven stone.

Ailín held Lila's hand tightly, small fingers trembling in hers.

THOTH activated external speakers.

"Caution. Immortal presence confirmed within twenty meters."

Lila scanned the ruins.

Twenty meters contained nothing but crumbling pillars and dark shadowed recesses.

"Where, "

A voice echoed from above.

"MacLeod."

Callum froze.

Lila followed his gaze upward.

Atop the highest remaining archway stood a tall figure, silhouette black against the bruised sky. The wind whipped his long coat around him. Even from a distance, something about his posture radiated discipline, painstaking, rigid control.

He descended without hurry, boots striking ancient stone with the soft, deliberate thud of someone who had trained his entire life to move quietly.

When he stepped into full view, Lila saw a man built like a

Highland stag: tall, powerful, weather-beaten with dark hair streaked with silver, sharp, perceptive blue eyes that matched the storm, a face marked with lines earned through battle, not age, and a claymore strapped to his back, not decorative, but worn from real fights

He stopped ten paces from them.

For several seconds, no one spoke.

Then Cadigan said, voice low and steady, "You took your time."

Callum held his ground. "I didn't expect you to answer."

Cadigan snorted faintly. "I didn't answer. You came."

Lila glanced at Callum.

He gave the slightest nod; this was their dance.

Cadigan studied him.

Studied Lila.

Studied Ailín.

When his eyes fell on the girl, Lila stepped instinctively in front of her.

Cadigan's expression didn't change.

"You brought a child to our meeting."

"She's under my protection," Callum said.

Cadigan raised a brow.

"Is that what you tell yourself?"

"What the hell is that supposed to mean?" Lila bristled.

Cadigan's gaze slid to her with polite, deadly interest.

"You're mortal."

"Thanks for the observation."

"You're also out of your depth."

"So are you," she fired back.

Callum almost, almost, smiled.

Cadigan ignored her and looked back at Callum.

"Why are you here MacLeod?"

Callum exhaled.

"We need your help."

Cadigan's jaw tightened.

"I do not help traitors."

The words cut sharper than steel.

Ailín gripped Lila's hand tighter.

Lila felt the muscles in Callum's arm coil, as if bracing for a blow he'd known was coming.

"Cadigan," Callum said quietly, "I never betrayed Duncan."

Cadigan stepped forward one pace.

"Then tell me why he died believing you did."

Lila inhaled sharply.

Callum didn't move.

Ailín hid behind Lila, her luminescent eyes peeking out fearfully.

Cadigan's gaze flicked toward her again, lingering only a moment.

"She's the reason you came," he said. Not a question, a statement.

"Yes."

"And the reason Duncan is gone."

Callum stiffened, "Don't you dare… "

"Don't what?" Cadigan's voice sharpened.

"Speak the truth? Duncan died protecting potential. Protecting the next generation. Protecting someone just like her."

He pointed toward Ailín, his gesture sharp as a blade.

"Your presence here tells me she is precisely what I feared."

Lila stepped in front of the child fully, anger rising.

"You have no right."

Cadigan's gaze snapped to her, ice-cold.

"Stay out of this, mortal."

Lila didn't flinch.

"Not a chance."

Callum moved between them.

"Cadigan. Enough. Your complaint is with me."

Something flickered in Cadigan's eyes, respect or recognition.

He crossed his arms, posture rigid.

"You have two minutes, Callum. No more. Say what you came to say."

Callum breathed, steadying himself.

"Renwick is moving."

No surprise.

But Cadigan's eyes narrowed.

"What did he do?"

"He's after her."

Callum motioned to Ailín.

Cadigan studied the girl again.

This time, something shifted in his expression.

Not warmth.

Not sympathy.

Understanding.

"She's awakened," he murmured. Too young. Too early."

"We need help," Callum said. "Yours."

Lila watched Cadigan's jaw tighten, a muscle jumping along the edge.

"No," Cadigan said.

"You don't need my help."

He stepped closer.

"You need my permission."

Callum blinked.

"Permission for what?"

Cadigan leaned in slightly, voice almost a growl:

"To restart the old alliance."

The air between them tightened.

Even the sea seemed to go quiet long enough to hear the weight of it.

Lila frowned.

"What alliance?"

Cadigan didn't look at her when he answered.

"The one Duncan died trying to rebuild."

The wind tore across the old monastery, rattling loose stones and whipping Cadigan's coat like a banner of some forgotten clan. Ailín pressed close to Lila's leg, her wide eyes fixed on the tall Immortal who seemed carved from the same stone as the ruins around them.

"The old alliance?" Lila repeated.

"You mean Duncan had... what, a team?"

Cadigan gave her a level look.

"A fellowship."

Callum closed his eyes. He knew this moment was coming. He just hadn't wanted to face it.

Cadigan stepped closer, boots crunching on gravel.

"Duncan believed the Game could be changed. Not by prophecy. Not by fate. By us. By Immortals who refused to become butchers."

The accusation in his eyes was unmistakable.

Callum didn't flinch.

"Duncan believed Immortals could choose mercy," Callum answered quietly. "He believed family meant something."

Cadigan's voice sharpened.

"And you!" pointing at Callum, " shattered that family."

Lila stepped between them before Callum could respond.

"Enough," she snapped. "You want to relive centuries of trauma, fantastic. You want to continue to play ancient Highland checkers, fine, do it on your own time. We have a child who's being hunted."

Cadigan's expression barely changed, but something flickered, irritation? amusement? It was impossible to tell.

"Chess." Then his gaze cut back to Callum.

Lila just rolled her eyes.

"If you came here to ask me to help you resurrect Duncan's idealism…"

"I didn't," Callum interrupted.

Cadigan blinked once.

Callum turned slightly, motioning to Ailín.

"She awakened too early. Too loudly. Renwick knows. Morrigan knows. Others will feel it soon."

Cadigan's jaw tightened.

"How old is she?"

"Eight," Callum said.

Cadigan swore under his breath in Gaelic.

"The Gathering isn't here yet," he muttered. "Not even close. This shouldn't be happening."

"It is," Callum said. "And it means something is shifting. The old patterns are breaking."

Cadigan stared at him, the wind swirling their words through the ruined arches.

"You want me to help her survive."

Callum nodded.

"Yes."

Cadigan exhaled slowly, a long breath that sounded like it had waited centuries to be released.

Cadigan exhaled slowly, arms folding across his chest.

"You'll need more than me."

Callum frowned.

"Who else?"

Cadigan glanced toward the dark ridge beyond the monastery, the moon revealing jagged ruins and shifting shadows.

"Someone older. Wiser. Infinitely more dangerous."

Lila raised a brow.

"I'm going to need more than adjectives."

Cadigan ignored her.

He stared at Callum.

"You'll need the one Duncan trusted when the world fell apart. The one who always survives."

Callum's breath caught, almost imperceptibly.

"...No."

Cadigan's lips curled mirthlessly.

"Yes."

Lila stepped forward.

"Okay, I'm clearly missing context. Who are we talking ab... "

Cadigan cut her off with a low voice that carried like a warning bell.

"The oldest of us."

The words fell heavily, like a stone dropped into deep water.

Lila blinked.

"That supposed to mean something to me?"

"It will."

Before Lila could reply, THOTH's voice chimed abruptly inside FENRIR's external speakers.

"Callum... internal diagnostic anomaly.

A resonance signature just appeared at ten meters.

It was... not there a moment ago."

Callum's eyes widened.

"That's impossible, "

A voice drifted from the broken archway.

"Please, MacLeod. 'Impossible' stopped meaning anything around the time you were still figuring out how boots worked."

Callum spun around, hand on his katana

Lila turned too, heart in her throat.

A man leaned casually against the low stone wall.

He was tall and Lean with brown hair, slight stubble, and a scarf loosely wraped abound his neck.

He could have passed for a handsome professor on sabbatical if he was wearing the stereotypical sport jacket with elbow pads.

Callum breathed the name.

"Methos."

Lila, confused:

"Who?"

Methos grinned.

"Exactly."

Cadigan nodded respectfully.

"Old man."

Methos winked.

"Jealous as ever."

Lila's eyes darted to FENRIR.

"THOTH, how did you not see him?"

The AI replied, almost offended.

"Because he was not present until he decided to be present."

Methos tapped the stone wall lightly.

"Five thousand years of practice. You learn how to keep quiet."

Callum stared at him.

"You heard everything."

"Of course," Methos replied. "I hear *most* things."

Lila stepped protectively in front of Ailín.

"What do you want?"

Methos's expression softened, surprisingly gentle, as he knelt to Ailín's eye level for a moment.

"To help," he said quietly.

"Because Duncan would have wanted me to."

Ailín blinked up at him.

"You're... really old."

Methos grinned.

"You have no idea."

He straightened and joined Cadigan and Callum beneath the arch. The night tightened around them.

"Well then... shall we talk about rebuilding an alliance we all swore we'd never attempt again?"

Cadigan remained rigid, arms crossed, watching the ancient

Immortal with the wary respect of someone who understood exactly what centuries of survival required.

Callum stood between them, shoulders tight, gaze flicking between old mentor, old rival, old... friend? Something too complicated for one word.

Lila hung back slightly with Ailín, protective but attentive, trying to piece together a millennium of tension unfolding in real time.

Methos gave them all a long, appraising look.

"Alright," he said. "Since you've dragged me out of my perfectly good hiding place... let's begin."

He approached the only intact stone table in the courtyard, brushed dust from its surface, and sat on the edge of it, long coat trAilíng behind him.

Cadigan didn't move.

Callum didn't either.

Methos watched their refusal with mild amusement.

"Sit," he said. "I promise not to decapitate anyone before tea."

Callum finally stepped forward, though tension radiated through him like a taut bowstring.

Cadigan joined, but only after a beat, a deliberate show that he was not responding to Methos's command, only to duty.

Lila escorted Ailín to a sheltered corner near the table's edge, keeping a clear line of sight to Callum.

Rain tapped lightly on the stones around them.

Methos folded his arms.

"So. Renwick."

Cadigan's jaw ticked.

Callum's expression hardened.

Lila stared.

Methos continued:

"He's been waiting for an excuse to make his move for centuries. The fact that he's chosen now... and chosen her..."

He gestured to Ailín.

"...means the Cycle is turning faster than expected."

"Why?" Lila asked. "Why her?"

Methos shrugged lightly.

"Ask the universe. Or the Veil, if you're feeling metaphysical. Some

Immortals awaken quietly. Some do it loudly. And some..."

His eyes softened toward Ailín in a way Lila hadn't expected.

"...shake the board when they arrive."

Ailín clutched her blanket.

"I didn't mean to,"

Methos stood, walked over to her, and crouched down again, gentle, patient, more teacher than warrior.

"Little one, no child ever means to shake the world."

He smiled faintly.

"But sometimes it needs shaking."

Ailín's pale blue glow flickered faintly under the skin of her hands.

Methos spoke softly.

"You remind me of someone."

"Who?" Ailín asked.

He straightened.

"Myself, a very, very long time ago."

Callum swallowed.

He had heard stories of Methos's early life, few good, fewer survivable.

Cadigan stepped forward, voice low sounding bored.

"Methos. The alliance."

Methos's expression shuttered.

He turned his gaze on Cadigan, no longer amused.

"You think you can rebuild what Duncan started? Now?"

"You came," Cadigan said.

"Yes, well," Methos replied, "I have a weakness for lost causes."

"You believed in it," Callum said. "Back then."

Methos scoffed.

"I believed in Duncan, not his crusade. The idea that Immortals could choose mercy? End the Game? Peace?"

He shook his head.

"It was noble and doomed and beautiful, and so bloody irritating."

Lila crossed her arms. "language."

Callum fixed his eyes upon him, "So you're here to tell us we're doomed and go home?"

Methos smiled thinly.

"If I wanted to leave, you wouldn't have seen me arrive."

Cadigan stepped closer.

"Methos. The girl is in danger. Renwick is rallying his allies. That means the old rules are collapsing."

Methos's eyes narrowed.

"No," he said. "It means Renwick intends to bend the rules."

Callum rubbed the back of his neck.

"He's using Helios to map Immortal activity through resonance signatures."

Methos gave a low whistle.

Lila asked, "If he finds us, "

"He will," Methos said, matter-of-fact. "Eventually. Men like him always do."

Callum stepped toward him.

"That's why we need you. Both of you. Duncan kept us together because he believed Immortals didn't have to be monsters. We can rebuild that."

"No," Methos said.

Silence fell across the ruins.

Lila felt her stomach drop.

Cadigan's expression hardened.

Callum stared at Methos, anger flickering behind his controlled exterior.

But Methos wasn't finished.

He stepped forward.

"No," he repeated, softer now.

"We can't rebuild what Duncan created. We can't resurrect something that depended on his heart, his integrity, and his maddening optimism."

Lila's heart hammered.

Methos looked at Callum, directly, deeply.

"But we can build something new."

Callum's breath caught.

Cadigan blinked in surprise.

Lila exhaled.

Methos continued:

"An alliance built on survival. On purpose. On the understanding that Renwick doesn't want to win the Game, he wants to rewrite it.

And if we don't stand together..."

He glanced toward the child.

"...Ailín becomes the fulcrum he uses."

The rain intensified, pattering on stone.

Callum stepped closer.

"Methos... will you join us?"

Methos looked at him for a long time.

A very long time.

"Yes."

Ailín's eyes widened.

Cadigan looked relieved, though he would have rather died than admit it.

Lila felt tension unwind in her chest she didn't realize she'd been holding.

But Methos wasn't finished.

He lifted a finger.

"On one condition."

Callum tensed.

"What condition?"

Methos stepped to Ailín, crouched again, and lifted her chin gently.

"You let me teach her."

Callum froze.

"Teach her what?" he asked.

Methos's gaze turned colder.

"What it means to survive five thousand years in a world that wants you dead."

Ailín stared.

Callum felt every instinct he had, protective, paternal, Immortal, flare at once.

He inhaled.

"Methos... she's just a child."

Methos nodded once.

"Exactly."

A pause, smiling at Ailín

"That's why she cannot afford to make the mistakes we made."

Callum stared at Methos, jaw set, muscles tight, torn between instinct and necessity.

"You want to teach her," Callum said carefully.

Methos met his gaze with an expression Callum had rarely seen on him: something between resolve and regret.

"I need to teach her," Methos corrected softly.

"Before someone else does."

Cadigan nodded once.

That alone told Lila how serious this was.

Ailín looked between them, confused, frightened, and trying not to show it.

Callum stepped forward protectively, too protectively, perhaps.

"She's a child," he said. "Not a weapon. Not a prophecy. Not an heir to the Gathering."

Methos tilted his head.

"You think I don't know that?"

"Do you?" Callum snapped. "You've seen more cycles than anyone. You've watched more children die than I've seen years."

Methos flinched.

The statement wasn't dramatic or theatrical...it was fact.

Because Callum was right.

And Methos had never truly forgiven himself for surviving when so many others hadn't.

He looked away.

"For five thousand years," Methos said quietly, "all I've ever done is survive, to hide and enduree."

He faced Callum again.

"She deserves better than that."

Ailín tugged Lila's sleeve, small voice barely audible:

"Are they fighting?"

Lila knelt down, brushing hair from the girl's forehead.

"No, sweetheart, They're trying to figure out how to keep you safe."

Ailín frowned.

"I want Callum to teach me."

Callum froze.

Methos looked at her with more patience than Lila expected.

"You will get both of us," he said. "Callum will teach you heart, courage, and Honor."

A pause.

"I will teach you how to live long enough to need them."

Silence.

Callum sighed, long, tired, and honest.

"Alright," he said finally.

"You can teach her. But I decide what she learns. And when."

Methos smiled faintly.

"Reasonable."

Cadigan exhaled, tension easing from his shoulders.

Lila stood, relief washing over her.

"So that's it? We're a team now?"

Methos snorted.

"This isn't a tavern brawl, doctor. It's an alliance."

"A very dysfunctional alliance," Cadigan added.

"I've seen worse," Methos muttered.

Callum gave a dry laugh.

"You were usually responsible for worse."

Methos shrugged.

"Details."

Ailín tugged on Methos's sleeve.

"Are you really the oldest?"

Methos crouched again, eyes softening.

"Older than the pyramids. Younger than regret."

The girl stared.

"…that doesn't make sense."

"It will," Methos said gently.

Callum turned serious again.

"Renwick's already moving. We need to get ahead of him."

Cadigan nodded.

"He'll go after Helios first. It's the easiest way to isolate you."

"And he'll send someone after the girl," Methos added. "Not himself. Not yet."

Lila stepped closer.

"Then we need a place safe enough for training and hidden enough to keep her off Renwick's radar."

Cadigan looked toward the far side of the island.

"There's a cave system beneath these ruins. It was used as a refuge during the Clearances. Hidden, stable, protected from storms.

Methos folded his arms.

"We start here. Tonight."

Callum shook his head.

"She's exhausted. We all are."

Methos nodded.

"Then we rest. But tomorrow… we begin."

Lila exhaled.

"And Renwick?"

Methos's expression turned cold.

"We keep him guessing. The worst thing you can give a strategist is predictability."

Callum met his eyes.

"Are you speaking from experience?"

Methos grinned.

"Always."

Later, after Cadigan scouted the perimeter, after THOTH re-established a stable encrypted net, and after Ailín finally drifted to sleep beneath a pile of old monastery blankets, Callum walked out onto the cliff.

Lila followed.

The moon hung low, pale light shimmering across the endless black sea.

"Are you alright?" she asked.

Callum gave a humorless laugh.

"No."

She stepped beside him.

"Methos scares you."

"Methos scares everyone," Callum said.

"But he's here," she said softly. "He came."

Callum looked at her, as if seeing her through centuries of battles and losses.

"You trust too easily."

"And you don't trust enough."

He didn't argue.

The wind wove around them, cool and constant.

"You did well today," Lila said quietly.

"So did you."

She shrugged.

"I'm making most of this up as I go."

"So is Methos," Callum said.
"That's how he's survived."

Lila glanced up at him.

"And how will *you* survive this?"

Callum turned back to the ocean.

"I don't know," he admitted.

She stepped closer.

"You have allies now. Real ones."

He didn't speak.

But his hand brushed hers, barely, and he didn't pull away.

Hundreds of miles away, in a glass tower overlooking Zurich's midnight skyline, Renwick watched a glowing map of Europe flare with new resonance data.

A thin smile tugged at his mouth.

"Found you," he murmured.

He didn't know exactly where Callum was yet.

But he knew enough.

He tapped a command on the interface.

A single red marker blinked over the western coast of Scotland.

"Send the Hunter," he ordered.

His lieutenant hesitated.

"Sir... we don't usually deploy him without full confirmation."

Renwick's eyes narrowed.

"This is not 'usual.' Callum has the girl. And he has help."

"Help from who?" the lieutenant asked.

Renwick's smile deepened.

"That," he said, "is what the Hunter will discover."

The tower lights flickered as a dark figure stepped out of the shadows behind them, silent, tall, hooded.

Renwick didn't turn.

"Go," he said.

The Hunter vanished like a knife sliding into darkness.

Back on Harris Island, Methos stepped to the monastery arch, leaning against the stone as he watched Callum and Lila on the cliffside.

Cadigan approached beside him.

"You think he can do this?" Cadigan asked quietly.

Methos watched the ocean.

The cliffs.

Callum.

Ailín sleeping nearby.

"I think," Methos said softly,

"Duncan believed he could."

Cadigan nodded slowly.

"And you?"

Methos smirked.

"I think believing in MacLeods has caused me nothing but trouble."

He paused.

"So let's cause some trouble."

Chapter 12

Morning came late to Harris Island. Clouds hung low, thick and gray, swallowing the horizon in a pale shroud. The ruins looked different in the cold light, less haunted, more ancient; less ominous, more enduring. Long grass bent with the wind, brushing the broken stones that had stood longer than any Immortal still living.

Inside the sheltered alcove beneath the monastery, the air was warmer, though not by much. Callum stood at the entrance, sipping the miserable excuse for instant coffee Methos had insisted "added character."

Lila approached from behind him, rubbing warmth back into her arms.

"Does the temperature ever go above 'Scandinavian fridge' out here?"

Callum allowed a faint smile.
"No."

"And you brought a child here."

"I brought a child here because it's silent, and because Renwick won't find her easily."

Lila nodded but kept her arms crossed, eyes scanning the fog.

"THOTH says external sensors are clean," she murmured. "No movement. No resonance outside of the three of you."

"Three?" Callum asked.

Lila tilted her head toward the training circle farther down the path. "You know exactly which three."

Callum sighed.

The makeshift training yard was a flat stretch of stone surrounded by broken pillars. Mist curled around the edges of the ruins, drifting over the ground in ghostly sheets.

Cadigan stood in the center like a statue carved from the earth itself, his claymore planted in the ground, his feet were anchored, and stance perfect.

A warrior entirely uninterested in compromise.

Methos sat on a fallen column behind him, peeling an apple with a small knife like this was a picnic.

He didn't look up when Callum and Lila approached.

"You're late," Methos said.

Callum checked his watch.

"It's 6:01."

Cadigan lifted the claymore with a single fluid motion.

"Training begins at first light."

"That *is* first light," Methos countered. "The sun's being lazy. Don't blame Callum."

Cadigan shot him a look.

Methos smiled innocently and took another bite of apple.

Lila whispered to Callum, "Are they always like this?"

"You have no idea."

Ailín stood barefoot at the edge of the training circle, wrapped in a thick wool coat, sleep still clinging to her eyes. Her small hands glowed faintly under her sleeves, that echo of early Immortality she couldn't yet control.

She looked up when Callum approached.

"Do I... have to fight?"

Callum crouched in front of her immediately.

"No," he said gently. "Not yet. Not today. Today is about listening. Learning. Feeling the world differently."

Ailín frowned.

"I already feel it differently. Everything is... loud."

Methos stepped forward, his usual sarcasm absent.

"Loud is normal," he said. "You're hearing things most Immortals don't notice until after their first death."

Ailín didn't look comforted.

Methos knelt beside her, lowering himself to her height with surprising softness.

"That's why we start now," he said.
"Before the world overwhelms you."

Cadigan nodded.

"Strength without discipline is a curse."

Lila met Callum's eyes.

"That sounds like something Duncan would've said."

Callum swallowed.

"It is."

Ailín looked between the adults, scared but trying very hard not to show it.

Callum touched her shoulder.

"You're not alone," he said softly. "You have me. You have Lila. And..."

He exhaled, glancing at the two other Immortals.

"...you have them. For better or worse."

Methos raised his apple.
"Mostly for worse."

Cadigan scowled.

Ailín giggled, a tiny sound, but warm.

Cadigan stepped forward.

"It's time."

Ailín's smile vanished.

Methos gave Cadigan a pointed look.
"Not combat."

"I know what I'm doing," Cadigan replied.

"You always *think* you know what you're doing."

"Would you like to lead this lesson?" Cadigan asked pointedly.

Methos waved him off.
"No thank you. I prefer to supervise and judge."

Lila muttered, "Shocking."

Cadigan turned to Ailín and gave the child something almost like a bow, stiff, deliberate, respectful.

"Lesson one," he said.

"Stillness."

Ailín blinked.

"What kind of lesson is that?"

"The one you need," he replied.

Methos leaned back on his stone seat.

"Consider yourself lucky. His lesson one for me was 'survive this cliff.'"

"It worked," Cadigan said flatly.

Methos looked mildly offended.

"I didn't *survive* the cliff. I fell off it."

"Same thing."

Callum pinched the bridge of his nose.

Lila whispered, "Is this... training?"

"For them? Yes," Callum said.

"For us? Therapy."

Ailín took a nervous step toward Cadigan.

"What do I do?"

Cadigan crouched to place a palm on the cold stone.

"The world speaks," he said. "Most Immortals only feel the Quickening when another Immortal is near. But some few, very few, can feel deeper."

He looked at her meaningfully.

"You are one of the few."

Ailín's luminescence grew slightly.

"I don't want the world to feel loud."

"I know," Cadigan said softly.

"But if you learn to be still, it will quiet on its own."

Methos added, "Stillness saves you more often than swords."

Callum nodded.

That actually sounded wise," Lila admitted.

"It happens sometimes."

Cadigan placed both hands on the stone.

Ailín mirrored him.

The wind shifted.

The fog seemed to curl inward.

A faint hum rose around the girl, soft but perceptible.

Methos's eyes sharpened.

Callum's breath hitched.

Lila felt goosebumps climb her arms.

Ailín's glow intensified…

…then settled.

She opened her eyes.

"Everything got quieter."

Cadigan nodded once.

"Well done."

Callum let out a breath he hadn't realized he'd been holding.

Lila smiled.

"You're incredible."

But Methos didn't speak.

Cadigan's eyes narrowed too.

Callum turned sharply.

Ailín noticed first, her luminescence spiking for a moment.

"What's wrong?"

Methos slowly rose to his feet.

"Stillness is useful," he murmured.

"Because it makes movement easier to hear."

Callum stepped forward, scanning the cliff.

"THOTH," he said urgently. "Report."

THOTH's voice came through Lila's wrist comm.

"One anomaly detected. Very faint. Not local. Pattern… unknown."

Methos unsheathed his small, concealed dagger, lazily, but purposefully.

Cadigan's hand fell to his claymore.

Ailín hid behind Callum instantly.

Lila froze, feeling a chill slip under her skin.

Callum's eyes hardened.

"That's not a signature," he said.

Methos nodded slowly.

"No. It's an absence."

Cadigan finished the thought:

"Something is hiding."

Callum's voice went cold.

"Renwick sent someone."

Methos exhaled.

"No. Not someone."

A pause.

"Something dangerous."

Cadigan's gaze swept the ruins.

"The Hunter."

Lila asked, "Who the hell is the Hunter?"

Methos glanced her way.

"The last person you ever want to meet."

Ailín trembled.

Cadigan stepped forward.

"Callum. We move her below. Now."

Methos nodded.

"I'll take the rear."

Callum lifted Ailín into his arms, heart pounding, the old Game roaring back through his veins.

Lila kept pace beside him, hands shaking but ready.

The fog thickened around the monastery.

Somewhere within it…

Something watched.

The Hunter had arrived.

The narrow stone passage twisted into the cliffs like something carved by monks or refugees long before Callum's time. Moss grew thick on the walls; the air smelled of damp earth and sea salt.

Ailín, "Is it coming after us?"

Callum hugged her tighter.

"No."

Methos corrected quietly from behind:

"Not yet."

Lila spun around.

"What do you mean 'not yet'? What is this thing? Someone explain this before I start panicking in a cave."

Cadigan strode ahead, his heavy boots echoing.

"The Hunter isn't a person."

Methos added, "He's an Immortal, technically. But that word doesn't really cover it."

Callum paused, glancing back at Lila.

"He's old. Older than Connor. Older than… most."

"Older than you?" Lila asked.

Methos chuckled softly.

"Older than me."

Lila gaped. "Is that even possible?"

"No," Methos said. "Normally. But he's… different."

Callum continued down the corridor.

"The Watchers called him a myth for centuries," he added. "A bogeyman they whispered about. But the truth is worse."

Cadigan stopped at a wooden door reinforced with corroded iron braces.

He faced Lila.

"The Hunter is the last survivor of a failed Gathering."

Lila's brow furrowed.

"A what?"

Methos's tone turned grave.

"A Gathering that shouldn't have happened. Before Connor's time. Before even the earliest chronicles."

Callum explained:

"He was one of the final two, the last duel. But something happened. Something no one recorded."

Cadigan opened the reinforced door, leading them deeper.

"He gained something he shouldn't have. Lost something, he shouldn't have. And what came out of that duel… isn't exactly a man anymore."

Lila swallowed.

"So he's an Immortal."

Methos corrected:

"He's a purpose."

The hidden chamber opened suddenly into a broad cavern lit by flickering lamps, a remnant of old emergency power routed from the monastery. Thick stone walls hugged the space, and a natural spring pooled quietly to one side.

Callum set Ailín on a narrow cot and tucked a blanket around her. She clung to his sleeve.

"Callum... why does it feel scary?"

Because the Hunter's resonance wasn't felt like other Immortals.

Because his presence felt like *nothing*, a void, a silence so complete that even Immortals felt hollow.

But Callum didn't tell her that.

He brushed her hair back gently.

"You're safe. All of us are with you."

She nodded, though not convincingly.

Lila turned to Methos.

"Why does Renwick think the Hunter can defeat Callum?"

Methos laughed.

A genuine, startled laugh.

"Oh, Doctor... Renwick doesn't think the Hunter can defeat Callum."

Lila blinked.

"Then why send him?"

Cadigan sat heavily on a stone bench.

"Because the Hunter doesn't *hunt* the strongest."

Callum finished:

"He hunts the most important."

Ailín shrank into her blanket.

Lila's voice tightened.

"You mean her. Renwick sent that thing for *her*."

Methos nodded slowly.

"He won't attack unless provoked. He won't kill unless guaranteed. And he won't pursue unless he sees the target."

"Wonderful," Lila muttered. "So basically: he's death with a tracking system."

"More or less," Methos said.

Cadigan straightened.

"We need a plan. Callum, what is THOTH reading aboveground?"

Callum tapped the wristpad THOTH had synced to his comms.

The AI's voice was low, filtered through the stone.

"Surface scan incomplete. Fog interference is significant.

However... one anomaly remains."

"What kind of anomaly?" Callum asked.

"Something blocking my sensors.
Something standing still."

Methos sighed.

"That's him."

Lila frowned.

"How do you know?"

Methos shrugged.

"Because nothing else is patient enough to wait."

Cadigan paced the perimeter.

Callum leaned against the cavern wall, thinking.

Lila rubbed her hands together, trying to stay warm.

Methos finally spoke again, quieter now.

"The Hunter wasn't always like this. Long before any of us, before Connor, before Duncan, there was a Gathering that failed."

Cadigan nodded.

"The final two fought for three days. Neither could land the killing blow. No Quickening. No end."

Callum added:

"And on the fourth day, one of them broke."

Lila hugged herself.

"What does that mean?"

Methos's voice was almost a whisper.

"He lost everything that made him human, except his purpose. A fragment of the Prize. Enough to follow orders without question. Enough to sense who the next key Immortal might be."

Cadigan sat heavily.

"He's not a contender. He's an enforcer, a slave to his owner."

Lila stared at all three Immortals.

"So... how do we fight something like that?"

Methos smiled without humor.

"You don't."

Lila froze.

Cadigan sighed.

"You run," he clarified. "You hide. You outthink him."

Callum stepped forward.

"And you train the one thing he doesn't understand."

Lila looked confused.

"What's that?"

Methos answered:

"Hope."

The room fell silent.

Ailín reached out, taking Lila's hand.

"Callum?" she whispered.

He knelt beside her.

"Yes, little one?"

She swallowed.

"Will he find us?"

Callum hesitated only a moment.

Methos watched him carefully.

Then Callum placed a gentle hand over Ailín's.

"No," he said softly. "Not tonight."

Cadigan stood.

"Then at first light, we begin real training."

Methos added with a slow exhale:

"And pray the Hunter loses interest before he decides to make his move."

Somewhere far above them, in the fog-covered ruins…

Something shifted.

Nothing loud.

Nothing seen.

Just a… wrongness.

A presence without weight.

The Hunter waited.

And the alliance knew he would not wait long.

Morning seeped reluctantly into the cavern, thin, pale light dripping through cracks in the ceiling far above. It was not a sunrise so much as a gradual surrender of the night.

Methos had been awake for hours.

So had Callum.

Lila, who had slept against the cool wall with Ailín tucked

protectively against her, stirred last. Cadigan, unsurprisingly, hadn't slept at all.

The oldest Immortal stood at the cavern's edge, hands behind his back, staring into the darkness as if expecting something, or someone, to emerge from it.

He turned as Methos approached.

"You saw something," Methos said.

Cadigan didn't turn.

"I felt nothing. That's how I know he's still out there."

Methos grimaced.

"He masks himself well."

"Too well."

Callum joined them, voice low.

"He won't move unless forced."

"That's what worries me," Cadigan replied.

Ailín woke slowly, blinking at the dim cavern and rubbing sleep from her eyes. The glow beneath her skin was quieter today, less scattered, more contained. Lila noticed immediately.

"Callum," she pointed, "look."

He did.

And his breath caught.

"Her resonance is smoother," he murmured. "More stable."

Methos nodded without surprise.

"Stillness always works quicker with the young."

Ailín sat up, stretching her arms under the blanket.

"Do I learn sword fighting now?" she asked brightly.

Cadigan stiffened, hand going to his claymore.

Methos raised an eyebrow at him.

"Down, Highlander."

Cadigan lowered his hand, slowly.

Methos knelt in front of the girl.

"You will learn the sword in time. But that is not your first lesson."

Ailín frowned.

"What is?"

Methos placed a hand over her small chest, near her heart.

"Your first lesson is here."

Ailín blinked.

"In my shirt?"

Methos smiled faintly.

"Inside you."

Lila hid a laugh behind her hand.

Methos turned serious.

"What you feel, what makes everything seem loud, is the beginning of the Immortal spark. It is power, yes. But power is only useful when it has shape."

Ailín considered that carefully.

"How do I shape it?"

Methos tapped his temple.

"With your mind. Not your hands."

She nodded, trying to look fierce and disciplined, mostly succeeding.

Callum's chest tightened.

It was like watching the early days of her inevitable future.

The first steps toward something she never asked for.

And something he was determined to guide gently, carefully... lovingly.

Cadigan stepped into the center of the cavern.

"Begin with grounding," he instructed. "The method Connor taught us."

Methos sighed heavily.

"Connor taught you grounding. He taught me running."

"That explains your technique," Cadigan shot back.

Callum sighed.

"Are we really doing this?"

Methos spread his arms.

"Of course we're doing this. It's tradition."

Lila stepped between them instinctively.

"Hold up, you both want to teach her the *first* lesson differently? Before she can even tie her shoes properly?"

Ailín lifted her hand.

"I can tie my shoes."

Lila smiled.

"Exactly. Let's keep it to skills at that level first."

Cadigan looked offended.

"Training must start properly or, "

Methos cut in.

"She's eight, Cadigan. If you push her like you push a new Immortal, you'll break her."

Cadigan's voice sharpened.

"The world won't be gentle with her."

"And we should be," Methos countered.

Callum finally stepped forward.

"Ailín will learn grounding. But *my* way first. Then yours. Then Methos's."

Cadigan blinked.

"That's a terrible system."

Methos smiled.

"Agreed. Perfect compromise."

Callum pointed at both of them.

"She is a child. I won't have the two of you turn her into a soldier."

Cadigan huffed.

"Every Immortal becomes a soldier eventually."

Callum glared.

"Not yet."

Methos leaned toward Lila and whispered:

"I give it two hours before they argue about sword forms."

Lila muttered back:

"They've already argued about breathing."

While the Immortals debated technique, Lila knelt in front of Ailín.

"Hey," she said softly. "I noticed something earlier."

Ailín tilted her head.

Lila pointed at the girl's hands.

"Your glow. It's less erratic today. Like you slept better."

Ailín nodded.

"My head wasn't buzzing as much."

Lila took a slow breath.

She'd treated countless patients with neurological hyperstim disorders. She knew the symptoms of sensory overload. She also knew the symptoms of trauma.

"Ailín," she said gently, "you might be able to feel the world more clearly, but your brain still needs time to grow. You can't be pushed too hard."

The girl frowned.

"I want to help."

"I know," Lila said, squeezing her hand. "But you have to stay healthy to do that."

She stood and called to Methos and Callum.

"Before training starts: she needs food. Hydration. Warmth. And breaks. You push her too fast, her developing brain won't integrate the resonance properly."

Methos raised a brow.

"Doctor's orders?"

"Yes."

Cadigan folded his arms.

"She must be prepared."

"She must be alive," Lila corrected. "And stable."

Methos nodded slowly.

"She's right. If you overwork a young Immortal before their first death, you risk destabilization."

Callum turned sharply.

"What destabilization?"

Methos glanced at the ceiling.

"Uncontrolled sensing. Loss of balance. Inability to mask her resonance. In extreme cases, spontaneous pre-immortal collapse."

Lila blanched.

"Excuse me, PRE-immortal *what*?"

Methos grimaced.

"Fainting. Think fainting. Dramatically."

Callum sighed.

"For the love of, please lead with that next time."

Ailín raised her hand again.

"I don't want to faint dramatically."

Lila put a hand on her shoulder.

"You won't. We'll pace you."

Methos smirked.

"So the doctor leads lesson plans now."

"Yes," Lila said.

"And you three follow."

Cadigan actually looked like he might argue.

Callum glared at him until he didn't.

THOTH chimed softly over the wristpad., "Callum. Incoming encrypted intercept from Helios Zurich node."

Callum froze.

Methos and Cadigan turned instantly.

Lila's heart sank. "What does it say?" she asked.

THOTH's voice lowered.

"Renwick has initiated a 'containment protocol' for all off-book Helios holdings."

Callum's blood ran cold.

"That includes this island."

Cadigan stepped forward.

"We need to move."

Methos shook his head.

"No. Moving is predictable. Renwick expects it."

Callum clenched his jaw.

"He's trying to corner us."

Methos corrected softly.

"He already has."

Ailín tugged Callum's sleeve.

"Callum... I'm scared."

He lifted her into his arms.

"I know, but you're not alone."

Methos stepped closer, his voice low, steady, ancient.

"We begin training now."

Cadigan nodded.

Callum swallowed.

Ailín held his neck tightly.

Lila placed a hand on both of them.

And in the shadows aboveground, beneath the shifting fog...

A silent figure moved.

The Hunter was watching.

And waiting.

The cavern felt smaller than it had an hour ago.

With Renwick tightening the Helios network and the Hunter occupying some invisible vantage point above, the air seemed to hold tension like static. Even the stones seemed to listen.

Ailín sat on a blanket in the middle of the training space, hands folded, breathing slowly on Methos's cue.

Methos stood over her with the relaxed posture of a man who had done this lesson a thousand times, indeed, he may have.

Cadigan watched with arms folded, foot tapping impatiently.

Callum leaned against a rock column, arms crossed, doing his best impression of calm.

Lila paced in a slow, anxious line near the back wall, glancing at the wristpad where THOTH's feed ran silently.

Methos crouched in front of Ailín.

"Now," he said softly, "return to the quiet place you found yesterday. The stillness. The small room in your mind."

Ailín nodded, eyes closing.

Her hands glimmered faintly.

Cadigan made a disapproving sound.

Methos didn't look at him.

"Don't push her," Methos warned.

Cadigan didn't back down.

"She needs discipline, not meditation."

Callum shot him a look.

"Discipline comes later. If she cannot control her resonance, she cannot fight."

Cadigan muttered, "A child shouldn't fight anyway."

Callum's gaze sharpened.

"No one said she would."

Methos smirked slightly.

"She will eventually."

"Not now," Callum snapped.

Lila cut in before the men escalated into another immortal pissing contest.

"Hey, centuries of experience or not, take a breath. All three of you."

Cadigan and Callum glared in opposite directions. Methos just looked amused.

Ailín, still breathing slowly, "It's easier today."

Callum crouched beside her.

"What do you feel?"

She opened her eyes and pointed toward the ceiling.

"That thing. Above us."

Lila swallowed hard.

Methos nodded.

"Good. Not afraid. Just aware."

"That's what 'stillness' buys her," Callum said to Cadigan sharply.

Cadigan reluctantly conceded with a nod.

"Now," Methos said, settling into a teacher's stance, "lesson two."

Ailín straightened.

Methos tapped her forehead.

"Control of fear."

Ailín blinked.

"I am scared."

Methos nodded.

"That's the point."

Lila frowned.

"Isn't that... a little much?"

Methos sighed patiently.

"Doctor. The first rule of an Immortal life is simple: fear keeps you alive. The second rule is harder: fear cannot rule you."

Ailín bit her lip.

"How do I do that?"

Methos sat cross-legged in front of her.

"By recognizing that fear tells you something important. But it does not get to decide who you are."

"Callum said I'm safe with you all."

Methos softened.

"You are."

Cadigan added gruffly:

"And you are never alone."

Ailín nodded.

Slowly, her glow stabilized again.

Methos glanced at Callum.

"She's progressing faster than you did."

Callum rolled his eyes.

"I was stabbed three times in my first week of training."

Methos shrugged.

"You were dramatic."

While the lessons continued, THOTH pinged Lila's wristpad with soft alerts. She frowned at the data stream.

"Callum," she said quietly.

He stepped over.

She rotated the pad so he could see.

"This doesn't make sense."

Methos and Cadigan joined them, curiosity piqued.

"THOTH's mapping Renwick's surveillance sweep," Lila explained. "He's pushing Helios network crawlers across the European grid zone. But look, "

She zoomed in.

A single blink on the map.

Then another.

A faint pattern.

Callum narrowed his eyes.

"That's not normal activity."

"No," Lila said.

"It's *delayed* activity."

Methos blinked.

"Explain it for the old folk."

Callum continued:

"Renwick's sweep is too clean. Too orderly. That means he's relying on Helios's predictive tracking... rather than a live feed."

Cadigan frowned.

"So?"

"So," Lila said, "that means Renwick doesn't know *where* you are. Only where you went."

Callum tensed.

"He's tracking FENRIR's last known vector."

"Exactly," Lila said. "But the predictive model assumes you flew in a straight line. You didn't. You zigzagged during the storm."

Cadigan's eyes widened.

"So he thinks we went west."

Methos nodded slowly, admiration flickering.

"But we came north."

"Which means," Lila continued, "Renwick's forces will search the wrong cluster of islands unless someone corrects the model."

Callum's voice was low.

"That buys us time."

Methos tapped the map.

"Enough to train her. Enough to prepare."

Cadigan exhaled.

"And enough time for the Hunter to get bored."

Methos shot him a look.

"The Hunter doesn't get bored."

Lila's stomach turned.

"So what's it doing now?"

THOTH's voice answered through the wristpad, soft, but chilling.

"Standing, watching, and waiting.

Ailín whimpered.

Callum scooped her into his arms. "Enough training for now. Everyone rests."

"We can't rest," Cadigan protested.

"We can," Callum growled. "And we will."

Methos stretched lazily.

"The boy's right. Fear training is exhausting. She's done enough for today."

Cadigan looked like he wanted to argue, then stopped himself when he saw Ailín's trembling hands.

"Fine," he said. Reluctantly.

Ailín buried her face into Callum's coat.

"I don't like it," she muttered.

"I know," he murmured, kissing the top of her head. "But we're here. We're all here."

Lila rested a hand on Ailín's back.

"It's alright, sweetheart. No one's getting to you."

"But what if the Hunter doesn't go away?" Ailín asked softly.

Methos's voice drifted in from the doorway.

"Then we'll make him."

Ailín slept in a small cot tucked beneath a thermal blanket, her tiny chest rising and falling in slow, even breaths. The soft flicker of the lantern cast warm ripples across the stone walls.

Callum stood watch nearby, but Lila could see the fatigue weighing on him now. His shoulders were slumped, his breathing uneven, his eyes too sharp for a man who desperately needed rest.

She approached slowly.

"You should sit."

Callum exhaled.

"I will."

"You said that an hour ago."

He didn't argue. He just looked at Ailín again.

"She's so small," he murmured.

"And she's safe," Lila countered.

"For now."

She stepped closer, her hand brushing lightly against his arm.

"Callum… she's not the only one who needs protection."

He turned toward her then, really turned, and she saw the centuries behind his eyes: the failure he feared repeating, the ghosts of the Immortals he couldn't save, the worry that he wasn't enough.

"You're carrying too much alone."

"That's how Immortals survive," he replied.

"But you're not alone anymore."

His jaw tightened.

"It doesn't matter," he said.
"She chose me. I have to be worthy of that."

Lila reached up and placed a hand on his cheek.

"You already are."

For a moment, Callum didn't breathe.

He leaned into her touch, barely, gently, before stepping back, eyes softening.

"Thank you."

Cadigan approached then, breaking the moment with the subtle grace of a man who absolutely knew he was interrupting something important but refused to care.

"We cannot keep running," he said.

"We cannot keep hiding. And we cannot hope the Hunter grows bored."

Methos sat on a rock nearby, boots crossed, whittling a piece of driftwood into the world's ugliest horse.

"Agreed," Methos said.

"But your solutions tend to involve breaking things we need intact."

Cadigan folded his arms.

"I know how to beat the Hunter."

Methos snorted.

"You can't."

"I can slow him."

Methos stopped carving.

That got his attention.

Callum straightened.

"How?"

Cadigan walked to the cavern wall and tapped a charcoal map THOTH had displayed earlier, a rough outline of the ruins above.

"The Hunter follows purpose," Cadigan said. "He doesn't track like we do. He doesn't feel Quickening the same way. He moves toward... significance."

Methos nodded grudgingly.

"Correct."

"So we create a false significance," Cadigan continued.

"A decoy."

Lila frowned.

"What would that be?"

Cadigan looked at Callum.

"You."

Callum blinked.

Methos groaned.

"Oh, brilliant. Use the man with the dragonhead sword and the impossible child as bait."

But Cadigan shook his head.

"No. We don't use Callum."

He pointed to the glowing map.

"We use Callum's Quickening."

Lila's jaw dropped.

"Excuse me, *how* exactly?"

Cadigan met her eyes.

"Callum can imprint resonance. Leave a fragment of himself in a place, a signature the Hunter will follow."

Callum stiffened.

"That's old magic," he said quietly. "It's not safe."

Methos stood slowly.

"It's worse than not safe."

He stepped closer.

"If Callum leaves a resonance imprint, it could drain him."

Cadigan didn't flinch.

"It could buy the girl time."

Lila stepped forward, furious.

"You're suggesting he weaken himself while we're being hunted by something that kills Immortals for fun?"

Cadigan met her anger with steady intensity.

"If we do nothing, the Hunter will find us in hours."

"A decoy buys us days," Methos added reluctantly.

"Maybe longer."

Callum clenched his jaw.

"I've only done it once."

"And it worked," Cadigan said.

Lila turned to him sharply.

"When?"

"Long ago."

She glared incredulously.

"Wonderful. Let's rely on ancient, half-remembered Immortal tricks while being stalked by the boogeyman."

Methos sighed.

"She's not wrong."

Cadigan gripped his claymore.

"She is not right either."

The tension spiraled between them like another fault line waiting for pressure.

And then,
THOTH chimed. "Callum. Update.
The anomaly has moved."
The cavern froze.
Callum's pulse spiked.
"How far?"
THOTH's voice wavered.
"...three meters."
Methos's face drained of all amusement.
"Three meters from what?"
A single beat.
A single breath.
Then THOTH answered:
"From where it was."
Cadigan swore.
Callum's eyes widened.
Lila covered her mouth.
Ailín stirred in her sleep.
And Methos whispered,
voice so soft it was almost lost in the dark:
"...He shifted. That means he made a mistake."
Cadigan turned sharply.
"Mistake?"
Methos nodded slowly, eyes narrowing.
"Yes. He moved too soon.
He knows we're underground...
but he doesn't know where."
Callum inhaled sharply.
"That means, "
Methos finished the thought.
"For the first time since he arrived...
the Hunter is guessing."
Lila exhaled sharply.
"And that means what, exactly?"
Methos grinned, a slow, dangerous grin that belonged to a man
who had outwitted armies and survived empires.
"It means we finally have leverage."

The cavern seemed to breathe with them.

Ailín blinked awake, rubbing her eyes.

"Callum… did something happen?"

Callum lifted her into his arms.

"Something good," he whispered.

"Did we beat the bad thing?"

"Not yet," he murmured.

"But for the first time…

he doesn't know where to look."

Methos nodded, sharpening the driftwood horse's "nose" pointedly.

"Now we plan."

Cadigan stepped forward.

"We move before he regains certainty."

Lila smiled faintly, adrenaline still racing.

"You mean we finally stop reacting?"

Callum nodded.

"Yes."

He glanced at Methos, then Cadigan, then Lila.

"The Hunter is guessing."

He tightened his grip around Ailín.

"And now it's our turn to act."

Chapter 13

The cavern felt different in the hours after THOTH's alert. Lighter, in a way Callum hadn't expected. Not safer, never safer, but shifted. For the first time since reaching Harris Island, the alliance was no longer waiting.

They finally had initiative.

Methos stretched with all the languid ease of someone who had survived more centuries than most languages, then rolled his shoulders.

"Well," he announced casually, "if we're going to survive this, we need a war room."

Cadigan frowned.

"We're in a cave."

Methos pointed at him with the driftwood horse he'd been carving into a vaguely threatening shape.

"Exactly. It's rustic. Inspiring. Druids would approve."

Lila rubbed her forehead.

"You want to plan a counterattack… in a damp basement under a broken monastery."

Methos nodded.

"Yes. You get it."

Callum exhaled and stepped into the center of the chamber.

"Alright," he said. "Enough sarcasm. We need to decide our next move."

Ailín sat up on her cot, blanket wrapped around her like a cocoon. "Are we leaving the island?"

Callum knelt beside her.

"Maybe," he said honestly. "If we must. For now, we plan."

Ailín nodded, trust shining in the quiet glow beneath her skin.

Lila joined Callum as the Immortals began gathering stones, crates, and old monastery debris to form a makeshift tactical table.

She touched his forearm.

"You're not alone in this."

He met her eyes, grateful, pained, relieved, before standing again as Methos slapped a dusty map down onto the stone table like a magician revealing his first card

It wasn't a map of Harris Island.

It was the northwestern coast of Scotland. It had wind patterns, topography, old ferry routes, abandoned fishing villages, ancient burial sites, and old Highland clan strongholds.

Marked in heavy charcoal across the edges:

RENWICK CONTACT NODES

"Where did you get all that?" Lila asked.

Methos shrugged.

"You don't live five thousand years without developing a hobby or two."

Cadigan cut in.

"These are Renwick's old staging points. Training halls. Temporary sanctuaries. Some from centuries past, some newer. All of them places he's used to gather or hide allies."

Callum studied the map's perimeter.

"And now he's mobilizing them."

Methos nodded.

"He's not stupid. He'll spread his people wide and wait for a signal from the Hunter. Once he gets even a whisper of our location, he'll collapse the grid inward."

Lila frowned.

"Like a net."

Methos snapped his fingers.

"Exactly."

Ailín tugged at Callum's sleeve.

"What does that mean for us?"

"It means," Callum said gently, "we need to stay ahead of him. Always."

Cadigan tapped the map near the coast.

"Before we leave this island, we need a real tactic. Something that forces Renwick off-balance."

Methos added, "And something that keeps the Hunter guessing."

Callum's eyes sharpened.

"I have an idea."

Cadigan stared at him skeptically.

"You always say that right before something explodes."

"This time," Callum said, "nothing explodes."

Methos snorted.

"Promise?"

Callum ignored him.

He pointed to a cluster of islands north of Harris, small, uninhabited dots in the stormy sea.

"The Hunter tracks intention. Purpose. But he struggles with misdirection."

Cadigan's eyes widened slightly, impressed.

"You want to hide our *purpose*?"

Callum nodded.

"Yes."

Lila blinked.

"What does that even mean?"

Methos leaned forward, suddenly more serious than she'd seen him all morning.

"It means he wants to mask our motive, not our location."

Cadigan added:

"If the Hunter can't tell what we plan to do next, he can't predict where to wait."

Callum straightened.

"And that gives us our only chance to move freely."

Lila exhaled slowly.

"So... strategy by emotional camouflage?"

Methos grinned.

"Exactly, doctor."

She shook her head.

"I hate that that's starting to make sense."

Callum smirked.

"You're adjusting faster than you think."

Before anyone could answer, THOTH's voice chimed through the wristpad.

Urgent.

"Callum, new Helios network intercept."

Callum's spine stiffened.

"What is it?"

"Renwick has issued a Class Red corporate directive."

Cadigan's eyes widened.

"That's not possible."

Methos swore softly under his breath.

Lila frowned.

"What's Class Red?"

Callum closed his eyes.

"It means Renwick has seized emergency control of *all* Helios resources."

Lila felt her pulse spike.

"What? How can he do that? You're the CEO."

Methos gave a grim half-laugh.

"And Renwick has clearly decided that doesn't matter anymore."

Cadigan's voice was tight.

"What did he invoke?"

The wristpad vibrated.

THOTH answered:

"Helios Charter Clause 0.

Threat: existential."

Methos dropped the carved driftwood horse.

"He's declared an existential threat?"

Lila froze.

"Who's the threat?"

Callum didn't answer.

THOTH did.

"Callum MacLeod."

Lila's breath caught, "How was he able to do that?"

"Apparently he's gotten to the board." Callum said as he was cursing himself for not thinking about that strategy.

"Most likely, he's blackmAilíng the board members with threats to harm their families. It's effectively a coup. It makes sense now why he went after Graham…he wanted him off the board."

Cadigan's expression twisted into something between fury and alarm.

Methos rubbed his forehead.

"Well… that escalated."

A long silence fell over the cavern.

Callum finally looked up.

He wasn't afraid.

He wasn't angry.

He was frustrated, and now he was determined.

"It's official," he said.

"We make the first move."

He turned toward the cavern entrance.

"We have a Hunter to mislead, a child to protect, and a madman with my corporation to stop."

Methos smirked, "Finally, A plan with teeth."

Cadigan drew a deep breath.

"We follow you."

Lila stepped beside Callum.

"And you don't do it alone."

Ailín reached out and took his hand.

"Callum… I can help."

He squeezed her hand gently.

"You already do, little one."

The cavern's war table had settled into a tense, charged silence.

The four adults, three Immortals, one mortal with more backbone than all of them combined, stood around the map spread across rough stone. Ailín hovered near Callum's side, small fingers looped through his, her glow faint but steady.

Renwick's Class Red directive hung in the air like a guillotine.

Methos broke the silence first.

"Well, in fairness, MacLeod… it *is* nice to finally be recognized as an existential threat. Most of us had to work centuries for that."

Callum didn't even blink.

"Methos. Focus."

Methos sighed dramatically and tapped the map with the driftwood horse.

"Fine. First rule: if Renwick thinks you're the threat, let him keep thinking it. That keeps his attention split."

Cadigan frowned.

"You want Callum to draw Renwick's eye while we move the girl?"

Methos shook his head.

"No. I want Renwick to *think* that's what we're doing."

Lila tilted her head.

"So, the key is not misdirection of location… but misdirection of intent."

Methos snapped his fingers.

"Exactly. The doctor gets it."

Cadigan leaned forward.

"Misdirection only works for so long. If Renwick has invoked Clause 0, he'll mobilize his entire security apparatus."

Lila stiffened.

"What does Clause 0 actually give him?"

Callum answered, voice taut.

"Everything. Full access to Helios satellites. Tactical drone fleets. Global AI analytics. If he pushes far enough, he can piggyback on NATO imaging. He can request emergency access to ESA orbital patterns. He can… "

Lila's face went pale.

"He can track every airborne craft on this side of the equator."

Methos groaned.

"Well. This will be a challenge."

Ailín tugged Callum's sleeve.

"Callum… does that mean he can see us now?"

He knelt to her level.

"No. THOTH's cloak is still holding. But we can't stay in one place forever."

Cadigan tapped a finger on the map.

"We must make the next location unpredictable."

Methos grinned.

"Unpredictable is my specialty."

Callum shot him a look.

"Methos. Not chaos. Strategy."

Methos rolled his eyes.

"Chaos is a strategy."

Lila crossed her arms.

"Not when a child's life is involved."

Methos paused.

Point for the doctor.

Cadigan leaned over the map, tracing his hand along the islands and coastal cliffs.

"There are three viable safe zones within travel distance," he said. "Each has different advantages. We have the northern sea caves; difficult to reach, natural resonance, and zero human presence." Moving his hand to another part of the map, "There is an abandon watch tower ruins on Boreray; it has high ground that I like, limited approach vectors, defensible but exposed." Moving his hand again, "The ancient burial cairns inland, here. Heavy stone interference, hidden chambers, and uninhabited last I was there"

Callum pointed at the cairns.

"That's the only site Helios satellites haven't logged."

Cadigan nodded.

"It's the least likely place Renwick will expect."

Methos folded his arms.

"Which is why it's exactly where he might guess."

Callum exhaled through his nose.

"We need something he won't predict at all."

Methos grinned.

"Finally, a man speaking my language."

Cadigan scowled.

"We are not adopting Methos's 'wing it and run' philosophy."

Methos raised two fingers.

"First of all, it's 'wing it, run, and improvise.' Second, "

Lila cut between them.

"Stop. Both of you."

The Immortals blinked.

She pointed to Ailín's glow, still faint, but no longer flickering.

"Your strategy has to consider *her condition*. Her resonance is irregular. It spikes around stress, fear, and hunger. If you push her too far, she'll become a beacon Renwick can track even without satellites."

Cadigan took pause, "You're saying her Quickening... broadcasts."

"Yes," Lila said firmly.

"And you three arguing over tactical philosophy is not helping."

Cadigan straightened, chastened.

Methos coughed awkwardly.

Callum looked at Lila with open gratitude.

"Thank you."

She nodded.

"We need a plan that protects her biology, not just your swordsmanship."

Methos cleared his throat.

"Which means we need a fourth location."

Cadigan frowned.

"What location?"

Methos smirked.

"One Renwick has never considered. One he does not know exists."

Lila raised an eyebrow.

"And where is that?"

Methos tapped the map.

But not on land.

Not even close.

He tapped the water.

"The sea?" Callum asked.

Methos nodded.

"The Hebrides are full of old smuggler coves, sunken fortifications, forgotten tunnels carved under the cliffs. Places no satellite sees because they're not on the ground, or the surface."

Cadigan stared at him.

"You're suggesting we move *underwater*?"

Methos shrugged.

"Not underwater. Under."

Cadigan's eyes widened.

"That could work. The Hunter relies on above-ground resonance traces. If she goes below the rock strata, "

Callum paused,", he loses line-of-sight perception."

Cadigan exhaled.

"That's... actually brilliant."

Methos grinned proudly.

"Yes. It is."

Callum scanned the map again.

"There's one place that fits what you're describing."

Cadigan's eyes narrowed.

"You don't mean, "

Callum nodded.

"Yes. The old Atlantic tunnel under the cliffs."

Methos blinked.

"Wait. That place still exists?"

Callum smirked faintly.

Ailín tugged Lila's sleeve again.

"Is the tunnel safe?"

Lila knelt.

"If the adults don't sabotage each other, it will be."

Methos laughed under his breath.

Meanwhile, far across Europe, in the high-security Helios Zurich tower, Renwick studied the predictive model THOTH had referenced earlier.

He frowned.

"Why would he deviate north?" he murmured.
"There were no islands of interest there."

His lieutenant stepped closer.

"Sir, the model assumes MacLeod fled west with the storm."

Renwick shook his head.

"No. He's smarter than that."

He pointed to the map's upper corner.

"Check the northern cluster. Expand resonance sensitivity."

"But sir, that region is stone-deaf. No readings will... "

Renwick turned, slow and sharp.

"Do it."

The officer swallowed hard and obeyed.

The map recalibrated momentarily and a faint blip pulsed. It wasn't strong, not Immortal, but something.

Renwick leaned forward.

"There," he pointed.

"It's subtle. But it's something."

He turned to his lieutenant.

"Inform the Hunter."

"But sir, he already moved."

Renwick smiled coldly.

"And now he moves again."

Far away, on Harris Island,

THOTH pulsed on Callum's wristpad.

"Warning. Renwick's predictive grid is now adjusting to northern vectors."

Lila's head snapped up.

"How?"

Callum's face hardened.

"He's guessing."

Cadigan tightened his grip on his claymore.

Methos cracked his knuckles.

"Then we stop giving him guesses."

Callum nodded.

"We move. Tonight."

Ailín swallowed but nodded bravely.

Lila took the girl's hand.

"We stick together."

Methos rose.

"Prepare the tunnel."

Cadigan followed.

Callum exhaled.

"We make our first move."

The fog above thickened once more,

And the Hunter turned its head.

Searching.

Still uncertain.

Still guessing.

For now.

The cavern rumbled faintly as the tide shifted beneath the cliffs, the muffled roar of the Atlantic echoing up the stone tunnels. Methos lit a lantern and hoisted it, illuminating the narrow stairwell descending deeper into the earth.

Cadigan took point, sword drawn, posture rigid as he scanned the shadows.

Lila followed close behind Callum, one hand clutching Ailín's as the girl clung to Callum's other side. The deeper they went, the colder it became, a cold that felt ancient, patient, and powerful.

The kind of cold that belonged in Highlander stories older than writing.

Methos spoke softly behind them.

"Keep your thoughts calm, princess. The Hunter can't sense your body, but he can sense your panic."

Ailín swallowed.

"I'm trying."

Callum crouched slightly to look her in the eyes.

"You're doing well. Remember what Methos taught you, quiet mind, steady breath."

She nodded, inhaling shakily.

Lila whispered from behind Callum, "I can't believe we're coaching a child through stealth evasion from an immortal nightmare."

Methos smirked.

"You get used to it."

Cadigan shot him a glare.

"Do not speak about this as if it's normal."

"Oh, please," Methos replied.

"I've been stalked by more monsters than you've had sword lessons."

"You trained me," Cadigan snapped.

"And look how far you've come," Methos replied, grinning smugly.

Callum cut them both off.

"Save it. Eyes forward."

The stairway funneled into a low stone corridor lit only by Methos's lantern and the pale natural glow of lichen along the walls. The air tasted metallic, iron, salt, and the faint hint of ancient tools.

Ailín wrinkled her nose.

"It smells like old coins."

Callum smiled faintly.

"It does."

"Why?"

"Because some metals remember the sea," Methos answered, stepping around a stalactite.

Ailín blinked up at him.

"Metals… remember?"

Methos tapped her forehead.

"Everything remembers."

Lila mouthed to Callum, "Comforting."

Callum replied under his breath, "This is how Methos talks. You get used to that too."

The corridor widened into a natural cavern where soft bioluminescent moss lined the walls, glowing blue-green. It cast a watery light across Ailín's face, and her own glow flickered in response.

"It's singing!"

Methos grinned.

"Good. You're learning to hear resonance."

Lila blinked.

"The moss… is singing?"

Methos waved his hand lazily.

"Everything sings. Most never listen."

Ailín placed her small hand on the moss-covered wall, eyes wide as the glow pulsed in harmony with her own.

Callum watched her carefully.

"Easy," he said softly. "Don't let it pull too much from you."

Ailín nodded… but Lila didn't miss the way Callum's breath hitched as he said it.

Or the way he rubbed the side of his ribs afterward.

As the group moved forward, Lila slowed her pace, watching Callum's posture. His steps were too deliberate, too careful. That wasn't like him.

"Callum, are you alright?"

He forced a faint smile.

"I'm fine."

Lila didn't buy it.

"I'm a trauma doctor. I know what 'fine' looks like. And this? Isn't it."

Methos overheard from behind.

"He's weakening. Resonance imprinting drains Immortals, it's why most never attempt it more than once."

Callum shot him a withering look.

"I haven't imprinted anything yet."

Methos gave a knowing shrug.

"Stress mimics it. So does prolonged proximity to a young Immortal awakening. Her spark pulls at yours."

Cadigan glanced back sharply.

"That's dangerous, Callum."

"I know," Callum said quietly.

"Then why didn't you say anything?" Lila asked.

Callum looked at her.

Because he didn't want to worry her.

Because he wanted to be strong.

Because he wanted to avoid the fear he saw in her eyes now.

But he didn't say any of that.

"I'm managing," he said.

Methos rolled his eyes.

"Ancient Immortal translation: 'I'm absolutely not managing and will collapse dramatically if pushed too far.'"

Cadigan did not laugh.

"You need to conserve energy."

Callum didn't argue,

which said everything.

Ahead, the natural tunnel narrowed to a bottleneck, a jagged choke point where stone walls squeezed together around a steep drop into black water far below.

Cadigan stopped abruptly.

"No. This won't work."

Methos stepped beside him.

"What do you mean 'won't work'? It's a tunnel."

"It's too exposed," Cadigan hissed. "One wrong step, and, "

Methos flicked his hand.

"Please. I've walked worse paths blindfolded and drunk."

"Which explains much about you," Cadigan muttered.

Lila stepped forward cautiously.

"Is it stable?"

Callum studied the rock.

"Stable enough."

Methos crossed his arms smugly.

"See?"

Callum added, "If we move one at a time and keep weight centered."

Cadigan shot Methos a glare.

"And does your ego know how to follow that rule?"

Methos grinned.

"My ego floats."

"Just go," Callum sighed, rubbing his temples.

As they prepared to cross the choke point, THOTH's voice chimed from Callum's wristpad, soft, tense, mechanical in a way THOTH rarely sounded.

"Callum...external anomaly has shifted again."

Callum stiffened.

"How far?"

"Eight meters. Direction: unknown."

Methos swore under his breath.

"He's triangulating."

Cadigan tightened his jaw.

"He's guessing again."

"No," Methos said.

Eyes narrowing.

Voice cold.

"This time...he's testing."

Ailín's glow spiked involuntarily.

She whimpered, clinging to Callum.

Lila bent down beside her.

"Hey, hey, eyes on me. Breathe. It's okay."

Ailín nodded shakily, trying.

Callum lifted her.

"We keep moving. We must reach the tunnel before he recalibrates."

Methos stepped to the edge of the choke point, lantern in hand.

"Let's hope the Hunter guesses wrong again."

He turned his head slightly, voice dropping to a whisper.

"Because if he guesses right...he'll come down here."

The cavern went still.

Even the ocean below seemed to quiet, and the alliance knew their window was closing.

The choke point was narrower than any of them remembered.

The passage constricted into a limestone wedge where centuries of erosion had shaved the rock into a knife-edge over a drop so deep the lantern light never reached the bottom. The air smelled of salt and ancient mineral dust, like a cathedral built by water instead of hands.

Cadigan stood at the lip of the passage, jaw set.

"This shouldn't be here," he said grimly. "Not like this."

Methos snorted.

"Rock tends to rearrange itself over a few centuries. Shocking, I know."

"No," Cadigan growled, his voice tight. "I mean I've seen this formation before."

Callum narrowed his eyes.

"When?"

Cadigan stepped forward, lantern light framing the hard lines of his face.

"Connor brought me here once," he said quietly. "After the Clearances. After... a fight he didn't speak of."

Methos's eyes sharpened.

"A fight? Here?"

Cadigan nodded.

"He said this tunnel was a place of endings. And that I should never enter it alone."

Lila's pulse quickened.

"Why not?"

Cadigan exhaled, a long breath filled with memory.

"Because he said only the desperate or the hunted ever made it this far."

Ailín whimpered, clinging tighter to Callum's coat.

"We're being hunted."

Methos placed a hand on the rough stone wall.

"Yes," he said softly, "But we are not desperate."

He stepped onto the first narrow ridge.

The ridge was barely two feet wide, slick with condensation, and angled just enough to send an untrained foot sliding into the black gulf below.

Methos sliced through the silence:

"One at a time. Cadigan, you next. Then Callum and Ailín. Lila stays directly behind them."

Cadigan glared.

"You want me behind you?"

Methos smirked.

"Darling, if I fall, I'll take you with me just to annoy you."

Cadigan stepped onto the ridge anyway.

Callum tightened his grip on Ailín's hand.

"Ready?" he asked softly.

She nodded, though her little fingers trembled.

Lila steadied her breathing.

"Careful steps. Think smooth, not strong. Slow is smooth."

Callum moved forward, boots placing each foot with a precision that came from centuries of training. But Lila saw it again, his balance was subtly off. His left foot paused too long. His right leg trembled under weight.

He was weakening.

And he was hiding it.

They were halfway across the ridge when Ailín gasped, grabbing her chest.

"Callum..."

Her glow exploded outward in a pulse of pale blue-white energy.

The ridge vibrated.

Dust shook loose from the ceiling.

Even the lantern light flickered.

"Callum!" Lila shouted.

He caught Ailín around the waist just before her knees buckled.

"It's okay, it's okay. Breathe."

But her glow was no longer faint, it was blazing, lightning under skin.

Cadigan turned back, eyes widening.

"She's resonating, too strongly!"

Methos dropped to one knee, gripping the ridge for balance.

"Ailín! Listen to me, this is just your sense reaching out. Pull it back!"

"I, I can't," she sobbed. "It's too loud!"

Lila's mind raced.

This wasn't a panic attack.

This wasn't sensory overload.

It was biological.

Her pre-Immortal resonance was overcharging,

feeding on the fear of the Hunter above.

"Callum," Lila said urgently, "you have to stabilize her!"

Callum nodded, but as he reached toward her glow, his hand trembled. His breath stuttered. His pulse hammered visibly at his temple.

Methos saw it instantly.

"Stop! Callum, you're too drained, touching that spark will floor you!"

Callum ignored him.

"It's fine, "

"No," Lila snapped, stepping onto the wet stone behind him. "It's not. You're not steady."

But Callum, stubborn and protective beyond reason, reached anyway.

The moment his palm met Ailín's shoulder,

A surge of resonance ripped through him.

His knees buckled.

His vision spun.

The ridge tilted sickeningly beneath his boots.

Lila lunged.

She grabbed Callum with one arm and Ailín with the other, bracing her full weight backward.

"Callum, look at me! Stay with me!"

His grip tightened on the ridge's edge.

Methos cursed.

"He's drawing her excess into himself, damn fool boy, Cadigan, get ready to catch them!"

Cadigan sheathed his sword and crouched low.

"Lila, pull them toward me!"

"I'm trying!"

Callum strained against the resonance tearing through his chest.

"Ailín... breathe..." he gasped.

Her glow reached a peak, a white-blue flare that hummed like a struck blade,

Then,

It collapsed inward.

Ailín fell forward, sobbing.

Callum nearly toppled with her, but Lila held him upright, boots scraping on the stone.

Cadigan reached and pulled all three onto the wider shelf beyond the ridge.

They collapsed in a heap, panting.

Callum's skin was pale, too pale, sweat coated his temples, and his breathing was shallow.

Lila grabbed his face gently.

"Callum. Focus on me."

He blinked slowly.

"...I'm fine."

"You are *not* fine," she snapped. "Your resonance field is unstable. You've absorbed too much."

Cadigan lowered Ailín to the ground gently.

"Methos, what's happening to him?"

Methos crouched beside Callum, studying him with a rare seriousness.

"He's not just drained. He's resonating in sync with her."

Lila stiffened.

"In sync meaning...?"

Methos met her eyes.

"Meaning her spark is feeding from him."

Ailín's breath hitched.

"I'm sorry, I didn't, I didn't mean to, "

Callum pulled her close.

"No. No, little one. You didn't do anything wrong."

Methos rubbed his forehead.

"This is why Immortal children were always rare. Their early resonance binds to the nearest Immortal guardian. It's instinct. Survival. But it drains the guardian until the equilibrium stabilizes."

Lila swallowed.

"How long does that take?"

Methos sighed.

"Days… if we're lucky."

Callum closed his eyes.

"We don't have days."

Cadigan knelt, voice low.

"There's no other way down this tunnel. We continue slowly. We rest often. We protect the girl."

Methos added:

"And we protect Callum."

Callum started to protest, but Lila pressed a hand over his mouth.

"No. For once, you listen."

He blinked.

She removed her hand

"You're allowed to be the one who needs protecting."

Ailín crawled into Callum's lap, small arms wrapping around him. "I'll be careful,"

"I know," he murmured.

Above them, far above, at the monastery ruins, the fog swirled. and the Hunter stepped forward.

Not aggressively.

He simply placed a hand on the stone.

As if testing resonance.

Sensing.

And then,

He turned his head toward the sea.

As if he felt the cavern system beneath the cliffs.

As if he understood the misdirection.

As if…

Methos suddenly went rigid.

His head snapped upward.

Callum looked at him, alarmed.

"What?"

"He's not guessing anymore."

Cadigan drew his sword.

"How do you know?"

Methos swallowed.

"Because the Hunter just made a sound."

A cold silence fell.

Lila's breath caught.

"What kind of sound?"

Methos's voice dropped to a frightened whisper she had never heard from him before.

"He laughed."

The cavern went absolutely still.

Callum instinctively clutched Ailín tighter.

Cadigan's grip tightened on his claymore.

Lila shivered.

"We need to move. Now."

The Hunter had never laughed before.

Now he had.

And that meant only one thing.

He'd chosen his moment.

And he was coming.

The tunnel widened into a cavern so vast it felt like they had stepped into the hollowed chest of a mountain. The thunder of the ocean cracked through unseen openings, reflecting off the jagged walls like distant rolling drums.

Moss glowed faintly along the ceiling.

Water trickled in slow, rhythmic drops into a pool that stretched out of sight.

The air tasted like iron and salt and something older.

"This is the heart of it."

Cadigan scanned the shadows.

"This is where the tunnel splits," he said. "One branch leads to the old smuggler's jetty. The other... deeper."

"And deeper is where we need to go," Callum said, voice tight.

Lila touched his arm.

"You can barely stand. You need to stop."

Callum shook his head.

"If we stop now, he'll reach the entrance to this level in minutes."

Methos inhaled sharply.

"He's coming faster now. His pace changed."

Cadigan tensed.

"That shouldn't be possible. He can't know where we, "

"No," Methos cut in.

"He doesn't know where we are, he knows where we're going."

Lila steadied him again.

"Callum, please, your resonance is unstable. Your pupils are constricted, your pulse is overclocked, your breathing, "

"It doesn't matter."

"Yes, it does!" Lila snapped.

"Your body is shutting down."

Methos stepped closer, voice grim.

"He's right on the edge. Her spark is draining him faster than it stabilizes."

Cadigan clenched his jaw.

"What happens if it doesn't stabilize?"

Methos didn't answer.

Ailín's voice trembled.

"What happens to Callum?"

Methos hesitated, something he very, very rarely did.

Finally, "He collapses, and he doesn't get back up."

Lila's eyes filled with tears.

Callum forced a hard breath, "We keep moving."

He made it exactly three steps, then his legs buckled; his hand slipped off the stone wall, his vision dimmed, and Callum MacLeod collapsed onto the cold cavern floor.

Ailín screamed.

Lila dropped to her knees beside him.

"Callum! Callum, look at me, Callum!"

His eyes fluttered, unfocused, struggling.

Methos tore the glove off his hand and pressed two fingers to Callum's throat.

A second.

A third.

A fourth.

Then, quietly:

"...his resonance is crashing."

Cadigan froze.

"Can you stop it?"

Methos shook his head. "This isn't physical. His spark is being siphoned."

Ailín's glow spiked, flaring white-hot.

"It's my fault," she cried. "I'm hurting him, I didn't mean to, I don't know how to stop it, "

Lila grabbed her shoulders.

"You're not hurting him, sweetheart. This is just something Immortals go through. You're not doing it on purpose."

Cadigan paced backward, muttering.

"This is why Connor warned me, why he said never to bring a child here, this place amplifies resonance, "

Methos spun.

"WHAT did you just say?"

Cadigan's face twisted.

"Connor said the heart of this tunnel magnifies Quickening signatures. It's why he hated the place. He said it was dangerous for any Immortal to stay long."

Methos paled.

"Oh...Oh, this is worse than I thought."

Suddenly, Ailín's glow didn't just flare, it shifted.

No longer erratic, no longer fearful.

It became warm, steady and focused like a heartbeat syncing with another.

Methos's eyes widened.

"No… no, she can't, she's too young, "

Lila held Ailín close.

"What's happening?"

"She's trying to stabilize him."

Cadigan stepped forward.

"Is that even possible?"

"No," Methos said.

Then corrected himself.

"…It shouldn't be."

Ailín placed her small hands on Callum's temples.

Her glow seeped through his skin like warm light through paper.

Callum exhaled, tension flowing out of him like smoke.

His pulse steadied.

His breathing eased.

His muscles relaxed.

Methos stared in awe.

"She's giving him resonance," he murmured.

"She shouldn't be able to give anything, she hasn't had her first death, she's not Immortal yet, "

"So she's healing him?" Lila asked.

Methos swallowed.

"She's protecting him."

Ailín opened her eyes.

They glowed brighter than the moss.

"Callum, you're not allowed to leave me."

Callum's eyelids fluttered.

His hand lifted weakly, brushing her cheek.

"I won't," he breathed.

Ailín collapsed into his chest, exhausted but safe.

Callum's color returned.

His resonance stabilized into a slow, steady hum.

Lila let out a shaky breath of relief.

Cadigan bowed his head in respect.

Methos exhaled like a man who had been holding his breath for a century.

"Incredible. The girl is… extraordinary."

Callum groaned softly and sat up, leaning into Lila's shoulder.

"Is she... okay?"

Lila nodded.

"She protected you."

His breath hitched.

"She shouldn't have to."

Methos knelt beside him.

"Welcome back. You nearly made me sentimental. Never do that again."

Callum smirked weakly.

"No promises."

THOTH chimed.

"Callum...external anomaly has entered the upper chamber."

Lila froze.

"He's here?"

Methos hissed.

"He's too close. We have minutes, maybe less."

Cadigan unsheathed his claymore.

"We stand and fight."

"No," Callum said, forcing himself upright. "Not here."

Methos pointed to the darkness ahead.

"Move into the deeper passage. Now."

Ailín clung to him, still glowing faintly.

Lila took his arm, steadying him.

Cadigan took point, blade raised.

Methos lifted the lantern and froze.

Because the air behind them changed.

A pressure.

A distortion. Something standing just beyond the choke point, on the far side of the ridge. The Hunter hidden in shadow, waiting.

Callum, "keep walking."

They didn't look back.

They moved deeper into the dark.

And the Hunter took a single step forward.

Chapter 14

Glen Lyon, Scotland , 1998

The Highland rain fell soft and cold, brushing against the windows of Duncan's secluded cottage. The fire in the hearth burned low, casting warm shadows across the room.

Callum sat opposite his mentor, a glass of whiskey untouched on the table between them.

Duncan looked older than Callum had ever seen him. Not physically, Immortals didn't age that way, but in the weight behind his eyes, the slump of his shoulders, the quiet resignation.

"Death comes for all of us eventually," Duncan said softly.

Callum's throat tightened.

"Not like this."

"It never comes the way we want."

Callum stared at him.

"Who?"

Duncan shook his head.

"No names. No vengeance. Just a path ending where it must."

He stood slowly and walked toward the mantle.

His hand closed around the hilt of the dragon-head sword.

The Katana.

His most iconic weapon.

He returned and placed it in Callum's hands.

"This belongs with you now."

Callum shook his head.

"I can't take this."

"You must," Duncan said, voice firm. "Not for the prestige. Not for the legacy. For the discipline it carries."

Callum swallowed hard.

"Duncan, "

"If you're going to live in this world," Duncan said, "you must choose who you become. Power will tempt you. Rage will stalk you. But remember this, "

He laid a hand over Callum's heart.

"You are not defined by the spark in your chest, but by the choices you make with it."

Callum's eyes burned.

"I don't want to lose you."

"You won't," Duncan said. "Not really. Everything you need... you already carry from our years together."

He stepped back.

"Promise me something, Callum."

Callum tightened his grip on the sword.

"Anything."

"Promise me you'll protect the ones who cannot protect themselves.

No matter the cost.

Even when you must stand alone."

Callum's voice cracked.

"I promise."

Duncan smiled.

Then embraced him.

Hours later, Callum buried his mentor beneath a quiet Scottish sky, the Katana at his side, and a vow echoing in his soul that would shape the rest of his immortal life.

The deeper passage swallowed them like the throat of the earth. The cavern narrowed into a winding corridor carved by a thousand years of tides. The roar of the ocean overhead faded to a low hum, as if the sea itself were holding its breath.

Callum leaned against the wall, steadier now but still weak from Ailín's resonance surge. Lila stayed at his side, guiding him carefully on uneven stone.

Ailín walked between them, her small hand gripping Callum's coat, still glowing faintly with a warmth that flickered like candlelight.

Methos carried the lantern, its golden glow pushing back the dark in flashes that made the shadows dance like living things.

Cadigan moved ahead, sword in hand, each step purposeful.

Behind them, the Hunter's presence pressed against the walls.

Not closer.

Not further.

Just there.

Shadowing.

Methos muttered under his breath.

"He's waiting."

Lila frowned.

"For what?"

Methos stepped over a shallow pool of water.

"For us to make a mistake."

Ailín asked, "What does he want?"

Cadigan answered without looking back.

"For us to go the wrong direction."

Lila raised an eyebrow.

"Wait. Is there a wrong direction?"

Methos gave a humorless laugh.

"Oh yes."

He pointed ahead to where the tunnel branched into two dark mouths.

"Connor wrote about this place," Methos said.

"Only one path leads to the old smuggler jetty. The other…"

He paused, inhaling deeply.

"…is a dead end. In every sense."

Lila swallowed.

"What killed the people who took the wrong path? The water? The fall?"

Methos shook his head.

"Their own hubris."

Cadigan added, tone low:

"And the fact the tunnel amplifies Quickening fields. The deeper you go the wrong way, the more it pulls you apart from the inside."

Lila stiffened.

"So if Callum, or Ailín, goes the wrong way…"

Methos finished grimly, "They burn out. Fast. Not to mention the hunter would have us cornered."

Callum braced himself against the wall.

"How do we choose the right path?"

Cadigan pointed to the darker of the two tunnels.

"That one."

Methos frowned.

"You're sure?"

Cadigan nodded.

"Connor showed me. Before he… before Duncan."

Methos gripped his shoulder.

"I trust you."

Cadigan blinked, surprised, then nodded once.

Callum motioned the group forward.

"We follow Cadigan."

The right-hand tunnel sloped downward, and soon the air grew warmer, too warm, like the inside of a smithy. Light shimmered on the walls, not from the lantern but from something within the stone itself.

Ailín gasped softly.

"It's humming again."

Lila tensed.

"Methos? Is that normal?"

He shook his head.

"Nothing about this place is normal. Welcome to Immortal architecture at its strangest."

Cadigan paused, placing a hand on the wall.

"This is where resonance moves through the rock. It's the only reason the Hunters of old never used this path, too unpredictable."

Callum felt the gentle tug of energy against his ribs, a pull he recognized from battles where two Immortals were too close in too tight a space.

Except this was coming from the **stone**.

"Methos," he said quietly, "is the tunnel reacting to Ailín?"

Methos hesitated.

"The tunnel reacts to *potential*. And she has more potential than the three of us combined."

Ailín squeezed Callum's hand.

"Is that bad?"

Callum knelt down beside her.

"No, not bad. Just... powerful."

They moved deeper until the tunnel opened again, this time into a dome-shaped hollow where the walls shimmered with reflected resonance.

Ailín froze.

The tunnel behind them shook.

Dust fell from the ceiling.

A sound echoed through the stone, .

A pulse like a heartbeat.

Slow and mechanical.

Methos whispered, face pale, "He's here."

Lila clutched Callum's arm.

Cadigan gripped his blade.

Ailín glowed brighter.

And Callum said the only thing he could, "Run."

The tunnel behind them pulsed again, A low, rhythmic thrum that vibrated through stone and bone alike.

Ailín clapped her hands over her ears.

"It's too loud!"

Callum lifted her instantly, holding her close.

"Stay with me. Breathe."

Cadigan took point again, sprinting down the narrow passage with a precision born from centuries of battlefield instincts.

Methos, for once, didn't joke, didn't smirk, didn't sigh dramatically. He ran.

And silently terrified.

Lila kept pace beside Callum as best she could, breathing hard.

"What *is* that sound? It's like a pressure wave."

Methos didn't look back.

"It's him."

"You mean the Hunter?"

"No," Methos said, voice tight.

"I mean his Quickening. He's using it like sonar."

Lila's face twisted.

"So he's... echolocating?"

"Yes."

"Through the rock?"

Methos nodded grimly.

"Through us."

Callum clenched his jaw.

"If he can sense us, "

"He can't *see* us," Methos corrected. "He can only sense movement."

Cadigan glanced back sharply.

"Which means... "

Methos finished, "Run smoothly and don't spike your resonance."

Ailín's glow suddenly flared.

Too bright.

Too abrupt.

She cried out.

"It hurts! It hurts, it's like he's grabbing my head, "

Callum stopped mid-step, nearly stumbling as he pressed his forehead against hers.

"Look at me. Look at me, Ailín. Focus."

Her small hands clutched his coat.

"I can feel him."

"So can I."

Methos swore.

"If she keeps spiking like that, he'll triangulate within minutes.

Callum, can you mask her again?"

Callum gritted his teeth.

"I can try."

But Lila grabbed his arm.

"No," she said firmly. "You barely survived the last surge. If you pull from her again, you'll pass out."

Cadigan turned back.

"We don't have a choice."

"Oh, we do," Lila snapped.

"But none of you ever consider the medical one."

Methos rolled his eyes.

"Doctor, this isn't exactly a clinic, "

"Quiet!" she snapped.

Methos blinked, surprised.

Lila knelt in front of Ailín.

"Honey, listen, your glow is responding to danger. Like adrenaline. But you're not in danger right now. You're safe because you're with us. So you need to tell your spark the truth."

Ailín blinked through tears.

"...the truth?"

"Yes," Lila said softly. "Tell it you're not afraid."

Ailín was shaking too hard to respond.

Callum touched her cheek.

"You're not alone," he whispered. "Fear doesn't get to decide who you are."

Ailín swallowed.

Her glow dimmed.

Slightly.

Then more.

Finally settling into a soft, warm pulse.

Methos stared.

"How in the hell..."

Lila smirked.

"A little grounding technique called trauma-informed care. You're welcome."

Cadigan murmured:

"Whatever works."

Then, the tunnel shook again.

Dust rained down.

The Hunter was closer.

Much closer.

Methos grabbed Lila and Callum both by their arms.

"Move! Now!"

They sprinted down the twisting tunnel.

The corridor widened into a chamber barely taller than Cadigan's shoulders, its ceiling bowed and warped by centuries of pressure. Torches long dead still lined the edges; their brackets rusted by salt.

Methos slowed.

His eyes were fixed on the wall.

A series of symbols, scratched into the stone.

Cadigan recognized them instantly.

"Connor," he whispered.

Callum stepped forward, brushing his fingers over the etchings.

"It's his handwriting," he said softly. "His style. He always carved his warnings low on the wall, right where you'd look if you were ducking a blade."

Lila leaned in.

"What do they say?"

Cadigan traced one line with reverence.

"It's old Gaelic. Very old."

"Translate," Methos urged.

Cadigan took a breath.

"'Beware the silence. For it forgets nothing.'"

Lila frowned.

"That's… cryptic."

Methos shook his head.

"No. It's literal."

Callum swallowed.

"It means the stone remembers. Everything. Every Immortal who passed through here. Every Quickening. Every death."

Ailín tugged Callum's sleeve.

"What does that mean?"

Callum knelt beside her.

"It means this place isn't just a tunnel," he whispered. "It's a memory."

Methos added:

"And the Hunter is using that memory to track us."

The ground vibrated again.

Stronger.

A louder hum echoed down the passage behind them,

The Hunter's pulse.

Cadigan tightened his grip on his claymore.

"We can't stay here."

Methos pointed to an arched opening on the far side of the chamber.

"There. That leads to the deep chamber. The one Connor sealed."

Callum stiffened.

"He sealed it for a reason."

Cadigan nodded.

"He did. And right now, that sealed door is the closest thing we have to a wall between us and that... thing."

Ailín trembled.

"Callum..."

He scooped her into his arms.

"We're going. Stay close."

As the group moved through the archway, a sudden shockwave hit the chamber behind them.

The stone itself *bent*.

A deafening pulse reverberated through the cavern.

Ailín screamed, clutching Callum's neck.

Callum winced, nearly dropping to one knee again.

Lila grabbed his shoulder.

"Callum!"

Methos spun.

"He struck the wall."

Cadigan's eyes widened.

"He's testing its strength."

Another pulse.

This one stronger.

A chunk of stone cracked off the wall and shattered on the floor.

A wave of pressure rolled through the chamber, followed by an eerie silence.

Methos pointed toward the sealed door ahead,
a massive slab of carved stone with ancient Gaelic runes spiraling across its surface.

"We don't run." A long breath, "We break the seal."

Cadigan gasped.

"No. Connor forbade anyone from opening that door."

"He said it was a place of endings."

Methos nodded.

"Yes, Exactly."

He stepped forward.

"And the only thing that stops the Hunter...
is an ending."

The stone behind them trembled again.

The Hunter moved.

And the alliance faced the door Connor never wanted opened.

The sealed stone door loomed ahead of them, carved with spiraling lines of ancient Gaelic that shimmered faintly in the lantern glow. The runes hummed as if the stone were alive, as if it had been waiting centuries for someone, *or something*, to approach it again.

Methos walked toward the door with slow, measured steps, the lantern trembling in his hand.

Cadigan reached out and grabbed his arm.

"Methos. Stop."

Methos shook free, eyes fixed on the ancient carvings.

"This door was never meant to be a barrier," he said softly.
"It was meant to be a warning."

Callum steadied himself on the wall, his balance faltering again, breath catching.

Lila moved instantly to support him.

"Callum, sit," she ordered. "You need to rest for at least a minute."

Before Callum could respond, a deep tremor surged through the chamber behind them.

A pressure wave.

A pulse of resonance.

A sound like stone *teeth* grinding.

Ailín gasped in terror.

"He's here!"

Methos spun.

"No, not at the door. Not yet. He's testing the outer wall."

Cadigan raised his claymore.

"He'll break through."

Methos nodded grimly.

"Yes. But he won't understand what he finds."

Lila moved Callum against the side wall where he slid down to one knee, trying desperately to hide the tremor in his hands.

"Methos," Callum said, voice hoarse, "tell us what's behind the door."

Methos inhaled deeply,
then exhaled slowly, as if in pain.

"Connor told me once," he said. "A long time ago. Before Duncan."

Cadigan frowned.

"He told *me* never to open it. But he never said why."

Methos nodded.

"He told me because he didn't trust himself."

Lila froze.

"What does that mean?"

Methos brushed his hand over the runes.

"This tunnel... this deep chamber... it doesn't just echo Quickening. It stores it."

Cadigan stiffened.

"No."

"Yes," Methos said.
"This is where Immortals left pieces of themselves. Fragments. Echoes of power."

Callum asked, "Like a sanctuary?"

Methos shook his head.

"No. Not a sanctuary. A burial."

Ailín's eyes widened.

"Something died in there?"

Methos looked at her gently.

"No, sweetheart. Nothing died."

He swallowed.

"Someone was *put* there."

Cadigan's voice cracked.

"Who?"

Methos hesitated.

"Connor's teacher."

Callum froze.

"Connor's, what? He had a teacher *before* Ramirez?"

Methos nodded slowly.

"An Immortal so old, so powerful, he went mad when the Gathering didn't come in his time. Connor defeated him, but he couldn't kill him. Couldn't take his head."

Cadigan added quietly, "So he sealed him alive."

"He sleeps. Or something like sleep. Connor bound him with the resonance of this place. He said the seal would hold for centuries."

Callum murmured, "Until now."

Ailín stepped toward the door as if pulled by invisible strings.

Callum reached for her,

But his hand faltered mid-air.

Lila held him upright.

"Ailín!" she called. "Stay close!"

But Ailín didn't respond.

Her glow intensified, soft at first, then brighter, responding to something in the stone.

Cadigan grabbed her shoulder.

"Don't, "

But the moment his hand touched her, a surge of blue light shot through the runes.

The carvings lit up.

The chamber hummed.

The sealed door…shifted.

Cadigan yanked his hand back, cursing under his breath.

"It responds to her!"

Methos went pale.

"Oh hell."

Lila stepped forward, voice trembling.

"What's happening?"

Methos shook his head slowly.

"Her resonance... is opening the seal."

Ailín's voice was small, frightened, "I didn't mean to..."

The door glowed brighter.

Cracks of light spidered through the carvings.

Cadigan raised his sword.

"Methos, what happens if it opens?"

Methos finally answered the question he'd hoped never to face.

His voice was quiet.

Broken.

"The Immortal inside wakes up."

Callum shot him a look.

"You knew?"

Methos stared at the door.

"I didn't *know*," he said quietly. "But I feared."

Cadigan stepped forward, jaw clenched.

"When Connor brought me here, he said the man behind this door was the reason he hated these tunnels. He said the man was once a friend."

Lila swallowed.

"What changed?"

"The Game." Cadigan said.

Methos closed his eyes.

"Some Immortals bend under centuries. Some break."

Ailín's glow flickered wildly.

Her fear made the resonance surge again,

and the seal glowed brighter.

Callum staggered forward.

"Ailín, stop. You have to calm your spark."

"I'm trying!" she cried.

Lila knelt beside her, gripping her hands.

"You're safe, you're safe. With us. With Callum."

But Ailín's panic was feeding the ancient stone.

The tunnel shook violently.
A sound rang through the stone, not a voice, not a breath,
A single knock.
Knock.
Everything froze.
Methos's face drained of all color.
"That's him,"
"The Hunter."
Cadigan's fingers tightened on his sword.
"That's the door behind us."
Methos nodded.
"He found the inner wall."
Another knock.
Harder.
Dust rained from the ceiling.
The air folded inward, pressure rising.
But the stone door glowed brighter still.
The sealed Immortal's prison hummed.
Cracked.
Shifted.
Methos, voice trembling:
"If the Hunter breaks through that wall…
the shockwave will break the seal."
Cadigan stepped forward.
"We need to divert him."
"How?" Lila hissed.
"No idea," Cadigan said.
Callum rose to his full height, barely, painfully, shielding Ailín with
his own body.
"We buy time," he said.
Another knock.
Closer.
Louder.
"…He knows exactly where we are."
The door behind them trembled.
The seal before them glowed.
Both dangers closing in.

And in that suffocating moment,
Ailín stepped forward.
Her glow surged,
The runes flickered.
The chamber hummed.
Callum stared in shock.
"Ailín, what are you doing?"
Her little voice was steady.
"Helping."
And before any of them could stop her,
She placed her hands on the seal.
The world shook.
The runes exploded with light.
Callum screamed.
Cadigan swore.
Lila reached for Ailín,
Methos yelled:
"NO, DON'T TOUCH HER!"
And the door,
opened a crack.
Enough for something ancient to stir.
Enough for something powerful to awaken.
Enough for a voice to whisper through the crack:
"...MacLeod..."
And Callum's blood ran cold.

The crack in the stone door widened only an inch, but that inch changed the entire chamber.

A pulse of cold air swept through the room, cold not from temperature, but from age. From forgotten centuries. From something that had been contained so long that even the air around it had become ancient.

Ailín recoiled, trembling.
Callum yanked her backward.
Lila grabbed her shoulders.
"Ailín, look at me. Stay back."

But the child stared at the crack in the stone with wide, glowing eyes.

"He knows my name."

Callum froze.

"What?"

"He said my name," Ailín announced.

"He whispered it."

Lila paled.

"That's impossible…"

Methos's voice was brittle.

"No. Not impossible. Dangerous."

Callum braced himself against the wall, voice sharp:

"Who is he?"

The whisper slid through the crack again,
a voice like a blade wrapped in memory:

"MacLeod…"

But it wasn't calling Callum.

It wasn't calling Ailín.

It was calling someone else.

Cadigan's face went white.

Cadigan's voice dropped to a raw whisper:

"Boroun."

Lila frowned.

"Who?"

Cadigan swallowed.

"Boroun of the Forgotten Isles."

Methos rubbed his face.

"Oh, for the love of, this is worse than I feared."

Ailín's glow fluttered.

"He feels sad."

Callum stiffened.

"What?"

"I can feel him," pressing her hands to her chest.
"He's sad. And angry. And… old."

Lila placed both hands on Ailín's cheeks.

"Honey, don't connect with him. You don't know what he's capable
of."

Ailín's lip trembled.

"But he's hurting."

Callum closed his eyes, heart tearing.

He knew that feeling.

He knew it too well.

Methos stepped forward, both hands held up toward Callum and Ailín as if trying to stop them from walking off a cliff.

"Listen to me carefully," he said.

"There are Immortals who live long. And Immortals who endure long. And then…"

His voice cracked, just barely.

"…there are Immortals who *survive* long."

He pointed at the crack in the door.

"That thing behind the stone? He survived five millennia before Connor sealed him."

Lila asked, "Why did Connor seal him?"

Methos met her gaze.

"Because Boroun was losing himself. His mind. His purpose. The world had changed too many times. His Quickening was fracturing. Breaking him."

Cadigan nodded shakily.

"Connor said Boroun started… hearing voices. Echoes. Past Quickenings. The memories of every Immortal he'd ever taken."

Callum ran a hand through his hair.

"He went mad."

Methos retorted, "No. Worse."

The tunnel vibrated again,

and the chamber plunged one shade darker.

Lila felt the cold seep into her bones.

"Methos. What's worse than mad?"

Methos stared at the crack.

"A mad Immortal with a cause."

A sound echoed down the passage.

Slow, measured footsteps.

Cadigan raised his claymore, stepping between the group and the tunnel mouth.

"Methos."

"I hear him."

"Callum."

"I know."

Ailín pressed her face into Callum's chest.

"He's right there…"

Lila turned toward Methos, panic rising.

"Methos, if the Hunter breaks through that choke point, what happens to the seal?"

Methos swallowed.

"It shatters."

The crack in the stone door pulsed with answering light,

As if *listening*.

As if *waking*.

Callum forced himself forward, lifting Ailín into Lila's arms.

"Cadigan," he said, voice like steel.

"We get her away from the door."

Methos pointed toward the far side of the chamber where a narrow passage slanted downward.

"There! That's the bypass tunnel, Connor mentioned it in passing. It might connect to the lower chambers."

Cadigan didn't hesitate.

He moved toward the opening,

And then froze.

Because a whisper drifted through the crack in the door:

"…MacLeod…you cannot…run…"

The cracked seal pulsed like a beating heart.

Light spilled from the runes, blue-white, blinding, alive. Dust rained from the ceiling as the ancient stone shuddered, reacting both to Ailín's resonance and to the Hunter's approaching force behind them.

The whole chamber vibrated with two competing frequencies:

Callum placed himself between Ailín and the sealed door, sword drawn despite the tremor in his hands.

Methos tightened his grip on the lantern hilt.

Cadigan raised his claymore higher, knuckles white.

Lila held Ailín close, heart pounding against her ribs.

And through the crack,

through that sliver of ancient darkness,

309

the voice whispered again.

"…MacLeod…"

Callum stiffened.

He could *feel* it now, not resonance, not Quickening, but something far older: a weight pressing against his lineage, tugging on his blood like an ancestral command.

Ailín whimpered, hiding her face in Lila's shoulder.

"He's calling you,"

"He knows you."

Callum swallowed hard.

"No. He knows my name. He doesn't know me."

Methos stepped closer.

"Callum, don't answer him. Not even in your mind."

Callum didn't speak…

but the door spoke again.

"…you brought…

…the child…"

Everyone froze.

Lila's breath caught.

Cadigan's voice cracked into a shout:

"Don't listen!"

"Callum, step away from the seal."Methos directed.

Callum forced his legs to move,

but then,

The light inside the crack surged.

A wind whipped through the chamber, though there was no place for wind to come from.

Ailín's glow reacted instantly, flaring, then shifting into something Callum had never seen before,

Recognition.

"He knows me, too."

Methos nearly dropped the lantern.

"Oh bloody hell."

Callum spun toward her.

"Ailín, do NOT look at the door!"

But she stepped forward, trembling but entranced.

"He's hurting," she said softly.

"He's trapped. He's alone."

Lila grabbed her shoulders.

"No, sweetheart, listen to me. What you're feeling? That's not empathy. That's resonance manipulation. He's trying to pull you toward him."

Ailín blinked up at her.

"But he's sad."

Lila's voice cracked.

"So is every predator."

The seal pulsed again.

"…release…me…"

Cadigan roared, "NO!"

And then it happened.

The Hunter reached the door behind them.

There was no scream, no growl.

Just silence.

And a hand.

A silhouette pressed through the stone slit at the entrance to the chamber,

Not a body.

Not a face.

Just a perfectly still shadow of a hand,

resting against the rock.

It wasn't trying to break through.

It was *feeling* the resonance.

Learning it.

Understanding it.

Methos mouthed, "He's mapping the seal."

Lila tightened her grip on Ailín.

"What does that mean?"

Methos swallowed.

"It means if he touches the crack on this side,

even once,

the shock will shatter the entire door."

Callum stiffened.

"So we stop him."

"We can't," Cadigan said. "He's too strong. And if we fight him here, the chamber collapses."

The sealed door pulsed again.

"…MacLeod…you cannot run…not with her…"

Callum's stomach dropped.

"He's talking about Ailín."

Methos nodded.

"Yes."

"He wants her."

Ailín hid behind him.

"I don't want to go."

Callum sheathed his sword long enough to cradle her face.

"You won't. Not ever."

Behind them,

another pulse.

Another movement.

The Hunter's hand was gone.

Silence.

Then,

BOOM.

A shockwave smashed through the tunnel wall behind them.

The Hunter had struck.

The chamber floor cracked.

The ceiling split.

Water rushed in from above, cold, black, violent.

Cadigan grabbed Lila and shoved her toward the lower passage.

"MOVE!"

Methos lunged for Callum.

"Take the girl!"

A second shockwave blasted through the stone.

The sealed door cracked open another half inch,

Releasing a surge of resonance so ancient and powerful that everyone dropped to their knees.

Ailín screamed.

Her glow burst outward, wild and bright, but somehow controlled.

Callum shielded her with his body as the door reacted to her spark.

Methos shouted, "CALLUM, TAKE HER BELOW NOW!"

Lila grabbed Ailín and pulled.

Cadigan held the collapsing ceiling with his own body long enough for them to pass.

Callum stumbled forward, almost falling,

But Ailín reached out and touched his forehead.

Just like before.

Just like the chamber had shown.

Her glow steadied him.

Warmed him.

Kept him conscious.

Methos stared in disbelief.

"She protected you AGAIN, Callum, MOVE!"

The Hunter struck the upper wall a third time.

Stone exploded.

Water poured.

The crack in the sealed door glowed, blindingly bright.

And from inside that ancient darkness, a voice whispered, not to Callum, not to Ailín…

but to Cadigan.

"…I remember you…"

Cadigan's face collapsed in horror.

"No…"

The Hunter's footsteps echoed closer.

Callum grabbed Ailín.

Lila grabbed Callum.

Methos grabbed them both.

And they fled into the deepest passage.

The chamber collapsed behind them.

The sealed door finally split,

Releasing Boroun's Quickening into the dark…

and letting the Hunter into the chamber.

Chapter 15

The collapse behind them sounded like the world trying to swallow its own heartbeat. Stone tore free from stone. Water thundered through gaps forced open by centuries of tension. And somewhere in the dark, two impossibly ancient forces collided.

Callum didn't look back.

He couldn't.

His hand clamped protectively around Ailín's wrist as he pulled her through the narrowing passage, Lila at his side, Methos close behind, and Cadigan bringing up the rear with his claymore raised in case the Hunter forced his way through the debris.

The tunnel leveled out abruptly, widening into a long corridor of black basalt. The ground vibrated beneath their feet, but the collapse noise softened, like a storm moving behind distant hills.

Lila exhaled, finishing a headcount with shaking hands.

"Everyone… still here?"

Callum nodded, breath ragged.

Ailín clung to him, glow dimmed to a soft pulse.

Cadigan sheathed his sword.

"For the first time since we entered this hole," he muttered, "I actually think we're past the worst of it."

Methos tapped dust off his coat.

"Careful. The universe loves to punish premature optimism."

Callum leaned against the wall, finally letting himself breathe, just breathe, for more than a few seconds.

Lila crouched beside him.

"You holding together?"

He nodded.

"I've been worse."

"You always say that."

"And it's always true."

She touched his arm gently.

"You scared me back there."

He gave a tired half-smile.

"You and me both."

Before she could reply, Ailín tugged on his sleeve.

"Callum... is he still behind us?"

The child's voice trembled, not from panic, but from clarity. She had felt something in that chamber none of them had: intention.

Callum knelt to her level.

"The Hunter?"

Ailín shook her head.

"The other one."

Methos stiffened.

Cadigan froze.

Lila's skin prickled.

"What do you feel, sweetheart?" Lila asked softly.

Ailín pressed a hand to her chest.

"He's... quiet. And sad again. But farther away now."

A pause.

"Like he's going back to sleep."

Methos exhaled in something close to relief.

"Thank God. The collapse helped. The pressure sealed itself."

Callum brushed Ailín's hair back gently.

"You did good. Very good."

"Did I hurt him?" she asked.

"No," Callum murmured.

"You helped us. And you kept me alive."

Ailín folded into his chest, exhausted.

Cadigan looked down the dark passage ahead, the only way left.

"We should move. Before the Hunter finds another way in."

Methos nodded.

"He won't follow immediately. He's recalibrating."

Lila frowned.

"What does that mean?"

Methos tapped his temple.

"He needs to understand what just happened.
Hunter or not... even he wasn't expecting Boroun."

Callum rose slowly.

"Then this is the moment we leave before either of them decide to try again."

Cadigan motioned ahead.

"The exit tunnel's not far. I remember Connor mentioning the sloped basalt corridor."

Methos chuckled.

"Connor always did love dramatics."

Callum took Ailín's hand.

"Let's go home."

"Home?" Lila asked.

Callum gave a faint, weary smile.

"Anywhere with sky."

They started moving again, together, shoulder to shoulder, breathing the recycled air of a tunnel that had not seen sunlight in centuries.

Behind them, the earth rumbled one last time.

A distant, muffled shift.

Then silence.

Boroun slept again.

The Hunter waited again.

And for the first time in hours, the alliance walked toward a place where daylight still existed.

The slope of basalt ahead rose gradually, forming a natural ramp carved by ancient tidal forces. The ground still trembled intermittently, aftershocks from the sealed chamber, but each tremor was softer, more distant. Like thunder rolling away across a valley.

Ailín kept close to Callum, her smaller hand locked around two of his fingers. Lila stayed beside them, watching his posture, the tightness in his jaw, the way he caught his breath when he thought no one was looking.

"Pain?" she murmured.

"A little."

She gave him a sharp look.

He amended.

"A lot."

She exhaled softly.

"We'll fix that when we're out of here."

Callum gave a tired smile.

"Promises, promises."

Ahead, Cadigan scouted with renewed urgency, sweeping his hand over the cavern walls. His steps had changed, lighter, quicker, impatient. The man wanted out. Desperately.

Methos followed, lantern held high, muttering calculations under his breath.

Callum finally asked, "What are you thinking?"

Methos didn't look back.

"Thinking? No. I'm *counting*."

"Counting what?" Lila asked.

"Minutes until the Hunter stops recalibrating."

Ailín shivered.

"He's not moving."

Methos nodded.

"Exactly. He's learning."

Cadigan stopped abruptly and turned.

"You mean he's adapting?"

Methos sighed.

"They always adapt. But this one… faster than most."

Callum tightened his grip on Ailín.

"How much time do we have?"

Methos took a long breath.

"If Boroun's resonance disoriented him enough? Fifteen minutes."

"And if not?" Lila asked.

Methos shrugged.

"Five."

"That's not a lot."

"No," Callum said. "But it's enough."

Cadigan pointed ahead.

"The incline ends up there. If Connor's map was right, the final chamber opens into the air shaft."

Lila frowned.

"The air shaft? Does it go outside?"

Methos gave a small nod.

"Eventually. This place is a labyrinth of old smuggler routes and forgotten Celtic ritual paths. But if we keep following the incline, we'll reach a fissure that opens to a cliffside."

Callum raised a brow.

"A cliffside?"

Methos shrugged.

"It's air. Stop complaining."

Ailín squeezed Callum's hand.

"I don't mind cliffs."

Lila smiled faintly.

"One brave girl we've got here."

A faint rumble passed through the stone under their feet.

Ailín stopped mid-step.

"He's moving again."

Callum swore softly.

"How fast?"

Ailín closed her eyes, as if listening.

"Slow... but getting closer."

"Still guessing?" Lila asked.

Ailín nodded.

"Yes. He doesn't know where we are. He just knows we're higher now."

Methos muttered:

"Good. Let him guess wrong."

They pushed forward faster.

The passage narrowed again, not as dangerously as the choke point, but tight enough that single-file was mandatory. Cadigan went first, carving the air with his steps, alert to every echo.

Methos followed, then Ailín between Callum and Lila.

As they entered the last stretch, the rumbling behind them intensified, closer, but still muted by distance and debris.

Callum, "He's following the resonance pattern."

Lila's voice was low.

"Can he climb through the collapse?"

"No," Methos said.

"That chamber is sealed under tons of stone. Even he can't push through fast."

Cadigan glanced back.

"Then where is he?"

Methos's expression tightened.

"Finding another way in."

A beat of silence.

Then Callum said what everyone feared.

"There's more than one way into these tunnels...Dozens."

Ailín trembled and looked back "Callum... he's not behind us anymore."

Callum froze. "What?"

Cadigan's expression hardened.

"Which direction?"

Ailín pointed, straight up.

Everyone looked at the ceiling.

Stone.

Methos's face drained of color.

"...He's in the upper labyrinth."

Lila's stomach dropped. "So he's ahead of us?"

Methos shook his head.

"No. He's searching the wrong branch. But he'll correct soon."

Ailín squeezed Callum's hand.

"Please... can we go faster?"

Callum lifted her into his arms.

"Hold on."

The incline steepened to nearly forty degrees. This slowed the group down; Their legs were burning, breath grew shorter.

The walls rumbled with shifting stone above.

But finally, finally, Cadigan reached a break in the darkness.

A faint draft – cold, clean, and carrying the scent of sea air.

He turned to them, relief cracking his stoic mask.

"There. Ahead!"

Methos nearly laughed.

"Sky. Blessed, miserable Scottish sky."

Lila caught Callum's arm.

"Come on. Almost there."

But Ailín looked over her shoulder.

"The Hunter's moving faster now."

Cadigan nodded.

"Then we move faster."

They pushed toward the faint glow of daylight slanting through cracks in the stone.

The tunnel behind them darkened again,

Not from the collapse.

Not from Boroun.

But from something else.

Something moving.

Something searching.

Methos, "He found the right path."

Callum tightened his grip on Ailín.

"Then let's get out before he finds us."

Together, they climbed toward the light.

The incline narrowed into a jagged break in the stone, a fault line carved open by time and storms.

Cold, salt-heavy air streamed through the cracks, carrying the spindrift of distant waves.

Cadigan climbed first, wedging his shoulders through the opening and hauling himself into a small chamber just beneath a fractured cliff ledge. He turned back, extending a hand.

"Give me Ailín."

Callum boosted her upward. Cadigan pulled her through with surprising gentleness for a man his size. She scrambled beside him, peering back down.

"Hurry," she announced. "He's coming."

Callum felt it too now, the low vibration in the stone. like a beast scraping its claws along the walls of the earth.

Methos came next, muttering under his breath.

"If we survive this, remind me to burn Duncan's old maps. Every last one."

Lila climbed after him, grunting as she squeezed through the rock. Callum lifted her by the waist to help her through the last tight stretch.

She exhaled hard once her boots hit the chamber floor.

"Never again," she panted. "Never again, Callum. I swear, "

He smirked despite everything, "No hiking adventure in our future?"

"At least try to avoid subterranean death tunnels next time." She retorted.

Ailín tugged Methos's sleeve.

"He's closer."

"Yes. Time to go."

Callum was last.

He wedged himself upward, braced his hands against the walls, and pushed until he cleared the opening. The pain in his ribs made him gasp, but Lila caught his arm, pulling him the rest of the way.

As soon as he was through, Cadigan shoved a boulder across the opening.

It scraped with a long, ringing groan, sealing the gap just as a burst of pressure shook the tunnel below.

Ailín flinched.

Callum crouched beside her.

"It's alright," he murmured. "He won't fit through that. Not for a while."

Methos nodded grimly.

"He'll search. But the collapse bought us minutes, maybe hours."

Lila brushed dust off her jacket.

"Then let's use them."

Cadigan pointed toward a brighter fissure in the upper wall.

"That's the way out."

The final climb was steep but mercifully short.

And then, the world opened.

They emerged onto a narrow ledge halfway down a sea cliff, the wind snapping at their coats and whipping Ailín's hair across her face. But the sky, the open Scottish sky, as the most beautiful thing any of them had seen in hours.

Clouds bruised with storm colors spread across the horizon. The sea crashed below in silver and gray. Sunlight filtered through breaks in the clouds like spears of gold.

Ailín sighed with relief, a small smile breaking through the fear.

"It's pretty."

Callum lifted her into his arms.

"It's freedom."

Methos inhaled deeply.

"Ah, fresh air. Salt. Danger. Reminds me of the old days."

Lila shot him a look.

"How old?"

Methos winked.

"Old enough that this feels nostalgic."

Cadigan ignored them, scanning the cliff edge.

"There's a path along the ridge. Leads to the north side. We can reach higher ground and regroup."

Callum nodded, steadying himself.

"Good. Let's put distance between us and the tunnels."

Ailín clung to him a little tighter.

"Is Boroun really going to sleep again?"

Methos crouched beside her.

"Yes. For now. The collapse sealed the chamber."

Lila frowned.

"And the Hunter?"

Methos gestured southward.

"He'll find another way out eventually. But we have a head start."

Ailín's glow pulsed softly.

Callum kissed the top of her head.

"That's enough for now."

They walked along the cliff ledge, boots scraping against wet stone. The wind tugged at their hair and clothes, a cold but welcome reminder that the open world still existed beyond tunnels, resonance, and ancient voices.

Lila moved beside Callum, her hand brushing his arm.

"You alright?"

He thought about lying.

He didn't.

"No."

She nodded once.

"Good. That means you're finally being honest."

He huffed a quiet laugh.

"Thank you. For earlier. You helped her... and me."

She squeezed his hand briefly.

"We take care of each other. That's how this works."

Ailín looked up at them.

"You both take care of me."

Callum smiled softly.

"Yes, little one. Always."

The group reached the top of the ridge, a windswept plateau dotted with heather and stone cairns. The storm clouds spread out below them in shifting layers.

Cadigan turned to Methos.

"Next move?"

Methos held up his wristpad.

But it wasn't THOTH's voice that greeted them.

Not Callum's AI.

Not an alarm.

A dry, wry voice crackled through the small speaker.

"Well. Took you long enough to climb out of that hole."

Callum blinked.

Lila frowned.

Ailín tilted her head, curious.

Methos beamed.

"Finally!"

Cadigan groaned.

"Oh no."

Callum stiffened.

"No. It can't be, "

The voice continued:

"Callum MacLeod, I swear, if you've woken another ancient lunatic, I'm going to strip your clan tartan off you myself."

Callum groaned.

"It *is* him."

Methos clapped Callum on the back.

"Welcome back to the land of the living, old friend!"

The voice replied:

"Methos… if you're laughing right now, stop. I can hear it."

Lila blinked.

"Who is that?"

Ailín smiled.

"He sounds funny."

Callum rubbed his eyes.

"That," he said, "is Joe Dawson."

The speaker crackled again.

"Callum? Pick up the damn line. We need to talk."

Chapter 16

The wind on the ridge was sharp enough to sting skin, but to Callum it felt like liberation, clean, cold air after the suffocating weight of stone and ancient resonance.

Ailín tucked her face into his shoulder, her small arms wrapped tight around his neck. He pressed a steadying hand against her back, not letting the wind tug her away.

Methos stood a few steps ahead, coat flapping, staring at the sky with a dramatic sigh.

"Ahh, freedom. Almost forgot what untainted oxygen tastes like."

Cadigan snorted.

"You complain about everything. Even the air."

"I'm a man of refined tastes," Methos replied.

"You're a man who survived plagues before soap existed."

Methos grinned.

"Exactly. I've earned my preferences."

Lila stepped beside Callum, her hair blowing wildly across her face.

"I never want to see another tunnel again," she said.

Callum nodded.

"Agreed."

A faint electronic chirp sounded from Callum's wrist.

He froze.

Lila's face brightened.

"Is that, ?"

Callum lifted his arm.

"Yes. THOTH."

The screen flickered to life, static at first, then stabilizing as the AI re-synced with satellite contact.

"Callum."

The voice that came through was calm, precise, a contrast to the chaos below the earth.

"Signal strength restored. Atmospheric conditions acceptable. Are you injured?"

Callum exhaled slowly.

"No serious harm."

Lila shot him a pointed look.

He amended.

"Some harm."

A more pointed look.

"…more than some."

THOTH replied:

"Noted. I will run a full medical scan once you are stationary."

Ailín perked up at the familiar voice.

"THOTH! We're out! We made it!"

THOTH's tone shifted, modulated, warmer.

"Good to hear your voice again, Ailín. You gave me quite a scare."

Ailín giggled.

"I scared *you*?"

"Terrified."

Methos shook his head.

"That AI worries more than half the Immortals I know."

THOTH answered immediately.

"Statistically accurate. Immortals experience fewer acute stress responses per lifespan hour."

Lila burst into laughter.

Callum hid a smile behind his hand.

Cadigan wasn't amused.

"THOTH. We need situational updates. Has Renwick mobilized forces to the islands?"

The AI's response came instantly.

"Affirmative. Three Helios reconnaissance drones have been deployed. Two are sweeping the southern coastline. The third is holding position above a secondary island nearly one kilometer east."

Callum stiffened.

"That's too close."

"Agreed," THOTH answered.

Methos folded his arms.

"The Hunter?"

A pause.

Then:

"His resonance signature remains below the island's surface. He has not breached an exit point yet."

Lila exhaled shakily.

"So we have time."

Cadigan shook his head.

"Not much."

THOTH continued:

"Renwick has also initiated a wide-net data sweep of all Helios transponder channels. Your jet, Callum, is being tracked by corporate-level pings."

Callum grimaced.

"That means he's taking full control of the company fleet."

"Worse," Methos added, "It means he thinks you're still on the island, and he's trying to cut off every escape route."

Ailín tugged Callum's sleeve.

"Callum… are we going home now?"

He wished he could say yes.

But the truth wasn't simple.

"No," he said softly. "Not yet."

Ailín's glow dimmed with worry.

"But we will," Lila assured her, brushing a strand of hair behind her ear.

"We just need to stay ahead of Renwick and the Hunter."

"This is the part where you say 'easy peasy,' right?" Ailín asked.

Lila chuckled. "Not exactly."

THOTH spoke again.

"May I recommend relocating? Coordinates suggest a minor storm approaching within ninety minutes."

Methos frowned.

"Oh wonderful. Rain. As if today wasn't dramatic enough."

Callum looked across the rugged island terrain.

"We need shelter. Higher ground won't stay safe."

Cadigan nodded.

"There's a bothy, an old stone hut, two kilometers north. Connor used it decades ago."

Methos arched an eyebrow.

"Of course he did. That man nested in every corner of Scotland."

Callum adjusted Ailín on his hip.

"Alright. Let's move."

As they started toward the ridge path, THOTH's voice chimed one more time.

"Callum... a message is waiting for you."

He stopped.

"A message? From who?"

Another pause.

THOTH's tone dropped to one of rare unease.

"...from a Watcher channel. Encrypted. Sender ID: Joe Dawson."

Methos grinned.

Cadigan groaned.

Lila sighed.

"Oh boy."

Callum closed his eyes briefly.

"Put it through."

The voice crackled, exactly as before, rough, weary, familiar:

"Callum, it's Joe. If you're getting this... things are worse than I thought. You need to call me back. Now. It's about Renwick, and it's about the girl."

Ailín tightened her grip on Callum's coat.

"Callum... what does he mean?"

Callum's stomach knotted.

"We're going to find out."

He looked at the others.

"Let's reach the bothy. Then we talk to Joe. Then we plan."

Methos cracked his knuckles.

"Finally. A proper plan."

Cadigan smirked.

"Famous last words."

Together, they moved into the windswept Highlands, THOTH guiding them through rough terrain as the storm built overhead.

The bothy appeared on the horizon like a stone tooth jutting from the hills. A squat, centuries-old structure built of rough granite, its roof sagging under years of rain and wind. Moss clung to the shaded side of it. A rusted iron latch hung crookedly from the door.

Cadigan exhaled as the group approached.

"There. Still standing. Connor always said this place would outlive him."

His voice tightened slightly.

"For once, I wish he'd been wrong."

Methos pushed the door open, stepping into the single-room shelter. Dust and peat-smoke residue coated the rafters, but the space was dry, insulated, sheltered from the wind.

"Home sweet ruin," Methos declared, dropping his pack dramatically on a creaking bench.

Lila guided Ailín inside, brushing the child's hair back from her face.

"You okay, sweetheart?"

Ailín nodded, still hugging Callum.

But her glow had calmed to a soft, steady warmth.

Callum set her down gently.

"Stay close to Lila."

Ailín nodded again and climbed into Lila's lap without hesitation.

Callum turned to THOTH's wristpad, jaw tightening.

"THOTH. Open the channel. Joe Dawson."

"Channel open."

Static crackled.

Then a voice carried through, rough, exasperated, strained.

"About damn time, Callum."

Methos smirked.

"He sounds less dead than usual."

Callum ignored him.

"Joe. We're aboveground. We're safe for now. What's going on?"

Joe let out a tired sigh.

"Wish I could say nothing, kid. But the Watchers are splitting down the middle. Renwick's made moves we never authorized."

Cadigan stepped closer to the wristpad.

"What kind of moves?"

Joe's tone hardened.

"He's weaponized corporate channels. He's broken the Code, publicly, loudly, and with a smile, and he's declared *you*, Callum MacLeod, an existential threat."

"Yeah," he said softly. "I got that memo."

Joe continued, "It gets worse. Renwick's using Watcher archives to dredge up anything he can on Immortal children."

Callum's heartbeat thudded painfully in his ears.

"What has he found?"

"He's reopened every ancient file on Immortal offspring, real, rumored, fabricated, forgotten. He's comparing them to your daughter, Callum."

Methos was the first to speak, "Renwick's not stupid enough to believe half of those myths."

Joe shot back instantly, "He doesn't have to believe them. He just has to *use* them."

Cadigan's face darkened.

"That means he's trying to build a case."

Joe sighed.

"More than that, Callum... he's trying to claim legal control."

Lila shot to her feet.

"Legal control of *what*?"

Joe hesitated.

"...of Ailín."

Callum's entire body went still.

Lila's voice dropped to a dangerous whisper.

"He wants custody of a child who isn't even his?"

Joe's response was grim.

"He's claiming she's an unregistered Immortal manifestation under corporate jurisdiction."

Methos threw up his hands.

"Oh, piss off, he's trying to turn Immortals into intellectual property."

Ailín looked up at Callum.

"What does that mean?"

Callum knelt beside her, voice steady but trembling at the edges.

"It means he's wrong. And we're not letting him anywhere near you."

Joe added quickly:

"Kid, Callum, listen to me. Renwick has Watchers on his payroll. He's ordering a global lockdown on any Immortal sightings. And he's spreading misinformation about you to justify hunting you down."

Cadigan's hand drifted toward his sword.

Methos muttered under his breath.

"So he's starting a war."

Joe didn't argue.

"He thinks he's protecting humanity...or power...or both. The man's gone full crusader."

Callum exhaled slowly.

"We need to disappear for a while."

"Exactly," Joe said, "And you need to get the girl somewhere Renwick can't track."

Lila frowned.

"And where is that?"

The pause on Joe's end was long.

"There's someone you need to see. Someone Methos knows."

Methos's eyes widened.

"Oh, hell no."

Joe pushed on.

"He's the only one who can help Ailín understand what she is."

Methos shook his head violently.

"Absolutely not. That man is dangerous."

Callum stiffened.

"Who?"

Joe's voice cracked slightly.

"An Immortal older than Boroun. One who can teach without

draining her spark."

Lila's stomach knotted.

"And his name?"

Joe hesitated again, "The Archivist."

The bothy felt suddenly colder.

Callum looked at Methos, "I thought he was a myth."

Methos closed his eyes.

"Oh, he's no myth"

Ailín leaned into Lila.

"Callum… are we going to see him?"

Callum swallowed.

"We might have to."

Methos muttered:

"And may God help us when we do."

Joe's voice drifted through the static one last time:

"Callum, time is running out. If Renwick finds you before the Archivist does…there won't be a future for the girl."

The channel cut.

Silence filled the bothy.

The storm rolled closer.

THOTH chimed softly.

"Callum. The decision is now yours."

Callum closed his eyes.

The storm pressed closer, wind rattling the bothy door and sending cold drafts through gaps in the stonework. The single-room shelter felt suddenly too small, too dim, too close to the danger Joe had just confirmed.

Callum sat on a low bench, elbows on his knees, staring at the floor as though expecting it to crack open into another tunnel.

Lila stood near the hearth, watching him with growing concern.

Ailín sat curled under one of the blankets, her glow barely visible beneath the wool.

Methos leaned against a wall, arms folded tightly.

Cadigan paced back and forth with long, deliberate steps.

Finally Lila broke the silence.

"We need to talk about this Archivist."

Methos groaned loudly.

"Or, hear me out, we don't."

Cadigan glared at him.

"Methos. Enough."

"No, not enough," Methos snapped.

"You all think Connor was dramatic? You haven't met the Archivist."

Callum lifted his head, voice quiet but firm.

"Then explain it. All of it."

Methos closed his eyes.

"Fine. But you're not going to like it."

Methos stepped forward, lantern shadows flickering across his face.

"The Archivist isn't just old," he began.

"He's deliberate. He's... careful. Too careful."

Callum raised an eyebrow.

"Meaning?"

"Meaning he never intervenes," Cadigan cut in.

"Not unless something threatens the old balance."

Lila frowned.

"What balance?"

Methos pointed to Ailín.

"The balance between Immortal memory and Immortal power."

Callum's stomach tightened.

"Explain."

Methos exhaled and paced slowly.

"You know how Immortals absorb memory through the Quickening. Every head taken, every mind, every emotion, it gets stored inside us."

Lila nodded.

"I've seen the aftermath. It looks... overwhelming."

"It *is*," Methos said.

"So imagine an Immortal whose entire purpose is to keep that memory intact. Catalogued. Organized. Preserved."

Callum blinked.

"Preserved?"

Methos nodded.

"The Archivist carries the memory of thousands. Maybe tens of thousands. His Quickening is... dense. Heavy. He remembers Immortals whose names humanity never learned."

Cadigan added:

"And some he wished he didn't."

Lila crossed her arms.

"So he's a historian?"

Methos shook his head.

"No. He's a guardian."

Cadigan finished:

"Of truth."

Lila considered that.

"And that's supposed to help Ailín how?"

Methos sighed.

"Because the Archivist is the only Immortal ever recorded who learned to manage external resonance. He could prevent echoes from tearing him apart. He could even... regulate it."

Callum's breath hitched.

"Regulate?"

"Yes," Methos replied.

"Meaning he can help Ailín control her spark. Maybe even hide it."

Ailín peeked out from her blanket.

"Can he fix me?"

Callum knelt beside her.

"You're not broken."

Ailín's voice quivered.

"But I made the stone angry. And I hurt Callum."

Lila pulled her close.

"You saved him. Twice."

But Ailín shook her head.

"My spark hurts people."

Callum pulled her into his arms.

"It won't. Not with help."

Methos nodded reluctantly.

"The Archivist *can* help her. But we need to prepare for the cost."

Lila stiffened.

"What cost?"

Cadigan stopped pacing.

"The Archivist only teaches those who can withstand what he is."

Callum tensed.

"What does that mean?"

Methos rubbed his face.

"It means he tests you first."

Lila's eyes narrowed.

"Tests? What kind of tests?"

Methos met her gaze.

"The kind that make Boroun look like a cranky uncle."

Ailín shrank into her blanket.

Lila swallowed.

"Then why the hell would we let him near a child?"

Before Methos could answer, THOTH chimed through the wristpad.

"Dr. Lila is correct. However…the Archivist is statistically the only entity capable of stabilizing Ailín's resonance without damaging Callum."

Callum blinked.

"You knew of him?"

"Only in fragments," THOTH said.

"His data appears in ancient Immortal metadata. Partial. Corrupted. Warning flags are present."

"Warning flags?" Lila echoed.

"Correct. Records indicate individuals who sought him often emerged… changed."

Methos groaned.

"See? Even your AI doesn't like him."

"But," THOTH continued,

"they emerged alive. And more stable."

Cadigan planted the tip of his claymore on the dirt floor.

"Callum. This is your decision."

Ailín crawled into Callum's lap, burying her face under his chin.

"Please don't be mad."

Callum gently stroked her hair.

"I'm not mad. Just scared."

She nodded.

"Me too."

Methos stepped closer.

"Callum... I've avoided the Archivist for centuries. Because I knew he could see through me. The oldest of us can do that. They know the things we hide."

Callum met his eyes.

"But you're not saying 'don't go.'"

Methos frowned, conflicted.

"No," he admitted.

"Because I've also seen what happens when a child Immortal grows without a guide."

"What happens?" Lila inquired.

Methos answered softly, "They burn out."

The room went silent.

Even the wind seemed to hold its breath.

Ailín tightened her grip on Callum's coat.

"Callum... I don't want to burn."

Callum wrapped both arms around her.

"You won't," he promised.

"We won't let that happen."

Lila moved beside him, resting a hand on his shoulder.

"We go," she said, "We find him."

Cadigan nodded once.

Methos shut his eyes, then opened them with a resigned sigh.

"...fine. We go."

THOTH chimed one last time.

"I have located a possible route to the Archivist's last known sanctuary."

Callum exhaled.

"Where?"

THOTH paused.

"...the Orkney Archipelago."

Methos's head snapped up.

"Oh. Wonderful.

Fog. Ruins. And sheep."

Cadigan smirked.

"You survived the Bronze Age. You can survive sheep."

Callum stood, lifting Ailín into his arms.

"Then Orkney it is."

The storm clouds had sunk low enough to cloak the entire ridge in mist. Wind howled against the granite walls of the bothy, rattling the loose stones and scraping dried heather against the roof.

Inside, THOTH's lens flickered on Callum's wrist.

"Routing parameters established."

Lila stepped closer.

"What's the safest path?"

THOTH answered without hesitation.

"None. However, the least dangerous route is a northern descent along the ridge to a sheltered cove. Coordinates uploaded."

Methos raised an eyebrow.

"A cove? On *this* rock? Excellent. We'll die in the most scenic fashion possible."

Cadigan ignored him, studying the map overlay THOTH projected.

"There's an old fishing hut at that cove. I remember it. Connor used it once to avoid unwanted Watcher attention."

Methos chuckled.

"Connor avoided attention the same way you avoid alcohol, badly."

Cadigan's glare was sharp enough to cut stone.

Callum stepped between them.

"How far?"

THOTH responded, "Approximately three kilometers over uneven terrain. Storm impact expected within twenty minutes."

Lila massaged her forehead.

"So we're racing the weather again."

Ailín crawled into Callum's arms.

"I don't like storms."

He kissed her hair gently.

"Neither do I. Let's stay ahead of this one."

Methos snapped his case shut.

"Good. Because the next storm is Renwick himself."

Cadigan sheathed his claymore.

"He'll deploy Helios drones. Maybe even private contractors."

Lila stiffened.

"He'd send mercenaries after a child?"
Methos gave a bitter smile.
"He thinks she's a resource."
Callum's grip tightened around Ailín.
"We leave. Now."

As the group stepped outside, the wind almost shoved them back through the doorway. Dark clouds swept sideways across the ridge in long, uneven sheets.
Cadigan squinted into the storm.
"We cut north around the ridge line. Keep low."
THOTH pulsed on Callum's wrist.
"Alert. Helios drone signature detected."
Callum snapped to attention.
"Where?"
"Above the southern basin.
Altitude high. Search pattern narrowing."
Methos muttered under his breath.
"He's triangulating our last known position."
Lila asked urgently, "Will they find the tunnel entrance?"
THOTH replied:
"Negative. Terrain obstruction remains significant. But aerial surveillance will expand."
Callum nodded.
"Then we keep moving."
They descended the ridge, boots slipping on wet stone, mist swirling around their legs. Ailín clung to Callum like a small lighthouse, her glow barely visible beneath the blanket Lila wrapped around her.
Lightning flashed somewhere far out over the sea.
Cadigan scanned the sky.
"Heavy rain coming from the west."
Methos scoffed.
"Rain? That's the least of our concerns."
A faint hum cut through the wind.
THOTH chimed sharply.
"New resonance detected."

Callum's chest tightened.

"The Hunter?"

"Affirmative."

Lila grabbed Callum's arm.

"Where?"

THOTH answered:

"Emerging from a secondary cave system. Approximately four hundred meters southeast."

Cadigan swore quietly.

"He found another exit."

Methos pressed a hand to his forehead.

"Of course he did. Because nothing is simple."

Callum turned to the group.

"We don't engage. We stay ahead of him."

Ailín whispered into his coat.

"He's angry."

Callum stiffened.

"You can feel that?"

She nodded.

"Yes. And… he's confused too."

Methos blinked.

"Confused?"

Ailín nodded again, eyes distant.

"He feels… wrong. Like something hurt him."

THOTH confirmed moments later:

"Correlation: resonance shockwave from Boroun's partial awakening has disrupted the Hunter's pattern."

Lila inhaled sharply.

"He's unstable."

Methos muttered, "Unstable is worse."

Callum adjusted his grip on Ailín.

"What's he doing now?"

THOTH's tone darkened, "He has paused."

Cadigan frowned.

"Paused?"

"Correct."

Methos's eyes widened and his voice dropped.

"It means he's thinking."

Callum cursed softly.

"Let's move. Now."

They reached the last ridge slope as thunder cracked overhead. The air filled with mist and the sharp scent of ozone. The sound of waves crashing grew louder as the cliffs dipped toward the northern coast.

Cadigan pointed ahead.

"There, down that slope. The cove is just beyond those rocks."

Methos squinted.

"Is that a boat?"

Callum narrowed his eyes.

"Yes. Looks abandoned."

Lila pulled her coat tighter.

"At least it means shelter."

Ailín tugged Callum's collar.

"Does the Archivist live near boats?"

Callum shook his head softly.

"No, little one. But he lives on an island. And islands sometimes need boats."

Ailín nodded, satisfied with the answer.

They moved faster, skidding down the wet slope as rain began to fall in uneven, cold spatters.

Behind them, the ridge trembled once more,

A pulse.

A whisper of resonance through the earth.

Ailín flinched.

Callum stopped immediately.

"Ailín? What is it?"

She pressed her face to his chest.

"He said something."

Lila knelt beside her.

"Who?"

Ailín shivered.

"The voice from the door."

Methos's face went stone still.

"What did he say?"

Ailín's glow flickered.

"He said…'Find him.'"

Lila looked sharply at Callum.

"Find who?"

Ailín whispered, "The Archivist."

The wind howled across the ridge.

Thunder cracked overhead.

THOTH's voice came through the storm:

"Callum. We must leave this island. Immediately."

Callum lifted Ailín into his arms.

"Then let's go."

The alliance moved toward the cove as the storm broke open above them.

Chapter 17

The descent into the cove was treacherous, wind howling across jagged stones, rain slicking the slopes, salt spray rising in cold spirals from the crashing surf below. The cliffs of Harris Island rose like black teeth around them, directing the storm's fury straight into the narrow inlet.

By the time the group reached the bottom, the waves were pounding the shoreline in unpredictable swells, surging up against the rocks with enough force to shake the ground.

Ailín clung to Callum's side, her cheeks red from wind and cold, but her glow steady, calmer than it had been in hours.

Lila brushed wet hair from Ailín's face.

"You holding up?" she asked gently.

Ailín nodded.

"It's cold. But it's not scary like the tunnels."

Callum smiled faintly.

"Good. No more tunnels for a long while."

Methos snorted as he hopped down the last rock.

"Speak for yourself. I once spent a decade living in a cave."

Cadigan rolled his eyes.

"You spent a decade *drinking* in a cave."

"Details."

THOTH chimed from Callum's wrist.

"You are approaching the coordinates. The hut is fifty meters ahead."

Callum squinted through the sheets of rain.

"Where?"

Then he saw it, a small weather-worn shack wedged between two rock outcroppings, its roof patched with driftwood, its walls leaning just enough to suggest one strong gust might finish the job.

Lila frowned.

"That doesn't look safe."

Methos shrugged.

"Safety is a spectrum."

Cadigan smirked.

"In this case, a very narrow one."

Callum led the way toward it, boots sinking into sand soaked by stormwater.

Ailín tugged on his coat.

"Callum… will the Archivist be scary?"

Callum hesitated, but only for a moment.

"Probably," he said honestly.

Ailín blinked.

"…oh."

Lila shot him a look.

"You're terrible at comforting children."

"I don't believe in lying to them."

Ailín piped up:

"No, it's okay. I already knew he'd be scary."

Callum raised a brow.

"How?"

She shrugged.

"My spark told me."

Methos blinked.

"That is… surprisingly accurate."

Cadigan lowered to her level.

"But scary doesn't mean bad. Some scary people are protectors."

Ailín nodded.

"Like Callum!"

Methos laughed.

"Kid's got a point."

Callum felt his ears warm, but the moment didn't last.

Because THOTH's voice cut sharply through the banter.

"Alert. Multiple Helios signals approaching. Distance: three kilometers and closing."

Lila stiffened.

"Drones?"

"No," Callum said quietly.

He had learned this pattern long ago.

"Corporate intercept craft."

Cadigan's expression darkened.

"They'll be flying low along the coast in this weather. Renwick's serious."

Methos muttered:

"Of course he's serious. He's cornered and thinks he's the good guy. That's the worst combination."

Callum lifted Ailín into his arms.

"Everyone inside. Now."

The interior was small but dry, barely. The floorboards creaked underfoot, and a small table wobbled near the wall. A rusted lantern hung from a beam overhead, swinging gently with the wind.

Ailín climbed into Lila's lap by the small window.

Methos shook rain from his coat.

Cadigan barred the door.

THOTH dimmed its display to avoid detection.

Callum stood in the center, wiping water from his face with the back of his hand.

"THOTH. Status."

"Renwick's craft will arrive within fifteen minutes. Possibly less depending on wind patterns."

Lila frowned.

"And the Hunter?"

"Stationary. But I detect rising resonance from the tunnels. He is recovering his stability."

Cadigan rested both hands on the table.

"So we're caught between Renwick on one side and the Hunter on the other."

Methos sat on a crate, rubbing his hands together thoughtfully.

"Then we don't stay between them."

Callum nodded slowly.

"We leave the island."

Lila blinked.

"…In what? There's no boat."

THOTH chimed:

"Incorrect."

The lantern flickered as a gust rocked the hut.

Callum frowned.

"Incorrect how?"

"There *is* a boat."

Cadigan turned toward the window.

"Where?"

THOTH responded:

"You were standing on it earlier."

Callum blinked.

"…the wreck by the rocks?"

Methos grinned.

"Oh, this will be fun."

Lila stared at them both.

"You expect us to sail a half-rotten boat through a storm?"

Methos shrugged.

"Sail? No. Drift? Maybe."

Ailín raised her hand.

"We can do it."

Lila looked at her in disbelief.

"Sweetheart, even Callum couldn't sail that."

Callum raised a hand.

"I heard that."

Ailín shook her head earnestly.

"No, I mean… THOTH knows how."

THOTH confirmed:

"I can interface with the craft's residual navigation system. Assuming it has not fully corroded."

Lila groaned.

"We're going to die."

Methos smirked.

"Not today."

Cadigan nodded.

"We reach the Archivist by water anyway. Might as well start early."

Callum adjusted Ailín in his arms.

"Alright. We take the boat."

Ailín tugged his collar.

"Callum."

"Yes?"

"Is the Archivist really expecting us?"

He considered this.

"No."

Ailín smiled.

"Then we'll surprise him."

Methos laughed.

"Oh, child… you have no idea."

THOTH interrupted, "Recommendation: depart within ten minutes. Renwick's craft has shifted to thermal scan mode."

Callum nodded.

"Then we move now."

He opened the door.

Wind and rain slammed into the hut.

Behind him, the sea roared like a warning.

Ahead of him lay a broken boat, a brutal storm, and the path to the one Immortal even Methos feared.

And somewhere far under the island,
the Hunter finally moved.

The wrecked boat sat half-buried in sand and kelp, its hull scarred and weather-beaten from years of storms. One side was split open where it had smashed against the rocks; the prow was intact but cracked; the rudder hung on a twisted bolt that looked ready to surrender to the next strong wave.

Methos approached it like a man evaluating a questionable horse.

"Well… it floats."

Cadigan snorted.

"That is not floating."

Methos kicked the hull lightly.

The boat rocked, sloshing rainwater inside.

"It's floating now."

Lila's eyes widened at the state of the craft.

"We are NOT getting into that."

Callum ran his hands along the chipped rail.

The wood was old, but thick.

Driven deep.

Reinforced poorly, but reinforced nonetheless.

"THOTH," he said quietly.

"Can you bring her back online?"

The AI processed for a moment before replying.

"Pre-Check: Hull, compromised but serviceable. Engine, destroyed. Primary battery, drained. Secondary battery, partial charge. Navigation system, minimal function."

Lila groaned.

"That's not reassuring."

THOTH continued:

"However... electrical contact is possible."

Methos grinned.

"So it runs on faith, fear, and luck. Perfect."

Cadigan broke apart an old crate nearby, producing two lengths of wood.

"We'll need oars."

Methos blinked.

"We? *I* don't row."

"Good," Cadigan replied.

"No one trusts you not to hit a rock."

Ailín stepped forward, eyes wide with concern.

"Callum... is this safe?"

Callum crouched beside her.

"No. Not really."

She nodded thoughtfully.

"But safer than tunnels?"

"Much."

Ailín nodded.

"Okay."

Lila stared at them both, incredulous.

"That's your safety metric now? The tunnels?"

Methos clapped her on the shoulder.

"Welcome to Immortal travel, Doctor."

THOTH chimed, its voice cutting through the wind.

"Alert. Helios craft approaching the island's northern perimeter."

Callum snapped to attention.

"How many?"

"Three. Thermal sweeps. Low altitude."

Cadigan grimaced.

"They'll see us if we linger."

Lila scanned the sky nervously.

"I don't hear engines."

Callum shook his head.

"Because they're electric. Quiet as sin."

THOTH added:

"They have not yet detected your heat signatures. The storm is interfering with their scans."

Callum lifted Ailín into his arms.

"That won't last long."

Cadigan grabbed the makeshift oars.

"Everyone aboard. Now."

Methos climbed into the boat first, muttering:

"If this thing falls apart, I'm haunting all of you."

Lila followed, settling Ailín between her and Callum.

Cadigan pushed off the sand, guiding the boat toward the foaming water.

The first wave struck the hull with a hard slap.

Ailín flinched.

Callum wrapped an arm around her.

"It's alright. The sea likes to test everyone the first time."

Ailín peered over the rail.

"Is it mad at us?"

Methos shook his head.

"No, no. This is its version of a handshake."

Lila shot him a look.

"You're not helping."

"I'm not trying to."

Cadigan shoved the hull deeper, wading waist-high into the surf.

"THOTH," he called, "is this angle good?"

"Adequate."

"Just adequate?"

"Adequate is optimal under these conditions."

Callum stepped into the stern, steadying himself as the boat pitched.

"Ready?"

Lila braced herself.

"Do we have a choice?"

Methos raised a hand.

"Wait for a lull, "

A massive wave surged toward them.

Cadigan shoved hard, launching the craft free of the sand.

The boat lurched violently, water splashing over the sides.

Ailín clung to Callum with both hands.

Lightning split the sky.

Thunder rolled across the sea.

THOTH activated from the wrist display, syncing with the flickering navigation panel.

"Stabilizing. Estimating drift pattern. Prepare for impact."

Methos yelled:

"Impact with what?!"

THOTH responded calmly.

"The ocean."

The boat crested a wave, then slammed into the trough with a crash that rattled every rib.

Cadigan dug the oars in, pulling with practiced strength.

Lila squeezed Ailín's shoulders.

"Stay low. Hold tight."

Ailín gulped.

"He's following."

Callum stiffened.

"The Hunter?"

Ailín shook her head slowly.

"No... the other one."

Methos paused mid-row.

"What do you mean the *other* one?"

Ailín stared out at the storm-dark sea, her eyes glowing faintly under the blanket's edge.

"He's awake again.

Just a little.

He's... watching."

Cadigan swallowed.

"Boroun."

THOTH chimed softly.

"Resonance confirms partial awakening. He is aware of your direction."

Methos muttered:

"Wonderful. We've become a beacon for ancient nightmares."

But Lila saw something in Ailín's face.

Not fear.

Not panic.

Something else.

"Sweetheart," Lila murmured. "What is he feeling now?"

Ailín shivered.

"He's... curious."

Callum's jaw tightened.

"We keep going."

Cadigan put his back into the oars.

Methos gripped the side rail.

Lila held Ailín tighter.

THOTH recalibrated drift.

The boat pushed deeper into the storm.

Rain struck the boat in sheets, driven sideways by the wind. The hull rocked violently as wave after wave crashed against it, the old wood groaning under each impact. The small craft lurched up the face of a towering swell, then dropped with stomach-turning force into a dark trough.

Ailín clung to Callum so tightly he could feel her pulse racing through her fingertips.

Lila wrapped her arms around both of them.

"Callum!" she shouted over the storm.

"We'll capsize if we don't angle starboard!"

THOTH corrected her immediately, "Port. Angle port by twenty degrees."

Cadigan pulled the oars with everything he had, water splashing across his face.

"I'm trying, THOTH, this boat is older than Methos!"

Methos rolled his eyes despite nearly losing his grip.

"Funny. Truly. Make jokes while we drown!"

A wave slammed into the hull, knocking Methos sideways. He slipped on the wet boards and nearly tumbled over the side.

Callum lunged, one arm hooking Methos's coat, yanking him back into the boat before the next surge could swallow him.

Methos coughed seawater and glared.

"I could've saved myself."

Callum shook his head.

"No. You couldn't."

Methos opened his mouth to argue,

then didn't.

He looked almost… shaken.

Not from the fall.

From something deeper.

Ailín tilted her head, staring at him.

"You're scared."

Methos froze.

Cadigan raised an eyebrow.

"Well? Explain."

Methos clicked his tongue.

"It's nothing."

Ailín shook her head.

"It's the other voice. The one from the door. He scares you more than the Hunter."

Callum met Methos's eyes.

"Methos?"

For once, the world's oldest Immortal didn't hide behind sarcasm.

He didn't deflect.

He didn't posture.

He just said quietly, "Boroun remembers me."

Cadigan nearly lost his grip on the oars.

"What?"

Methos stared out at the black horizon.

"I knew him. Before Connor. Before any of you. Before... damn near everything you call history."

Callum felt his stomach drop.

"You never said, "

"No," Methos cut in.

Lila frowned.

"Why not?"

Methos laughed dryly.

"Because I had hoped to never see him again."

Ailín pulled her blanket tighter.

"He sounded lonely."

Methos swallowed, hard.

"Lonely is not the same as safe, little one."

The sea roared beneath them as the storm intensified, wind whipping across the surface in sheets. Thunder rolled like cannon fire.

THOTH chimed with sudden urgency, "Alert. The Hunter is moving. Resonance indicates rapid relocation."

Callum straightened.

"How rapid?"

"Very. Trajectory shifting, correcting course."

Lila's eyes widened.

"He's tracking us?"

"No," THOTH corrected. "Tracking something else."

Methos cursed softly.

"Then we have to hurry."

A massive breaker struck the hull, nearly knocking Cadigan off the bench.

Lila braced herself against the rail.

352

"THOTH, how much farther?"

"Two hundred meters to open sea."

Callum nodded.

"Cadigan, hold steady. Methos, keep balance aft."

Methos scoffed.

"Balance is my specialty."

The boat lurched left.

"A specialty I'm currently ignoring," he muttered.

Callum steadied himself, adjusting Ailín's blanket as she clung to him.

"Sweetheart... what else do you feel?"

Ailín trembled, her glow pulsing faintly.

"The sad one is whispering again," she said softly.

"Not words. Just... feelings."

Lila swallowed.

"Is he trying to hurt you?"

"No."

Ailín shook her head.

"He's trying to follow me."

Methos swore again.

Cadigan gripped the oars tighter.

Callum kissed Ailín's forehead.

"We won't let him reach you. Either of them."

"But he's not the scary one.

The scary one is, "

A sharp tone from THOTH cut her off.

"Renwick's craft have changed course.

They are heading directly toward your position."

Lila's stomach twisted.

"How? They can't detect us in this storm."

Another pause.

Then THOTH spoke quietly, "I am detecting a secondary signal.

It is not coming from Renwick."

Callum's grip tightened.

"Then who?"

THOTH answered:

"Unknown source.

Transmission pattern resembles Immortal resonance... mixed with electromagnetic interference."

Methos's eyes narrowed.

"Oh no..."

Cadigan kept rowing.

"What now?"

THOTH finished:

"Someone is guiding them. Someone who wants them to find you."

Callum's voice dropped.

"Who?"

The AI replied:

"Possibly... the Archivist."

Wind slammed the boat sideways.

Ailín's glow pulsed.

And far out on the horizon, through lightning flashes, a single beacon of pale white light flickered in the mist, as though someone were lighting the path for them.

Or luring them.

The storm rose to its full height as the battered boat finally broke past the last line of rocks. The sea surged beneath them in monstrous, heaving swells. Waves towered over the small craft like walls of liquid iron, crashing down with explosive force.

Cadigan's oars strained against the currents, every stroke a battle.

THOTH crackled through the rain, "Warning: velocity increase detected...storm intensity escalating...hold bearing five degrees westward."

Callum tightened his grip around Ailín, bracing his legs as the hull slammed into another trough.

Lila steadied herself with one hand while keeping the other around Ailín.

"We're not going to make it like this!"

Methos barked a laugh despite the chaos.

"Optimism! I knew you'd get there eventually!"

A massive wave pitched the boat sideways.

Lila screamed.

Cadigan almost dropped the oars.

Methos was thrown across the benches.

Callum held firm, shielding Ailín with his body.

THOTH cut through the noise, "Callum! Bearing correction required: twenty degrees starboard!"

Cadigan heaved the oars, pulling with strength born from centuries of war.

"Push! Push!" he shouted over the thunder.

Lightning spidered across the sky, illuminating the horizon,

And there it was again.

The pale white beacon...flickering.

Methos wiped rain from his face.

THOTH chimed urgently, "Brace! Wave impact imminent!"

The boat hit a towering swell.

Wood groaned.

The hull almost capsized.

Cadigan yelled:

"CALLUM, HOLD HER!"

Ailín clung to him, shaking.

The next wave rose higher,

too high,

a roaring wall that would swallow them whole.

Lila's voice cracked with terror.

"CALLUM! WE'RE NOT GOING TO CLEAR IT!"

Methos stared up, eyes wide.

"Well. It's been a long life."

Callum held Ailín tightly against his chest.

"Stay with me," he whispered.

Ailín's glow burst outward,

Not with fear.

Not wild.

Not chaotic.

But controlled.

Her eyes shone like polished silver.

She raised her small hands.

And the wave,

broke around them.

Split cleanly down the center

like a curtain of water parting for a stage.

Spray fanned out in two massive arcs, racing past the boat.

Lila gasped.

Cadigan dropped the oars in shock.

Methos swore violently.

THOTH chimed, almost sounding impressed, "Ailín has manipulated kinetic force."

Ailín collapsed into Callum's arms, exhausted.

He held her, stunned.

"Ailín... what did you do?"

"I didn't want it to hurt us."

Callum kissed her forehead.

"You saved us."

But Methos breathed, "No... she did more than that."

Lila turned to him.

"What do you mean?"

"Only Immortals who survived the Great Ages could part water like that. and only with centuries of mastery."

Callum frowned.

"So how did she, ?"

"Because someone amplified her," Methos finished.

THOTH confirmed with eerie calm, "Resonance overlap detected. Source: unknown Immortal beacon ahead."

Callum's heart froze.

"The Archivist."

Ailín lifted her head.

"He's calling us."

Another flicker of white light pulsed across the waves, not lightning, ancient, and deliberate.

Lila trembled.

"What does he want?"

THOTH answered, "Destination reached in twenty-two minutes."

Methos gave a humorless smile.

"What does he want? Oh, very simple."

Callum narrowed his eyes.

"What?"

The next flash of white lit the horizon, illuminating a silhouette on a distant island's highest peak.

Methos finished quietly, "He wants the girl."
And the storm roared around them.

Chapter 18

The storm eased as abruptly as it had come. Not gradually, unnaturally. One wave hammered the boat, hard enough to tilt Methos off his seat, and the next rolled toward them in a gentle, almost ceremonial swell.

The sky did not clear, not really, but the thunder faded like someone had closed a distant door.

Cadigan lifted the oars, chest heaving.

"That's... not normal," he said between breaths.

Callum adjusted the blanket around Ailín, who slept fitfully in his arms, worn out from whatever force she had channeled.

"No," Callum murmured, "It isn't."

Lila wiped seawater from her face. She'd been watching Ailín, not the storm.

"She's still warm," she said, checking the girl's pulse. "Still responding normally."

Callum exhaled in quiet relief.

"I don't want her to use that ability again," he said softly.

Methos scoffed.

"Oh yes, tell the sea not to be wet while you're at it."

Lila shot him a look.

"You think I enjoy watching a child nearly drain herself?"

Methos raised both hands defensively.

"Just saying, she didn't 'use' it. It used her. That's how resonance works with the young."

Cadigan steadied the boat.

"And how the Archivist is using her now."

Callum frowned.

"You're sure?"

Cadigan nodded at the horizon.

"Look."

The clouds shifted. For the first time since they'd fled the tunnels, the horizon opened enough to reveal land, jagged cliffs rising sharply from the water, shaped by thousands of years of wind and tide. Sparse grass clung to the rock. Old stone pillars dotted the ridgeline like sentinels.

Methos leaned forward, squinting.

"That's no natural formation."

Lila blinked.

"The pillars?"

"No," Methos said.

"The gaps between them."

Callum saw it, too.

Even in the storm's dying gloom, the pillars were arranged with uncanny precision. Not symmetrical, purposefully asymmetrical, angled like a sundial built to measure something older than time itself.

Ailín stirred, voice small.

"Callum... where are we?"

Callum stroked her hair gently.

"We're almost there."

She blinked, eyes silver in the half-light.

"It feels... quiet."

Lila smiled softly.

"Quiet is good."

Ailín shook her head.

"No. Not *that* kind of quiet."

THOTH spoke, voice low and modulated, "Coordinates confirmed. This is the correct island. Local designation lost.

Historical records: incomplete."

Lila frowned.

"Why incomplete?"

Methos answered before THOTH could.

"Because the archivist erases the parts of history he doesn't like."

Cadigan nodded grimly.

"And leaves only what he wants others to find."

Another wave carried them closer to shore.

A narrow beach stretched in a crescent at the base of the cliffs, sand the color of bone, not black volcanic rock like Harris Island.

Callum eyed the landing.

"We can bring the boat in there."

Methos scoffed.

"Better than smashing into the rocks, I suppose."

Lila steadied herself as Cadigan angled the boat.

"I'd complain, but this is the smoothest the water's been all night."

Callum said nothing, but his eyes were sharp, scanning the cliffs.

Something felt wrong. Nothing dangerous or threatening, but intentional. It's as if someone has prepared for this moment.

Ailín sat up, rubbing her eyes.

"We're here."

"Yes," Callum said.

Methos leaned over the side.

"We're being invited."

Cadigan glared.

"How do you know?"

Methos pointed.

There, at the waterline, stood a tall iron torch, lit with a pale white fire that did not flicker in the wind.

Lila gazed out toward the landing, "That was not there a moment ago."

"No," Callum agreed, "It wasn't."

Ailín stared at the flame.

"He's waiting."

Callum tightened his grip around her.

"Yes, and now we find out what he wants."

The boat slid gently onto the sand.

The pale fire burned steady.

And above it, carved into the cliff face,
a single ancient symbol glowed faintly,
older than Gaelic, older than the clans.

Methos confirmed, "The mark of the First Witness."

They had arrived.

The boat hissed across the pale sand, dragged upward by the outgoing swell as if the tide itself had offered them safe landing. The storm that had threatened to rip the boat apart just minutes before now seemed to brood offshore, its clouds clinging to the horizon like a predator waiting its turn.

Callum stepped off first, boots sinking an inch into the cool, powder-fine sand. He lifted Ailín to the ground carefully. She blinked up at the sky, glow pulsing with cautious curiosity.

Cadigan secured the boat with a length of worn rope.
Lila wrapped Ailín's blanket more securely around her shoulders.
Methos remained at the waterline longer than necessary, staring up at the cliffs.

Callum turned to him.

"You alright?"

Methos didn't answer right away. His eyes followed the pale fire of the torch, steady, unnatural, emotionless.

Finally, he said, "I've walked onto many islands in my life."
A long breath, "I've never walked onto one that watched me back."

Ailín turned toward him, "You feel it too."

Methos nodded.

"I'd be worried if I didn't."

The sand changed character as they moved inland,
from the smooth powder near the water to a gritty, black-speckled texture that reminded Callum of volcanic beaches in the far north. But this island wasn't volcanic.

No storms had sculpted these patterns.
No tides had shaped this gradation.

Ailín knelt, touching the sand with her fingertips.

"It feels warm."

Lila crouched beside her, "From the sun?"

Ailín shook her head, "No. From underneath."

Callum stiffened, "Below the island?"

Ailín nodded softly.

"Yes. It feels... awake."

Methos immediately scanned the cliffs again.

"He activated the island."

Cadigan frowned.

"What does that mean?"

Methos looked at him, eyes darker than usual.

"The Archivist has lived here long enough that the ground remembers him."

Lila blinked.

"So... everything is imprinting?"

Methos nodded.

"Everything."

She shook her head slowly, "everything really is a riddle with you..."

"Everything. It keeps it interesting."

Callum looked up at the towering stone pillars.
Carved spirals and recesses marred their surfaces, not mere erosion, but deliberate shaping.

Cadigan placed a hand on one.

"Late Bronze Age," he murmured. "Or older."

Methos huffed.

"Definitely older."

THOTH chimed from Callum's wrist.

"Correction: current geological assessment suggests initial shaping during the early Neolithic era."

Lila exhaled in disbelief.

"So the Archivist has been here for thousands of years?"

THOTH paused.

"...or he inherited it from someone older. We just don't know because there are no records."

That made the air colder.

Even Methos stiffened.

"There were few older."

Callum rested a hand on Ailín's shoulder.

"You feeling anything now?"

Ailín closed her eyes.

Her glow pulsed once.

Twice.

Then she inhaled sharply.

"It's like…everyone who was ever here is whispering."

Lila wrapped an arm around her.

"Is it hurting you?"

"No. Just loud."

Callum exchanged a look with Cadigan.

"This island is a memory vault."

Methos nodded slowly.

"A place where Immortal echoes don't fade."

"He built this place as a sanctuary. Or a trap."

"Which one?" Lila asked.

Methos, "Depends on who you are."

The moment they stepped deeper inland, the wind shifted.

THOTH chimed, "Topographical update. Callum, a path has appeared ahead."

Lila blinked.

"A path? I don't see… "

And then she did.

The long grass parted in a slow ripple as if brushed by invisible hands. For a heartbeat, the blades lay flat, revealing a narrow track of compacted soil that hadn't been visible seconds before.

Ailín squeezed Callum's hand.

"He's showing us where to go."

Cadigan moved ahead, hand on his claymore, scanning the cliffs. But nothing moved. Nothing stirred.

Callum stepped onto the path. Ailín matched his stride; Lila stayed close. Methos followed reluctantly; Cadigan remained at the rear, guarding their back.

THOTH reported, "Environmental readings stable. But resonance on this island is… anomalous."

Callum frowned.

"Define anomalous."

"Interference. Like walking through someone's memories."

"That's not comforting." Lila said.

Methos chuckled humorlessly, "It's not supposed to be."

Ailín lifted her head suddenly.

"He's close."

Cadigan drew his claymore.

"Where?"

Ailín pointed ahead, toward a narrow cleft in the cliff base.

"It feels like…he's behind the stone."

Methos exhaled sharply.

"Oh. Then we are definitely expected."

Callum tensed.

"How close?"

Ailín whispered:

"Very."

The path narrowed into a fissure framed by stone pillars so tall they seemed carved from the sky itself. The pale fire of the shoreline torch cast shifting shadows across their surfaces, revealing faint spirals etched into the rock, patterns reminiscent of the earliest Neolithic monuments.

But these weren't carved by human hands.

Cadigan placed a hand on one pillar.

"It's warm," he murmured. "Stone shouldn't be warm."

Methos stepped forward, frowning.

"It's not stone, Not exactly."

Lila blinked.

"What else would it be?"

Methos ran his fingers over the symbols.

"Condensed Quickening. Solidified over centuries."

Callum paused mid-step.

"You're telling me the Archivist carved these pillars with… resonance?"

Methos snorted, "Carved? No. He *grew* them."

Ailín trembled slightly beside Callum.

"It feels like… singing."

Lila knelt.

"Singing?"

Ailín nodded.

"Yes. Like…if stones could hum."

Methos exhaled.

"They're responding to her."

Cadigan glanced sharply at Ailín.

"Is it safe?"

Before anyone could answer, the rock tremored underfoot.

A rumble rolled through the cliffs, not violent, but resonant.
Deliberate.

Callum stepped in front of Ailín.

Cadigan drew his claymore.

Lila pulled Ailín into her arms.

Methos braced himself on the wall.

THOTH chimed, voice lower than usual.

"Callum, proximity shift detected."

Callum tensed.

"What kind of shift?"

"The stone is moving."

The fissure ahead warped ,
the walls widening
as if the cliff inhaled.

A breeze swept through the passage, warm, stale and very old.

Ailín gulped.

"He opened the way."

Lila tightened her grip.

"Ailín, honey, how do you know that?"

Ailín, "Because he whispered to me."

A silence fell.

Callum knelt in front of her, forcing calm into his voice.

"What did he say?"

Ailín blinked, her eyes glowing faintly silver.

"He said…'Do not fear.'"

Lila looked sharply at Callum.

"That is NOT reassuring."

Methos shook his head.

"Nor is it an accident. The Archivist speaks to resonance, not minds. But she heard him. Directly."

Cadigan placed a hand on Callum's shoulder.

"That means the Archivist wants her specifically."

Callum rose slowly.

"He's not taking her."

Lila stepped in front of him.

"Callum. Stop pretending you're not terrified."

He froze.

Methos winced.

Cadigan looked away.

Ailín hugged her blanket.

Lila continued, voice softening.

"You've been running on fear since Harris Island. Afraid of Renwick. Afraid of the Hunter. Afraid of Boroun. Afraid of losing her."

She touched Ailín's hair.

"Afraid of the thing she's becoming."

Callum's throat tightened.

"That doesn't matter. I keep her safe."

"But you don't have to do it alone."

Ailín took his hand, small fingers wrapping around his.

"I'm not scared if you're here."

His resolve cracked.

A moment.

A breath.

Enough to make him steady again.

He squeezed her hand gently.

"I'll always be here."

Methos cleared his throat loudly.

"Touching. Truly. And embarrassing for Callum, Now let's enter the gaping supernatural corridor before Renwick drops a drone on us."

Cadigan gave him a shove.

"Let them have a moment."

"No," Methos muttered, brushing sand from his coat.

"We don't have moments. He's watching."

Callum's eyes narrowed.

"You feel him?"

Methos nodded once, slowly.

"Yes. The Archivist is fully awake now."

And with a final rumble,

the fissure widened into a proper passage ,

a doorway of living stone.

THOTH scanned the opening.

"Callum, Energy readings are highly abnormal."

"Define abnormal," Lila muttered.

"This passage predates recorded Immortal history."

Methos turned pale, "Then we're walking into a myth."

Ailín stepped forward, glow brightening.

"No, We're walking into his home."

Cadigan drew his sword.

"Stay close."

Callum lifted Ailín into his arms.

Lila followed at his side.

Methos brought the lantern forward.

And together,

they crossed the threshold

into the Archivist's sanctuary.

The moment the group crossed beneath the arched mouth of the fissure, the air changed to warm and dense.

The walls no longer felt like carved stone, but like compressed memory. Layered strata of Immortal lives, etched into the earth long before humans recorded history. The light was dim but steady, emanating from no source they could identify. It was as if the stone itself glowed with faint golden veins of Quickening.

Lila reached out instinctively, but Methos caught her wrist.

"Don't touch the walls."

She looked startled.

"Why? Will it hurt?"

Methos's eyes were unusually serious.

"Only if you dislike sharing your memories with the dead."

Ailín's glow intensified.

"It's humming again."

Cadigan stepped forward, sword drawn tight to his chest.

"Humming?"

Ailín pointed at the walls.

"They're talking."

Callum tightened his grip on her, not possessive, but protective.

"Don't engage with it," he directed.

"We don't know what it does."

A chime from Callum's wrist made them all jump.

THOTH.

But its voice crackled like a radio losing static war.

"Cal...um... con...nection... destabilizing."

Lila gasped.

"THOTH? THOTH, can you hear us?"

"Re...sonance... interference... ex...treme..."

Callum raised his wrist.

"THOTH, what's happening?"

A burst of static.

Then THOTH's voice came through clearer, but urgent.

"Callum, listen.

Drones... have triangulated my location...I must relocate... now."

Callum's chest tightened.

"What? Where?"

THOTH's audio stuttered.

"...moving to high-altitude shell pattern...You will lose contact... temporarily."

Lila pressed closer.

"THOTH, wait, Ailín still needs your... "

The connection fractured.

A tone cut through the passage.

Then silence.

THOTH was gone.

The sanctuary swallowed the last echo of his voice like it had consumed countless voices before.

Ailín clutched Callum's collar, suddenly small again.

"He's gone."

Callum kissed the top of her head.

"He'll be back. He just needs to hide."

Methos exhaled sharply.

"Losing THOTH is… not ideal."

Cadigan added:

"We're blind without him."

Callum adjusted Ailín in his arms.

"No. We're not."

He looked ahead.

Toward the corridor that opened into a vast chamber lit by ancient, impossible light.

Toward the heart of the sanctuary.

Toward the presence Ailín had been sensing since they arrived.

The Archivist.

A soft vibration rolled through the floor, not like the Hunter's violent resonance, nor Boroun's ancient gravity.

Ailín trembled.

"He wants to talk to me."

Lila stepped in front of Callum.

"And we want to talk to *him*. But no one touches her. No one separates her from us."

Her voice trembled with fear she refused to show.

Callum nodded.

"We stay together."

Methos breathed shallowly.

"Together is good.

Just remember, he hasn't seen company in centuries.

His social skills may be… rusty."

Cadigan muttered:

"That's one word for it."

They moved forward into the sanctuary.

The tunnel opened into a massive circular rotunda, its ceiling so high it vanished into shadow. Monoliths encircled the chamber, each carved with shifting symbols, curling like script, humming like distant thunder.

At the center stood a single stone dais.

Empty.

Lila looked around.

"Where is he?"

Ailín's glow pulsed once.

Twice.

Then she pointed to the dais.

"He's here."

Methos looked alarmed.

"Ailín, there's no one, "

The ground beneath them thrummed.

The air thickened, vibrating with energy.

And then, the symbols on the monoliths shifted.

Rotated, turned inward like a dozen massive eyes focusing at once.

Lila froze.

Cadigan lifted his claymore.

Methos mouthed:

"No...No, no, no..."

Callum stepped forward, placing himself between the dais and his family.

Ailín's glow intensified until silver light bled through the blanket.

And then a voice, soft, calm, and ancient echoing through the chamber.

"Welcome, Callum MacLeod. I have waited a very long time."

The monoliths pulsed.

The dais illuminated.

And the Archivist stepped into existence as though he had been carved from the air itself.

He was tall and lean, draped in ancient robes of woven gray, long unkept, disheveled beard. He looked like he could have come right out of and Arthurian novel. His eyes shimmering blue with an eternity of stolen memory.

Ailín gasped and buried her face into Callum's neck.

Callum held her tightly.

Lila reached for him, breathing hard.

Cadigan stepped forward, blade raised.

Methos whispered a single, trembling word:

"Arthis."

The Archivist smiled faintly.

"Hello, old friend."

Chapter 19

The Archivist, Arthis, stood with the stillness of a monument, yet the chamber itself seemed to breathe with him. Light shimmered faintly along the woven gray fabric of his garments, not reflective but resonant, as if each thread held strands of Quickening older than any living Immortal.

His eyes were the most unsettling part.

Not bright, not menacing, just ancient.

Ancient in a way that no human could ever mimic.

Eyes that had seen the first Immortal rise. Eyes that had watched the first Quickening in the age before memory. Eyes that, without trying, could look through a person and see every ghost they carried.

Methos visibly recoiled when those eyes turned toward him.

Arthis lifted a single hand in greeting.

"It has been… many lifetimes, Methos."

Methos looked away.

"Not long enough."

Cadigan stepped forward, claymore angled protectively.

"If you mean us harm, you'll regret… "

Arthis didn't raise his voice.

He didn't move.

He simply *exhaled*.

A soft, controlled breath.

Cadigan staggered backward two full steps, nearly dropping his blade.

Lila rushed to steady him.

"What did he do?"

Methos swallowed hard.

"Nothing. That's the point."

Callum held Ailín close, Ailín's small hands gripping his coat like she was anchoring herself.

Arthis's eyes softened when he looked at her.

"The girl is stronger than I expected."

Lila stepped in front of Callum and Ailín, arms outstretched in a defensive posture.

"She's a child. You don't touch her. You don't go near her. You don't even breathe in her direction without our permission."

Arthis blinked slowly, as though contemplating the concept of boundaries like one might contemplate a museum artifact.

"Your devotion is admirable, Doctor Lila Serrano."

Lila stiffened.

"You know my name."

"I know many names," Arthis replied simply.

"What do you want with her?"

Arthis tilted his head.

"To witness her."

"No," Callum snapped, "She's not a specimen."

"She is not," Arthis agreed, "Which is precisely why she must be seen."

Ailín peeked over Callum's shoulder, silver eyes wide.

"You're sad."

Arthis's expression didn't change.

"Am I?"

Ailín nodded, "You feel like…like a room that has too many things in it, and not enough windows."

For the first time, Arthis blinked in surprise.

Methos exhaled.

"She sees resonance. She *reads* it."

Arthis nodded slowly.

"A rare gift, and a dangerous one."

Callum stepped back half a pace.

"That's why we came, she needs help, not theories, not riddles.

Arthis looked at Callum for a long moment, and his gaze was not unkind.

"You love her."

Callum's teeth clenched.

"Of course I do."

Arthis nodded.

"Then you have brought her to the only place where she can learn to survive her spark."

Cadigan finally found his breath again.

"Survive it? What does that mean?"

Arthis turned slightly, robes whispering like ancient parchment.

"It means she carries the echo of the First Immortals. And if not trained, that echo will consume her."

Lila's heart dropped.

"Consume her? How?"

Arthis looked at Ailín again.

"By tearing her apart from the inside."

"What does she need?"

Arthis raised one hand.

"Step forward."

Lila stepped in front of Callum so fast her boots skidded on the smooth stone.

"Absolutely not."

Arthis regarded her like she was a curious but admirable phenomenon.

"Your courage is noted, but unnecessary."

Callum's heartbeat slammed in his chest.

"You don't lay a hand on her."

Arthis lowered his hand calmly.

"Then we begin with you."

Callum froze.

"What?"

Methos groaned quietly.

"Here we go."

Arthis stepped toward Callum, not threateningly, but with the gravity of someone approaching an altar.

"Your bond with the child is the first tether. Before I can teach her, I must understand what ties you together."

Callum's voice cracked with equal parts fear and instinct.

"You're not touching her."

Arthis shook his head.

"No. I am touching *you*."

The room dimmed; the monoliths pulsed. The stone beneath their feet vibrated.

And Ailín grabbed Callum's coat, whispering:

"Callum...he's reading you."

Callum braced himself,

The chamber dimmed as though someone had drawn a veil across the light. The monoliths' pale lines of Quickening flared, then narrowed to thin pulses, like a slowed heartbeat.

Arthis lifted one hand toward Callum.

Not to touch him, just to begin.

A pressure brushed Callum's chest, like static electricity gathering beneath the skin. Not painful, yet, but overwhelmingly intimate. It felt like someone leafing through his memories without his permission.

Callum stiffened.

"What are you doing?"

Arthis's voice was calm.

"Reading the tether."

Ailín clutched Callum's coat.

"No."

Arthis's eyes shifted, just slightly, to her.

"Child, I am not harming him."

She shook her head fiercely.

"He doesn't like it."

Arthis's eyebrow lifted.

"You sense that?"

She nodded.

"He feels like... like someone's pulling on his story."

Callum's breath hitched.

Images flickered at the edge of his mind.

He growled, trying to shove Arthis's resonance away.

"I said stop."

Arthis didn't.

Not out of malice,

but out of intent.

"You resist. Good."

Lila stepped in front of Callum, hands raised like a shield.

"Back off. Right now."

Arthis's gaze moved to her, patient and unnervingly gentle.

"Doctor Serrano... "

Lila didn't let him finish.

"I don't care who or what you are. I don't care how old you are. He's *hurting*. You stop."

She reached for Callum's arm,

A pulse erupted from the monoliths.

Lila was thrown backward, skidding across the floor.

"LILA!" Callum yelled, lunging forward,

But Ailín reacted first.

Her glow blazed white.

She flung her arms out,

and the pulse hit an invisible barrier around her, rippling like heat on stone.

Arthis blinked.

Actually blinked.

A flicker of genuine surprise.

"Interesting."

Lila groaned, sitting up with her hair sticking to her face.

"What the hell was that?!"

Methos moved to her side, helping her up.

"Arthis doesn't like anyone interrupting. He didn't hurt you. That was... a warning reflex."

Lila spat a curse, "His reflex sucks."

Cadigan planted himself between her and Arthis.

"You do that again, and I swear.. "

Arthis didn't turn.

"Ye cannot harm me, Cadigan Ross."

Cadigan's grip on his claymore tightened.

Methos shook his head.

"He isn't bragging. He's stating fact."

Callum grit his teeth as the resonance brushed deeper into him.

"What are you looking for?"

Arthis lowered his hand slightly.

"I am not searching, I am listening."

Callum breathed hard.

"To what?"

Arthis's eyes flickered with something almost reverent.

"To the oldest echo that follows you."

Methos groaned.

"Oh no. Not this again."

Lila blinked rapidly.

"What echo?"

Methos ran a hand through his hair, suddenly exhausted.

"Callum... you're not carrying just your own memories. Every Immortal carries echoes of the ones they've taken. But rarely, *rarely*, does one carry a First Echo."

Callum's skin chilled.

"What's a First Echo?"

Arthis stepped closer.

"The memory of one who lived in the dawn of our kind."

Callum swallowed.

"That's not possible."

Methos exhaled.

"Possible? Not probable, but you were trained by Duncan, and before him, Connor. Both old. Both exposed to older."

Arthis finished:

"One of the echoes inside you is not theirs."

A shiver ran down Callum's spine.

Ailín hugged him tight.

"Callum... I don't like this."

He placed his hand over hers.

"Neither do I."

Arthis finally lowered his hand fully.

The pressure ebbed.

Callum gasped as if surfacing for air.

Arthis studied him with unsettling calm.

"You carry a fragment of Arkael."

Cadigan froze.

Methos stepped back.

Lila blinked, confused.

"Who?"

Methos said, "One of the First Immortals. One of the ones even I never met.

Old as myth. Older."

Arthis nodded.

"His echo is faint. Dormant. But present."

Callum stared, stunned.

"That's impossible."

Arthis's voice turned solemn.

"Nothing is impossible for the First. Not memory. Not reach. Not prophecy."

Ailín's glow flickered gently.

"Is he bad?"

Arthis shook his head slowly.

"No, child. He was… a beginning."

Callum inhaled deeply, steadying himself.

"What does this have to do with Ailín?"

Arthis looked at her, really looked, for the first time.

"She recognized the echo without knowing its name."

Methos muttered:

"Oh, that's… that's not great."

Ailín's voice was small.

"Callum isn't scared of him."

Callum frowned.

"No. I'm not."

Arthis nodded.

"That is why you are her tether."

Ailín leaned into him.

"And why she trusts you above all others."

A soft warmth filled the chamber around them for a moment, almost comforting.

Then Arthis stepped back.

"Now that I understand your resonance...we can begin her training."

Callum stiffened.

Lila grabbed his arm.

"No. Not without conditions."

Arthis tilted his head faintly.

"There are no conditions. Her spark is awakening faster than expected. If you deny her this path, she will die."

Ailín trembled.

Callum wrapped both arms around her.

Lila stood tall, shaking but resolute.

"Then we need to understand exactly what you're going to do."

Arthis regarded her.

"You will."

He turned,

And the monoliths lit in a spiraling pattern.

A pathway opened deeper into the sanctuary.

Arthis stepped forward.

"Come, the first lesson begins now."

Arthis moved through the sanctuary with soundless steps, his robes brushing the stone like whispers. The deeper they went, the more the architecture changed. The rough, ancient rock gave way to polished surfaces, smooth as obsidian, marked with fractal patterns that resembled the branching of lightning.

Ailín clung quietly to Callum, her small hand wrapped tightly around his thumb. Her glow pulsed in a steady rhythm that seemed to sync with the faint vibrations in the floor.

Lila walked beside them, on alert.

"Callum," she said softly, "we need to be careful here."

He nodded.

"We will be."

But his eyes remained fixed on Arthis, tracking every movement.

Methos trailed behind them, unusually quiet, scanning the chamber with deep unease.

Cadigan walked rear guard, claymore out, ready for anything.

The passage widened into a great circular hall, the true heart of the sanctuary.

Dozens of monoliths formed a spiral around a sunken basin in the center. The basin itself glowed faintly with soft white light, like shallow water reflecting dawn.

Arthis extended a hand toward it.

"This is where she begins."

Callum immediately stepped forward.

"No."

Arthis lowered his hand.

"Callum MacLeod, If you want her to live, she must learn control."

Lila moved in front of Ailín, voice trembling but firm.

"You're not putting her into anything glowing, humming, vibrating, or remotely mystical until you explain exactly what it does."

Arthis regarded her with calm neutrality.

"You fear for her, that is expected."

"Expected or not," Lila snapped, "you start talking."

Methos cleared his throat uneasily.

"Lila... be careful. He isn't used to being challenged."

Lila squared her shoulders.

"He's about to get a crash course."

Callum held Ailín close, his breath warming her hair.

Arthis looked at Lila.

Then at Callum.

Then at Ailín.

Finally, he nodded.

"The basin is not dangerous. It is memory. It will not harm her. It will show her what she carries, and what she must control."

Lila scowled.

"You expect us to throw her in a puddle of ghost soup?"

Methos muttered:

"That's... not an inaccurate description."

Ailín tugged Callum's collar.

"Callum... I feel it."

He knelt.

"What do you feel?"

She pointed to the glowing basin.

"It's warm...like...like when I hug you."
Callum's heart twisted.
"You're not going anywhere alone."
Arthis stepped closer, but not threateningly.
"No. She does not go alone. You go with her."
Cadigan frowned.
"Why him?"
Arthis looked at Callum with something approaching respect.
"Because he is her tether. Her anchor. The one echo she trusts above all others."
Ailín leaned into Callum.
"I'm not scared if you come too."
Lila looked up at Callum, eyes softening despite the danger.
"You don't have to do this."
Callum brushed Ailín's hair gently.
"Yes, I do."
He rose, stepping toward the basin,
But Methos grabbed his arm.
Callum stopped, surprised.
"Methos?"
The oldest Immortal swallowed.
"Before you step into that...you need to understand something."
Callum frowned.
"What?"
Methos glanced at Arthis, then at the basin, then back at Callum.
"Arkael... wasn't just a First Immortal."
Lila blinked.
"You said he was ancient. That's all."
Methos shook his head.
"I didn't say the rest because I hoped it wouldn't matter."
Callum's jaw tightened.
"Methos. Tell me."
Methos exhaled, voice lower now, weighted with centuries of memory.
"Arkael was the First Witness. The one who remembered everything...Everything."
Cadigan's grip on his claymore slipped.

"Wait, if Arthis is the Archivist, then Arkael."

"Was his predecessor," Methos finished, "And the echo you carry? It means Arkael touched your lineage, Connor, Duncan, somewhere along the chain."

Callum's breath trembled.

"And Ailín?"

Arthis stepped forward.

"She does not carry Arkael's echo. She carries something older."

Silence fell.

Ailín tucked herself against Callum's shoulder.

Callum swallowed hard.

"Older?"

Arthis nodded.

"The spark that awakened in her is not from one of us. It is something new."

Lila felt her knees weaken.

"New... how?"

Arthis raised his hand, and the basin brightened.

"Come, Callum. The only way to understand is to see."

Ailín squeezed his hand.

"I want to try."

Callum kissed her hair.

"I'll be right there."

Lila grabbed his arm before he could move.

"Callum...

just promise me something."

He looked at her.

"Anything."

"Come back."

He nodded once.

"I will."

Then he stepped down toward the basin, Ailín in his arms,

And the moment their toes touched the glowing surface, the sanctuary ignited with light.

Ailín gasped.

Callum staggered.

And through the blinding brightness, Callum saw something vast and impossible, A towering figure of pure energy, no face, no form watching him, watching *them.*

Arthis whispered, "The First Light."

Callum asked back:, "What is she?"

Arthis answered, "The future."

The moment Callum and Ailín stepped into the basin, the world dissolved.

The glowing surface spread beneath their feet like warm water, yet it felt weightless, neither liquid nor stone, neither air nor energy. It absorbed sound, swallowed the echoes of their breath, and left only a single hum vibrating through the chamber.

Ailín gasped, clinging to Callum's neck.

"Callum... everything is shining."

He held her close.

"It's alright. I've got you."

The basin pulsed, once, twice, and then the sanctuary blurred away. In its place came light.

White.

Gold.

Silver.

Shifting like the inside of a star.

A figure formed from the radiance.

Not a man.

Not a woman.

Not any recognizable shape ,

just a looming silhouette woven from pure Quickening.

Tall as a tree.

Vast as a memory.

Silent.

Yet the silence carried meaning.

Ailín pressed her glowing forehead to Callum's shoulder.

"He's... not scary."

Callum's chest tightened.

"You can see him?"

Ailín nodded.

"He feels like... sunlight."

Callum blinked through the haze of brilliance.

"Who are you?"

The figure did not answer with words.

Instead,

A rush of images flooded Callum's mind:

A desert of red stone.

A night sky with moons that no longer exist.

A man awakening alone under the stars.

The first Immortal breath.

A sword hammered in fire older than civilization.

A storm of Quickening that split mountains.

Callum staggered.

Ailín lifted her head, eyes glowing brighter than ever.

"He's the first one, the very first."

Arthis's voice echoed from nowhere and everywhere.

"Behold the First Light. The echo from which all Immortal sparks descend."

Callum's breath caught.

"This isn't memory."

"No."

Arthis's voice softened, "This is origin."

Ailín held out a hand toward the spectral figure.

The light bent toward her, like grass bending toward the sun.

Callum instinctively reached to stop her, but Arthis's voice cut through:

"Do not interfere."

Callum growled, "She's a child."

"She is more than that."

Ailín whispered, "He knows me."

Callum's heart clenched.

"How?"

The First Light shifted, tilting its head, if it had one, toward Ailín. The surrounding brilliance dimmed for a moment, focusing entirely on her.

Cadigan's voice echoed faintly from beyond the basin:

"Callum! What's happening?"

Callum barely heard him.

The First Light extended a tendril of energy toward Ailín's chest,
But before it could reach her, Ailín's glow exploded outward.

Silver.

White.

Blue.

Power radiated from her in ripples, distorting the very air.

The First Light recoiled slightly, not from pain, but from recognition.

Lila screamed from outside the basin:

"Ailín! AILÍN!"

Callum shielded the girl as best he could.

"Ailín! Sweetheart, slow down! Breathe!"

She trembled violently.

"It's... too big..."

Arthis spoke, steady and measured, "Let it come."

Callum shouted, "She's not ready!"

Arthis stepped to the edge of the basin.

"No, But the spark does not wait for readiness."

A second burst erupted from Ailín ,
this time so strong that the monoliths around the chamber resonated, trembling with her energy.

Methos shouted, "That's not normal! Arthis, stop her!"

Arthis raised a hand, "This is her awakening."

Ailín's glow shifted, brightened, deepened.

Her eyes opened, only silver.

No pupils.

No irises.

She whispered a word Callum had never heard, *"Primara."*

Callum froze.

"What did she say?"

Arthis inhaled slowly.

"The original word for Firstborn."

Lila's voice broke, "What does that mean?"

The First Light leaned in ,
acknowledging her, answering her.

Arthis's eyes shone for the first time.

"It means she is not descended from us."

Methos staggered.

"What?"

Arthis spoke with reverence and dread intertwined, "She is the spark of something new. A bridge between what we were...and what Immortals will become."

Callum stared down at Ailín, his heart torn between awe and terror.

"What does that make her?"

Arthis stepped onto the basin itself, the glow bending around him.

"She is the Firstborn of the next age."

The First Light bowed, to *her*.

Ailín, "I'm scared..."

Callum held her tight.

"I'm right here. I won't let anything happen to you."

Arthis spoke again, voice heavy with ancient certainty:

"You cannot stop what she is. But you can guide her."

Callum looked up, eyes burning.

"Then teach me, Teach *us*."

Arthis nodded.

"Then your first lesson begins now."

A deeper tremor rolled through the sanctuary.

Outside, distant thunder rumbled.

Ailín's glow dimmed gently as she rested her head on Callum's shoulder, exhausted but alive.

The First Light slowly faded.

Arthis turned to the group.

"The world outside moves against you. Renwick hunts. The Hunter approaches. Boroun awakens, and she is the key to all of it."

Callum swallowed hard.

"What do we do?"

Arthis's expression turned grave, "Prepare."

Chapter 20

The basin's glow dimmed until only faint silver tendrils remained along its surface. The First Light's presence faded like a memory dissolving beneath dawn. Callum's breath slowed as the chamber returned to shape around him, monoliths, stone, spiral engravings, and the faint hum that never fully went away.

Ailín sagged against his shoulder, exhausted but peaceful in a way she hadn't been since Harris Island.

Lila rushed toward them, sliding into the basin's shallow edge.

"Callum! Ailín! Are you both okay?"

Ailín murmured softly.

"I'm tired, Lila."

Lila touched her cheek gently.

"You did so well."

Callum stepped out of the basin, holding Ailín close as though she might vanish if he loosened his grip. His eyes locked on Arthis.

"You said this was the first lesson."

Arthis nodded.

"Yes."

"And what exactly did she do just now?"

Arthis looked at the girl with an expression Callum couldn't decipher, not affection, not calculation, but something quieter.

Ancient.

"She greeted the First Light."

Methos scoffed.

"Most Immortals spend centuries trying to brush against an echo of the First, and your… " He caught himself, gesturing at Ailín, "…your little spark just introduced herself like she was born for it."

Arthis did not disagree.

"She was."

Lila frowned.

"Born for what?"

Arthis turned away, robes whispering.

"The next age."

"Arthis. What's happening outside this island right now?"

The Archivist did not turn but raised one hand. A ripple of energy pulsed along the chamber floor and up the monoliths.

The air shimmered. Mist collected into rough forms. Shadows gathered into moving shapes; Renwick's drones circling overhead like metal vultures circling carrion.

Lila inhaled sharply.

"He found us."

Arthis spoke calmly.

"No.

He found where THOTH was."

Callum stiffened.

"And the Hunter?"

The mist shifted.

A new silhouette approached, tall, broad, monstrous in presence rather than form.

Slower now, but purposeful.

Methos, "He's heading toward the sea."

Cadigan swore quietly.

"He's following our wake."

Callum's voice was tight.

"Can he get onto the island?"

Arthis finally turned.

His answer was quiet.

"He will, and so will Renwick's men."

A chill passed through the chamber.

Ailín pressed her face into Callum's shoulder.

"Callum... I don't want them to come."

He kissed her hair.

"They won't reach you. I promise."

Arthis stepped closer.

"Promises will not stop them."

Callum glared.

"Then what will?"

Arthis lifted a hand toward the monoliths.

"Her becoming what she must."

Lila's eyes widened, full of fear and fury.

"She's a child."

"Yes," Arthis said simply. "And that is why her training must begin immediately."

Callum tightened his grip on Ailín, jaw clenched hard enough to ache.

"You're asking too much."

Arthis studied him.

"You have not yet seen what pursuing forces will do when they discover what she is. You underestimate their desperation."

Cadigan stepped forward.

"Then tell us."

Methos nodded.

"Yes. Enough riddles, Arthis. Spit it out."

Arthis didn't sigh, but the air around him seemed to.

"Renwick has convinced the surviving Watcher Council that Ailín is an existential threat to humanity."

Lila staggered.

"What?! Why?"

Arthis answered without hesitation.

"Because she represents an Immortal child with no cyclical limitations. A spark that grows outside the rules. A spark that could learn without killing."

Methos inhaled sharply.

"Holy hell."

Cadigan's voice dropped.

"So… she could surpass all of us."

Arthis nodded.

"She will. If she survives."

Ailín trembled.

"Callum… I'm scared."

He held her tightly, voice breaking at the edges.

"I know, little one. I know."

The chamber rumbled, not violently, but insistently, like a warning timed with the storm outside.

Arthis turned toward the deeper passageway into the sanctuary.

"We begin now. Time is shorter than even I predicted."

Callum's eyes narrowed.

"How short?"

Arthis answered, "Renwick's men will land within the hour. The Hunter will follow and Boroun watches from far below."

Ailín pressed her hands to Callum's cheeks.

"Don't leave me."

Callum kissed her forehead.

"I won't."

Arthis nodded once.

"Good, because you will train together."

Methos threw his hands up.

"Oh, this should be fun."

Cadigan gripped his sword.

"Callum… whatever happens, we stay with you."

Lila touched his arm.

"And with her."

Callum drew a long breath.

Then another.

He met Arthis's ancient gaze.

"Then let's begin."

The chamber vibrated again. This time, deeper. Heavier.

Like something big and old and inevitable was drawing nearer.

Arthis raised his hand, and the monoliths brightened in a slow spiral, illuminating the next chamber's entrance like the iris of an ancient eye. The glow was neither harsh nor warm, just steady, deliberate, alive.

Ailín stared at the pulsating light, her small fingers tightening around Callum's shirt.

"Callum, it feels like it's waiting for me."

Lila stepped forward immediately.

"Then it can wait longer. She needs rest."

Arthis turned, his expression calm but absolute.

"If we delay, she will not survive the next resonance wave."

Lila stiffened.

"Resonance wave?"

A rumble traveled through the stones beneath their feet, distant, like the heartbeat of something buried deep in the earth.

Methos swallowed hard.

"Boroun."

Cadigan braced a hand on the monolith nearest him.

"He's stirring again?"

Arthis nodded once.

"His awareness… is growing. He senses her awakening."

Ailín buried her face against Callum's neck, trembling.

"I don't want him to see me."

Callum stroked her hair.

"He won't. I'll make sure of it."

Arthis stepped closer, voice still even.

"You cannot shield her from what she is, but you can help her control it, if you allow this."

Callum bit back a surge of instinctive refusal.

Lila grabbed his arm.

"Callum, she's exhausted. Look at her. She can't…"

Ailín lifted her head, eyes shining faintly.

"I can try."

Callum shook his head.

"No. You don't have to… "

Ailín cupped his face with both hands.

"No… I *want* to. I want to stop being scared."

The room fell silent.

Lila closed her eyes, heart twisting.

Cadigan exhaled slowly.

Methos muttered under his breath, "…damn brave kid."

Callum kissed her forehead.

"Alright. I'm with you."

Ailín nodded and wrapped her arms around his neck.

"Together."

Arthis gestured toward the spiraling chamber.

"Then step forward."

While Callum and Ailín approached the glowing entryway, Methos and Cadigan turned toward the corridor leading back outside.

Methos cracked his neck.

"Well, while you two explore the cosmic toddler school, Cadigan and I will try to keep the island from becoming a parking lot for Renwick's army."

Cadigan smirked despite the tension.

"Aye. Someone must greet our guests with proper Highland hospitality."

Methos grinned.

"You mean stabbing."

"Exactly."

Lila rushed to them.

"Wait, what are you two going to do?"

Methos gave her a flat look.

"What we always do when disaster strikes: improvise and attempt not to die."

Cadigan nodded, "The sanctuary amplifies Immortal signatures. If Renwick's men breach the shore, we'll know. If the Hunter arrives first..." He rested a hand on his claymore, "We'll make sure he doesn't reach the child."

Lila's face paled.

"Just the two of you?"

Methos clasped her shoulder.

"Relax, Doctor. I've survived worse odds."

Cadigan added, "And I've survived Methos."

"Hey."

"Come Methos, let us prepare for our guests."

The sanctuary trembled again. This time the quake was sharper.

Arthis raised his head.

"The first helicopter has landed. Half a mile east."

Callum froze, "You can sense them?"

"Yes."

Lila's stomach dropped.

"How many?"

Arthis answered without hesitation, "Many...four helicoptors total."

Callum did some quick calculations, "Four strike teams... that's twenty-four men total. Heavily armed. Renwick is not taking chances."

Outside Methos and Cadigan didn't have much time to look around before they heard the first incoming helicopter approaching. They got to a point that jetted out above the beach that they arrived at just in time to see the fist helicopter touchdown and three others on final approach.

Methos muttered a curse.

"Bloody hell."

A smile came to Cadigan's face, "Ah Methos, It'll be a skoosh, do not worry my friend."

The cliffs above the sanctuary shuddered as another helicopter banked low, cutting a tight arc over the island. Its rotors whipped the mist into spiraling sheets of rain and spray. Searchlights swept across jagged stone, chasing shadows that refused to hold still.

Methos and Cadigan crouched behind a narrow ridge, cloaks pressed flat against the wind.

Cadigan's hand rested on the hilt of his claymore.

Methos's hand rested on nothing.

He didn't need it.

Cadigan eyed him sidelong.

"Please tell me you have a weapon."

Methos scoffed.

"I *am* the weapon."

Cadigan rolled his eyes, "You never get tired of saying that, do you?"

"No," Methos said, "Because it keeps being true."

Below them, Renwick's strike teams hit the ground in staggered formations, black-clad operatives with compact carbines, thermal visors, and drone uplinks feeding battlefield data into wrist-pad HUDs.

Modern weapons. Modern training. Modern intent.

But this was not a modern battleground.

Cadigan's expression hardened.

"Twenty-four men. Four teams. Advanced tech. Tight formation."

Methos smirked.

"And no idea what they've just walked into. I do love an optimist."

Cadigan scanned the teams.

"They're branching. Pairing off into two-man sweeps. Thermal scans active."

Methos grinned.

"Thermal scans? Oh, bless their little hearts."

He stood up.

Cadigan hissed.

"What are you doing?"

"Announcing myself."

"Don't, !"

But it was too late.

Methos stepped into the storm-swept clearing with the casual posture of a man strolling into a pub.

The first two mercenaries turned, rifles snapping upward.

"Hands up!"

Methos raised one hand.

A friendly wave.

"Hello! Yes, very intimidating. Please don't faint."

They fired.

Twin bursts of suppressed gunfire cracked through the air.

Methos tuck and rolled before the sound finished, a ripple of motion faster than the eye could track.

He wasn't in the clearing.

He was *behind* one of the mercenaries.

A single strike to the helmet, a twist.

The soldier crumpled silently.

The other pivoted, firing wildly, but Methos flowed around the bullets as if he were smoke.

Cadigan burst out of hiding.

393

"Methos!"

"What?" Methos called, "It's been centuries since I had cardio!"

Cadigan vaulted down the slope, crashing into the second operative like a battering ram. He slammed the man into a rock face so hard the helmet cracked. A precise pommel strike to the visor dropped the man instantly.

Two down.

Twenty-two to go.

Cadigan retrieved the fallen rifle, checked the chamber, and slung it over his shoulder.

Methos wiped rain from his face, "You always were unsubtle."

Cadigan's smirk was sharp.

"And you always were a show-off."

The wind shifted.

Voices carried up from farther down the ridge.

"They're splitting wide," Methos said, "Smart. They'll try to flank."

Cadigan drew his claymore, "Then we hit them first."

Gunfire can be heard in the distance.

Then, a different pulse; low and cold. Wrong.

Ailín whimpered.

"He's here..."

Callum's looked to her, "Where?"

Arthis lowered his voice.

"The Hunter has reached the shoreline. He is... evaluating the island."

Arthis nodded.

"He senses the old energy. He senses Boroun; He senses her. He does not yet know which direction to take."

Lila shakily, "So we have... minutes? Hours?"

Arthis turned toward the glowing doorway.

"You have but this moment, no more."

Callum stepped into the spiraling chamber with Ailín in his arms.

The air shifted immediately, no longer heavy like the outer sanctuary, but lighter, warmer, humming with potential.

Ailín gasped softly.

"It's like the ground is breathing."

Callum held her closer.

"I'm right here. Whatever happens."

Arthis stood at the threshold.

"Put her down, Callum."

Callum hesitated.

"No."

Arthis's eyes softened.

"Trust me, she will not fall."

Ailín looked up at Callum.

"It's okay."

He knelt slowly and set her on her own feet.

Her glow brightened.

The chamber responded. Symbols ignited in the floor. The walls glowed faintly. The entire room shifted from silver to gold.

Ailín reached out a hand.

"Callum… something's inside me."

Callum steadied her.

"What is it?"

"A door."

"What happens if you open it?"

Ailín looked up at him, eyes bright silver glowing; fear and courage intertwined.

"I think…everything."

The chamber roared with light.

A trio of Renwick's men advanced along the ridge trail, rifles raised, rain streaking off their visors. Their leader barked orders through a commlink.

"Thermal sweep shows two unidentified signatures, moving fast."

A second team answered:

"Copy. Engage."

Too late.

Cadigan dropped from above like a stone, his claymore flashing in the stormlight. He moved with precision, not brutality: a parry, a blade flick at the rifle barrel, a strike to the shoulder that disabled the weapon. A sweep of his leg took the man down.

Methos slipped past Cadigan like shadow, slamming his elbow into the second soldier's visor and wrenching the rifle free.

The third backed away, stumbling.

"S-stand down!"

Methos tilted his head.

"Oh, sweetheart. No."

The mercenary froze, trembling.

Cadigan grabbed the soldier by the vest, lifted him slightly.

"Tell your boss," Cadigan growled, "that he doesn't belong here."

Methos said with amusement, "And mention that his fashion sense is terrible."

Cadigan shoved the man backward.

"GO."

The soldier sprinted downslope, slipping and scrambling in panic.

Methos raised a brow.

"Letting him live? How noble."

Cadigan's jaw tightened.

"He's just a hired man. I don't take heads unless they deserve it."

Methos smirked, "Adorable. You've become soft."

Cadigan pointed his sword at him.

"You're next."

Methos stepped back, laughing, "Oh, if you insist... "

A crack of thunder cut him off.

But not thunder, something else.

The ridge vibrated violently beneath their feet.

Methos's smile vanished, "Oh... that wasn't weather."

Cadigan's eyes widened.

"The Hunter."

Methos nodded grimly.

"And he's almost here."

They stood on the windswept ridge, soaked, armed, aware.

Both Immortals instinctively fell into a stance older than nations Cadigan, sword anchored low, body set to block or cleave, Methos, empty-handed but coiled, a predator in human skin

Cadigan whispered, "You feel it?"

Methos nodded, "Oh yes. He's close.

And he's hungry."

The ground trembled again , heavier this time,closer,
like footsteps large enough to make the island's bones shake.

Methos gave Cadigan a sidelong look.

"Do we run or do we pretend we stand a chance?"

Cadigan rolled his shoulders.

Rain dripping from his hair.

Claymore gleaming.

"We fight."

Methos grinned through the storm, "Excellent. I was hoping you'd
say that."

The ridge lit with lightning , and something vast moved within the
mist below.

The Hunter.

Still distant.

But unmistakable.

Methos exhaled, steadying his breath, "I'll distract him."

Cadigan stared.

"You'll *what*?"

Methos shrugged.

"Relax. I'm very good at not dying."

Cadigan growled, "Just be good at keeping him away from the
sanctuary."

Methos winked, "Always my plan."

They descended into the mist as the Hunter drew near.

And inside the sanctuary, Ailín took her first step toward the door
inside herself.

The mist crawled across the ridge like a living thing, dense enough
that visibility dropped to only a few yards. Wind whipped the fog into
spiraling tendrils that coiled and uncoiled along the ground.

Methos and Cadigan moved down the slope in silence.

Even Methos didn't joke now.

That alone told Cadigan how serious this moment truly was.

The tremor came again, longer this time, like the earth itself
flinched.

Cadigan tightened his grip on his claymore, "Methos... you ever
fought one of these before?"

Methos, without humor, "Once. It didn't go particularly well."

Cadigan swallowed.

"What happened?"

Methos kept walking, "I survived."

A shadow formed in the mist below them, large, indistinct, shifting with predatory patience.

Cadigan lifted his blade.

"Methos... he's tracking by resonance now, not scent."

"Yes," Methos said quietly.

"Which means he knows we're Immortal."

Cadigan exhaled.

"How close do you think he is?"

Methos stopped walking.

"Too close."

The mist ahead moved, parting, inhaling, exhaling.

Something massive shifted its weight.

A low rumble vibrated through Cadigan's boots.

Cadigan murmured, "He's standing right there."

Methos raised both hands slightly, not in surrender, but in readiness, "Hello, old friend..."

But the Hunter did not reveal itself.

Instead, A whisper cut through the fog, "MacLeod..."

Methos froze, "Did he just... "

The mist exploded.

A dark silhouette lunged through the fog, its presence alone knocking both Immortals backward. Methos rolled with the impact, narrowly avoiding being crushed beneath a stone that shattered under the Hunter's weight.

Cadigan brought up his claymore just in time to deflect a sweeping attack that sent sparks flying as ancient steel clashed with something harder than bone.

Cadigan grunted.

"By the clans, he's stronger than rumors!"

Methos kicked off the ground, grabbing Cadigan by the collar and yanking him aside as a massive arm slammed into the earth. The ground cracked.

"Don't admire him!" Methos yelled, "He'll kill you!"

Cadigan spat rain from his mouth.

"I wasn't admiring!"

The Hunter lunged again. This time, they saw it. Not fully, not clearly, but enough. It was tall and broad; a silhouette shaped like a man but moving like an apex predator. It's eyes glowing faintly white through the mist. Pure focus. Pure purpose.

Cadigan attacked first, claymore slicing through the fog.

The Hunter caught the blade mid-swing.

Cadigan's entire body jolted with the force, not breaking the blade, just stopping it. Stopping a sword swung by an Immortal like a toy.

Methos shouted, "CADIGAN, MOVE!"

Cadigan twisted, breaking free just as the Hunter hurled him backward. He slammed into a boulder; breath knocked from his lungs.

Methos darted left, sweeping the Hunter's legs with a fluid motion that would've toppled most Immortals.

It barely made him shift.

Methos's eyes widened, "He's stabilizing."

Cadigan coughed and pushed to his feet.

"What does that mean?!"

"It means," Methos grunted as he dodged a crushing blow, "he's adapting faster than he was in the tunnels!"

Cadigan wiped blood from his lip.

"Then we adapt faster."

Together, they engaged, Methos moving with ancient speed, Cadigan with brutal precision.

For a moment, just a heartbeat, they held him at bay.

Then the ground trembled again.

All of them froze.

"That wasn't him."

Methos looked at the ground.

"No... that's something else."

Inside the Sanctuary

Arthis's eyes snapped open as a deep vibration passed through the sanctuary.

Lila gasped.

"What was that?"

Arthis's voice was grave, "Boroun, he stirs."

Callum jerked his head up from where he knelt with Ailín.

"He's waking?"

Ailín trembled.

"I feel him…he's calling something."

Arthis stepped toward the glowing doorway, worry showing on his face for the first time, "The island cannot hold all three forces at once."

"What three?" Lila asked.

Arthis turned, "The Hunter outside. Boroun below, and the spark in this child."

Callum stood, shielding Ailín.

"What do we do?"

Arthis's gaze was steady, "Finish the lesson."

The mist thinned, just enough to see the ridge clearly.

Renwick's second strike team was arriving from the west, weapons raised.

Cadigan wiped rain from his eyes.

"Great. Hostiles at our back, monster at our front."

Methos cracked his knuckles.

"Well, Cadigan…let's show them why Immortals don't retire."

The Hunter roared.

Renwick's men advanced.

Methos grinned.

"Finally. Some chaos I understand."

Cadigan lifted his claymore with a warrior's calm.

"On you."

Methos crouched low.

"Try and keep up."

And together, they charged.

Callum knelt beside her.

"Ailín… look at me."

Her silver eyes met his, glowing with fear and something else, something rising.

"I can hear the door again…"

He held her hands tight.

"You're not alone. We're opening it together. Only as far as you can go."

She nodded.

Arthis stepped closer.

"Begin."

Ailín inhaled sharply.

The chamber darkened.

The monoliths pulsed.

"I've got you." Callum said.

"I know."

The air cracked with energy,

And Ailín, opened the door.

A shockwave blasted through the sanctuary.

Outside, the Hunter froze mid-strike.

Methos stumbled.

Cadigan steadied his blade.

Renwick's men collapsed to their knees, clutching their helmets.

A light, silver and gold, shot into the sky above the island.

Arthis declared, "The next age begins."

Callum shielded Ailín from the burst of energy.

"We're not ready!" he yelled.

Arthis replied softly,

"She is."

Chapter 21

The shockwave rolled across the island in a blinding flash, white-gold fire spiraling upward like a helix before dissolving into the storm-heavy sky. Every stone pillar in the sanctuary hummed simultaneously, vibrating with a resonance older than any living Immortal.

Callum gasped as the energy rippled through him, knocking him to one knee. His vision blurred at the edges, the world warping into streaks of light and shadow. Ailín clung to him, her small hands glowing like molten silver.

"Callum!" Lila cried, rushing toward them.

Callum forced breath into his lungs, "I'm...I'm alright."

Arthis stepped between them, eyes narrow, watching the last strands of light coil back into Ailín's body, "Do not interrupt. This resonance must settle."

Lila bristled.

"She's a child, not a conduit! She needs space, not rituals!"

Arthis met her gaze calmly, "And I am giving her that space."

Callum held Ailín tightly as her glow dimmed from blinding brilliance to a trembling pulse. Her breathing steadied, but her voice was small.

"I didn't mean to... I barely touched the door..."

Arthis knelt directly in front of her, closer than he'd dared before.

"And yet you opened it more than any Immortal has in ten thousand years."

Ailín stared at him, frightened, "Did I... do something bad?"

"No," Arthis said softly, "You did something inevitable."

Lila's face tightened.

"That's not comforting."

Arthis stood, "It was not meant to be."

The shockwave struck like a battering ram.

Cadigan staggered backward, claymore slipping from his grip. Methos dropped to one knee, clutching his head in both hands.

"Resonance, too strong, !"

Renwick's mercenaries convulsed in synchronized chaos, dropping weapons, tearing off helmets, scrambling back from the epicenter.

The Hunter...

The Hunter froze.

For the first time since his appearance, he was still completely.

Motionless in the mist.

Cadigan panted, forcing himself upright.

"Methos... you alright?"

Methos shook his head sharply, blinking away disorientation.

"No. But I'm alive. Which is something."

Cadigan retrieved his sword.

"What did she do?"

Methos stared at the sky, where faint tendrils of silver still glistened, "She made the island remember something."

Cadigan swallowed.

"Is that... good?"

Methos gave a thin, humorless smile.

"We're about to find out."

The Hunter took a step forward.

Cadigan's grip tightened.

"He's moving again."

Methos muttered:

"Of course he is."

But the Hunter wasn't charging.

He was...tracking the energy trail left by Ailín's surge.

And he wasn't heading toward Methos or Cadigan.

He was heading toward the sanctuary.

Cadigan's blood ran cold, "He's locked onto her."

Callum set Ailín on her feet.

"Sweetheart, can you stand?"

Ailín nodded shakily, "I'm okay... just tired."

Lila brushed hair from her forehead.

"You did enough for one lifetime."

But Ailín shook her head.

"No, Callum needs to do something now."

Callum froze.

"What do you mean?"

Ailín pointed toward the basin.

"The door... opened a tiny bit. And something pushed back. It wants you, too."

Arthis turned toward Callum.

"Her spark recognized you as tether. But for her to stabilize, you must take the next step."

Callum's stomach dropped.

"What step?"

Arthis motioned to the basin.

"You will let me read your resonance fully. No resistance. No shielding."

Callum stepped back, "No. Last time nearly tore me apart."

"This time," Arthis said, "you will not fight me."

Lila stepped between them instantly.

"Absolutely not, not until we understand what just happened to her."

Arthis turned to her patiently.

"What happened to her was awakening. What must happen to him is understanding."

Lila's breath trembled.

"You're not touching him again."

Arthis lowered his voice, "Doctor Serrano...Renwick moves closer. The Hunter approaches, and Boroun stirs."

The ground trembled underfoot, as if to agree.

The sanctuary hummed.

Light flickered across the monoliths.

Callum exhaled.

"Arthis is right. We don't have time."

Lila grabbed his arm, eyes blazing.

"You're not sacrificing yourself for prophecy!"

He touched her cheek gently.

"This isn't sacrifice. It's connection."

Ailín tugged his sleeve.

"Callum…if you don't learn how to hold it, I can't either."

He nodded.

"Alright. We do this together."

Arthis stepped back.

"Prepare yourself."

Callum stepped toward the basin.

Lila, "Callum… please come back."

He kissed her forehead, "I will. I promise."

He placed a hand into the glowing surface, And the chamber erupted.

A second shockwave tore through the sanctuary.

Not as large.

But deeper.

Callum's eyes widened as the world fell away again.

Outside, the Hunter froze, then turned directly toward the sanctuary entrance.

Methos muttered, "Oh hell. He felt him."

Cadigan steadied his blade.

"Felt who?"

Methos answered:

"Callum."

Lightning illuminated the ridge.

And the Hunter stepped forward.

Light surged around Callum's hand the moment he touched the basin again, not blinding this time, but dense, concentrated, almost tactile. The surface pulsed beneath his palm like the skin of a great animal breathing slow and deep.

Ailín steadied herself beside him, her glow faint but steady.

Arthis watched with the calm detachment of a historian observing the unfolding of long-predicted events.

"Do not resist this time, Callum."

Callum grit his teeth as the hum coursed up his arm and into his chest, "I'm… trying."

Arthis moved closer, voice lowering.

"What she unleashed a moment ago was not power. It was instinct. Untrained. Unanchored."

Ailín's voice was small.

"It scared me."

Callum squeezed her hand.

"Then we learn how to control it. Together."

The basin pulsed again.

This time the resonance didn't knock him backward. Instead, it flowed into him, warm at first, then growing heavier, like water filling a vessel too quickly.

The ridge overlooking the sanctuary had become a battlefield. Mist swirled. Sleet drove sideways in sheets. Lightning crawled like white fire across the low clouds.

Renwick's strike teams regrouped after the shockwave, shaken but reorienting with soldierly precision.

"Team Delta, sweep left!"

"Thermals unstable, we lost half our readouts!"

"Something's moving in the fog, eleven o'clock!"

Cadigan took a defensive stance.

"Methos… that shockwave made them erratic."

Methos cracked his neck, "Which makes them unpredictable. And twitchy. And very likely to shoot at anything with a pulse."

Cadigan lifted his claymore.

"Good thing we can't die."

Methos smirked.

"Speak for yourself. I quite enjoy staying alive."

Cadigan gave him a hard look.

"And staying alive means stopping the Hunter here. Away from her."

Methos's humor faded, "Agreed."

Down the slope, Renwick's mercenaries formed staggered lines, rifles raised, scanning the mist with twitchy, uncertain movements.

"Thermal picking up one... no, two signatures, closing fast!"

"Negative, resonance distortion...something's interfering with sensors!"

From the fog, two shapes emerged.

Cadigan.

Methos.

The soldiers fired.

Methos ducked under a volley of suppressed rounds, shifting sideways with uncanny speed, impossibly fluid. Cadigan parried incoming fire with the flat of his claymore, sparks showering into the night.

A soldier shouted, "What the *hell* are they?!"

Cadigan answered by closing the distance in three strides and knocking him unconscious with a single strike.

Methos disarmed two others, but then, a new tremor.

Closer.

Too close.

Methos froze mid-block, "Oh no."

Cadigan swung around, "What now?"

Methos's face tightened, "He's found a path."

Cadigan's stomach dropped, "The Hunter?"

Methos nodded, gaze fixed on the shifting fog.

"He's not tracking us anymore. He's tracking *them.* Callum and the child."

Cadigan raised his sword.

"Then we make damn sure he doesn't reach them."

Methos muttered,

"I'll do my best not to get ripped in half."

Cadigan smirked, "You've survived worse."

Methos gave a nervous laugh.

"Actually... no. Not really."

Callum gasped as a wave of resonance pushed into him. It wasn't painful, not like the first time, but overwhelming. He fell to both knees, still holding Ailín's hand.

Arthis leaned forward, watching with hawklike focus.

"Good. You endure more than most."

Ailín's glow brightened, "Callum... the door is opening again."

Arthis stepped closer, "Then step through."

Callum blinked, "What?"

Arthis extended a hand toward the basin., **"She showed you the First Light. Now it will show you something else."**

The basin shifted beneath them, shimmering, swirling, deepening.

Ailín grabbed Callum's hand tighter.

"Callum... I'm scared again."

He squeezed back, it's alright. We do this together."

Arthis nodded.

"Yes. Together. For what lies beyond this threshold cannot be borne by one alone."

Outside, the fog parted.

The Hunter stepped into view.

Methos inhaled sharply.

"Cadigan...no running. No retreat."

Cadigan raised his claymore.

"Wouldn't dream of it."

Inside the sanctuary, Callum's hand plunged deeper into the basin's light,

The door opened wider.

The door of resonance opened fully around Callum and Ailín.

The basin dissolved beneath their feet, replaced by a landscape that was not a place at all, an expanse of shimmering air where echoes of Immortals drifted like afterimages, their shapes half-formed, translucent, weighted with memory.

Ailín clung to his hand, breath shallow, "Callum... they're looking at us."

Callum swallowed, "There are too many...Dozens. Hundreds.

As if the entire lineage of Immortals had gathered inside this one vision-space.

Arthis's voice echoed faintly from outside the basin.

"These are not ghosts, not lives you took. These are the unborn echoes. The future that follows you."

Ailín tugged on Callum's coat.

"Callum, one of them is calling me."

Callum knelt beside her.

"Which one?"

She looked around, eyes glowing silver,

and pointed at a figure standing farther back in the shifting haze.

Tall.

Still.

Hollow around the edges, like a memory not yet formed.

Arthis's voice sharpened,"Do not go to it."

Ailín frowned.

"Why not?"

Arthis answered:

"Because that one is not yours. That is *who hunts you.*"

Callum stiffened.

"The Hunter?"

Arthis's voice echoed like stone cracking.

"No. What he once was."

Ailín's eyes widened, "He's sad."

Callum pulled her close.

"Don't go to him."

She nodded, "I won't."

The vision-space pulsed. Shadows warped.

Something darker moved behind the gathering of echoes,

something with vast shoulders

and a presence that made the air colder.

Ailín whimpered.

"That's the scary one."

Callum whispered, "Boroun."

Arthis's voice answered faintly, "Yes. He watches the door too."

The echo-shadow leaned in.

Ailín grabbed Callum's hand tighter.

"But he doesn't want to hurt me...

not yet."

Callum's breath caught.

"Then what does he want?"

Ailín whispered:

"To be... whole."

The fog split open with a violent gust as the Hunter stepped fully onto the ridge.

Rain sheeted off his armor in streams. Cracks of Quickening pulsed along his chest and shoulders like scars that refused to heal.

Cadigan planted his feet.

"Methos, left side."

Methos nodded, slipping into a stance that was too calm for the circumstances.

"Try not to get decapitated. I don't want to be the one to drag your head home."

"Focus," Cadigan growled.

The Hunter tilted his head, eyes glowing dim white, not with emotion but with calculation. He had no rage. No hesitation, only *purpose.*

He moved faster than either of them expected.

Cadigan brought his claymore down in a defensive arc. The Hunter caught it mid-swing, *caught a two-handed blade in one hand*, and twisted, nearly wrenching the weapon from Cadigan's grip.

Methos darted behind him, striking at the back of his knee, but the Hunter shifted weight instantly, forcing Methos to dodge a stomp that cracked the ground open.

Cadigan shouted, "He's faster than before!"

Methos ducked another blow.

"Because he's stabilizing! Ailín's surge woke *something* in him!"

Cadigan's eyes widened.

"Lucky us...then we move faster."

Methos smirked.

The Hunter lunged again.

This time, he grabbed Cadigan by the throat, lifting him clean off the ground.

Cadigan kicked, metal screeching under his boot as he tried to break free.

Methos sprinted forward, but the Hunter backhanded Methos so hard he skidded across wet stone, carving a groove into the mud.

Methos groaned, "That… was unpleasant."

He rolled sideways as the Hunter's foot smashed into the earth where his head had been a heartbeat earlier.

Cadigan gasped, still held aloft.

The Hunter turned, toward the sanctuary.

Toward Ailín.

Cadigan's eyes went wide, "No, you're not, getting to her!"

With a burst of Immortal strength, Cadigan shoved his sword upward, slicing through the Hunter's armor at the shoulder. Sparks and Quickening burst out like shattered ice.

The Hunter dropped him.

Cadigan hit the ground hard but rolled away instinctively.

Methos was on his feet instantly, "You bought us ten seconds. Don't waste them."

They braced for another attack,

But the Hunter didn't charge them.

He turned he looked toward the sanctuary entrance, and

And he *started walking.*

Purposefully.

Methos uttered, "…oh, that's not good."

Callum pulled Ailín close, turning her away from the Boroun-shadow.

"Ailín, look at me.

Don't look at him.

Don't listen."

She breathed fast, panicked.

"He's asking something…"

Callum tightened his grip.

"What is he asking?"

Ailín swallowed.

"He wants…

to know my name."

Callum went cold.

"No. He doesn't get that. He gets nothing."

Arthis's voice cut through the vision, "Good. Do not share names with the old ones."

Lila paced the basalt floor outside the basin, voice cracking.

"What the hell does that mean?!"

Arthis replied calmly:

"Names carry power in resonance realms. If she gives him her name, he will have a claim on her."

Callum stiffened.

"No."

Ailín buried her face into his chest.

"I didn't tell him."

He exhaled shakily.

"Good girl."

Arthis stepped closer.

"Callum. The time for gentle revelation has passed. She must learn control not later, not soon, now."

Callum lifted her.

"Then show us how."

Arthis extended his hand.

The sanctuary shook again.

Outside, Methos and Cadigan both turned toward the entrance.

Methos, "He's coming to her."

Cadigan tightened his grip, "Then let's make sure he dies trying."

Inside the resonance realm, Boroun's shadow leaned closer.

Ailín whimpered, "Callum...he knows we're here."

Callum held her tight.

"He's not taking you."

Arthis raised both hands.

"Prepare yourselves."

The basin flared.

Outside, the Hunter reached the sanctuary doorway. And everything predicted by Arthis started to converge.

Callum could feel Ailín shaking in his arms.

The resonance vision pulsed around them, echoes swirling, shadows shifting, the not-yet-formed specter of Boroun pressing against the half-opened door. The air trembled with a pressure that felt like the entire history of Immortals was leaning forward, waiting for Ailín to make a decision she didn't understand.

Ailín clung to Callum desperately.

"Callum… the door… it's trying to open by itself…"

Callum knelt and wrapped both arms around her.

"Then we stop it."

A whisper rumbled through the echo realm, deep and mournful.

Not words.

A plea.

Ailín whimpered, "He's sad…He's so sad…"

Arthis's voice echoed from outside the basin.

"Sorrow can be a weapon, child.

Do not let it pull you in."

Callum shifted, shielding her.

"What does he want?!"

Arthis answered, "Everything."

Ailín breathed faster.

"He wants me to help him."

Callum stiffened.

"No. You don't help him. You don't *answer* him."

Ailín pressed her forehead to his.

"I'm trying! But he's so loud…"

Arthis stepped forward, voice rising for the first time.

"Close the door, Ailín."

She shook her head, "I don't know how!"

"Then *I* will show you," Arthis said, reaching toward the basin.

Callum looked up sharply.

"What are you… "

BOOM!

The sanctuary shook violently.

Dust fell from the ceiling.

Monoliths flickered.

The echo realm wavered.

Arthis's eyes snapped toward the entrance.

"He is here."

Rain hammered the sanctuary's carved archway as the Hunter emerged from the mist, stepping onto ancient stone with slow, inexorable certainty.

Methos staggered, clutching his ribs.

Cadigan raised his claymore, chest heaving.

"Hold...the...Line."

The Hunter tilted his head, studying them both.

He moved.

Methos intercepted, but the Hunter batted him aside like an insect.

Cadigan swung his blade, the Hunter caught it again.

Twisted.

Snapped it nearly in half.

Cadigan flew backward into a stone pillar.

Methos roared, "CADIGAN!"

But Cadigan was unconscious, body slumped at the base of the monolith.

The Hunter turned.

Not toward Methos.

Toward the sanctuary's entrance.

Toward Ailín.

Methos forced himself upright, every instinct screaming.

He ran.

"HEY!...HEY!...OVER HERE!"

He hurled a broken spear from the ridge's debris,

It hit the Hunter's shoulder and shattered like glass.

The Hunter did not look back.

Methos raggedly, "Oh no. No, no, no..."

Ailín screamed.

The echo realm convulsed as the not-yet-formed Boroun pressed harder against the door. Callum held her, eyes burning from the strain.

"Close it! Close it now!"

Ailín sobbed.

"I'm trying, !"

Arthis stepped into the basin, placing both hands on its trembling surface.

"Callum, lend her strength."

Callum grabbed Ailín's shoulders.

"You're not alone. I'm here. I'm with you. Always."

Ailín's glow brightened.

The echo realm pulsed.

Arthis extended both hands.

"Together!"

Callum shouted, "CLOSE IT!"

Ailín yelled, and slammed the door.

Light exploded outward. Boroun's shadow recoiled. A shockwave ripped through the sanctuary. Stone pillars cracked. Monoliths shuddered. The basin threw Callum backward, but he held Ailín tight against him, turning mid-air to shield her as they hit the floor.

Lila rushed to them.

"Ailín! Callum!"

Callum gasped for breath, hugging Ailín close.

"I'm here...I'm here..."

Ailín buried her face in his shoulder.

"It's closed...I did it..."

Arthis exhaled, "Good. Very good."

Then his eyes snapped toward the sanctuary entrance.

A dark silhouette filled the arched doorway - silent and massive, Dripping with rain and resonance.

Ailín's glow flickered.

"Callum..."

Lila's breath caught in her throat.

"No..."

"He has come for her,"said Arthis.

Callum rose slowly, placing Ailín behind him.

"You don't touch her."

The Hunter stepped forward, but froze.

Not because of Callum.

Not because of Arthis.

But because Ailín stepped into view beside Callum, trembling but radiant with a faint silver glow.

The Hunter's head tilted.

He inhaled.

As if sensing her essence.

Ailín uttered, "I know you."

Callum flinched.

"Ailín, don't, "

The Hunter took a single step forward.

Ailín stepped back.

Callum reached for his sword.

Arthis raised a hand,

"He will not strike yet."

Callum shouted, "Why?!"

Arthis's eyes locked on the Hunter.

"Because she closed the door."

Callum stared.

"So he can't take her?"

Arthis shook his head slowly.

"No. Because now… he wants to open it."

The Hunter took another step.

Ailín whimpered.

Callum held her tight, voice breaking, "You'll have to get through me."

The Hunter's eyes flared white.

Chapter 22

The sanctuary fell utterly still, not quiet, still. As if even the air knew something terrible had stepped inside. The Hunter stood framed in the ancient archway, a silhouette carved from shadow and storm. His cracked armor gleamed faintly in the monolith-light, beads of rain sliding from his shoulders like molten silver. The faint white glow in his eyes pulsed once, slow, deliberate, predatory.

Ailín's small hand trembled as she clutched Callum's sleeve.

"Callum...he's so loud now."

Callum positioned himself squarely between her and the creature.

"I know. Stay behind me."

Lila circled around, pulling Ailín into her arms, but Ailín struggled, refusing to hide completely. Her glow brightened at the edges, not consciously, but in fearful instinct.

The Hunter's gaze snapped to that glow instantly.

Arthis stepped forward, standing between the monoliths like a sentinel carved from history.

"Hunter."

The creature turned its head toward him.

Arthis continued, "You step into my sanctuary uninvited."

The Hunter did not speak.

He never spoke.

But his presence pressed outward, an oppressive, heavy force that tasted of violence, hunger, and inevitability.

Methos staggered in through the archway, bloodied and barely upright.

"Callum, you need to move.He's locked onto her."

Cadigan stumbled in after him, claymore broken, one arm limp at his side.

"He nearly killed us both."

Lila pulled Ailín behind her.

"You can't have her," she said, voice shaking, "You can't."

The Hunter took a single step forward.

The sanctuary itself reacted.

The monoliths flickered.

The stone floor vibrated.

Dust rained from the ceiling in delicate threads.

Arthis spoke softly, almost reverently:

"He is drawn to what she is becoming. Not her life, her spark."

Callum's jaw clenched.

"He's not touching her.

Not while I'm breathing."

Arthis looked at him.

"Then prepare yourself."

The Hunter took another step.

He was enormous up close, not a giant, but impossibly dense, radiating a pressure that made Callum's bones ache.

The creature stopped just a few feet away, head tilting, studying Callum as a wolf studies a wounded stag, assessing, calculating, deciding how best to break him.

Callum squared his stance.

"If you're after me, you go through me."

The Hunter's eyes flickered,

Not dismissal, just recognition.

Arthis murmured, "He remembers you from the tunnels. You wounded him."

Methos wheezed a laugh, "Well done, Callum. Now he'll kill you first."

The Hunter stepped closer.

Callum drew the Katana in a slow, deliberate motion. The ancient katana hissed as its edge caught the sanctuary's glow, reflecting it in a line of white fire.

Ailín inhaled softly.

"It doesn't like that sword."

Arthis nodded.

"No. It remembers that blade as well."

The Hunter extended one hand, slowly, toward Callum's chest.

Callum raised the Katana.

"No further."

For the first time since entering the sanctuary, the Hunter stopped. Waiting.

"He's not getting past me."

Ailín squeezed Lila's hand.

"He's waiting…
for something."

Cadigan spat blood.

"What? Permission?"

Methos shook his head, eyes widening, "…no. He's waiting for the next surge."

Ailín stiffened.

Callum turned.

"What surge?"

Ailín's voice trembled:

"He wants me to open the door again."

Callum's blood ran cold.

"No. Absolutely not."

Arthis whispered, "And yet… she may have to."

Callum rounded on him.

"Why?!"

Arthis answered:

"Because only someone who has touched the door can push him back."

Ailín whimpered.

"Callum…"

He knelt immediately, holding her face in both hands.

"You're not opening anything.
Not for him.
Not ever."

Ailín's eyes filled with tears.

"But if I don't...he'll hurt you."

Callum swallowed.

"I'd rather die standing in front of you than live knowing you opened that door for him."

The Hunter took another step forward.

Arthis held out a hand.

"Prepare yourselves."

Callum rose, sword ready.

Lila stepped beside him.

Methos and Cadigan took their positions, bloodied but unbowed.

Ailín's glow flickered violently as she grabbed Lila's sleeve.

"Something else is coming..."

Arthis inhaled sharply, "Yes.Boroun."

The sanctuary shook.

Cracks spiraled across the floor.

A distant roar vibrated through the island's bones.

The Hunter stood still,
as if savoring the storm.

Arthis declared, "The last time these forces converged... the world changed."

Callum lifted the Katana.

"Then let's make damn sure it changes our way."

The Hunter stepped forward,

For a heartbeat, no one moved.

Callum, sword raised.

The Hunter, looming over them.

Ailín, trembling like a flickering candle.

Lila, shielding her with bare hands and all the courage in the world.

Methos, leaning on a cracked pillar, refusing to fall.

Cadigan, half-conscious but lifting his broken claymore anyway.

Arthis, still as a carved god.

The sanctuary groaned under the weight of Immortal power converging in one place.

The Hunter struck first.

A blur of motion, silent, impossibly fasta blow aimed directly at Callum's chest.

Callum braced, the Katana absorbing the full force with a burst of white sparks.

The impact hurled Callum backward, sliding across the stone floor.

Lila screamed.

"CALLUM!"

He hit the ground hard but rolled, coming up with the blade between himself and the monster.

The Hunter didn't press.

Not immediately.

He had seen Callum survive similar blows before.

He was learning.

Methos spat blood and pushed off the wall.

"Callum! He's reading your stance, don't let him fix your rhythm!"

Callum moved sideways, adjusting his grip.

Lila pulled Ailín behind a monolith, but Ailín refused to fully hide. Her silver glow pulsed in sync with the sanctuary's heartbeat.

The Hunter felt it.

He turned toward her.

Ailín whimpered.

"Callum... he's pulling again... like before..."

Callum roared, "HEY!...I'm your fight!"

He charged.

A rare thing happened then,

The Hunter turned back to face him.

Not out of fear.

Not out of threat.

Respect.

Or something like it.

Callum swung the Katana in a clean arc. The Hunter caught the blade with his forearm, but this time, unlike the broken weapons of before, the Katana *bit* into him.

A spray of white-blue Quickening burst from the wound.

The Hunter froze.

Callum stared.

"Did I, ?"

Arthis answered without turning:

"Yes. You wounded him. Again."

The Hunter's head snapped toward Callum, And the roar that followed was unlike anything human.

Cadigan staggered to his feet, clutching his fractured claymore.

"If he bleeds… we can kill him."

Methos shook his head, "No. He bleeds because he wants to. It tells him something."

Cadigan frowned, "Tells him what?"

Methos, "Where to strike next."

The Hunter launched forward.

Callum barely got the Katana up in time before the creature seized him by the throat and *lifted him off the ground.* His boots kicked, scraping stone. His grip loosened. His vision blurred.

Lila cried out, "NO!"

Ailín screamed, reaching out blindly, and her glow erupted.

A shockwave blasted from her tiny form, smashing into the Hunter's back. The creature staggered forward, dropping Callum as the energy rippled through his armor.

The Hunter turned.

Slowly and deliberately.

He looked at Ailín, not with hunger. Not with curiosity.

Ailín yelled, terrified, "Don't look at me!"

Callum crawled between them.

"Stay back! Stay with Lila!"

But the Hunter stepped toward them.

Arthis finally intervened.

He lifted his hand,

Stone beneath the Hunter's feet rippled like water,

and giant slabs of basalt rose from the floor, slamming into the creature from both sides.

The Hunter caught one slab mid-swing and broke it with a single punch.

A cloud of stone dust filled the air.

Cadigan stared, "Arthis, what are you?!"

The Archivist ignored the question.

He raised both hands.

The monoliths brightened.

The sanctuary floor trembled.

Ancient resonance flared like a tidal wave.

Arthis spoke, "Leave this place."

The Hunter took a single step forward and shattered Arthis's resonance wave like ripping silk.

Arthis recoiled, a flicker of shock crossing his ancient features.

Methos hissed through his teeth.

"He countered the Archivist. That's... new."

Lila pressed Ailín against her chest.

"Callum, what do we do?!"

Callum rose unsteadily, Katana shining in his hand.

"We fight. We hold him as long as we can."

Ailín grabbed his hand.

"No...we run."

Callum froze.

"What?"

Ailín trembled.

"Callum...this place is too loud."Tears filled her eyes, "He's not alone... Boroun's coming too..."

Arthis's expression sharpened.

"The barrier between realms is thinning. Boroun senses her awakening."

Methos and Cadigan exchanged horrified looks.

Lila shook her head.

"We can't fight both. We can barely fight one."

Arthis spoke plainly, "You must flee deeper into the sanctuary. To the inner vaults."

Callum's grip tightened around the Katana.

"We can't outrun him."

Arthis locked eyes with him.

"No. But you can outlast him... if you move now."

The Hunter took another step.

Ailín started to cry softly, "I don't want him to take me..."

Callum sheathed his fear.

He lifted her into his arms, "He won't."

He looked at Lila.

"Stay close."

He turned to Methos and Cadigan.

"Hold the door."

Methos cracked his neck, bloody but defiant, "I was planning on it."

Cadigan raised his broken blade.

"Aye. We'll send him to hell."

Callum nodded once.

"Thank you."

Arthis extended his hand toward a cavernous passage behind the monoliths.

"Go. Now."

Callum ran.

Lila at his side.

Ailín glowing in his arms.

The sanctuary shook again, a deeper, older rumble, Boroun awakening in the dark below.

Methos and Cadigan stepped between the Hunter and the passage.

The Hunter leaned forward, eyes blazing.

Methos murmured, "Come on then, monster…let's dance."

The moment Callum, Lila, and Ailín vanished into the inner corridor, the Hunter moved.

Cadigan barely got his broken claymore up before the creature struck. The blade snapped the rest of the way, clattering across the stone. Cadigan absorbed the blow with his forearms, bone crunching under the force. He flew backward and skidded across the basalt floor, gasping.

Methos didn't hesitate.

He didn't run.

He didn't shout.

He didn't posture.

He hurled himself at the Hunter with the desperation of someone who understood exactly how thin the margin of survival truly was.

His fist connected with the Hunter's jaw, not enough to harm, but enough to pull his attention.

"Over here, you prehistoric arsehole!"

The Hunter turned.

Methos grinned through blood.

"Good. Now follow directions."

He dove sideways as the Hunter lunged, the creature's arm smashing into a monolith with a sound like thunder. A spiderweb crack spread across the ancient stone pillar.

Cadigan pushed to his feet again, grimacing as he relocated his dislocated shoulder with a sickening pop.

"Ye big bastard…"

The Hunter pivoted toward Cadigan.

Methos launched himself onto the Hunter's back, locking his arms around the creature's neck.

From the doorway, Arthis shouted, "METHOS, DON'T, "

He was too late.

The Hunter grabbed Methos by both arms and threw him over his shoulder. Methos hit the stone hard enough to crack it, collapsing in a heap.

"ow."

Cadigan snarled, charging forward with nothing but fists and fury. He slammed into the Hunter's torso, grabbing the creature's cracked armor plates and driving him backward.

The Hunter dug his heels into the floor, unmovable.

Cadigan gritted his teeth, "You're not going, through, that, door!"

The Hunter lifted Cadigan by the throat and slammed him into the wall.

Cadigan's vision flickered.

Methos staggered upright.

"Cadigan, stay with me, stay, "

The Hunter turned as if swatting an insect and struck Methos across the face with an open hand.

Methos flew sideways, hitting a stone column and crumpling.

For a split second, everything stopped.

The Hunter stood alone in the chamber.

Cadigan lay gasping. Methos was dazed but alive.

Arthis watched, eyes narrowed, hands twitching with restrained energy.

From the corridor, the sanctuary shuddered again, the deep,

resonant groan of something vast stirring beneath the earth.

Boroun.

"The convergence draws near..." Arthis said.

Callum ran with Ailín held close, Lila matching his pace, breath sharp and fast.

The inner corridors of the sanctuary were different, narrower, smoother, carved with lines that glowed faint blue instead of silver. The air felt charged, as though the walls themselves were alive.

Ailín trembled, "He's coming."

Callum held her tighter, "He's not reaching you. Not here."

Lila touched Ailín's hair.

"We're going to be okay. We have to be."

A series of carvings illuminated across the walls, reacting to Ailín's glow. Each line brightened as they passed, forming a path ahead.

Lila pointed, "Look, it's guiding us."

Callum slowed for a heartbeat.

"Arthis said the inner vaults are older. Who built these?"

Ailín leaned her head against his shoulder.

"Not him."

Lila frowned.

"Not Arthis?"

Ailín shook her head.

"No. Someone... before."

Callum's chest tightened.

"How far before?"

Ailín looked up at him with silver eyes.

"Before everything."

Rain pounded the sanctuary's exterior as Renwick's strike teams finally reached the carved threshold. Four soldiers crouched in formation, weapons raised, scanning the archway with wide eyes.

"Team Lambda, movement inside, unknown hostile, high thermal distortion!"

"Is that...is that a man?!"

"Negative, readings unstable."

Then the Hunter stepped into view.

A hush fell over the comms.

The team leader whispered, "...what the hell..."

The Hunter looked at them with the same attention one might give a falling leaf.

Then he moved.

One soldier fired a burst,

the bullets ricocheted off the Hunter's armor and hit the wall.

Another soldier backed away.

"What *is* that?!"

The Hunter grabbed the nearest operative by the vest and lifted him off the ground. The man screamed until the Hunter snapped his neck with a twist.

Chaos erupted.

Gunfire, shouts, and panic

Cadigan, still shaking, crawling toward Methos, breathed, "They're dead...all of 'em."

Methos grabbed Cadigan's arm, pulling him behind a fallen column.

"Let them run. If they survive, good. If not, less noise."

Cadigan coughed blood.

"You've a dark sense of humor."

Methos spat red.

"It's gotten me this far."

Callum slowed as they entered a vast, circular chamber.

This one was different – colder, older.

A massive stone mosaic covered the floor, etched with swirling patterns that radiated outward from a central emblem, a shape resembling a sun split into three pieces.

The moment Ailín stepped inside, the chamber hummed.

Ailín clutched Callum's shirt.

"It doesn't want me here."

Lila touched the central emblem.

"What is this place?"

Callum turned to Ailín.

"Ailín... talk to me."

She looked around, eyes wide.

"It's a prison."

Callum froze.

"For who?"

Ailín pointed at the center of the mosaic.

"For him."

Callum swallowed.

"Boroun."

Ailín nodded slowly.

"He's not in it… but it remembers him."

"What does that even mean?"

Ailín didn't answer.

She stared at the emblem, her glow intensifying against her will.

"Callum…he's calling me again."

Callum dropped to his knees in front of her.

"You don't listen. You hear me? You don't answer."

She shook.

"But he's here…"

The chamber trembled. Stone dust fell from the ceiling, and a low moan echoed through the vault.

Boroun was waking.

The Hunter stepped over Renwick's fallen men and re-entered the sanctuary, rain trAilíng off his armor.

Methos forced himself upright, positioning his body between the Hunter and the inner corridor.

Cadigan groaned but mirrored the stance.

Methos wiped blood from his lip.

"Cadigan…I think we're out of clever ideas."

Cadigan managed a smile through the pain.

"Aye… but we've no shortage of stubbornness."

The Hunter moved toward them.

Methos inhaled sharply.

"Then remember, head or heart, nothing else slows him."

Cadigan nodded once.

"Together?"

"Together."

They charged.

The Hunter met them halfway.
The chamber shook with the impact.

Back in the vault, Callum held Ailín as she trembled violently.
Lila looked at the trembling stone beneath their feet.
"Callum…if this is a prison…"
Callum uttered, "It's fAilíng."
Ailín cried softly.
"He's waking up…
and he's so… hungry."
Callum lifted her up, heart pounding.
"We're leaving. Now."
A deep voice breathed from below.
Callum held Ailín close.
Lila backed against him.
From outside the vault, faint and fading, Methos screamed, "CALLUM, RUN!"
The vault rumbled.
The door sealed behind them with a grinding, ancient finality. Dust rained from the seam where the stone met the frame. No hinges. No handles. No mechanical systems. Whatever locked them in had been built into the bones of the earth.
Lila rushed to the door and slammed her palms against it, "ARTHIS! OPEN THIS! ARTHIS!"
Her voice echoed in the chamber, swallowed by the cold, still air.
Callum held Ailín tight, her glow flaring in frightened pulses.
"Callum…" she whimpered, "it's getting louder."
Callum knelt, placing a steadying hand against her cheek.
"What is?"
Ailín pointed downward.
"The sad one."
Callum's throat tightened.
"Boroun."
Ailín nodded.
"He's pushing. Trying to reach us – me.

The floor trembled again, a deep, rolling vibration like something enormous shifting far beneath the stone mosaic.

Lila spun, panic creeping into her voice.

"Callum, that floor isn't just reacting, it's *responding* to her!"

Callum rose slowly, sword drawn, scanning the chamber with a warrior's instinct.

"Arthis said this place predates him. So if it's responding… it's by design."

Lila shook her head.

"Design by who?"

Ailín whispered, almost inaudibly, "By the First."

Before Callum could ask what she meant, the mosaic beneath them lit with faint white lines,

thin veins of Quickening crawling outward like cracks in ice.

Lila grabbed Callum's arm.

"What the hell is happening?!"

Ailín shivered violently.

"He's calling me…

but something else is too…"

Callum's grip tightened on the Katana.

"We're not answering either."

Ailín's lip trembled.

"It hurts…"

Callum knelt and pressed his forehead to hers.

"Stay with me, little one. You hear me? Stay with me."

She nodded weakly.

The impact of the Hunter's blow sent Methos and Cadigan skidding across the sanctuary floor. Cadigan's back hit a cracked monolith, knocking breath from his lungs.

Methos rolled to his feet, barely.

"Cadigan, up!"

Cadigan pushed through the pain.

"I'm up! I'm up, ye bastard, "

The Hunter advanced, moving with terrible calm.

Methos spat blood and cracked his neck.

"Alright. Round nine hundred."

Cadigan raised the shattered sword blade like a dagger.

"We can't let him get past us."

Methos grinned through the exhaustion.

"Funny. I was thinking the same."

The Hunter lunged.

Cadigan threw himself into the path, smashing the broken blade against the Hunter's wrist. Methos struck from behind, slamming a knee into the creature's spine.

For one glorious second, the Hunter staggered.

Then he seized Cadigan by the torso, lifted him into the air, and hurled him into Methos.

They hit the floor in a heap, both groaning.

Cadigan wheezed, "We're losing…"

Methos wiped blood from his lips.

"We lost five minutes ago. Now we're just being dramatic about it."

The Hunter advanced.

One blow.

That's all it would take.

He raised his arm.

Methos, "…Callum… hurry…"

Ailín gasped as a cold wave of resonance surged from the mosaic.

Callum caught her.

"Ailín, !".

She was listening.

Her silver eyes widened.

"Callum… he's talking."

"What is he saying?"

Ailín's voice went hollow.

"He says…'I am broken. Help me.'"

The chamber trembled.

Lila stepped back, terrified.

"No. No, Ailín, don't answer him, don't *think* toward him, "

Ailín flinched as another wave hit.

"It hurts… he's hurting… everything hurts…"

"Sweetheart, look at me!" Callum cupped her face. "Ailín! You don't answer him!"

But Ailín looked past him.

Down.

Through the floor.

Her eyes glowed brighter.

"Callum...he says he knows you."

Callum froze, "What?"

"He knows your echo."

The Katana hummed in his hand, vibrating against his palm.

Lila stepped back.

"What echo?!"

Callum clenched his jaw.

"If he's talking to her through resonance, he might be sensing Arkael, "

Callum's stomach dropped.

"Arthis said Arkael was one of the First."

Ailín trembled.

"And Boroun says...Arkael was the one who locked him away."

The chamber convulsed.

Stone cracked under their feet.

Boroun stirred violently, shaking the vault.

Callum pulled Ailín close.

"You don't talk to him, Ailín. You don't owe him anything!"

Ailín sobbed.

"He's so lonely..."

Lila grabbed Callum's arm.

"Callum, if she breaks here, "

"I know."

He stood, holding Ailín, sword in hand.

"Then nobody gets in. Nobody gets near her."

The vault shook harder.

A massive crack split the mosaic.

A low, mournful rasp rose from the depths,

The voice of something ancient.

The Hunter reached Methos and Cadigan.

He raised both hands.

Two quick deaths.

Cadigan shakily braced his broken sword.

Methos lifted trembling fists.

The Hunter lowered his arm to strike,

And the floor exploded beneath him.

A blast of ancient energy erupted from the vault below, ripping upward like a geyser of white-blue resonance.

Methos and Cadigan were thrown back again.

The Hunter stumbled, armor splitting further, white light pouring from the cracks.

The Hunter roared, for the first time, a sound of shock and rage.

Arthis stepped forward.

"Boroun... awakens."

The vault cracked open beneath Callum's boots. He held Ailín tight as the entire chamber shifted, stone grinding loudly.

Ailín screamed, "CALLUM, HE'S COMING!"

Callum lifted her.

"I've got you, just hold on... "

Lila grabbed his shoulder.

"What do we do?!"

Callum's eyes locked on the widening crack, "We run."

Above them, the Hunter regained balance, glowing brighter, drawn not just to Ailín now, but to Boroun's awakening.

Chapter 23

The floor split beneath Callum's feet with a sound like the earth itself was tearing apart. A wide crack ripped across the central mosaic, glowing white-blue as raw resonance bled upward from the darkness below.

Ailín screamed and wrapped her arms around his neck.

"CALLUM, !"

"I've got you!" Callum shouted, clutching her with one arm while bracing the other against the collapsing stone.

Lila grabbed his coat, pulling herself toward him as the vault pitched violently to the side.

"What's happening? What's happening?!"

Ailín gasped, face buried against Callum.

"He's waking…he's waking now…"

Callum didn't need Arthis to explain.

Boroun.

The ancient Immortal they'd only glimpsed as a shadow in the resonance realm…was rising, And the vault, his prison, was shattering.

Callum pulled Ailín tighter and shouted over the roar:

"We need to move, now! The floor's going to give!"

Lila nodded, coughing through the dust as she scrambled to her feet.

"Which way? CALLUM, WHICH WAY?!"

Callum looked around desperately.

The only exit, the sealed door, was still shut tight, the stone glowing faintly as ancient mechanisms strained against the energy rising beneath them.

Callum cursed.

"Damn it, open! OPEN!"

He slammed his shoulder against the door.

Nothing.

Another crack shot across the floor, splitting a portion of the mosaic clean in half. A massive slab dropped several inches, tilting downward into a widening abyss.

Ailín shrieked, "HE'S COMING UP!"

Callum turned, and saw a faint silhouette in the darkness below.

Not a form, Not a body, but something like a man-shaped void. A presence pulling itself closer into the world through the cracks. Just an outline of blackness etched in white resonance.

Callum's heart clutched.

"BOROUN"

The vault buckled again, throwing all three of them sideways. A tile the size of a car wrenched loose, crashing into the pit. A pulse of energy blasted out of the darkness. Callum shielded Ailín with his body. Lila shielded them both with hers.

The blast subsided.

Ailín's glow flickered violently.

"Callum… he wants something…"

Callum grabbed her face.

"What does he want?!"

Ailín sobbed mid-breath.

"He wants to be WHOLE."

Callum froze.

Lila's face went white.

"Oh God…"

Callum swallowed, heart hammering.

"Whole… how?"

Ailín shook her head violently.

"I don't know! I don't, "

The vault cracked again.

The silhouette rose higher.

And Callum saw something impossible, Boroun's shape was missing pieces. Like his resonance had been ripped apart. Like parts of him were lost. Like he was reaching because he needed something he no longer had.

Callum's blood chilled, "No, he can't have it; He can't have her."

Ailín whimpered into his neck.

"He wants me…"

Callum held her so tight he felt her heartbeat against his ribs.

"I won't let him."

Methos slammed into a monolith again, sliding down its cracked surface. Cadigan staggered toward him, limping, one eye swelling shut.

The Hunter's glow intensified.

Methos spat blood.

"Cadigan…he's not trying to kill us anymore."

Cadigan panting:

"Then what the hell is he…"

The Hunter turned toward the vault's sealed entrance.

Methos's eyes widened with horror.

"He feels Boroun."

Cadigan's grip tightened around the broken sabre shard.

"And the child."

Methos forced himself upright, leaning heavily on a column.

"Then we hold him one more time."

Cadigan nodded.

And together,

they stepped in front of the doorway

for a fight neither expected to win.

Outside the sanctuary, Renwick's surviving strike teams regrouped near the cliff, thunder rolling overhead.

The squad leader barked, "Push forward! Whatever's happening in there, we can't let the target disappear!"

A younger operative hesitated.

"Sir... our sensors are, our readings are, Sir, this isn't right, "

"MOVE!"

They advanced into the sancturary's entrance tunnel,

Just as another shockwave erupted from the vault.

One man was thrown backward out of the archway.

Two more stumbled as their gear shorted out.

The last, wide-eyed, muttered, "What the *hell* is in there..."

The vault ceiling groaned. A massive slab of stone sheared off and plummeted straight toward Callum and Ailín.

Arthis appeared in the doorway at the last possible second,

"ENOUGH."

His voice boomed with ancient resonance.

Time slowed.

Stone hung in the air for a fraction of a heartbeat.

Then Arthis flicked his hand.

The slab shattered into dust.

Callum stared, panting, "Arthis, what do we do?!"

Arthis looked down into the rising silhouette of Boroun with eyes full of dread and memory.

"We run."

Callum blinked.

"What?"

Arthis pointed to the far wall.

"Behind the mosaic, there is a secondary passage. We go now. Before he ascends."

The vault cracked wide.

Boroun's silhouette rose another foot.

The resonance screamed.

Ailín cried out.

Callum grabbed Lila's hand.

Arthis slammed both palms onto the mosaic.

A circle of light erupted around them.

Stone split.

A hidden stairway opened beneath the wall.

Callum ran.

Ailín held tight.

Lila followed.

Behind them, Boroun whispered again,

Not words.

Not a plea.

Just a single, mournful vibration, "…whole…"

The hidden stairway yawned open behind the cracked mosaic like a throat carved into the earth. A rush of cold, stale air blew upward, carrying with it the scent of old stone, deep water, and something far older.

Callum didn't hesitate.

He lifted Ailín into his arms and vaulted down the first steps.

Lila followed immediately, one hand on his coat, the other pressed over her heart.

"Callum, how deep does this go?!"

Arthis descended behind them,

"Far enough to survive what comes next."

A thunderclap rippled through the sanctuary.

Boroun roared, a sound like mountains grinding together.

Ailín screamed and clung to Callum's neck, her glow flickering so intensely it illuminated the staircase.

"He's angry, he's waking, he's *breaking things open*, "

Callum whispered into her hair:

"Hold on. Just hold on. We're almost clear."

The stairs trembled.

Dust rained down.

A long fracture snaked down the stone wall beside them.

Lila shouted:

"This passage isn't stable!"

Arthis did not look back.

"It was not designed to be stable."

Callum's breath hitched.

"What the hell does that mean?"

Arthis's tone cooled.

"It was designed to collapse behind us."

And it did.

With a deafening boom, the vault above gave way fully, stone slamming down into the pit behind them, sealing the door completely and cutting off the rising silhouette of Boroun.

Ailín sobbed.

"He's screaming..."

Callum tightened his grip.

"Don't listen. Don't listen, just focus on me."

Lila squeezed Ailín's hand gently.

"You're with us, sweetheart. He can't reach you down here."

Ailín's glow steadied slightly.

But the staircase continued to rumble.

Arthis quickened his pace.

"Move faster."

Callum didn't argue.

The ground above the sealed vault buckled.

Dust blasted upward from the cracks as Boroun's partial awakening sent resonance through every stone.

The Hunter froze mid-step.

His white eyes flared. He inhaled, that strange, predatory intake of breath not meant for air but for energy.

Methos steadied himself on a broken pillar.

"Oh no. No, no, no..."

The Hunter leaned down, placing one hand on the cracked mosaic, sensing the disappearance of his quarry.

Cadigan, barely conscious, breathed, "Did they... did they get out...?"

Methos nodded, "Yes. But he felt it."

The Hunter stood to his full height.

He turned toward the sealed vault entrance.

He placed both hands against the stone.

The chamber shook.

Methos's eyes widened.

"He's trying to break through."

Cadigan forced himself upright, swaying.

"Not on my watch."

Methos grabbed his arm.

"Cadigan, no. This isn't a fight we win."

Cadigan blinked through blood, but his voice was steady.

"It's a fight we stall."

He stepped forward.

Limping. Barely balanced.

The Hunter pressed his hands deeper into the stone.

Cracks spiderwebbed outward.

Methos under his breath, "Callum... for once in your long life... hurry."

Far above the vault area, at the sanctuary's main entrance, Renwick's last functional strike team advanced through the mist. Their weapons trembled in their hands.

"Steady, move slow, thermal's not reading, "

"Sir, radiation spike, what is this place?"

"We stick to objective, extract the child alive, "

Another shockwave hit.

Every soldier stumbled.

One dropped to his knees, vomiting.

The team leader cursed.

"Resonance event, again?!"

A young operative choked out, "Sir...this is not a human operation anymore."

A distant roar erupted inside the sanctuary.

The Hunter.

The team froze.

The leader swallowed audibly.

"Eyes up, weapons ready, whatever's in here..."

The Hunter burst through the stone archway.

Not attacking but moving toward the vault.

The strike team screamed.

Gunfire erupted.

Bullets ricocheted harmlessly off the Hunter's armor.

The creature didn't even turn its head. It simply walked straight through them as though they were reeds in a river. Bodies slammed against stone.

Weapons flew.

Two men hit the wall so hard their bones cracked.

And the Hunter kept going.

The stairway curved downward sharply.

Callum's boots skidded on dust-covered steps.

Arthis's pace did not slow.

Callum yelled up at him, "Arthis, where does this lead?!"

Arthis answered without turning.

"To the lowest vault. Boroun's resonance cannot reach you there."

Callum swallowed.

"And after that?"

Arthis looked back at him with ancient calm.

"You must learn the truth about Boroun."

Lila's pulse spiked.

"Which truth?"

Arthis stopped abruptly at the landing.

The tremors strengthened.

Dust fell like rain.

He turned fully toward them.

"That he was not imprisoned for what he did."

Ailín shivered.

"He was imprisoned...for what he *is*."

Lila asked, "What is he?"

Arthis spoke softly.

"The first Immortal who tried to become whole by taking the spark from a child."

Silence.

Callum tightened his grip.

"So he's trying again."

Arthis nodded, "Yes, and this time... he has found one with a spark unlike any before."

Ailín's tiny voice quivered.

"He means me..."

Callum kissed the top of her head.

"No one is taking you."

Arthis lifted a hand. The wall beside them pulsed. A hidden tunnel split open.

"Then we must go deeper."

The lower tunnel narrowed into a steep passageway with walls of smooth, obsidian-dark stone. The air was cold, unnaturally still, no drafts, no echoes, no outside noise. The deeper they descended, the more the passage seemed to swallow sound, as though they were moving into the lungs of the island itself.

Callum slowed, adjusting Ailín's weight in his arms. Her glow had dimmed to a pale shimmer, flickering like a candle struggling against a storm.

"Ailín... talk to me. How's your breathing?"

She pressed her forehead into his collarbone.

"It's heavy... the air here feels heavy."

"It's alright, sweetie. Just breathe with me. Nice and slow."

Callum touched Lila's arm.

"You okay?"

Lila nodded shakily.

"No. But I'm here."

Arthis kept walking, his robes brushing the stone with soft whispers.

"The lower vault suppresses resonance. It will calm her spark."

Callum frowned.

"Suppresses?"

Arthis nodded.

"Yes. It dampens Immortal energy. Boroun cannot sense her here. Nor can the Hunter."

Lila exhaled.

"Finally, good news."

Arthis stopped abruptly.

"No."

They froze behind him.

Arthis's voice lowered.

"The suppression cuts both ways."

Callum shifted Ailín protectively.

"What does that mean?"

Arthis turned slowly to face them, his expression heavy.

"It means your own spark will weaken the deeper we go."

Callum stared, "Meaning what exactly?"

Arthis's tone was grave.

"Your strength. Your senses. Your healing. Everything you rely on as Immortal... will fade."

Lila tensed.

"How much?"

Arthis answered without hesitation.

"To near mortal levels."

Ailín gripped Callum's coat.

"Callum... I don't want you to get hurt."

Callum kissed her head.

"Hey. I'm not going anywhere. Spark or not."

Arthis turned again and resumed walking.

"We must use the suppression carefully. The Hunter will struggle the deeper he descends. But we must reach the lowest vault first."

Lila frowned.

"What's in the lowest vault?"

Arthis answered without turning:

"The truth of Boroun's imprisonment."

Stone cracked like splitting bone.

Methos dragged Cadigan behind a fallen monolith, coughing blood.

Cadigan wheezed:

"Methos, we can't stop him, "

"I know," Methos rasped. "We're not trying to stop him. We're trying to slow him."

The Hunter slammed his fist into the vault's stone seal again.

A massive chunk shattered off.

A second blow widened the gap.

Methos wiped blood from his mouth.

"He's breaking through."

Cadigan nodded grimly.

"He wants the child."

"He wants Boroun." Methos pointed.

The Hunter paused, his head tilting, sensing the distant tremors below. Then he roared. A deep, resonant bellow that shook dust from the ceiling and made Methos's vision blur.

Cadigan braced his body against the broken stone.

"We need to give Callum more time."

Methos shook his head.

They stepped forward again.

Barely able to stand.

Barely healed. Barely alive, But standing.

The passage angled sharply downward. Carvings appeared on the walls, spirals, branching arcs, symbols that looked like early proto-writing but older than any known script.

Lila ran her fingers over one.

"These aren't decorative."

Arthis nodded, "They are warnings."

Ailín shivered.

"I don't like them…"

Callum looked at Arthis, "Warnings about what?"

Arthis stopped at the next landing, "About what was sealed below."

Callum's pulse spiked.

"You said Boroun was imprisoned above this."

Arthis corrected, "Boroun was sealed *away from* this. This is deeper."

Lila's eyes widened, "So Boroun isn't what's at the bottom?"

Arthis turned, "No."

Ailín began to cry softly.

Arthis placed a steady hand on the wall.

The stone rippled and shifted; it opened into a vast chamber.

"Welcome to the First Vault."

The chamber was enormous, larger than any part of the sanctuary above. A vast circular hall carved from solid stone, its ceiling lost in shadow. The air vibrated with suppressed resonance, like a heartbeat slowed to a crawl. In the center of the chamber stood a single object - A stone pedestal. And atop it, A dark, metallic sphere, cracked along its surface like fractured obsidian.

Ailín whimpered, "Callum…that's where the other piece is…"

"What?"

Ailín clung to Callum's shirt, "Boroun...he's missing something."

Callum's heart pounded.

"And it's in that sphere?"

Ailín nodded slowly, "That's why he wasn't whole. That's why he's reaching..."

Arthis stepped closer, "Yes, The First Vault contains the part of him that was torn away. The part that made him unstoppable."

Callum asked, "You cut him in half?"

Arthis met his eyes, "We broke him. Because we had to."

The vault trembled again.

Boroun roared somewhere above them.

The Hunter answered with a roar of his own.

Arthis turned sharply toward the passage.

"They race toward this place. Both of them."

Callum lifted the Katana, "Then we protect her. And we protect that sphere."

Arthis shook his head.

"No.You must destroy the sphere.

Arthis placed a hand on the pedestal.

"Callum... the Katana."

Callum raised it instinctively.

"What about it?"

Arthis pointed to the sphere.

"It can cut what others cannot."

Callum swallowed.

"You want me to destroy this."

Arthis nodded.

"If you do not, Boroun will reclaim it. And once whole, he will be beyond containment."

Lila, "So we destroy it."

Ailín clutched Callum, "No. If you hurt it... he'll hurt me. He's tied to me..."

Callum froze.

"Ailín, how do you know that?"

Her voice trembled.

"Because when he pushes...I feel it."

Arthis's expression darkened.

445

"The old connection is forming. We are out of time."
Before Callum could respond,
BOOM
A deafening impact shook the entire chamber.
Stone splintered above them.
A long crack shot down the wall behind the pedestal.
Lila gasped.
"What was that?!"
"The Hunter."

Up in the corridor above, Methos and Cadigan limped forward, battered and half-conscious. The tunnel walls trembled with every step the Hunter took, vibrating the stone like a drum.

Cadigan gasped:
"He's... faster now..."
Methos nodded, wiping blood from his mouth.
"Because Boroun is waking.
He's feeding off resonance.
And the Hunter is feeding off him."
Cadigan stumbled.
"We can't, we can't face him again. Not like this."
Methos grabbed his arm and pulled him upright, I know."
The Hunter appeared in the tunnel behind them, a towering silhouette wreathed in pale glow, cracking with the energy flowing from Boroun's awakening.
Methos swallowed hard.
"Cadigan...run."
Cadigan blinked.
"What?"
Methos pushed him, "RUN!
The Hunter followed the resonance trail.
Downward toward the First Vault.
Toward Ailín.

Cracks deepened along the sphere, glowing brighter.
Ailín clutched Callum's sleeve.
"He's here...

Arthis's voice sharpened, "Callum. Destroy the sphere now!"

Ailín sobbed.

"No! If you do, I'll feel it, I'll break, "

Callum's heart twisted painfully.

He held her face.

"Ailín. Look at me."

Her shimmering eyes locked on his.

"I will protect you.

From him.

From all of them.

But I need you to trust me."

Ailín cried.

"I do...but I'm scared..."

Callum pulled her into his arms, "So am I.

But we do this together."

A massive blow struck the vault door.

Stone cracked.

Lila screamed.

"He's here!"

Callum stood.

Arthis stepped away from the pedestal.

"The sphere must be destroyed before either of them reach this chamber."

Callum raised the Katana.

His hands shook.

"Tell me this doesn't kill her."

Arthis held his gaze, "It will hurt her, but it will save her."

Another massive blow.

The vault door bent inward.

Dust rained from the ceiling.

Lila pulled Ailín behind a pillar.

"Callum, HURRY!"

Callum looked at the sphere.

Then at Ailín.

Then at the sword.

"Please..." Ailín whispered, "Don't let him take me..."

Callum's jaw tightened.

He lifted the Katana overhead, when the vault door shattered inward.

The Hunter stepped through the debris in a burst of dust and white glow.

Lila screamed.

Arthis's eyes went wide, "CALLUM! DO IT NOW!"

The Hunter locked onto the sphere.

Boroun's roar echoed from below,

Ailín clung to Lila,

And Callum brought the Katana down.

Chapter 24

The Katana struck the cracked sphere. For a heartbeat, nothing moved. Light froze mid-air. Dust suspended itself in the beam of Ailín's glow. Even the Hunter halted mid-stride, white eyes widening as if time itself had stalled.

Then the world shattered. A flash erupted from the sphere, not an explosion, but a violent pull, a vacuum of resonance imploding inward. The carving lines of the First Vault lit all at once, casting the chamber in blinding white.

Callum felt the energy rip through the sword, through his arms, through his ribs, as though the blade had struck the heart of a star.

Ailín screamed.

Lila grabbed her and shielded her body with her own, sobbing against the blast.

The sphere cracked open completely, splitting along its deepest fracture, and a wave of ancient, agonized resonance tore outward in a ring.

Arthis planted his hands against the stone and roared, "SHIELD THEM!"

A shimmering barrier flared around Ailín, Lila, and Callum, a dome of fractured light that vibrated like struck glass.

The resonance wave hit it like a storm hitting a cliff.

Callum staggered, still gripping the sword, still forcing the blade

down as the sphere screamed beneath him,
a sound not of metal, not of stone,
but of something old
and broken
and alive.

The Hunter roared in answer, not in pain, but in recognition. Boroun's essence surged upward from below, reaching, pulling, desperate to reunite with the fragment inside the sphere.

Ailín's glow flared violently.

"Callum! CALLUM, IT'S HURTING ME!"

Callum lowered to one knee, trying to shield her with his body even as the backlash sent fire through his arms.

"I know, I know, baby, hold on, just hold on, !"

Arthis shouted over the roar, "Callum, finish it! If the sphere opens, Boroun will reclaim his spark!"

The sphere cracked further.

A black vapor, thick and oily, began to leak from the fracture, spiraling toward the ceiling.

The Hunter stepped toward it.

Cadigan, half-conscious, dragged himself through the broken doorway and shouted:

"CALLUM, HIT IT AGAIN!"

Methos, bloodied, barely able to stand, grasped a pillar and rasped:

"CALLUM, NOW!"

Callum lifted the blade,

Every muscle screaming,

every bone trembling.

Ailín cried out:

"CALLUM, DON'T, IT FEELS LIKE I'M BREAKING!"

He hesitated.

Just long enough.

The black vapor twisted in the air,
and shot downward
toward Ailín.

Arthis reached out to intercept, but the Hunter intercepted Arthis, grabbing the Archivist by the throat and slamming him into the wall with earthshaking force. Arthis roared in pain.

Lila screamed.

Ailín's glow flickered dangerously.

Callum's heart tore in two,

"NO!"

He swung.

The Katana hit the sphere a second time.

This time, it broke.

Light burst outward in a shockwave so violent the floor split open. The vault rippled like water.

The broken fragment of Boroun's essence howled as it tore free, not into the Hunter, not into Boroun, but into the only open vessel in the room.

Ailín.

The black vapor slammed into her chest.

Her glow erupted with blinding force.

She screamed, a raw, shrill, terrified sound that echoed through every chamber of the sanctuary.

Callum lunged for her.

"Ailín!"

Lila grabbed her too.

Ailín convulsed, clutching at her chest with small trembling hands.

Her silver glow turned black at its edges.

Callum's voice cracked, "No…no no no, Ailín, baby, stay with me."

Arthis staggered to his feet, eyes wide with horror.

"CALLUM, GET AWAY FROM HER!"

Callum shook his head violently.

"NEVER, !"

Arthis shouted harder:

"CALLUM, BOROUN'S ESSENCE HAS ENTERED HER, IF YOU TOUCH HER, IT MAY GO INTO YOU TOO!"

Callum's eyes filled with tears.

"I am not leaving her."

Ailín's glow flared again, white, silver, black; intertwining violently.

And then, she fell unconscious. Her body went limp in their arms.

Lila sobbed into her hair.

Callum held her like a drowning man clinging to a rope.

He whispered into her ear, "I've got you. I've got you. Don't leave me. Don't you dare leave me."

The Hunter froze completely.

For the first time since their encounter, his white eyes dimmed. as if he sensed a change in her - A change in what she was.

Arthis uttered a single word, "…impossible."

Methos staggered into the vault, coughing.

"What, what happened, "

Arthis pointed with shaking hands.

"Boroun's essence…has bonded with the child…"

Cadigan's eyes widened.

"That means…"

Arthis finished quietly, "She is no longer just awakening. She is ascending."

Callum looked up from her limp form, tears streaking his face.

"What does that mean?! WHAT DOES THAT MEAN FOR HER?!"

Arthis's expression was grim, "It means the endgame has changed."

The Hunter stepped forward, slowly, head tilting. Not approaching as a predator but as if observing something sacred.

Callum rose, sword in hand, holding Ailín close with his other arm, "You stay away from her."

The Hunter paused. Completely.

Arthis swallowed, "Callum…he isn't coming for her anymore."

Callum's eyes narrowed.

"Then what does he want?"

Arthis met his gaze.

"He wants to protect her."

The vault trembled. Boroun roared far below.

Ailín lay limp in Callum's arms, her breath shallow but present. A faint shimmer radiated from beneath her skin, no longer purely silver. A darker hue threaded through the glow, like ink bleeding through water.

Lila pressed trembling fingers to the child's pulse.

"She's alive. God, she's alive…"

Callum rocked her gently, unable to stop the tears streaking his cheeks, "Come on, sweetheart… breathe for me. I'm right here."

Ailín exhaled weakly, but her body remained still. Too still.

Arthis approached slowly, eyes locked on the faint glow flickering beneath her ribs.

"Callum...she's carrying two sparks now."

Methos slumped against a cracked pillar, face pale and streaked with blood.

"Two...? Arthis, that's not possible."

Arthis shook his head slowly.

"It should not be. And yet it is."

Cadigan limped toward them, clutching his shattered sword hilt.

"How can a child hold two Immortal sparks?"

Arthis answered without looking away from Ailín, "Because one spark is not Immortal."

Callum's heart clenched.

"What does that mean?"

Arthis turned to him, expression grave.

"The spark she was born with is something new, something that was forming outside the cycle of the Game. Boroun's essence, broken and incomplete, saw that spark and attached itself to it."

Lila frowned.

"Attached? As in... bound?"

Arthis nodded.

"Yes."

Callum shook his head, voice raw,

"So she's... what? Is she in danger?"

Arthis hesitated just long enough to terrify everyone, "Yes. But not from death."

Cadigan blinked.

"Then from what?"

Arthis gestured at the sphere's shattered remains.

"Boroun's fractured essence is chaotic. Unstable. It will try to rebuild itself using whatever vessel it finds."

Callum's grip tightened around Ailín's tiny shoulders.

"You're saying she's in pain because he's inside her."

"No," Arthis said softly, "I am saying she is in pain because she is resisting him."

Ailín stirred weakly at the sound of voices.

"Callum... hurts..."

He kissed her forehead.

"I know. I know, baby. I'm here."

The Hunter stepped closer, not menacingly, but with an odd, almost hesitant stillness. His cracked armor hummed faintly, white sparks flickering along the fractures.

Lila pressed her back against Callum protectively.

"Keep him away!"

But the creature didn't attack.

He knelt. Slowly before Ailín.

Arthis inhaled sharply.

"This...should not be possible."

Methos winced.

"Oh, wonderful. Another impossibility."

The Hunter bowed his head.

A gesture no one had ever seen him make.

Ailín's glow pulsed in response,

weak but unmistakably aware of him.

Ailín whispered without opening her eyes:

"He's...quiet now."

Callum's breath caught.

"What? Who?"

Ailín breathed softly, "The loud one...the hunter...he's not loud anymore..."

Arthis stepped forward cautiously.

"He feels her now. Not as prey. As... something else."

Cadigan wiped blood from his mouth.

"Why? What changed?"

Arthis gestured toward the cracked pedestal.

"The Hunter was created, shaped, really, by the old ones to track and kill powerful Immortals. But Boroun's essence, even a fragment of it, outranks anything in his nature."

Lila's eyes widened.

"You're saying the Hunter sees her as, what? A higher authority?"

Arthis nodded slowly, "He will not strike her. He will not harm her. He may even defend her...as long as her sparks remain stable."

Methos groaned.

"Oh terrific.
We've accidentally adopted a homicidal bodyguard."
Callum glared.
"I don't trust him."
"You should not," Arthis replied.
"He is only following instinct. He has no loyalty. Only resonance."
Ailín shifted weakly.
"He's looking for the broken one…"
Callum stiffened.
"Boroun."
Ailín nodded faintly.
Callum touched her cheek gently.
"Tell me what you need, sweetheart. Anything."
"I need it to stop hurting."
Callum swallowed hard.
"We'll fix it. I swear."
Arthis stood and walked slowly to the fractured pedestal.
"There is a way."
Callum rose sharply.
"How?"
Arthis placed his hand on the broken artifact.
"The fragment inside her must be stabilized. Re-shaped. Contained."
Lila asked softly:
"By who?"
Arthis turned to Callum.
Then to the Katana.
Then back to Callum.
"By you."
Callum blinked.
"By me? How?!"
Arthis stepped forward.
"Because your spark carries the echo of Arkael, the one who broke Boroun the first time."
Methos's eyes widened.
"Oh, hell."
Cadigan, "He's the only one who can finish what the First did…"

Arthis nodded.

"Yes."

Ailín whimpered.

"Callum… I'm scared…"

Callum held her tight, voice trembling:

"It's okay.

I'm right here."

Arthis stepped closer, voice lowering to a near-whisper, "Then you must step into the echo. And she must follow."

Callum stared at him.

"You're insane."

Arthis's expression didn't change.

"It is the only way she survives this."

Behind them, the Hunter rose slowly to his full height,

Not attacking.

Waiting.

For her.

The vault trembled again.

Boroun roared from deep below.

Arthis looked down the stairs they had descended.

"The deeper vaults will not hold much longer."

Callum closed his eyes, tears slipping down.

Then he looked at Ailín.

Then at Lila.

Then at the glowing fissures in the sphere.

Then at the Hunter.

Then at Arthis.

"Tell me," Callum, voice breaking, "exactly what I have to do."

Arthis nodded grimly.

"Prepare yourself."

Ailín trembled in Callum's arms, her light dimming and flaring in unsteady rhythms. Each pulse was accompanied by a small, pained whimper, not a cry, not yet, but the edge of one.

Callum brushed her hair back gently.

"Stay with me… please stay with me."

A faint glow pulsed beneath her ribs, a mixture of her silver spark and the dark resonance now housed within her chest.

Methos pushed himself off the pillar, face weary but alert.

"Arthis. Enough riddles. What does he need to do?"

Cadigan leaned heavily on a pillar, one hand pressed to his ribs.

"Aye. Words, man. Not poetry."

Arthis stepped into the center of the vault, near the cracked remains of the sphere, and gestured for Callum to come closer.

Callum held Ailín carefully and approached.

Arthis spoke quietly:

"Her spark is in conflict. Part hers. Part his."

Callum's jaw clenched.

"Meaning, ?"

Arthis gestured toward Ailín's chest.

"Meaning she is carrying two resonances that do not understand each other. They are fighting, and she is the ground between them."

Arthis stepped closer.

"Callum. You carry the echo of Arkael. That makes you the only one who can pull the broken resonance out of her."

Callum shook his head.

"So I tear it out of her? How? With what?"

Arthis met his eyes.

"With your spark."

Callum went cold.

"You're telling me to put my spark into her?"

Arthis nodded.

"Yes."

Arthis didn't flinch.

Callum frowned, "My spark doesn't carry anything special."

Methos exhaled sharply, "Oh it does, Callum. It does."

The Hunter turned his head slightly, as if listening.

Arthis continued, "You are descended, not by blood, but by lineage, from Arkael's teaching. All Immortals carry echoes of those they learned from, but your echo…is different."

Callum took a step back, holding Ailín tighter.

"What are you saying?"

Arthis forced the words:

"Arkael's spark bonded with yours long before you realized what you were."

Silence.

Methos stared.

"...Arkael chose you."

Callum shook his head.

"No... Arkael never, "

Arthis cut him off.

"He knew your potential. He knew what you could do. You were his legacy. Even if he never said it."

Callum felt his throat tighten.

"I'm not him."

"No," Arthis said.

"You are something new, and Ailín needs *that* Callum, not the warrior, not the survivor , but the echo that learned from the First."

A low rumble shook the chamber.

Stone dust fell like soft rain.

Lila's breath shook.

"He's... coming back up."

Arthis nodded.

"Boroun can feel the broken part missing. He will come for her, or for what she now carries."

Ailín whimpered louder.

"Callum...he's pulling me again..."

Callum held her tightly.

"I've got you. He's not taking you."

The Hunter stepped closer, slowly, kneeling again, watching Ailín with an unsettling stillness.

Methos was surprised, "That thing is treating her like she's... some kind of queen."

Cadigan nodded.

"Aye. Queen, goddess, ancestor...something beyond him."

Arthis turned to Callum.

"Your spark can shield her, but only if you step into the echo and draw Boroun's resonance out before it settles."

Callum's voice broke:

"And if I can't?"

Arthis didn't soften the truth.

"Then Boroun will rise, and Ailín will lose herself to his broken spark, and we all will likely cease to exist."

Ailín reached up with trembling fingers to touch Callum's cheek.

"Callum help me…"

His heart nearly shattered.

He knelt with her in his lap, hands shaking, forehead against hers.

"I will. I swear I will."

He looked up at Arthis.

"Tell me how."

Arthis placed a hand over Callum's heart.

"Open your spark. Let her resonance touch yours. And when the broken essence inside her reaches for you, *do not let it in.* Pull it out."

Callum swallowed.

"And what happens to it?"

Arthis stepped back.

His voice turned ancient, "You absorb it."

Callum stared down at Ailín.

At her trembling hands.

At her flickering glow.

"I love you, little one. I'm right here."

"Don't let him take me…"

He kissed her forehead.

"I won't."

He looked at Arthis.

"I'm ready."

The Hunter rose behind them.

Boroun roared again from the depths.

Callum knelt with Ailín in the center of the First Vault, the shattered pedestal behind them glowing faintly from the wound Callum had carved into the sphere. The Katana lay beside him, humming softly, as if sensing what was about to happen.

Ailín trembled in his lap, her glow flickering between silver and a darker, fractured pulse, the echo of Boroun's broken essence.

Callum brushed her hair from her eyes.

"I'm right here, sweetheart. Look at me."

She opened her eyes slowly, silver irises trembling.

"Callum… it hurts… it hurts a lot…"

Callum kissed her forehead, tears gathering.

"I know. I'm going to make it stop. I promise."

Arthis stepped forward cautiously.

"Callum. You must open your spark."

Lila hovered to the side, gripping her trembling hands together.

"He can do this. I know he can."

Methos coughed up dust but stood tall, jaw set.

"And so it begins…"

Cadigan gave a weary nod.

"Do it, lad. Whatever it takes."

The Hunter stood behind the group, towering and still, his white eyes dim but focused on Ailín, watching, waiting, sensing every shift in resonance.

Callum closed his eyes.

He hadn't opened his spark fully in decades.

Not since the last time he'd lost someone he loved.

He exhaled slowly and whispered, "…okay. Come on then."

A faint hum vibrated around his ribcage. Silver light seeped from his chest, soft at first, then brighter, pulsing in steady waves.

Ailín gasped and clutched his shirt.

"Callum… I feel you…"

"Good. Stay with me."

Arthis spoke quietly, voice steady but urgent.

"Let her spark reach into yours. Guide her. Do not force her."

Callum nodded.

"Ailín… reach for me. Just like when we held the basin. You remember?"

A weak nod.

She reached her tiny hand toward his chest,

and her spark flared.

Light connected them.

A shimmering thread of resonance bridged between their hearts, humming like a string pulled taut.

Callum gasped.

Ailín whimpered.

Cadigan uttered, "…bloody hell…"

Methos clenched his teeth.

"Arthis, if this goes wrong, "

Arthis didn't look away.

"It cannot go wrong.
It can only go forward."

Callum grit his teeth as the resonance thread thickened, tightened, pulling him and Ailín into perfect alignment.

He whispered to her:

"That's it, sweetheart. Just like that."

Her voice cracked.

"It hurts… something is pulling… pulling hard…"

Callum braced her shoulders.

"That's Boroun's shard. Don't let it win. Push it toward me."

Ailín shook violently.

"I'm scared…"

Callum's voice broke.

"Then take my strength. All of it."

Ailín screamed,
a high, piercing sound as dark resonance flared from her chest, surging along the thread into Callum's spark.

Callum arched, gasping.

Dark energy wrapped around his ribs, scorching like fire and freezing like ice simultaneously.

Lila cried out:

"CALLUM!"

Methos grabbed her.

"No! Don't touch them! You'll break the link!"

The Hunter stepped closer, instinct rising, protective, confused, trembling with the sense that something profound was happening.

Arthis lifted his hands.

"Callum, listen to me! Do NOT let Boroun's essence take root inside you!"

Callum roared through clenched teeth:

"THEN TELL ME, HOW THE HELL DO I STOP IT?!"

Arthis answered sharply, "Pull and claim."

Callum's eyes widened.

"What, ?!"

"CLAIM IT, CALLUM! Make the broken spark answer to YOU, not her, not Boroun, YOU!"

Ailín convulsed in his arms, screaming again.

Black resonance tore from her chest like smoke, funneling into him. His spark flared wildly, cracking through the vault like lightning. Stone shuddered. Dust fell.

Callum shouted into her hair:

"I've got you! GIVE IT TO ME! GIVE IT HERE!"

Ailín sobbed, "Take it, take it, take it!" With one final, ragged cry, she pushed. The dark essence surged fully into Callum. He felt it slam into his spark, a broken echo ancient, agonized and he did what Arthis commanded:

He claimed it.

Callum roared as his spark swallowed the fragment whole.

Light burst outward in a shockwave,

white, silver, and black intermingling.

The entire vault lit up.

Ailín collapsed against him, unconscious.

Callum fell to one knee, panting, trembling as the last strands of Boroun's essence wound into his own.

Arthis muttered, "...Arkael's echo awakens..."

The Hunter stepped back sharply.

Methos stared.

"Callum...what did you just become?"

Lila rushed forward as the glow faded.

"Callum? CALLUM!"

He lifted his head slowly.

His eyes glowed faintly,

not silver like Ailín's,

not white like the Hunter's,

not black like Boroun's,

but all three at once, swirling like a storm.

Callum cradled Ailín gently.

She breathed evenly.

Peacefully.

Her glow was pure silver again.

Callum confirmed, "She's okay. She's okay..."

Lila sobbed in relief.

Arthis lowered his head.

"The broken shard has been silenced…
but not destroyed."

Methos approached cautiously.

"And where is it now?"

Callum inhaled slowly. It hurt. Not physically, but in a way he had never felt before., "…inside me."

The vault trembled.

A roar erupted from below,

Boroun's full voice.

Arthis's face drained of color, "He felt the change."

Methos lifted his sword fragment.

Cadigan steadied his stance.

Lila grabbed Ailín protectively.

The Hunter turned toward the stairs, rage igniting through his cracked armor,

And Callum rose, the Katana in one hand, Ailín held safely in the other arm.

His new spark hummed in his chest.

Boroun roared again.

Callum looked up, "…he's coming."

Arthis nodded gravely.

Chapter 25

The roar from below shook the entire First Vault, rattling dust loose from the ceiling in long gray streams. The deep stone groaned beneath their feet, pulsing as if the earth itself had a heartbeat.

Ailín stirred in Callum's arms, breathing faint but steady. Silver light shimmered faintly under her ribs, no trace of the dark resonance remained.

She was clear.

Safe.

But Callum was not.

His own spark still thrummed unevenly, a strange, heavy pulse mixing with his natural resonance. The fragment of Boroun inside him pressed outward like a fist against a locked door.

Lila slipped a steadying hand on his arm.

"Callum... you're shaking."

He swallowed hard.

"I know."

Cadigan staggered closer, his shirt torn and stained with blood.

"Lad... what's wrong with ye?"

Callum stared at his own hands.

They trembled.

Not from fear.

"I can feel him," he whispered. "Boroun. He's reaching through me. Searching for what he lost."

Arthis stepped forward, face grim.

"He senses the shard is no longer in the vault. He senses you."

Methos shook his head.

"Oh, splendid. Callum just became a walking homing beacon."

Callum gritted his teeth.

"Callum… your light is different…" Ailín pointed out.

He looked down at her, eyes softening.

"How different?"

She reached up and touched his chest with small fingers.

"It has three voices now."

Lila stiffened.

"Three?"

Ailín nodded weakly.

"Yours…the sad one…and the old one."

Arthis inhaled sharply.

"Arkael."

Methos blinked.

"He can feel *Arkael's* echo now?"

Ailín nodded again.

"Arkael is quiet… like a shadow behind you."

Callum closed his eyes for a moment. In the drifting resonance around him, he could faintly hear something, not words, not thoughts, but a presence ancient, still, and waiting.

He mouthed, "…Arkael…"

Arthis stepped closer.

"He was your ancestor in the lineage of blades and thought. No Immortal alive today carries more of his echo than you."

Methos rubbed his forehead, "And now Callum also carries a piece of the most dangerous Immortal ever imprisoned. Lovely combination."

Cadigan muttered, "Balance of fire and ice…"

The tremor from below intensified. A sound followed, low, resonant, and hungry. Boroun's full self was rising.

Arthis turned toward the vault entrance.

"We must go. Now."

Lila nodded quickly.

"Where? Every direction feels worse than the last."

Arthis pointed toward a tunnel on the far side of the vault, a narrow, descending corridor carved with unfamiliar symbols.

"To the Echo Chamber."

Methos groaned.

"That sounds like a place where definitely nothing good happens. Seriously....can't immortals make their magical echo chambers in the sunny warm Caribbean for once?"

Arthis gave him a look.

"It is the only place Callum can stabilize the fragment inside him before Boroun arrives."

Callum looked down at Ailín's peaceful face.

"What happens if I don't?"

Arthis didn't hesitate.

"Then Boroun will reclaim his spark from your body."

Lila's face paled.

"Reclaim... how?"

Arthis answered plainly, "He will kill you."

Ailín whimpered, "No... don't let him take Callum..."

Callum hugged her gently, soothing.

"I'm not going anywhere. Not again. Not ever."

The Hunter stepped forward suddenly, towering over them with cracking armor and quiet intensity. He lifted his head, listening to the tremors through the stone.

Arthis murmured:

"He senses Boroun as well."

Cadigan gripped the broken claymore hilt.

"Well, at least he still looks ready to kill something."

Methos shook his head.

"No. He looks ready to defend the girl...and maybe Callum too."

Callum stared at the Hunter.

"Then stay out of my way, Because if Boroun wants what's inside me, he'll have to go through the Hunter, then me, then the girl."

The Hunter cocked his head.

A faint pulse of white light flickered across his armor.

Arthis nodded.

"Then let us move before we face both monsters at once."

Callum shifted Ailín in his arms, grabbed the Katana, and nodded toward the tunnel.

"Let's go."

Behind them, the vault shook violently as Boroun's roar tore through the stone, closer than ever.

The tunnel led into a steep, slanted hallway of smooth basalt, the kind of stone polished not by hands but by centuries of resonance flow. Strange markings danced across its walls, glowing faintly as Callum passed. Some symbols brightened near Ailín; others dimmed, almost recoiling from her presence.

Ailín stirred in his arms, eyelids fluttering.

"The walls... they're whispering."

Callum's grip tightened.

"What are they saying?"

Ailín whispered:

"They know you."

He nearly stumbled.

"Me?"

Ailín nodded weakly.

"They say... you've been here before."

Callum's stomach tightened.

He'd never set foot on this island until today.

Methos, limping slightly, overheard.

"Callum, don't read into that. These vaults are older than written language. They imprint echoes. Patterns. They might be reacting to Arkael's resonance inside you."

Arthis corrected, "Not reacting. Recognizing."

Lila exhaled stiffly.

"Wonderful. So the walls know him. Can we get to a room that doesn't think?"

But two steps later, the tunnel did the opposite of quieting.

It awakened.

A low vibration traveled down the stone like a ripple, meeting Callum's presence and flaring brighter as he stepped forward. The cracks in the walls pulsed softly in response.

Arthis slowed.

"The Echo Chamber is awake."

Methos groaned.

"That sounds... bad."

Cadigan crossed his arms (or tried to, his left shoulder still hung loose).

"Nothin' good ever happens when rocks change color for ye."

Callum ignored them, focused entirely on Ailín.

She curled into his chest, her small fingers resting over his spark.

"It's humming. Like when we touched the basin..."

"Is it hurting you?"

She shook her head.

"No... it's humming *with* yours."

That terrified him more than the alternative.

The tunnel opened into a vast, circular chamber. The chamber was shaped like a sphere sliced in half: a bowl of polished stone with no pillars, no seams, no carvings, just smooth, curving walls that rose a hundred feet overhead. At its center was a flat stone platform the size of a dinner table, carved with a single symbol - A sun split into three shards.

Callum recognized the emblem, "That's the emblem from the upper vault mosaic."

Arthis nodded.

"This is where it was created. This is where Arkael broke Boroun."

Methos whistled low.

"So this is the birthplace of one of the darkest chapters in Immortal history."

Cadigan stepped forward.

"It feels... wrong."

Lila hugged herself.

"It feels... heavy."

Ailín trembled against Callum.

"It feels... familiar."

Callum kissed her forehead.

"You okay?"

She nodded.

"It's calling me."

Arthis pointed to the central platform.

"Lay her down, Callum."

Callum hesitated.

"What happens when I do?"

Arthis didn't soften it.

"Her spark will align with yours.
And the fragment inside you will try to escape."

Lila choked.

"Callum, "

He cut her off gently.

"I know."

He brushed Ailín's cheek.

"Sweetheart, I need you to lie right here, okay? I'll be right beside you."

She swallowed hard.

"Promise?"

"Always."

He set her gently on the stone.

The surface lit beneath her body.

Ailín gasped.

"It knows me…"

Callum's chest tightened.

He knelt beside her and placed the Katana on the platform edge.

Arthis circled around them.

"Callum. When the fragment pushes out, your spark must take control. If you hesitate, just once, Boroun will reclaim his essence."

Callum closed his eyes.

"I won't hesitate."

Lila moved beside Ailín, trembling but firm.

"I'll talk her through it. She'll hear my voice the whole time."

Cadigan and Methos moved to guard the chamber entrance, weapons ready.

The Hunter stood behind Callum, waiting.

A thunderous crack echoed from above the chamber, followed by another roar, much closer, much stronger.

Arthis froze.

"He is near."

Methos snapped to alertness.

"How near?"

Another tremor.

Dust fell.

Cracks spread like veins across the upper stone.

Cadigan gritted his teeth.

"He's comin' down the bloody stairs."

Arthis shook his head.

"No. He is coming through the walls."

Callum's eyes widened.

"He can do that?"

"He's not whole…but he's strong…"

Arthis turned sharply to Callum.

"We must begin. Now. Before he breaks through."

Callum nodded, took Ailín's hand, and breathed deeply.

His spark began to glow from within his chest, silver-white with streaks of black flickering like distant lightning.

Arthis raised both hands.

The chamber responded.

The walls hummed. The stone vibrated. Runes that weren't visible moments before brightened in a spiral around them.

Ailín cried out softly.

"It's starting…"

Callum squeezed her hand.

"I'm right here."

Arthis commanded:

"Open your spark!"

Callum inhaled, and let the resonance inside him unfurl.

Light burst outward from his ribs, surrounding both him and Ailín in a sphere of shimmering white-silver-black. Ailín arched, crying out as her spark flared in response.

Lila held her hand tight.

"It's okay! You're safe! We're right here!"

The Hunter stepped closer,

drawn in by resonance instinct,

his armor cracking with pulses of white.

Methos pointing out the obvious, "…this is going to tear the place apart."

Cadigan muttered:

"And us with it."

A thunderous blast rocked the chamber, Boroun smashing against the outer walls.

Callum grit his teeth as the fragment inside him surged, pressing outward, violently, furious.

Ailín screamed.

The resonance sphere flickered.

Callum shouted:

"TAKE IT FROM ME, NOT HER!"

Arthis roared:

"CLAIM IT, CALLUM! NOW!"

Callum reached into his own spark, into the storm inside him,

The chamber pulsed like a great, stone heart.

Cracks snaked across the ceiling. Chunks of rock fell in sharp echoes. The air vibrated with low, bone-deep hums, a warning, a signal, a pulse of ancient fear.

Ailín cried out as the resonance sphere around her flickered violently. Her small hands grasped at Callum's wrist, nails biting into his skin.

Callum held her tighter.

"I've got you, I've got you, breathe with me, "

She screamed again as her spark surged, ripping through her tiny frame like a wild current. The silver glow around her intensified, streaked with faint black tremors, the last of Boroun's essence still inside her.

Lila stroked Ailín's hair with shaking hands.

"It's okay, stay with me, sweetheart, stay with me, listen to my voice, "

Ailín's sobs turned frantic.

"It hurts! It hurts! It hurts, !"

Callum's spark pulsed outward in response, glowing brighter, wrapping around Ailín like a resonant cocoon.

But the fragment inside him pushed back.

Hard.

Dark tendrils of broken resonance clawed through Callum's spark, ripping along his ribs like burning threads.

He gasped.

Pain tore through him.

Not quite physical or emotional, but Primordial.

Arthis stepped forward, eyes wide.

"Callum, he knows exactly where the fragment is, and he is reaching for it!"

A thunderous pound shook the outer vault wall.

Cracks spread deeper.

Boroun roared.

Methos flinched.

"That's the real voice! That's the whole of him!"

Cadigan braced himself.

"Aye, and he's nearly here."

The Hunter stood like a gargoyle between the group and the outer corridor, back arched, shoulders broad, white glow flickering through cracked armor.

He wasn't attacking.

He was bracing.

Protecting.

Arthis's voice dropped low.

"He recognizes the new resonance forming."

Callum gritted his teeth as dark energy surged through his chest.

"It's… inside me…

fighting back…!"

Arthis shouted:

"CLAIM IT! Do not let the fragment take control!"

Callum threw his head back in a wordless roar as the shard inside him flexed, filling his veins with raw, ancient malice.

Ailín felt it too.

Her scream choked into silence as her eyes opened, glowing silver with black veins radiating outward.

"Callum…

he's calling me again…"

Callum grabbed both sides of her face, pulling her forehead to his.

"No. He's calling me now. Not you."

Her breath hitched.

Her body shook in his arms.

Arthis lifted both hands, channeling resonance into the chamber floor.

Symbols ignited in a spiral around them.

"Callum! You carry Arkael's echo, use it!"

Callum blinked through the pain.

"I don't, know, how!"

Arthis's voice cracked for the first time.

"You DO! Arkael taught through instinct, not memory!"

Methos staggered forward, holding his cracked ribs.

"Callum, listen to me! Arkael was the only Immortal to ever defeat Boroun because he didn't overpower him, he outmaneuvered him! Use your spark the way he did, use the *echo!*"

Another crash. Stone burst inward as a massive fist punched through the outer wall.

A pitch-black arm, large, jagged, dripping resonance, slid through the crack.

Lila screamed.

Cadigan muttered a terrified prayer.

Arthis went still.

"He is breaching the vault. We have seconds."

Callum's heart pounded like a war drum.

He pressed Ailín to his chest and whispered, "I'm here, sweetheart. Give me everything you've got."

Her small voice shook:

"I'm scared..."

"So am I."

He closed his eyes.

He reached into his spark,

And found a door.

Not a literal door. Not a vision. A sensation.

A memory that wasn't his.

A stillness that belonged to someone who had lived in an age before words.

A shadow of Arkael.

Callum whispered, "...show me."

The echo responded.

Light burst through his chest,

silver on one side, black on the other, white at the core.

Arthis stepped away in awe, "He's doing it..."

But the moment Callum's spark opened fully,

Boroun reacted.

The black arm tore the remaining stone free.

A massive, jagged silhouette burst into the chamber,

Roaring, screaming, hungry for what was taken.

Arthis shouted:

"CALLUM, NOW!"

Callum pulled the shard out of himself with a cry that shook the vault,

Ailín's light snapped violently the Hunter advanced Boroun howled the chamber cracked

The resonance thread ripped free with a sound like metal shearing underwater.

Callum screamed, the force of it tearing through his throat, echoing through the chamber like a tortured storm. A spray of silver-white-black energy erupted from his chest as the fragment of Boroun, twisted, jagged, alive, tore free of him and writhed in mid-air like a living shadow.

Ailín gasped as her glow snapped back to pure silver. She slumped into Lila's arms, unconscious but finally free.

Callum collapsed to one knee, chest heaving, eyes burning with the after-image of something ancient.

Cadigan took a step toward him.

"Lad, !"

Methos threw an arm out.

"Don't touch him! The resonance hasn't settled!"

But the warning was too late.

Because Boroun had arrived.

The chamber wall gave way completely. A massive figure forced itself through the stone, a towering, jagged silhouette of cracked obsidian-like flesh. Black resonance pulsed inside the fractures like veins of molten glass. His presence filled the vault with suffocating heaviness.

Boroun stood fully revealed for the first time, taller than the Hunter, broader than any Immortal they had ever seen. Entirely whole, except for one thing, the thing Callum held inside his spark only seconds ago. His face was carved, ancient, emotionless, yet unmistakably aware.

Boroun's hollow, glowing eyes fixed immediately on the fragment floating in the air above Callum.

He reached out a hand.

The fragment shrieked at the sight of him, twisting away like a frightened animal.

Callum rose to his feet, still trembling, still flickering with the echo of Arkael.

"NO!"

His voice boomed with something that wasn't entirely his own, the resonance of a First echo, an authority older than the Game.

Boroun hesitated.

The chamber fell still. Even the fragment froze in the air.

Arthis inhaled sharply.

"...he hears Arkael in you..."

Methos, "Oh, that's not good."

Cadigan nodded. "It's definitely not good."

Lila clutched Ailín tighter.

"What does that mean?!"

Arthis answered without blinking.

"It means Boroun will not kill him outright."

For a half second, that sounded like relief, until Arthis continued.

"It means Boroun will try to reclaim him."

Callum staggered backward, hand reaching blindly for the Katana.

The Hunter roared, not in defiance, not in hunger, but in protection.

He leapt between Callum and Boroun, cracked armor splitting open as raw resonance surged through him. His white glow intensified until it burned almost silver.

Arthis stared in disbelief.

"He is imprinting on her...and on him."

Lila said, "He's protecting them both..."

Methos groaned.

"That… complicates things."

Boroun stepped forward. He reached again for the fragment.

The Hunter struck.

He slammed into Boroun with enough force to shake the chamber, and Boroun didn't budge.

Instead, Boroun lifted a hand and backhanded the Hunter so violently that the creature flew across the chamber like a ragdoll.

He smashed into the stone with a thunderous crack and collapsed in a heap, unmoving.

Lila screamed.

"NO!"

Cadigan swore.

"We are so very outmatched…"Methos said.

The fragment shrieked, an echo of resonance, lost and afraid.

Boroun extended his hand toward it again.

This time, the fragment did not resist.

It drifted toward Boroun, drawn like a spark back to its flame.

Callum forced himself upright, legs shaking.

"NO! You're not whole yet, she stripped that from you! You don't get it back!"

Boroun's hollow gaze turned toward him.

And for the first time, Boroun spoke,

A deep, resonant voice that rattled the air, "You carry my pain."

Callum's heart lurched.

Boroun took one slow step toward him , "You carry my echo."

Callum swallowed.

He could feel the fragment he held only moments ago.

The pain it carried. The loneliness.

The need to be whole.

He shook his head, "I won't give it back."

Boroun's voice rumbled, "Then you are mine."

Arthis shouted, "CALLUM, MOVE!"

Callum grabbed the Katana,

The fragment darted toward him,

Boroun roared,

The walls fractured,

Ailín stirred in Lila's arms,

And in a surge of pure instinct, pure echo...

Callum swung.

The blade cut directly through the fragment just as it reached for Boroun.

A burst of black resonance exploded outward, blowing both Callum and Boroun off their feet.

Boroun roared in fury.

The vault cracked from floor to ceiling.

Callum collapsed again, eyes glowing with white-silver-black light.

Arthis screamed over the devastation:

"HE HAS CHANGED THE GAME!"

Methos shielded his face from the falling stone.

Cadigan grabbed Lila and Ailín, pulling them to safety.

Boroun roared again, louder than before, a sound of betrayal, rage, and ancient grief.

Callum slowly pushed himself up.

His spark pulsed.

Different.

He whispered, almost afraid of his own voice, "...what did I just do?"

Arthis answered him with a whisper of awe and dread, "You just became the first Immortal in history to wound Boroun twice."

The chamber collapsed further.

Boroun advanced with murderous intention.

Chapter 26

The First Vault groaned under its own weight, the walls trembling as Boroun took another thunderous step forward. Every fractured inch of his obsidian-like frame glowed with violent resonance, black veins pulsing like molten glass through cracked stone.

Callum stood his ground, chest still glowing faintly with the echo that had awakened inside him. His breath came ragged, but he did not step back. Not this time.

Ailín stirred in Lila's arms, her voice barely a whisper.

"Callum... don't let him take you..."

He looked over his shoulder and forced a steady voice, "He won't."

Boroun's hollow, ancient eyes locked onto him. Not at Ailín. Not at the shattered fragment drifting away into nothing. At him. At the Immortal who had taken a piece of Boroun's essence and refused to give it back.

Boroun spoke again, his voice deep enough to vibrate the marrow in their bones, "You carry what is mine."

Callum tightened his grip on the Katana.

"Not anymore."

Boroun tilted his head.

A terrifyingly human gesture.

"Return it."

Callum stepped forward, "My name is Callum MacLeod from the Clan MacLeod...No."

A low rumble tore from Boroun's chest, not a roar, not yet, but something close.

The ground shook beneath them. Dust rained from the ceiling. The vault walls groaned.

Methos raised what remained of his sword.

"Callum, PLEASE tell me you have a plan."

Cadigan staggered to his feet.

"Or at least a death wish!"

Boroun took another step, cracked stone blistering under his weight.

Arthis raised both hands.

"Stand back!"

He slammed his palms against the vault floor. Lines of ancient symbols erupted outward in a spiral, pulsing with light. A resonance barrier formed between Boroun and the group, thin, shimmering, trembling like stretched wire.

Boroun stopped.

He stared down at the barrier...then slowly reached out and pressed a hand against it. A jagged crack formed.

Arthis's eyes widened.

"Impossible. This barrier held him for several millenia, "

The crack widened.

Boroun pushed harder.

Arthis staggered, "CALLUM, HE IS BREAKING THROUGH!"

Callum stepped forward instinctively.

"No, stay behind me."

Lila cried out:

"Callum, NO!"

But Callum had already moved, planting himself between Boroun and everyone else.

Cadigan lunged to join him.

Methos grabbed Cadigan's arm.

"No. Let him go."

Cadigan snarled.

"I'm not lettin' him die alone!"

Methos shook his head.

"He's not dying. Not today.
Look at him."

Cadigan hesitated.

Callum stood alone before Boroun, spark glowing, blade ready eyes burning with three colors at once.

Something inside Callum had awakened. Something ancient. Something that even Boroun recognized.

Arthis whispered:

"He carries the echo of Arkael."

Methos added softly, "And now… a shard of Boroun himself."

Boroun glared at Callum, resonance boiling through his cracked frame.

"You are not whole."

Callum lifted the Katana.

"Don't need to be."

Boroun pressed harder.

The barrier shattered like glass.

The shockwave slammed Cadigan, Lila, and Methos back against the wall.

Arthis stumbled, nearly collapsing.

Only two remained standing when the dust settled – Callum and Boroun.

Boroun lowered his head, ancient hatred simmering behind hollow eyes, "Then I will take what you stole."

Callum inhaled through the pain burning in his spark.

"Come take it then."

Boroun roared.

The Hunter, silent until now, rose from the rubble with a guttural metallic screech and launched himself at Boroun with feral speed.

Boroun caught the Hunter by the throat.

Effortlessly.

And threw him across the chamber with such force the cracked armor tore open mid-air.

The Hunter hit the far wall and slid to the floor, unmoving.

Ailín whimpered, tears forming.

Callum exhaled shakily.

He stepped forward.

"Ailín, stay with Lila."

Ailín, trembling, reached out toward him with small, desperate fingers.

"Callum… don't go…"

"I'll be right here."

He turned toward Boroun.

The chamber shook violently.

Boroun took a step.

Callum took one to match.

Boroun's voice boomed ,"Arkael is dead."

Callum declared, "I'm not Arkael."

Boroun leaned forward, towering over him.

"Then you will die."

Callum raised the Katana.

"Try."

Boroun stepped toward Callum with ground-shaking weight, each movement rippling with unstable resonance. Fractures pulsed along his obsidian frame, bright, jagged veins of blacklight flowing like magma beneath ancient stone.

Callum matched the step with one of his own.

His knees trembled. His breath came ragged. The shard he'd ripped from himself left a burning hollow inside his spark, but the echo that remained, Arkael's echo, held him upright.

Held him steady.

Held him *ready.*

The chamber floor split as Boroun's foot struck the ground. A wave of resonance rolled outward, knocking Cadigan and Methos against the far wall again.

Arthis managed to remain upright, though barely. His hands shook.

"Callum… remember, Boroun's full strength is not physical.
It's resonant. Guard your spark first. Your blade second."

Boroun's voice rumbled through the vault like thunder rolling through stone.

"You carry what belongs to me."

Callum tightened his grip on the Katana.

481

"Not anymore."

Boroun tilted his head, studying him like a predator inspecting something it had never seen before.

"Arkael hid behind tricks. Behind illusions. Behind echoes."

Callum stepped forward, jaw tight.

"I hide behind nothing."

Boroun leaned down slightly, hollow eyes narrowing.

"Then you will break."

And he moved.

Boroun lunged with terrifying speed, far faster than something so massive should move. He swung an arm like a falling mountain, aiming to crush Callum beneath sheer force.

Callum braced,

The impact threw him backward across the chamber, crashing into the stone floor hard enough to crack it.

Lila screamed:

"CALLUM!"

He slid, rolled, forced himself to his knees.

His spark flared instinctively, absorbing the worst of the blow. Pain radiated through his ribs, he wasn't fully healed, not even close, but he stood.

Boroun turned, surprised he was upright at all.

Callum spat blood.

"That all you've got?"

Boroun's eyes flared.

"You cannot bear my resonance."

He struck again.

Callum raised the Katana,

The blade met Boroun's arm with a clash that sent tremors through the pillars.

Black Quickening flashed where the blade struck his stone flesh.

Boroun staggered half a step back.

Just half.

But enough to show it meant something.

Methos blinked through blood.

"...he hurt him. Again."

Cadigan grinned through the pain.

"That's the lad."

Arthis shook his head in awe.

"Not hurt. He *interrupted* his resonance."

Callum rolled out of Boroun's reach, sparks flickering around his hands where his spark remained half-open.

Arthis shouted, "Callum! Break his rhythm! He cannot be defeated by force, only by disrupting his resonance!"

Callum hissed back:

"Then tell me how!"

But Boroun answered for him.

He slammed his foot into the floor, the chamber rippled outward like a stone dropped into water.

The shockwave hit Callum full-force.

His spark buckled.

His knees hit the ground.

Ailín cried out:

"CALLUM!"

He forced himself up again, breath shaking, spark flickering violently.

Boroun advanced, voice low.

"You are not whole. You are not ready."

Callum raised the Katana again.

"I'm enough."

Boroun raised both arms.

"You cannot stop me."

The shattered armor creaked.

A white light flickered.

And the Hunter rose from the rubble.

His movements were unsteady, joints cracking, but his purpose clear, unwavering, instinctual.

He staggered between Callum and Boroun, arms wide.

Protective.

"He has imprinted." Arthis stated, "He thinks Callum and the child are his priority now."

Methos muttered, "Great. The murder machine imprinted is our babysitter."

Cadigan shook his head.

"Now *this* I've got to see."

Boroun looked down at the Hunter with something like disgust.

"You were made to serve me."

The Hunter's hollow eyes glowed brighter.

He roared.

The sound echoed in every direction, deep, metallic, furious, and charged Boroun head-on.

Boroun caught him mid-charge and *slammed* him into the stone wall so hard it cratered.

But the Hunter clawed free and attacked again.

Again. Again.

Each hit shook the chamber.

Each counter tore stone from the walls.

Callum seized the opportunity, spark flaring.

He dashed forward, Katana blazing, slicing through the air toward Boroun's scored left side, the weaker side, the fractured side, the side where the shard had once been.

Boroun sensed it and turned, but not fast enough.

Callum struck.

The blade pierced the obsidian flesh again, deeper this time.

Boroun roared, staggered, backhanded Callum away, but the hit didn't send him flying across the chamber as before.

Callum slid, but stayed on his feet.

His spark flared brighter. Fiercer.

Methos breathed out:

"…he's adapting to Boroun's tempo."

Arthis nodded.

"Arkael's echo is guiding him."

Boroun steadied himself.

He stared at Callum with something new in his hollow gaze.

Recognition.

Callum lifted the blade.

"I know your rhythm now."

Boroun's voice dropped to a whisper that chilled the chamber,

"Then I will change it."

A deep rumble echoed through the vault.

Boroun lifted both arms, the stone around him cracked, pulled outward and glowed black,

He was changing his resonance pattern.

Arthis recognized, "CALLUM, MOVE, NOW!"

Callum dove,

The chamber erupted.

Black resonance detonated outward in a shockwave so violent the entire sanctuary shuddered.

The Hunter was thrown across the room. Cadigan and Methos hit the floor. Lila shielded Ailín with her body. Arthis fell to one knee.

And Callum, Callum crashed into the far wall, spark flickering, chest burning with the shard's phantom pain.

Boroun advanced through the smoke, voice like breaking stone,

"You cannot match me, Echo-Child."

Callum rose, eyes burning with three colors.

"I'm not done yet."

The blast wave faded, leaving dust hanging in the chamber like a fog. Massive cracks webbed the walls, and the floor sank several inches where Boroun's resonance had detonated. The ancient sanctuary, built to contain the impossible, was starting to lose the fight.

Callum pulled himself upright, ribs screaming in protest. His spark flickered sharply, white, silver, and black twisting like a storm. Every time Boroun shifted resonance, the shard inside Callum's memory burned like a reopened wound.

Boroun stepped from the settling dust, towering over Callum.

He lowered his head.

Not to charge. To listen.

Callum felt the hairs on his arms rise.

Boroun was adapting. Not just physically, **resonantly.**

Arthis gasped.

"He's shifting frequency. He's trying to collapse your spark from the inside!"

Callum flinched as a spike of pain ripped through his chest.

"Yeah, I noticed!"

Boroun's voice rumbled, "You carry my echo...and the echo betrays."

Callum spit blood.

"You broke yourself long before I got here."

The chamber vibrated.

Ailín cried out, clutching her chest.

"Callum,

he's hurting me again!"

Callum froze.

He turned to Arthis sharply.

"Why is she feeling it?! I pulled the shard out!"

Arthis's face tightened.

"You pulled most of it out."

Callum's breath stopped.

"What?"

Arthis stepped forward, voice low and urgent.

"Boroun's resonance is reacting to her spark because her spark remembers him."

Lila gasped.

"But she's pure again! You said she was clear!"

Arthis nodded.

"She is. But resonance memory lingers. She is attuned to him, and he senses it."

Another shockwave rippled through the chamber.

Ailín cried louder.

Lila held her close, voice breaking.

"Callum, do something!"

Callum turned toward Boroun.

Breath trembling.

Eyes glowing with three converging sparks.

"STOP HURTING HER!"

Boroun's head snapped toward him.

The resonance in the room stalled.

Holes burned in the dust.

Every crack in the stone glowed at once.

Boroun's voice shook the air,

"She carries what I was denied."

Arthis hissed sharply.

"Callum, move! NOW!"

But Boroun wasn't moving toward the girl.

He was moving toward Callum.

Methos raised a shaking sword fragment.

"Callum! Don't let him get close, if he touches your spark, "

Cadigan shouted, "He'll rip the shard clean out of ye!"

Boroun leveled his hollow gaze.

"Return what you carry…and she will not suffer."

Callum shook with fury.

"She suffers because of YOU!"

Boroun stepped closer.

The Hunter leapt forward, roaring with feral rage.

Boroun caught him by the head, and crushed half of his helmeted skull inward.

The crack echoed through the chamber.

The Hunter's body spasmed and dropped to the floor, twitching.

Ailín screamed.

Lila covered her mouth.

Cadigan whispered, "…dear God."

Methos stumbled back.

"Callum, he's unstoppable. We need to retreat… "

Callum ignored them all.

He stared Boroun down.

His spark pulsed so bright the cracks in the floor illuminated beneath him.

Ailín cried again.

"Callum… he's hurting me, it hurts…"

Callum's voice was low, shaking with fury and love and the echo of Arkael rising like a tide.

"No one hurts her."

Boroun's glow intensified.

"Then return the shard."

Callum shook his head slowly.

"No."

Boroun's entire body flared with violent resonance.

Arthis, terrified, "He's about to collapse the vault, everyone get DOWN!"

The chamber buckled. Stone split.

A shockwave gathered inside Boroun's chest like a storm about to break.

Ailín whimpered, "Callum…"

And Callum stepped forward.

In front of Ailín.

In front of Lila.

In front of everyone.

His spark burned brighter, white, silver, black, intertwined.

He shouted:

"I am not your vessel!"

Boroun roared and unleashed the shockwave.

Callum thrust the Katana forward and screamed,

And the two forces collided.

Light exploded. Stone shattered. The entire vault convulsed.

Methos yelled, "CALLUM!"

Lila screamed, "NO!"

Ailín reached out, crying, "CALLUM!"

The collision of resonance hit the chamber like a supernova.

Callum's spark blasted outward from his chest in a tri-colored wave, white, silver, black, while Boroun's dark resonance surged forward like a tidal force of cracked obsidian light.

The two energies slammed together mid-air.

The explosion was devastating.

The walls bowed outward. Stone split. Monolith tiles shattered into dust. Every light in the vault flared and then dimmed in unison.

Methos hit the ground hard. Cadigan shielded his head with his forearm. Lila wrapped Ailín in both arms and braced herself against the floor.

Arthis alone remained standing, barely, his hands raised to shape the resonance flow enough to keep the entire vault from collapsing.

"Callum, HOLD YOUR SPARK TOGETHER!"

Callum screamed as Boroun's force pushed him backward, sparks skittering off his skin like burning snow.

His knees buckled.

His lungs burned.

His heart felt like it was tearing.

But he didn't let go.

He drove the Katana forward again, forcing his spark into the clash.

"YOU DON'T TOUCH HER!"

Boroun roared, a sound like mountains collapsing.

"RETURN WHAT IS MINE!"

Cracks split across Boroun's torso, bright, jagged lightning lines of resonance where Callum's strike and stolen shard had once lived.

Callum saw it.

His eyes widened.

"That's your weakness…"

Boroun's head snapped toward him.

Callum pushed harder.

"You're not whole because of *me*."

Boroun snarled, stepping forward even through the blast stream.

"YOU CARRY MY PAIN, AND MY POWER, AND MY END."

Callum flinched, the last word echoed inside his spark like a buried truth awakening.

His knees faltered.

Boroun surged forward.

The resonance blast drove Callum back against the floor,

until Ailín screamed.

"STOP! STOP HURTING HIM!"

Her raw, terrified cry tore through the chamber,

and the resonance inside her flared pure silver.

A wave of **Ailín's** spark burst outward, weak but impossibly clean, radiating through Callum's tri-colored storm.

The shockwave hit the mid-air collision,

And for the first time, Boroun staggered.

Callum felt it. Saw it.

He used her spark's pulse like a foothold, like a grip, like a lifeline.

He pulled himself upright again, blade trembling in his hands.

Boroun lurched backward a step.

Only one.

But it was enough.

Cadigan mouthed, "…sweet mercy…"

Methos blinked in disbelief, "She... she *stabilized* his spark."

Callum rose to one knee.

His spark flared brighter, the black streaks tightening, the silver threads bracing the white core, the three energies harmonizing into something terrifying and beautiful.

Boroun froze, head tilting like an animal hearing a distant, ancient sound.

Callum lifted his head.

Every breath hurt.

His spark burned.

His bones felt like they would crack beneath the power he was holding, but he stood anyway.

He looked Boroun in the eye and and yelled, "You don't get to claim me."

The vault trembled.

Boroun leaned forward slowly, studying him with hollow, glowing eyes that flickered with something almost like...

...fear.

Arthis inhaled sharply.

"Callum...he recognizes the change."

Callum steadied the Katana.

"What change?"

Arthis swallowed.

"You are no longer just carrying Arkael's echo.

Or his shard."

Callum frowned.

"Then what am I?"

Arthis met his gaze.

His voice was heavy.

Ancient.

"An Immortal with a First resonance. The first of your kind."

Boroun roared in fury, a roar of denial, rage, loss.

The entire vault shook, and then collapsed inward just as the ceiling gave way.

Arthis screamed,

"MOVE! NOW!"

Callum grabbed Ailín and shielded Lila.

Methos and Cadigan ran toward the far corridor.

The Hunter, barely functioning, dragged himself upright.

Boroun lunged.

Callum turned, spark blazing, and the vault came crashing down around them.

Chapter 27

The world disappeared in stone and dust. The vault ceiling gave way with a grinding roar, stone slabs breaking free in cascading slabs that crashed down like falling cliffs. The sound swallowed everything, the screams, the thunder, Boroun's furious bellow. Then nothing but crushing darkness.

Callum hit the ground hard. Pain shot through his spine. Dust filled his lungs. Ailín screamed into his chest, "CALLUM!"

He tightened his grip around her and rolled, shielding her body as stone debris scattered across his back.

He grunted through clenched teeth.

"Stay with me, Ailín, I've got you, "

Ailín clung to his shirt, sobbing.

"It's dark, it's so dark, Callum, I can't see, "

"I know, hold on, don't let go."

Lila's voice came through the settling dust, coughing, panicked.

"CALLUM, WHERE ARE YOU?!"

He shifted, feeling the weight of debris pinning his legs.

"Here, over here!"

She crawled toward his voice, hands scraping across broken stone, her silhouette emerging through the haze.

"Oh thank God, Ailín, baby, are you hurt?"

Ailín sniffled and raised her head weakly.

"I'm okay… Callum kept me safe."

Lila brushed her hair from her face.

"Of course he did…"

Methos' groan came from somewhere behind them.

"…damn, bones intact, probably, Cadigan, you breathing?"

Cadigan answered with a strained cough, "Aye, barely. Me arm's pinned, but I'm alive."

Arthis's voice followed next, steady but winded.

But one voice was missing.

Callum's breath froze.

"The Hunter…?"

Silence.

Then, A metal scrape. A grinding sound. A heavy thud.

The Hunter dragged himself out from under a massive stone slab, half his faceplate crushed inward, one leg twisted, one arm hanging from frayed cables and shattered armor.

He rose slowly.

Painfully.

Deliberately.

Lila recoiled.

"Oh God…"

But Ailín whispered, "He's hurting…"

The Hunter staggered toward them, just limping forward like a wounded animal trying to locate its pack.

Callum shifted protectively in front of the child.

"Easy… slowly… show me your hands."

The Hunter stopped, head bowed, resonance flickering weakly across his cracked armor.

Arthis observed him carefully.

"He is damaged. Severely. But his instinct remains the same."

"What about Boroun?"

Arthis expression tightened.

He pointed upward toward the massive collapsed ceiling, where faint tremors continued to vibrate the stone.

"Listen."

They all fell silent.

K. A. Beaulieu

Through the thick, choking dust…through the rubble…through the layers of shattered vaults…a low, furious roar rumbled beneath them.

Boroun.

Alive.

Enraged.

Digging.

Callum clenched his jaw.

"He's coming back up."

Methos swore.

"Oh, bloody wonderful."

Arthis turned to them, his robes torn, his face streaked with dust.

"We must move. Now. Before he reaches us, and the tunnels collapse further."

Callum nodded, shifting Ailín into his arms.

She pressed her face into his shoulder.

"Callum… I'm scared…"

His voice softened even as adrenaline surged through him.

"I know, sweetheart. But we're together, and we're getting out of here."

Lila placed a hand on his arm.

"Where do we go? Everything's blocked."

Arthis stepped forward and pointed toward a narrow gap where the stone had broken unevenly, forming a slanted channel leading deeper, not upward, but down.

Lila froze.

"No. Down? Absolutely not."

Arthis met her eyes.

"It is the only surviving access tunnel. Every upper passage is crushed. Boroun will force his way toward us if we linger. We must descend, to the old transit tunnels beneath the sanctuary."

Methos groaned.

"Of course. Downward. Always downward."

Callum asked:

"What's in the transit tunnels?"

Arthis replied without hesitation, "The last route off this island."

Boroun roared again, closer now.

The ground trembled beneath their feet as stone shifted above.

Callum tightened his grip around Ailín and looked at the team, Lila, Methos, Cadigan, Arthis, and the limping Hunter.

"Alright. We move. Stay together. We get to those tunnels, we get off this island, and we regroup."

He turned to the rubble-choked descent.

The only path left.

"Let's go."

And as the first stone shifted beneath their feet, another roar echoed through the broken vault, shaking dust free from the walls.

Boroun was coming.

The slanted break in the collapsed vault was narrow enough that Callum had to turn sideways, shielding Ailín with both arms as he maneuvered through jagged stone. Dust filtered in thin shafts of light, hazing the air with a gritty, choking fog. The debris shifted under each step, grinding in low groans like the island itself was unsettled.

Lila followed close behind, one hand on Callum's back and the other steadied against the wall. Her breathing was sharp, panicked but controlled.

"Careful, there's a drop here."

Callum tested the edge with his boot, finding only loose rubble and a narrow, sloping descent.

He nodded.

"Stay behind me. If anything gives, I'll take the weight."

Ailín clung to him, her small fingers locked in the fabric of his jacket.

"It feels cold down here…"

Her voice trembled, but Callum kissed her temple.

"I'm keeping you warm. Just breathe with me."

Behind them, Methos grumbled as he maneuvered through the rubble, wincing at every movement.

"This is absurd. Tunnels under tunnels under vaults under ruins. What was this place, a stone onion?"

Cadigan grunted, hauling himself over a broken slab.

"I'll take a stone onion over facin' that monster again."

The Hunter, half-crippled, sparks flickering through his shattered armor, lurched behind them. Limbs dragging, metal grinding, but unwaveringly following.

Lila glanced back uneasily.

"Callum... is he... is it safe with us?"

Callum didn't look back.

"Yes. For now."

Ailín whispered against him:

"He won't hurt us."

Lila blinked.

"How do you know?"

Ailín's voice was faint.

"Because... he feels what Callum feels."

Methos froze.

"Oh that's *not* comforting."

Arthis, climbing carefully behind them, murmured:

"His instincts have shifted. He is responding to Callum's changed spark."

Callum exhaled.

"Whatever's happening, we need him. Boroun will tear through these tunnels like paper."

The ground rumbled above them, deep, powerful, inevitable.

A layer of dust fell like gray snow.

Lila flinched.

"Is that him?"

Callum answered quietly, "Yes."

The tremor pulsed again.

Closer.

Cadigan muttered, "He's diggin' through stone. Who does that?!"

Methos replied under his breath, "An immortal who used to be unstoppable on the battlefield."

Ailín whimpered.

"Callum... hurry."

He shifted her weight and kept moving.

As they reached the bottom of the slanted collapsed section, the rubble gave way to a long, narrow tunnel carved with perfect geometric precision, far older than the sanctuary above.

Lila stared in awe.

"This doesn't look like the other vaults."

Arthis nodded faintly.

"It isn't. This predates the sanctuary."

Methos raised an eyebrow.

"Predates the, what, the island?"

Arthis touched the smooth wall.

"No. Older than the island. This passage is part of the original structure, before the sanctuary was built, before Boroun's imprisonment."

Callum frowned.

"So this was here first."

"Yes."

Ailín clutched his shirt tighter.

"It feels… empty. And sad."

Arthis nodded.

"It has been sealed for millennia. Waiting."

Methos snorted.

"Waiting for what? Us to stumble into it running from a cosmic lunatic?"

Arthis didn't answer immediately.

His silence said enough.

Lila gasped suddenly.

"Callum, light up ahead."

Callum adjusted his grip, leaning forward to peer down the tunnel.

Faint illumination glowed in the distance, soft, cold white, pulsing like breath. Not torchlight. Not resonance glow.

"That's not Boroun."

Arthis's eyes narrowed, "No. It is not."

Cadigan's fingers tightened around his broken blade.

"Then what in hell's name is it?"

Arthis stepped past Callum, robes brushing the stone as he moved deeper.

"The transit chamber."

Methos muttered, "Oh, lovely. A room with a name. That always bodes well."

Arthis turned to them.

His expression tightened, and for the first time, Callum saw something in the Archivist's eyes he had *never* seen before.

Fear.

"We must reach the chamber before Boroun does."

Callum nodded, "Then we hurry."

He picked up the pace, running now, boots striking stone in quick, steady rhythm. Lila followed close, supporting Ailín's small arm as she lay against Callum's shoulder. Methos kept pace despite the pain. Cadigan limped but didn't complain. The Hunter moved like a wounded predator, dragging, sparking, relentless.

Behind them, the tremor grew louder.

Closer.

Boroun was nearly upon them.

Callum ran faster.

The tunnel took a sudden downward slope, sharp enough that Callum had to slide the last few feet, keeping Ailín pressed firmly against him.

The group regrouped at the bottom.

Arthis stepped ahead, breath unsteady.

"Just beyond this next turn. The transit chamber lies there."

Another tremor shook dust from the ceiling.

Lila inhaled sharply.

"We have to move, now!"

Callum ran.

A final turn.

A final stretch.

The light grew brighter, illuminating the carved archway ahead.

Callum stopped at the threshold, eyes widening.

Ailín's breath caught.

"Oh… now that's new." Methos said.

Arthis closed his eyes briefly, as if mourning something long gone.

Cadigan muttered, "Bloody hell…"

Because the chamber before them wasn't just old.

It wasn't just deep.

It was impossible.

A massive circular hall spiraled downward like an ancient transit hub, rail lines of stone running in three directions, each carved with symbols that glowed faintly with power older than Immortal memory.

At the center of the chamber…stood something enormous buried under stone.

Something humanoid. Armored

A colossal stone construct; a sentinel

Sleeping.

Waiting.

Ailín whispered, "Callum…he's waking up."

Callum gripped her tighter.

"Oh, hell…"

Arthis exhaled a long, haunted breath.

"We were not meant to come here. Not yet."

Behind them,

Boroun roared and the Sentinel's eyes began to glow.

For a heartbeat, no one moved.

The chamber breathed, if stone could breathe, and the low, pulsing glow radiating from the Sentinel's carved armor cast long shadows across the circular hall. Dust shifted down from the vaulted ceiling in soft curtains. The air carried a faint metallic hum, vibrating deep in Callum's bones.

Ailín clung to him, trembling.

"Callum…he's waking up."

Callum swallowed hard, scanning the massive stone figure.

The Sentinel stood twice the height of a man, carved in a humanoid shape but with armor plates fused into its stone body. Ancient runes spiraled across its limbs, chest, and helmet, glowing faintly in rhythmic pulses that matched the tremors in the floor.

It looked like a knight, a statue…and something much older.

Arthis stepped forward, breath hitching.

"This cannot be…"

Methos groaned as he leaned against the wall.

"Please tell me this is not another Immortal."

Arthis shook his head slowly.

"No. Much worse."

Cadigan frowned.

"Worse than Boroun?"

Arthis didn't answer.

The Sentinel's eyes flared brighter.

Two perfect circles of pale blue light.

Callum shifted Ailín against his chest and lowered his voice.

"Arthis. Talk."

Arthis hesitated, longer than he ever had.

"The Sentinels were not Immortals. They were the First Guardians."

Lila blinked.

"Guardians of what?"

Arthis pointed to the deep spiral structure below.

"Of the originals. The ones who came before the First Immortals."

Methos froze mid-breath, "...that's impossible."

Arthis shook his head.

"Nothing about this island was accidental. This chamber was ancient long before Boroun or Arkael or any of the early Immortals existed."

Cadigan spat dust, You're sayin' this... stone giant is older than all o' ye?"

Arthis nodded.

"Older than all of us put together."

A tremor shook the chamber.

The Sentinel's arms shifted, stone grinding against stone, as he slowly pulled free from the carved alcove. Ancient moss fell from his armor plates in brittle flakes. Dust cascaded from his joints.

His head turned toward the group.

Toward Ailín.

Arthis's eyes widened.

"Callum, back away! He senses her spark."

Callum tightened his grip instinctively.

"No."

Lila stepped behind him.

"WHAT does he want with her?"

Arthis exhaled shakily.

"He was built to identify anomalies in resonance."

Methos's voice lowered.

"Anomalies like... children with two sparks."

Arthis nodded.

"Exactly."

Callum's jaw tensed.

"You mean he thinks she's a threat?"

"No. He thinks she's an activation event."

Ailín whimpered, her small hands shaking.

"Callum... he's looking inside me..."

Callum stepped forward, placing himself between her and the Sentinel.

"Not happening."

The Sentinel's glowing eyes brightened in response. The runes along his chest ignited.

Cadigan lifted his broken blade.

"Tell me how to kill it."

Arthis snapped a glare at him.

"You don't kill a Sentinel. You survive it."

Methos groaned, "Oh perfect.

A guardian with no off-switch."

The Sentinel's chest opened with a low grind, a series of stone plates shifting in ordered sequence. Inside the armor cavity, a swirling sphere of faint resonance pulsed, similar to the artifact Callum shattered, but distinct.

Ailín gasped.

"It's calling me..."

Callum gritted his teeth.

"No. You ignore it."

But Ailín shook her head.

"It's not bad...not angry...it feels lonely."

The Sentinel stepped forward.

The ground quaked beneath each movement.

Arthis raised both hands, shouting,

"STOP! SHE IS NOT AN ACTIVATOR, SHE IS A CHILD!"

The Sentinel ignored him.

Callum hissed, "Arthis, what does it want!?"

Arthis's face went pale, "It wants to test her spark."

Lila nearly screamed.

"TEST HER HOW?!"

Arthis clenched his fists.

"By resonance."

Methos froze.

"...it's going to try to *synchronize* with her."

Ailín whimpered.

"I don't like this, I don't want it, Callum, "

Callum lifted her tighter and stepped back.

"You're not touching her.

The Sentinel's chest closed again, runes spiraling faster.

"Callum...you have to get her out of here."

Cadigan pointed upward.

"And where do ye suppose we go? Boroun is still comin' through the ceiling!"

The tremor above intensified, dust raining down in thick sheets.

A muffled roar echoed through the stone.

The Hunter staggered to his feet, sparks flickering along his half-crushed form. He positioned himself between the tunnel and the chamber, not attacking the Sentinel, but preparing to intercept something behind them.

Callum tightened his grip on the Katana.

"Arthis.

Tell me what happens if the Sentinel touches her."

Arthis said, "...her spark might stabilize."

Lila blinked.

"Might?!"

Arthis continued,

"Or the Sentinel may strip the memory of Boroun's shard from her spark."

Callum tensed.

"And the worst-case scenario?"

Arthis hesitated.

"Might" was gone from his tone.

"Her spark could collapse."

Ailín's breath hitched into panic.

"No, no, Callum, don't let him, "

Callum stepped forward, shielding her fully.

"I said NO."

The Sentinel paused.

For the first time.

His glowing eyes dimmed slightly.

As if measuring Callum, not with hostility, but with recognition.

A resonance flickered through his stone frame.

Callum's spark answered with a pulse of its own.

Arthis froze.

"…he recognizes *you* too."

Methos muttered:

"Oh that's just great. Now the ancient stone guard likes him as much as the murder robot."

The tremor above deepened. Stone cracked. Boroun roared, closer than ever.

Ailín gasped.

"He's right above us, "

Callum set her gently down behind him and lifted the Katana.

"Arthis, can we stop the Sentinel?"

Arthis answered quietly, "No."

"Can we outrun him?"

"No."

Callum's spark flared.

"So what's left?"

Arthis met his gaze, "You talk to him."

Callum blinked, "You want me to talk to a ten-thousand-year-old stone warrior?"

Arthis nodded.

"You carry the echo of Arkael. The Sentinels knew the First."

Methos groaned.

"Oh, he is NOT going to like that."

Cadigan muttered, "I'll guard the lass. Ye go have a chat with the giant."

The Sentinel stepped forward, glowing and waiting.

Callum stepped toward him, Katana lowered but ready.

He lifted his voice and spoke through the resonance in his spark:

"I am Callum MacLeod of the clan MacLoed."

The Sentinel's eyes flickered.

White runes pulsed across his core.

Callum continued, "I carry an echo of the First."

Silence.

Then…

The Sentinel kneeled.

Lila covered her mouth.

Cadigan muttered, "Bloody… hell…"

Methos stared.

Arthis exhaled a single breath.

"He recognizes Arkael's echo. You haven't angered him. You've awakened him."

But before Callum could respond, Boroun roared.

Stone shattered and dust exploded from the ceiling above.

Boroun was breaking through.

The ceiling above the transit chamber split with a jagged, deafening crack. Dust billowed downward in a choking cloud as Boroun's obsidian fist tore through the stone. Shards of rock rained down, smashing into the floor like dropped boulders.

Boroun's roar thundered through the fracture, raw, furious, ancient.

Arthis whispered, almost reverently, "He will not stop. He will dig until the world itself cracks."

Another blow. Another burst of falling stone.

Methos cursed, "Well this is lovely. One unstoppable monster above us, and an ancient stone guardian waking up in front of us. Perfect symmetry."

Lila looked up at Callum desperately.

"What do we do?"

Callum tightened his grip on the blade.

"We make sure she survives this."

The Sentinel's runes pulsed brighter and he rose from his kneeling position, slowly, deliberately, like an ancient machine waking from a long sleep. His stone joints ground against each other with a rumble that echoed through the cavern.

He towered above them, helm angled toward Callum.

His eyes glowed brighter.

A resonance ripple passed through him and outward into the chamber.

Ailín gasped.

"He's... talking..."

Callum knelt beside her, brushing her hair from her face.

"What do you hear?"

She pointed a shaking finger toward the Sentinel.

"He says...you woke him. Not me. You."

Callum blinked.

Arthis stepped forward.

"Callum. This is important."

Callum stood, holding the Katana at his side.

"Explain."

Arthis swallowed hard.

"Sentinels served Arkael. Not Boroun. Not any Immortal. Only Arkael and the originals."

Methos's voice dropped.

"Meaning the Sentinel thinks he's seeing Arkael standing in front of him."

Arthis shook his head.

"No. Not Arkael."

Callum frowned.

"Then what?"

Arthis faced him with somber eyes.

"He thinks you are the heir."

Silence filled the chamber.

"...heir?"

Arthis nodded.

"You carry Arkael's echo. You carry Boroun's shard-memory. And now you stand before a Guardian who knows the First."

Cadigan muttered, "So he's bowin' to him like a bloomin' king."

Methos added, "This is the worst idea the universe has ever had."

The Sentinel shifted slightly.

He extended one massive stone arm, not in attack, but in offering.

A symbol.

Service.

Arthis breathed, "Callum...he's choosing you."

Lila almost choked.

"Choosing him for WHAT?!"

"To lead him."

Callum recoiled.

"No. No, no, no. I don't control him. I don't control ANY of this."

Another crack split the ceiling.

Boroun's roar thundered again, shaking the floor violently.

A massive chunk of stone crashed down, barely missing the group.

Methos staggered back.

"Callum! The giant rock god is bowing to you! USE IT!"

Callum stared up at the Sentinel.

The Sentinel's eyes flared.

A pulse rippled across his chest, a command sequence waiting expectantly for input.

Callum looked back at Ailín.

Her tiny fingers clutched Lila's shirt.

Her eyes were full of fear.

He turned back to the Sentinel.

"You protect her.

Not harm her.

You hear me?"

The Sentinel flared with bright resonance.

A hum vibrated through the floor.

Then, in a voice like an avalanche rolling across a frozen mountain, "ACKNOWLEDGED."

The ground shook again as the ceiling split open completely, Boroun forcing his massive form through the collapsing stone.

His roar echoed with rage.

The Sentinel turned its head sharply, for the first time aware of the threat in full.

A deep pulse vibrated through the chamber.

Callum lifted the Katana.

"This ends now."

Then he shouted to the others, "RUN!"

Arthis grabbed Lila and Ailín. Cadigan supported Methos. The Hunter limped behind them.

Callum stayed where he was, between the Sentinel and Boroun, between two primordial forces that should never have awakened in the same age.

The Sentinel stepped forward, massive and ancient.

Boroun dropped from the ceiling with a crash that shook the entire chamber apart.

The two giants turned toward each other,

And the island trembled.

Chapter 28

The impact of Boroun's landing detonated through the chamber like a subterranean earthquake. The floor buckled. Ancient runes flared. Dust and shards of stone blasted outward in a violent storm.

Callum shielded his face with his forearm as the blast wave hit. Ailín buried herself in Lila's arms as Arthis pulled them toward a lower alcove in the transit hall.

A single figure did not move.

The Sentinel.

He stood unmoved as the shockwave tore past him, his stone armor absorbing the force like it was nothing more than a desert wind. A faint hum rippled across his carved surface, recognition of threat.

Boroun rose to full height, towering in the slanted beam of light pouring through the collapsed ceiling. His cracked obsidian form pulsed with molten-black resonance, his hollow eyes burning brighter than before.

When he spoke, the chamber vibrated.

"You are not of this age."

The Sentinel stepped forward.

The sound of stone grinding against stone was thunderous.

He replied in a voice older than the sanctuary, older than the

Immortals themselves,

"I AM OF ALL AGES."

The runes across his torso ignited in cold blue light.

Boroun's glow flared.

"You serve him."

The Sentinel's eyes shifted from Boroun to Callum.

Then back.

"I SERVE THE ECHO."

Callum's breath caught.

"…me?"

Arthis leaned in, whispering urgently.

"The Sentinel follows resonance, not allegiance. He senses Arkael's echo within your spark. He follows the authority that echo gives you."

Methos muttered, "So Callum is now the world's least-qualified general of an ancient golem. Wonderful."

Cadigan smirked despite the tension.

"Well… he's doin' better at gettin' bowin' respect from giants than I ever did."

Callum ignored them, eyes locked on the two colossal beings.

Boroun took another step, threatening.

The chamber groaned under his weight.

"You kneel to a mortal child wearing my pain."

The Sentinel's glow brightened.

"THE CHILD IS UNDER MY WATCH."

Boroun's voice deepened, almost a snarl.

"HE STOLE FROM ME."

Callum lifted the Katana.

"I didn't steal anything, and what I carry isn't yours anymore."

Boroun's head snapped toward him with terrifying speed.

"THEN I WILL TEAR IT FROM YOU."

The Sentinel stepped between Callum and Boroun, massive arms extending outward like a stone bulwark.

"YOU SHALL NOT PASS."

The words were slow, resonant, and final.

Boroun roared and launched himself forward, and the transit chamber shook as the two ancient beings collided with earth-shattering force.

The impact cracked the floor.

A blast of resonance tore outward.

Methos and Cadigan dove behind a stone support.

Lila fell to her knees, shielding Ailín as Arthis covered them with a protective ward.

The Sentinel grappled Boroun, stone fingers digging into cracked obsidian flesh. Boroun struck back with violent resonance, shattering plates of the Sentinel's armor.

The clash was brutal, primal, older than any duel of Immortals.

Callum watched with mounting dread.

"They're going to bring this whole island down…"

Arthis nodded grimly, "The Sentinels were never meant to fight a fully awakened Immortalm, and Boroun was never meant to face a Guardian alone."

Callum lifted the Katana, eyes narrowing.

"What do we do?"

Arthis answered without hesitation, "We run."

Methos blinked.

"Run? Run WHERE? Those two are blocking the only exit!"

Arthis pointed to the far side of the transit chamber where three spiral-cut transit rails descended into darkness.

"Those tunnels lead to the deep sea causeways. If the mechanisms still function, we can escape."

Cadigan raised a brow, "If they don't?"

Arthis replied calmly, "We drown."

Methos groaned, "Perfect. Always wanted my obituary to say 'died in ancient underwater death-maze.'"

Lila grabbed Callum's arm.

"What about the Sentinel? He's fighting for us!"

Callum looked back at the clash,

the Sentinel's fist smashing into Boroun's jaw, Boroun driving his jagged elbow into the Sentinel's side, resonance exploding in sparks across the hall.

"He's buying us time," Callum said quietly.

"And we're not wasting it."

Ailín tugged weakly at his sleeve.

"Callum...?"

He turned to her gently.

"Yeah, sweetheart?"

Her silver eyes were wide with fear.

"Don't let him hurt the big stone man..."

Callum brushed her hair softly.

"I won't. But we need to get you safe first."

She nodded, trusting him completely.

Behind them, another quake.

The Sentinel slammed Boroun into the far wall with a sound like an avalanche. The chamber shook violently. Cracks spread across the ceiling.

They didn't have long.

Arthis pointed to the descending transit rail.

"There! Move!"

Callum hoisted Ailín into his arms, nodded to Lila, and sprinted toward the far tunnel.

The Hunter limped after them, sparks trAilíng from exposed wiring.

Methos and Cadigan brought up the rear, battered but unbroken.

Behind them,

Boroun roared. The Sentinel answered.

Stone shattered.

The chamber trembled.

Callum didn't look back.

The transit tunnel sloped downward at a steep angle, carved from ancient stone so smooth it felt almost unnatural beneath their boots. Bioluminescent moss clung to the walls, casting faint green light across the pathway. The air grew colder with each step, too cold for a natural cavern.

Ailín shivered in Callum's arms.

"It feels like water... like being underwater..."

Lila kept close, one hand on her back.

"You're doing great. Just keep breathing."

Behind them, the crashing battle of giants echoed through the transit chamber. Stone cracked. The ground trembled. The roar of Boroun reverberated like a living nightmare.

Cadigan muttered as he limped, "He's not stoppin', is he?"

Methos winced as he maneuvered around a fallen pillar fragment.

"He's Boroun. Stopping isn't in his vocabulary."

Arthis slowed, placing his hand on the wall. His eyes narrowed, "The resonance here is different."

Callum frowned.

"How different?"

Arthis's voice dropped into something close to reverence.

"This tunnel predates Immortal resonance entirely. It was carved by the original builders, long before Boroun was born."

Methos stared.

"Arthis, enough of the history lessons, let's get out of here."

Arthis nodded, "Yes.

Ahead, the tunnel divided into three circular passages, each branching outward like spokes of a wheel.

Ailín lifted her head weakly.

"I know this…I saw it in a dream…"

Lila asked, "What do you mean?"

Ailín nodded, "I saw three doors…and the middle one was broken…"

Callum raised an eyebrow at Arthis.

"She's seen this before?"

Arthis rubbed the wall thoughtfully.

"Children with early resonance sensitivity sometimes dream of places they've never visited. Their spark orients itself to powerful sites."

Methos scoffed.

"Yeah, well her spark can orient us toward the quickest route out of here. Boroun's about to punch through the ceiling."

Cadigan stepped to the central passage and tested the ground.

The floor vibrated with a sickening rhythm, a pulsing that felt like the beating of a heart deep below.

He flinched.

"That middle one is no' right."

Arthis nodded.

"It leads to the core. We must avoid it."

Ailín grabbed Callum's shirt.

"Left...

left is safe..."

Callum didn't question it.

He trusted her.

"Left it is."

They moved together down the left passage, the Hunter limping behind them, dragging sparks with each tortured step.

Behind them,

another earth-shattering roar.

Another collapse.

Stone screamed.

Dust billowed.

Then,

A sound none of them had expected.

A metallic chime. Soft. Ringing once. Then again.

Arthis froze, "Oh no..."

Callum spun.

"What is that?"

"The transit system is waking." Arthis stated.

The tunnel lights brightened.

The moss glowed brighter.

A low thrumming filled the passage.

Ailín whimpered:

"He's coming..."

Footsteps boomed behind them.

Heavy.

Enraged.

Getting closer.

Callum lifted the Katana.

"Everyone run."

They sprinted down the tunnel,

as the ancient transit network came alive around them.

The transit tunnel vibrated as if waking from a long, uneasy sleep.

Lines carved into the stone, so thin they had seemed invisible until now, ignited one after another, glowing in pale blue-white pulses. The pattern spread outward like veins of light racing through a colossal creature buried beneath the earth.

Ailín clung to Callum.

"It's waking up...it's waking up like the island..."

Arthis nodded sharply, voice tense:

"It is reacting to the resonance in your sparks. Move, now!"

Callum sprinted down the widening corridor, Ailín pressed tightly to his chest. Behind him, Lila kept close, Methos limped with grim determination, Cadigan cursed at the dust and the incline, The Hunter dragged metal limbs, sparks flickering behind him, and and overhead, the Sentinel and Boroun tore the chamber apart

The tunnel opened abruptly into a massive stone basin, circular, bowl-shaped, with a single cylindrical capsule in its center.

It wasn't metal. It wasn't technological. It was a hollowed stone cylinder carved from the same basalt as the vaults, its sides inscribed with resonance glyphs now glowing faintly.

Methos skidded to a stop, "That's not a pod, That's a coffin with ambition."

Arthis shook his head urgently.

"It is a resonance capsule. The First used them to move between the sections of the island. Get inside!"

Callum didn't hesitate.

He stepped into the capsule, the stone interior surprisingly smooth and warm beneath his palms, almost alive. Ailín's spark pulsed gently as she touched the wall.

"It recognizes us..."

Arthis ushered Lila in, then climbed in himself. Methos entered with a grunt, followed by Cadigan who practically dove to avoid falling rock.

The Hunter stumbled in last, nearly collapsing, but forced himself upright with mechanical determination.

The moment Callum touched the center glyph,

the stone iris sealed shut.

The glyphs on the walls brightened,

pulsing in rhythm with Ailín's heartbeat.

Then with Callum's.

Then with the Hunter's flickering core.

"It's reading us..."

Arthis steadied himself, "It is attuning to your spark. You carry Arkael's echo, that will guide the capsule."

A soft hum grew beneath their feet.

The floor of the stone capsule vibrated.

Light spread along the outer rails, not electric light, but resonant light, pure and ancient.

And then,

the world dropped.

The capsule launched forward with breathtaking force, hurtling down the sloped stone rail like a stone bullet going down the barrel of a gun. The acceleration wasn't mechanical, it felt like being pulled by a current of energy rather than pushed.

Ailín squeaked in surprise and clung to Callum.

Lila gripped his arm, eyes wide.

"The capsule, how is it moving?! There's no engine, no track, no, "

Arthis answered through gritted teeth, "Resonance pressure! It's pulling on their sparks like magnets!"

Methos slammed against the smooth wall.

"I hate ancient elevators. I hate them so much."

The tunnel blurred by in streaks of light and shadow.

The hum deepened into a rhythmic pulse.

Cadigan yelled:

"Brace yerselves, something's changin'!"

The capsule tilted upward,

then angled sharply toward a pinpoint of blue light ahead.

Callum's spark flared instinctively in response.

The capsule flared back.

Ailín gasped.

"It's listening to Callum, he's guiding it!"

Callum opened his eyes, sparks flickering along his skin.

Somewhere deep in his chest, Arkael's echo stirred.

And the capsule surged forward toward freedom.

Light blasted into the capsule as it shot from a carved stone aperture halfway up a sheer cliff. The capsule burst free of the mountain like a bullet from an ancient cannon, arcing over the roaring waves below.

515

Salt air rushed in through the seams.

Wind whipped through cracks in the iris door.

The vast, gray ocean spread beneath them.

Arthis shouted, "HOLD ON, IMPACT!"

The capsule slammed into the turbulent water, sending spray high into the air.

It rocked violently, then stabilized as the resonant energy powering it dissipated into the stone.

The hum faded.

The glyphs dimmed.

The capsule settled as a buoyant stone cylinder on the waves.

They were out.

They were safe,

for the moment.

Methos hauled himself upright, soaked and shaking.

"Well...that was horrible. Absolutely horrible. Let's never do that again."

Lila let out a breathy, astonished laugh.

"I'll take ocean chaos over being crushed underground any day."

Ailín curled against Callum, exhausted but relieved.

"No more tunnels..."

Callum pressed a kiss to her hair.

"No more tunnels."

The wind pulled back the clouds. Sunlight glittered on the waves.

Ahead, a small fishing vessel drifted, unaware of the ancient capsule floating nearby.

Callum sighed with deep relief.

"Let's get you home."

For a moment, the ocean was the only sound.

The stone escape capsule bobbed gently on the cold gray swells, its outer glyphs flickering faintly like embers in a dying fire. Ailín rested against Callum's chest, exhausted, still trembling from the violent escape. Lila stroked her back, whispering reassurance into her hair.

Methos peeked out the cracked iris seam and exhaled a long, relieved breath.

"No falling rocks. No roaring gods. No ancient magic trying to eat my organs.

Cadigan eased himself upright, pressing a hand against his ribs.

"Speak for yerself. Me bones are complainin' louder than that monster's roarin'."

Arthis settled against the curved wall, robes soaked but composed.

"We will not have long before Renwick begins sweeping this coastline."

Callum nodded.

"We'll get moving."

He lifted Ailín carefully and pushed the iris door outward. It resisted for a moment, then loosened with a wet grinding sound as seawater spilled into the capsule's lower lip.

Cold wind washed over them.

Salt stung the air.

And ahead, rocking gently on the water, was the old fishing vessel he'd spotted through the capsule's cracks.

An older man aboard the vessel stared at the enormous basalt cylinder drifting toward him with wide, disbelieving eyes. He made the sign of the cross.

Methos muttered:

"Can't blame him. We look like we crawled out of Atlantis."

Callum raised a hand.

"Ahoy! We need assistance!"

The fisherman hesitated, then shouted back, "What in God's name are ye floatin' in?!"

Cadigan cupped his hands around his mouth.

"A very long story!"

Lila sighed.

"Understatement of the year."

The fisherman, an older Boston transplant named Grady with sun-weathered skin and friendly suspicion, helped them aboard, one by one. He frowned at the stone capsule.

"Never seen anythin' like that."

Callum forced an easy smile.

"Old research equipment. We had a mishap."

Grady eyed their soaked clothes, injuries, and the Hunter, who Callum had ordered to remain inside the capsule to avoid terrifying the man.

"Mishap lookin' that rough, huh?"

Methos smiled weakly.

"Fieldwork is brutal."

Grady grunted.

"Sea's gettin' choppy. Best get you folks ashore."

Ailín leaned into Callum's shoulder, exhausted.

"Callum… we go home now?"

He kissed the top of her head.

"Yes. Just not the home we used to know."

Lila placed a hand on his back.

"We'll make this work."

Callum nodded, meeting her eyes.

"We will."

As Grady steered the boat toward the mainland, the ancient stone capsule drifted slowly behind them, sinking deeper as its resonance faded completely.

Arthis watched it disappear beneath the waves.

"The island sleeps again… for now."

Callum stared at the horizon.

"No.

It's not done with us yet."

A faint vibration pulsed from Callum's jacket.

The dormant AI whispered, "…Callum…I am minimizing all external emissions. Renwick cannot detect me…for now."

Callum murmured back:

"Stay quiet until we reach the new base."

"Affirmative."

Ailín stirred.

"He's sleepy… like me…"

Callum tightened his hold on her.

"Rest now. We're safe."

The boat cut through the waves, heading toward the mainland.

Behind them, the island sank into a storm of stone dust and collapsing cliffs, Boroun's roar echoing faintly and then fading into the ocean wind.

Callum looked up at the sky.

"Time to disappear."

Methos sighed, leaning on the rail.

"I suppose we'll need a new name for the group. Something catchy. Something heroic."

Cadigan snorted.

"Somethin' that keeps us alive."

Lila smiled tiredly.

"Let's settle for 'breathing' for now."

Chapter 29

The fishing boat cut through the gray water, its engine humming steady and low as the coast drew nearer. The cliffs of the Pacific Northwest rose in jagged silhouettes, shrouded in mist and the pale light of an early afternoon sun. After the claustrophobic darkness of the tunnels and the suffocating pressure of the island, the open sky felt unreal, vast, endless, almost too large to comprehend.

Ailín sat bundled in Lila's jacket, her small frame pressed against Callum's side. She'd drifted in and out of sleep since they boarded the vessel, worn thin by fear, resonance surges, and exhaustion. Every so often her fingers twitched, as if feeling phantom echoes of the chaos they'd just fled.

Callum brushed a strand of hair from her forehead.

"You're safe."

Her silver eyes opened just enough to look at him.

"Promise?"

Callum's chest tightened.

"Always."

Lila sat opposite them on a wooden bench, watching the shore approach. Her eyes were puffy and red, her hair matted from seawater, but she looked more at peace than she had since leaving the hospital days ago.

"You realize," she said quietly, "that this is the first time in… I don't know how long… that the air doesn't smell like dust or stone."

Callum smiled faintly.

"I hadn't noticed."

"You noticed. You just weren't going to say anything."

He chuckled once, tired, but real.

She leaned back, exhaling.

"I could actually cry from the smell of pine trees right now."

Methos limped over from beside the wheelhouse, wincing at every step. He dropped onto the bench beside Cadigan with a pained grunt.

"I have survived plagues, crusades, volcanic eruptions, the fall of Rome, and two ex-wives," he said, "but that island is easily in the top five most unpleasant experiences of my immortal life."

Cadigan snorted.

"That's 'cause ye kept gettin' thrown at walls."

Methos raised a finger.

"I would have you know I threw myself at those walls with dignity."

Callum shook his head with a soft smile. The bickering was grounding, almost comforting. Something about normalcy creeping back into their reality felt necessary, like oxygen returning to a collapsed lung.

Arthis stood near the starboard rAiling, staring toward the horizon where the island once stood. His robes fluttered in the wind. He didn't speak. He didn't need to. His eyes carried centuries of knowledge, and the weight of what had just awakened beneath the Earth was etched in his expression.

He turned as Callum approached.

"Your spark has stabilized," Arthis said quietly. "For now."

Callum nodded.

"'For now' seems to be the theme of my life."

Arthis folded his hands behind his back.

"Be grateful. You survived a resonance transformation no Immortal in living memory has endured. The echo of Arkael… the shard of Boroun… and your own spark… they sit uneasily within you."

Callum frowned.

"Meaning what?"

Arthis met his gaze steadily.

"Meaning you are no longer bound to the same limitations as other Immortals."

Methos cleared his throat loudly.

"Meaning he's dangerous."

Arthis didn't deny it.

"Meaning he is necessary," he corrected.

Callum's grip on the rail tightened.

"I didn't ask for this."

Arthis gazed out at the sea.

"Few who matter ever do."

Lila came over and rubbed Ailín's back, "We'll get her somewhere safe. Somewhere quiet. She needs rest. We all do."

Callum nodded, "And we will. I know where we're going."

Methos raised a brow.

"You mean that thing you forgot to tell us about? The 'luxury bunker'?"

Callum gave him a look that was half apology, half exhaustion.

"It's off-grid. Cash-purchased. Not in my name. No digital footprint. No corporate ties."

Cadigan nodded approvingly.

"Well that sounds lovely. Fancy a pint and a bed."

Methos added, "And a shower. And heat. And food that isn't cave dust."

Lila smirked.

"And maybe, just maybe, a locked door between us and whoever Renwick sends next."

At the sound of Renwick's name, Callum's jaw tightened. He reached into his jacket where THOTH's dormant sphere rested.

The AI announced softly:

"…Renwick is expanding surveillance nets……caution is advised…"

Arthis turned to Callum.

"When we reach the shore… I must go my own way. The Archivist has paths untouched by mortals."

Callum stiffened but nodded.

"I won't stop you."

Arthis dipped his head.

"You were not meant to."

Methos added, "Cadigan and I can do some scouting. Old contacts. Old libraries. Old problems. We'll find what you need."

Cadigan gave a small nod.

"Aye. I'll go where ye point me."

Callum looked down at Ailín, who was finally beginning to breathe evenly.

And he understood what had to come next.

"We disappear," he said softly. "All of us. New names. New lives. Off the grid."

Lila squeezed his arm.

"We'll figure it out."

Callum looked ahead toward the quiet safety of a forgotten Cold War relic buried beneath the Earth.

And toward the storm he knew was coming.

The calm ocean swelled beneath the hull.

The sky opened in a break of cloud.

And the boat carried them toward the next chapter of their new lives. The fishing boat eased into the sheltered harbor of Tarbert, a quiet coastal village nestled along the western edge of Scotland. Whitewashed cottages dotted the hillside above the marina, and the smell of woodsmoke drifted faintly from the chimneys. The water was calm, still gray, still cold, but no longer oppressive. Here, the sea felt like a boundary between chaos and refuge.

Callum stepped onto the small wooden dock first, holding Ailín tight against him. She had fallen asleep again, her tiny frame curled under Lila's jacket. The girl didn't stir, even when a gull cried overhead.

Grady, the fisherman who'd rescued them, tossed a rope over a cleat and climbed onto the pier with a grunt.

"Well, that's as far as I can take you," he said. "Tarbert's quiet, but people talk. You lot look like trouble that washed ashore."

Methos limped down the ramp after him, muttering, "You have no idea."

Arthis stepped lightly onto the dock, his soaked robes trAilíng behind him.

"This village suits us for regrouping. Temporarily."

Cadigan rubbed his hands together.

"And it has a pub. I can smell it from here."

Lila shot him a look. "Food first. Sleep second. Pub third."

Callum pressed a folded stack of bills into Grady's hand.

"For the rescue," he said softly. "And the silence."

Grady looked at the cash, then at the weary, battered group.

"You've got an odd feel about you," he muttered. "Like you've seen storms no sailor should."

Callum nodded.

"We're trying to get away from them."

Grady pocketed the money with a nod.

"Aye. Then move quick. A place like Tarbert forgets strangers fast... but it notices 'em first."

The group made their way up the narrow street into Tarbert proper. The village was quiet, midday fishermen hauling gear, a few locals chatting outside a shop, the distant clang of a boat's mast in the breeze.

Ailín woke slowly, blinking up at Callum.

"...Where are we?"

"Scotland," Callum whispered. "Safe land."

"No more tunnels?" she asked.

"No more tunnels," he promised.

Her shoulders relaxed.

The door chimed softly as they entered the little harborside café. Warmth washed over them, radiator heat, the smell of fresh baked rolls, and the low murmur of conversation.

A couple of locals looked their way but didn't stare long. Travelers passed through Tarbert often enough.

They took a table tucked into the corner, away from windows.

Ailín slid into the booth beside Lila, leaning her head gently on her shoulder.

Callum sat across, finally easing the weight of the world off his back for the first time in days.

A waitress approached with a polite smile.

"Tea, coffee, soup? Ye all look chilled tae the bone."

Methos raised a hand dramatically.

"Everything hot you have, please."

Cadigan added, "And anythin' with meat."

Callum offered a tired smile.

"Soups, sandwiches, tea. Thank you."

Warm soup bowls arrived. Ailín took slow sips, her eyes half-lidded.

Lila rubbed her back gently.

"This is what she needs. Real food. Quiet."

Arthis sipped his tea with a thoughtful calm.

"This place is far enough from Watcher outposts," he said.

"But Renwick will cast his net over the UK soon."

Callum nodded.

"We need to be in the air within hours."

Methos leaned back, sipping tea with regal satisfaction.

"I have contacts. Old ones. Very old. Men who owe me favors for wars they caused and wars I ended."

Lila raised an eyebrow.

"And they can get five soaked strangers onto a plane without passports?"

Methos smirked. "My dear, I can get five goats and a piano onto a commercial flight with no questions asked."

Cadigan grunted.

"Seems like ye've tried."

Methos shrugged. "Long story."

Callum glanced toward the window.

"Private airports. Cash charter. No manifests. No questions."

Arthis added:

"And your THOTH must remain dormant until we reach the silo."

Callum nodded.

"I'll keep him wrapped and powered down. Renwick's sweepers can't detect what isn't emitting."

"He's quiet… like he's sleeping."

Callum touched the sphere hidden inside his jacket.

"He'll wake when we're ready."

After eating, they gathered supplies from the small market across the street, water, warm clothing, burner phones, backpacks, and a prepaid satellite locator that Methos tossed immediately into a trash bin.

"Too traceable," he muttered. "We're ghosts now."

The next step was clear:

Callum lifted Ailín again. She wrapped her arms around his neck.

"Where are we going now?"

Callum kissed her forehead.

"To a place where we won't have to run for a while."

Lila walked beside him, her eyes softening.

"Let's get moving."

They headed for the edge of the village.

Behind them, the ferry horns echoed over the water.

Ahead, the road stretched quiet and empty toward the mainland.

And the long journey to Montana, their hidden refuge, was about to begin.

The road leading out of Tarbert wound through rolling green hills and dense pockets of evergreen forest. The air smelled of damp earth and pine, and a cool breeze carried the distant cry of gulls from the harbor. The village slowly disappeared behind them as they walked toward a gravel pull-off where Methos insisted a car would be waiting.

Callum shifted Ailín higher in his arms, her sleepy weight resting warmly against him. Lila walked close on his right side, scanning the rural road with a cautious eye. Cadigan and Arthis followed behind, while Methos strode confidently ahead, hands tucked into his jacket as though leading a tour group instead of five fugitives from a supernatural disaster.

After several minutes of walking, Methos suddenly stopped.

"There it is," he said proudly, gesturing like a man unveiling a masterpiece.

Parked beneath a cluster of trees was a dark blue Land Rover Defender, older model, rugged, clean, and unremarkable in the best possible way.

Lila blinked.

"You had this waiting?"

Methos smiled with the smugness of a man who had rigged empires to fall.

"My dear, I never set foot in Scotland without at least one getaway vehicle strategically hidden within walking distance."

Cadigan whistled.

"Is that how ye survived all those angry husbands and kings?"

Methos grinned. "That, and charming modesty."

Callum approached the Land Rover.

"Is it fueled?"

Methos winked.

"It's mine, Callum. Of course it's fueled."

Arthis tilted his head.

"Is it registered?"

Methos scoffed.

"With who? The dinosaurs?"

Callum exhaled, relieved.

"Good. Let's get moving."

He opened the back door and helped Ailín settle onto the seat. Lila climbed in beside her, making sure she was wearing the small blanket they'd taken from the café. Arthis slid into the front passenger seat, robes gathered neatly. Cadigan took the back with a grunt.

Methos hopped into the driver's seat.

"Next stop," Methos announced, "Oban Airport. Private hangars. Friendly staff. Even friendlier bribe policies."

He turned the key.

The engine rumbled to life.

They pulled onto the narrow country road and accelerated toward the mainland.

For nearly two hours, the Land Rover wound through the sweeping Highlands, green hills rolling like waves, rugged cliffs rising along the coastline, and distant sheep wandering freely across stone walls earlier than anyone should.

Ailín slept most of the drive, her head resting on Lila's lap. Lila brushed her hair gently whenever she twitched.

Callum glanced back often.

"She's exhausted," he murmured.

Lila offered a small smile.

"She's also incredibly strong."

Callum nodded, looking out the window.

"She shouldn't have to be."

"None of us should," Lila replied, "but here we are."

Arthis turned from the passenger seat.

"The girl's spark has endured more resonance trauma in a handful of days than some Immortals experience in centuries."

Methos snorted.

"Brilliant. Add 'walking resonance magnet' to her list of accomplishments."

Arthis frowned.

"It is no small thing. The shard she touched, the echo within Callum, the brush of Boroun's rage. Her mind is still forming... yet she carries all of this without collapsing."

Callum said quietly, "She's just a child."

Arthis met his gaze in the mirror.

"And children are often stronger than we realize."

The road curved, and the peaks of the Grampian Mountains rose ahead.

Methos tapped the wheel lightly.

"Oban's fifteen minutes out. Once we're there, we need to keep it simple. No names, no forms, no conversations longer than ten words."

Cadigan squinted.

"Ye really have a man for every situation, don't ye?"

Methos smirked.

"I have favorites."

Callum leaned forward.

"Just tell me no one will recognize you."

Methos shrugged.

"Oh, they might. But I promise they won't remember me afterward."

Lila blinked.

"What does that mean?"

Methos winked.

"Bribery, dear. Bribery."

The Land Rover rolled onto the outskirts of Oban, winding through the outskirts until the small regional airport came into view, white hangars, private airstrips, and a few parked charter planes glinting in the late afternoon sun.

Methos slowed the vehicle behind a row of maintenance sheds.

Callum shifted.

"How do we do this?"

Methos pointed with theatrical flourish toward a small, windowless office near the runway.

"One of my contacts runs a private charter outfit. He owes me for the time I saved him from being deported for smuggling French champagne into London."

Cadigan snorted.

"Seems like a noble cause."

Methos smiled.

"I thought so too."

Arthis leaned toward Callum.

"Once you enter the United States, the federal Watchers will be alert to unusual movement. You must mask your resonance."

Callum nodded.

"I feel stable again. I'll focus on suppressing it."

Ailín stirred, mumbling softly.

"He's looking for you…
the bad one…"

Callum touched her cheek.

"We're far away from him now."

Arthis frowned quietly.

"Distance does not always diminish resonance."

Lila set her jaw.

"Then we'll keep moving."

Methos clapped his hands once.

"Excellent attitude. Now everyone look moderately wealthy, completely anonymous, and slightly bored. That's how you pass as normal in private aviation."

Cadigan raised his hand.

"What if yer none o' those things?"

Methos patted his shoulder.

"Fake it."

Methos approached the office with Callum beside him, Lila staying back to watch Ailín. The man inside, a balding Scotsman with a weathered face, looked up and froze.

"Methos? Bloody hell, I thought, "

Methos held up a hand.

"Don't finish that sentence. Time is money. We need a bird in the air. Cash."

The man's eyes flicked from Methos to Callum.

"No paperwork?"

"No paper," Methos repeated, sliding a thick envelope across the counter.

The man peeked inside.

"…Aye. Plane's yours."

Callum exhaled relief.

The man leaned forward.

"Methos… trouble followin' you?"

Methos smiled pleasantly.

"When isn't it?"

They moved quickly toward the hangar where a white mid-range charter jet was being prepped. The engines whirred softly as ground crew fueled her.

Callum helped Ailín up the steps. She looked back toward the Highlands, sleepy-eyed.

"Are we leaving Scotland?"

Callum nodded gently.

"For now."

Lila squeezed her hand.

"It'll be a long trip. But you can sleep."

Ailín smiled faintly.

"I like sleep."

Cadigan laughed softly.

"Smart lass."

Methos paused at the base of the stairs, staring at the horizon as if looking for something. Or someone.

Callum asked quietly:

"You okay?"

Methos exhaled.

"Just thinking. Scotland always brings back old ghosts."

He forced a smile.

"Let's go before they notice."

They boarded the aircraft.

The door sealed.

The engines roared.

And for the first time since the storm hit the island, Callum felt a sense of forward motion, away from danger, toward safety.

Toward Montana.

Toward the silo.

Toward the quiet they desperately needed.

The plane lifted off the runway in a smooth arc, banking over the dark green quilt of the Scottish Highlands before climbing into cloud. Ailín, exhausted beyond comprehension, fell asleep again before they reached cruising altitude. Lila tucked a blanket around her small frame and gently brushed a curl away from her forehead.

Callum watched the land recede beneath them until nothing but gray mist and sky remained. This time, leaving Scotland didn't feel like exile. It felt like necessity. Survival. A chance to breathe before the next storm.

Cadigan exhaled deeply in his seat, sinking back with a grunt.

"Feels wrong being in a plane and not expectin' it to blow up."

Methos sipped the miniature bottle of scotch he'd commandeered almost immediately.

"Oh, don't be so dramatic. Only half the planes I've ever flown in have exploded."

Arthis turned a slow, grave look toward Methos.

"That is not comforting."

Methos shrugged.

"Life isn't comforting."

Callum smirked despite himself.

The flight was long and quiet. The jet skimmed above the Atlantic through long stretches of turbulence. Each pocket of rough air made

Lila grasp the armrest with a tight breath.

Callum placed his hand over hers.

"You're safe," he said softly.

She nodded, eyes closing.

"I know. I just, after everything that happened, it's hard to stop expecting the floor to fall out from under us."

He squeezed her hand.

"Not this time."

Arthis sat across from them, looking contemplative, as though calculating something deeply ancient and complex. His eyes kept drifting toward Callum, not in worry, but in evaluation.

Finally, he spoke.

"Your spark is… different."

Callum met his gaze.

"Define different."

Arthis tilted his head, studying him.

"Stronger. Wilder. Less tethered.

The echo, the shard, and your own spark are no longer competing. They are beginning to align."

Callum exhaled slowly.

"And what does that make me?"

Arthis answered without hesitation.

"Something new."

Methos muttered from across the aisle:

"That's exactly what I didn't want to hear."

Cadigan stabbed a chunk of cheese with a plastic fork.

"Aye. New things tend ta cause old problems."

Hours later, the pilot announced descent toward a small private airfield in North Dakota, intentionally off the main grid, a ghost airport with minimal staffing and almost no digital oversight.

Methos's contact had arranged the landing with a level of casual bribery that would've impressed even Cadigan.

The jet touched down quietly, wheels squeaking on the deserted tarmac. Only a handful of hangars and a single airfield operator were visible from the windows.

Callum adjusted Ailín in his arms as she woke, her eyes blinking slowly.

"Did we fly around the world?"

Callum smiled.

"Yes."

"Can we sleep now?"

"Very soon."

Cold Midwestern air hit them as they stepped onto the tarmac. The sky was vast, endless blue with streaks of gold as the sun dipped toward the horizon.

Methos took a deep breath.

"American soil. Guns, trucks, fried food, and too many people who ask too many questions. Delightful."

Cadigan laughed.

"Ah, ye love it."

The airfield operator didn't ask questions, he merely accepted the thick envelope Methos handed him and pointed toward a row of abandoned rental sheds where several old vehicles were stored.

Arthis raised his hood.

"The journey continues. But my road diverges soon."

Callum turned to him.

"You're leaving?"

Arthis nodded.

"The Archivist's path is not one of shelter or sleep. I must seek answers this land has forgotten it holds."

Ailín looked up at him.

"You'll come back... won't you?"

Arthis gave her a rare, gentle smile.

"When the time is right."

He bowed slightly to Callum.

"Guide her well. Your journey is far from over."

And without another word, he stepped into the tall prairie grass and began walking toward the distant horizon.

Methos watched him walk away, and turned to Cadigan with a smile, "He looks like a nursing home patient wandering away."

Cadigan replied, "Be careful, he probably heard that .

Methos tossed a set of keys to Cadigan.

"Come on, old man. We've got contacts to shake down, bars to search, libraries to raid, and a few secret government files to misplace."

Cadigan grinned despite his injuries.

"Lead the way, ye mad bastard."

Methos tipped an imaginary hat to Callum.

"We'll find intel on Renwick, on Boroun, and on anything else waiting to kill us all. Try not to break anything while we're gone."

Callum smirked.

"No promises."

Methos winked and walked toward a beat-up Jeep with Cadigan hobbling behind him.

Ailín waved.

"Bye, Mister Methos!"

Methos looked back, softening for just a moment.

"Stay safe, little flame."

Cadigan called over his shoulder:

"Keep an eye on yer dad, he's trouble."

Callum snorted.

"Pot. Kettle."

They drove off in a cloud of dust.

Now alone on the tarmac, Callum adjusted Ailín and turned to Lila.

"That bunker... how far?"

She exhaled.

"Maybe... twelve hours south by car, depending on how much we avoid major roads."

Callum nodded.

"We'll stay off the grid."

Ailín yawned.

"What's a bunker?"

Callum smiled gently.

"It's a safe place. Underground. Warm. Quiet."

Her eyes brightened slightly.

"No tunnels though... right?"

He shook his head.

"No tunnels. Just a home. Our home. For now."

Lila locked eyes with him.

"Then let's get going."

Callum lifted THOTH's dormant sphere from his jacket and wrapped it in a thick, insulated bag, sealing every micro-seam.

"Rest now, THOTH. I'll rebuild you when we get there."

A faint whisper responded:

"…Acknowledged…

…low-power silent mode engaged…"

And then he went quiet.

Callum placed the bag in the backseat of an old Suburban they found in the rental shed, a vehicle with no digital systems, no GPS, and no black box.

Exactly what they needed.

Callum slid behind the wheel.

Lila buckled Ailín in beside her.

The sky was turning orange as the sun began to sink.

And as Callum pulled the truck onto the old access road leading toward Montana, he allowed himself, for the first time since the island, to breathe.

The fugitive era had begun.

But so had their chance at peace.

Chapter 30

The Suburban's tires hummed across the cracked asphalt as Callum steered south through the plains. The world outside stretched wide and empty, flat fields of dry grass extending to the horizon, broken only by the occasional windmill or abandoned farmhouse. The sky above them was an enormous bowl of fading gold, the sun melting into streaks of crimson and violet.

Ailín slept in the backseat, curled up under a blanket Lila tucked around her. The soft rise and fall of her breathing was the only sign that the girl hadn't simply dissolved under the weight of the last week. Every once in a while, her small fingers twitched against the seatbelt, echoes of resonance she couldn't yet control.

Callum watched her through the mirror.

Every twitch tore at him.

Lila glanced over.

"You're doing it again."

"What?"

"Staring at her like you expect her to disappear."

Callum's grip on the wheel tightened slightly.

"She's been through hell. We all have. I just… want her somewhere she can sleep without fear waking her."

Lila reached out and placed her hand over his.

"And we're almost there."

The plains darkened as twilight deepened. An expanse of stars unfurled overhead, far more than anyone living in a city ever saw. Lila leaned back in her seat, watching them.

"It's strange," she murmured. "The sky feels so big here."

Callum nodded.

"Montana does that. Makes you feel like you're a guest in a world much larger than you imagined."

Lila smiled faintly.

"Kind of like traveling with immortals."

"That too."

They drove in silence for a time.

Only the hum of the engine.

Only the whisper of wind through cracked window seals.

Only the stars watching their slow migration across the dark prairie.

Then Lila asked softly:

"Callum... what happens when we reach the bunker?"

He glanced at her.

"We rest. We plan. We rebuild THOTH."

"And then?"

Callum looked back at the road.

"I don't know," he said honestly.

Lila studied him, her voice barely above a whisper.

"You carry so much. You always have."

Callum didn't respond immediately.

Finally he said quietly:

"She deserves better than what she's been dragged into. And you,
"

Lila reached over, gently touching his arm.

"Don't finish that sentence. We're here because of choice. Not accident."

His jaw loosened, and something softened in his expression.

A small voice broke the silence.

"Where are we...?"

Callum glanced into the mirror.

Ailín had pushed herself upright, her eyes still foggy with sleep.

"We're in America now," Lila said warmly. "On our way to a safe place."

Ailín blinked.

"Is it under the ground?"

Callum nodded.

"It is. But it isn't like the tunnels. It's warm. Dry. Safe. Built for people to live in. It'll feel like a home."

Ailín hugged the blanket around her shoulders.

"Can I draw on the walls?"

Lila laughed softly.

"Probably not the real walls. But I'm sure we'll find paper."

"And my own bed?"

Callum nodded.

"Yes."

"And no scary stone men?"

Callum hesitated, just a fraction of a second, but she didn't miss it. Her face fell.

"They're gone... aren't they?"

Callum reached back, brushing her hair.

"The one that protected us isn't chasing us. That's all that matters right now."

Ailín nodded slowly.

"Okay... I trust you."

Hours later, they stopped at a lonely gas station lit by a single buzzing fluorescent light. The station attendant didn't even lift his head as Callum paid in cash for fuel and bottled water. They climbed back into the Suburban and resumed driving.

But something changed.

Callum felt it first, a tightening in the air.

A tension just beneath the surface.

THOTH's dormant sphere vibrated faintly from the duffel bag in the back.

Just one flicker.

Callum stiffened.

Lila felt it too.

"Callum... is he, "

"No. That was a passive resonance pulse. Not active."

Ailín looked up.

"It's not the bad one. It's… someone else. Someone looking."

Callum inhaled sharply.

"Renwick."

He glanced at Lila.

"We have to assume he knows we're back in the States. He'll monitor movement, buy satellite data, scrape thermal signatures from half the damn country if he has to."

Lila frowned.

"How much time do we have?"

Callum thought for a long moment.

"Hours," he said.

"Maybe less."

He pressed harder on the accelerator as the empty road swallowed them.

They turned off the highway after midnight, driving along an unmarked gravel road that vanished into an expanse of dark prairie. The stars overhead were dizzying, like scattered diamonds on black water. The wind howled across the plains, rustling dry grass for miles.

"I hear… quiet." Ailín said.

Callum smiled.

"That's what it's supposed to sound like here."

The Suburban climbed a shallow ridge and descended into a shallow valley. Tucked into the earth, beneath a grassy slope, illuminated only by moonlight and the faint glow of the headlights, lay what looked like an abandoned cattle shed and a rusted metal hatch half buried in soil.

To anyone else, it was nothing.

To Callum, it was home.

Lila stared.

"This is it?"

Callum nodded.

"It's disguised on purpose. The real entrance is under the shed."

Cadigan would've approved. Methos too.

But they weren't here.

It was just the three of them now.

Callum parked the truck and exhaled, long and deep.

"We're here."

Ailín smiled sleepily.

"Home..."

Lila rested her head back.

"God... finally."

Callum stepped out of the truck and breathed the cold Montana air. He felt the quiet. The safety. The isolation.

A man could disappear here.

A family could disappear here.

He looked up at the stars.

"Let's go inside."

Callum stepped into the chill Montana night, the cold air wrapping around him in a way that felt strangely familiar, clean, unpolluted, almost sacred. The wind rustled across the tall prairie grass, carrying with it the scent of sagebrush and distant pine. Overhead, the Milky Way stretched in a sweeping arc, brighter than the lights of any city back home.

Ailín blinked the sleep from her eyes as Callum lifted her out of the Suburban. She nestled immediately into his shoulder.

"It's cold," she shivered.

"It's dry cold," Lila said, coming around the truck. "Montana kind. You get used to it."

Ailín yawned and nodded softly.

Lila stepped beside Callum, looking up at the star-splashed sky in awe.

"I've never seen so many stars."

"This land was built for silence," Callum murmured. "And secrets."

She smirked lightly.

"Fitting."

Callum motioned her toward the shed.

"Inside. Let's get out of the wind."

To anyone passing by, the small wooden structure looked like a rundown cattle shed: warped boards, peeling paint, a door swollen from winter frost. Callum jiggled the handle twice, then lifted the latch in a specific pattern, one Methos would've appreciated for its subtlety.

A soft mechanical thud answered the motion.

The door swung inward.

Ailín wrinkled her nose.

"It smells… dusty."

"It hasn't been opened in years," Callum said. "But it's safe."

The inside of the shed was empty except for a concrete floor and an old feed bin. Callum stepped to the center and brushed aside a layer of loose hay.

A steel hatch waited beneath.

Lila let out a low whistle.

"Well… hello Cold War luxury."

Callum pulled the heavy latch, one solid pull, then a slow twist. The hatch hissed faintly as air pressure equalized.

"Stand back," Callum said.

He lifted the hatch.

A faint, warm glow rose from below, gentle amber lights flickering on automatically as the opening widened. A cool breeze drifted upward, like air circulating through a deep, quiet cavern.

Ailín leaned forward from Lila's arms.

"It's… pretty."

Callum smiled.

"Wait until you see inside."

He descended the metal ladder first, boots clanging softly against aged steel. Lila handed Ailín down to him, then climbed after. When they reached the bottom, the hatch closed behind them with a soft hydraulic click, sealed, secure, invisible from above.

Warm, filtered air greeted them in the main entry chamber, a small, round room with reinforced concrete walls and embedded LED strips set into the flooring. A control panel flickered to life as Callum approached it, reacting automatically to motion.

Lila's eyes widened.

"This is… surprisingly modern."

Callum nodded.

"It was a top-of-the-line civilian conversion when it was built.

private buyer hired a company to turn the old launch control center into a full-suite luxury shelter. Handed down through two generations before it landed in my hands."

Ailín tugged his shirt.

"Is this where we live now?"

"For a while," he said gently.

Ailín peeked around him, her voice barely above a whisper.

"It's warm."

"Intentionally," he said. "Let's go deeper."

He led them down a short corridor. Soft amber lighting illuminated murals of mountain ranges painted on the walls, someone's attempt to make the underground space feel more like home.

They passed through a heavy blast door and emerged into a spacious main living area.

Lila actually gasped.

A large circular room stretched before them, a full kitchenette, a sectional couch, soft carpeting, bookshelves, a built-in fireplace heater, polished countertops, a small dining nook, and a private sleeping corridor branching off to the right

There were no windows, only simulated daylight panels set in the ceiling. They cast a warm glow across the space, creating the illusion of a morning sun.

Ailín's eyes grew wide.

"It's... it's like a real house!"

Callum chuckled softly.

"Better than tunnels, right?"

She nodded vigorously, her exhaustion fading slightly as excitement took over.

Callum set Ailín down and let her wander the space. She shuffled over to the couch, ran her hand across the cushions, then peeked around the rooms branching off the main hub.

She pointed.

"Is that a bed?"

Her voice cracked with hope.

"It sure is," Callum said.

She looked at him as if she needed confirmation that it wasn't a trick.

"For me?"

"For you," Lila said, stepping beside Callum.

Ailín's face lit up in a way Callum hadn't seen since the hospital.

Ailín raced (as much as a half-swaddled exhausted child can race) into the small bedroom, soft bed, plush blanket, dimmable bedside lamps. A child's-sized paradise compared to everything she had lived through this week.

Callum leaned against the doorframe, watching her bounce experimentally on the mattress.

"Careful," he said.

She giggled.

"I like it."

Lila rested her hand on Callum's arm.

"She needs this. Hell, we all do."

He nodded.

"I know."

Callum returned to the living area, lifting the duffel bag with THOTH's sealed sphere inside.

"I need to hide him until I can rebuild the system."

Lila frowned.

"Somewhere Renwick can't detect?"

"Exactly."

Callum approached the bunker's old control center, an armored room with thick copper shielding. Once used to monitor launch protocols, it was now a dead zone for signal: no Wi-Fi, no cellular leakage, no resonance propagation.

He set the bag gently inside.

A faint whisper emanated from within.

"...location secure...signal suppression detected...entering deep-silence now..."

Then silence.

Lila exhaled.

"That's one problem handled."

Callum locked the control room.

"One of many."

Later that night, after showers, clean clothes, and the first hot meal they'd had in days, Ailín curled under her blanket in her new bed.

Callum sat beside her.

"Callum?"

"Yes?"

"Will we stay here forever?"

He smoothed her hair, heart tight.

"No. Just until it's safe."

"Will it be safe soon?"

He hesitated.

Then lied gently:

"Yes."

She reached out, small fingers touching his.

"Will you be here when I wake up?"

Callum nodded.

"Always."

She fell asleep within seconds.

Lila leaned in the doorway, watching.

"You're good with her."

Callum stood slowly.

"She's been hurt enough."

Lila stepped closer.

"So have you."

He swallowed.

"So have we all."

Callum and Lila retreated to the living area, soft lights glowing, heater humming quietly, the heavy earth above muffling every sound from the world outside.

Ailín slept peacefully. THOTH was shielded. Renwick had no clue where they were. For the first time in days, maybe years, Callum felt safe.

Lila sat beside him.

"Welcome home."

Callum rested his head back.

"Feels strange," he said softly. "Being still."

Lila nodded.

"Get used to it. Because tomorrow... we start planning."

Callum stared at the ceiling panels.

And for the first time, the quiet didn't feel threatening.

It felt earned.

Morning came slowly in the bunker.

Callum awoke to simulated "sunlight" brightening gradually across the ceiling, soft, warm, almost convincing. The air held a faint scent of cedar from the artificial diffuser system built into the ventilation unit. It was comfortable. Controlled. Quiet.

Too quiet.

Callum sat up on the couch, rubbing the stiffness from his neck. For a moment he lay still, listening, trying to decide whether the quiet meant safety or simply the eye of another storm.

Lila's footsteps approached softly.

"Morning," she said.

He turned.

She stood by the kitchenette, hair pulled back loosely, wearing a fresh shirt and jeans someone left in the bunker decades ago. She looked more rested than he'd seen her in days, still tired, but human again.

"Morning," he said.

She poured coffee into two mismatched ceramic mugs and handed him one.

"You slept on the couch?"

Callum nodded.

"You needed the bedroom."

"And what about you?"

He shrugged.

"I didn't want to leave Ailín alone her first night."

Lila smiled softly.

"You're allowed to rest too, you know."

"Eventually."

A sleepy voice rose from the hallway.

"Callum...?"

He stood immediately, coffee forgotten.

"I'm here, sweetheart."

Ailín emerged, still clutching her blanket, her hair sticking out in soft curls in all the wrong directions. She looked like a small, bewildered bird finding itself in an unexpectedly warm nest.

She blinked.

"I'm… not in the stone place."

Lila knelt.

"No tunnels. No cliffs. Just us."

Ailín shuffled forward and hugged Callum tightly.

"It wasn't a dream?"

"No," he said, kneeling to her height. "This is real."

Her silver eyes softened.

"Good. I like it here."

Callum lifted her.

"Hungry?"

She nodded against his shoulder.

"Starving."

Lila reached into the fridge, stocked with long-term supplies, freeze-dried meals, canned goods, and a surprising amount of pre-packaged oat bars, and pulled out a carton of eggs and a packet of bacon.

"You eat eggs?" she asked.

Ailín's face lit up.

"Yes!"

Lila beamed.

"Then eggs it is."

Breakfast felt… normal.

Almost painfully normal.

Ailín chattered softly as she ate scrambled eggs and toast. She swung her feet under the table, humming a little tune that sounded like something she'd heard long before the tunnels and resonance and ancient horrors.

Lila watched her with quiet joy, relief written in every line of her face.

Callum sipped his coffee, letting the taste anchor him.

For once, they weren't sprinting through collapsing chambers, dodging blades, or bargaining with millennia-old threats.

They were just eating breakfast.

For ten minutes, Callum let himself breathe.

And then,

A faint hum vibrated through the bunker.

Ailín froze.

Lila looked at Callum.

"THOTH?"

Callum shook his head, tense.

"No. THOTH is in deep-silence mode."

Ailín's voice was a whisper.

"It's not the quiet one. It's... someone else."

Callum felt his pulse spike.

"Ailín, what do you feel?"

She pointed upwards, toward the earth overhead.

"Someone is searching."

Callum swallowed.

"Renwick?"

Ailín shook her head slowly.

"No... not him. Someone older."

Lila's face paled.

"Boroun?"

"No," Ailín whispered. "He's still trapped. Angry. But far."

Callum knelt down to her level, his voice calm and steady.

"Who, then?"

Ailín's eyes drifted to the left, as if she could see beyond the walls, through the concrete, across the continent.

Her voice trembled.

"Someone with a spark......looking......but not at us. Not yet."

Callum frowned.

"A Watcher?"

Ailín shook her head again.

"It's not a Watcher."

She pressed her hands to her temples.

"It feels like... someone who knows you."

Callum froze.

Lila stiffened.

"Callum... who would know he's alive?"

Callum stood slowly, jaw tightening.

"There are only a few Immortals who could sense a resonance shift across continents."

Methos.

Cadigan.

Arthis.

But Methos and Cadigan were on their own missions. Arthis had left. None of them would project their spark this far.

Which left someone else.

Someone ancient.

Someone attuned to the same echo now embedded in Callum's spark.

Callum exhaled sharply.

"Someone who knew Arkael."

Lila stared at him.

"Is that possible?"

Callum didn't answer immediately.

Finally he said:

"Anything's possible now."

Lila placed a hand on his chest.

"Callum... we came here to hide. To rest. To plan."

"We will," he said gently.

"But this means Renwick isn't our only problem."

Ailín tugged at his shirt.

"Will he find us?"

Callum crouched again, holding her face gently in his hands.

"No," he whispered. "Not here. Not today."

Ailín leaned into him.

"Okay..."

Callum stood and looked around the bunker, at the comfort, the warmth, the fragile safety.

"We stay quiet," he said. "We stay off-grid. And we keep THOTH silent until I can rebuild him."

Lila nodded firmly.

"And in the meantime?"

Callum's eyes hardened, not with fear, but with resolve.

"In the meantime... we prepare for whoever comes next."

Ailín pressed close to his leg.

Lila slid her hand into his.

And for the first time since they escaped Scotland, Callum felt something that almost resembled clarity.

Not peace.

Not yet.

But direction.

The quiet of the bunker settled into something deeper as the day wore on, weaving itself into the walls, the lights, even the rhythm of their breath. After breakfast, after the uneasy conversation, after Ailín retreated to her room for a desperately needed nap, Callum finally allowed himself to sit.

He sank into the couch, elbows on knees, staring at the softly glowing ceiling.

Lila sat across from him, watching him quietly.

"You're somewhere else," she said.

Callum didn't deny it.

He ran a hand along his jaw.

"For the first time in days... I can think. And my head isn't sure if that's a blessing or a curse."

Lila leaned back.

"Depends what you're thinking about."

"Everything," he said. "Renwick. Boroun. Whoever Ailín felt out there. Methos and Cadigan. Arthis. This place. Us."

His voice softened on the last word.

Lila swallowed.

"We'll figure it out. Together."

He looked up at her, eyes tired but steady.

"I don't know what comes next, Lila. I really don't. But I'm not letting anything, Watcher, Immortal, or otherwise, take her away. Or you."

The room fell into a comfortable hush.

Hours later, as the simulated daylight dimmed, a sharp cry cut through the bunker.

Callum bolted up.

"Ailín!"

Lila was already running.

They reached her small bedroom as she thrashed on the bed, tiny fingers clenched around the blanket. Her breath hitched in panicked gasps.

"No, no, stay away, Callum, !"

Callum knelt beside her.

"It's me. I'm here. Wake up, sweetheart."

Ailín jerked awake with a gasp, tears streaming down her cheeks.

Lila gathered her gently.

"What happened?"

Ailín shook, pressing her forehead into Callum's shoulder as he lifted her onto his lap.

"He, he was shouting, he was breaking everything, and the lights were falling, "

Callum stroked her hair.

"It was just a dream."

"No…" she whimpered. "It was him. The broken one."

Callum's jaw tightened.

Boroun.

Even oceans and continents away, even underground, his presence still clawed at her spark.

Lila held Ailín's hand.

"Look around. Do you see stone walls? Darkness? Tunnels?"

Ailín sniffed.

"…No."

"You see a room," Lila said gently. "A soft bed. Warm lights. A blanket that smells like detergent instead of dust."

Ailín nodded timidly.

Lila smiled. "We're safe here."

Ailín leaned into her.

"I want to sleep with you both tonight."

Callum exchanged a glance with Lila.

"Of course," he said softly.

Later, after settling Ailín between them in the larger bedroom,

Callum turned off the artificial daylight and dimmed the warm amber floor lights.

Ailín curled into his chest.

Lila lay beside them, the quiet settling around the three like a heavy, comforting quilt.

"Thank you," Lila whispered in the dark.

"For what?" Callum asked.

"For bringing us here. For keeping us alive. For being... you."

Callum exhaled, long and slow.

"I'm just doing what I can."

Lila shifted closer.

"That's all any of us can do."

Silence wrapped around them,

For the first time since the island, the silence felt like a friend.

Ailín's breathing slowed into sleep, small fingers curled in Callum's shirt.

Lila reached across her and brushed his knuckles gently.

"Get some rest."

Callum nodded.

But he didn't sleep.

Not yet.

Not with whatever Ailín had sensed still echoing faintly in the back of his mind.

Not with Renwick out there tightening his nets.

Not with Boroun's rage pulsing somewhere in the deep dark beneath the earth.

Not with another ancient spark reaching across the continent...

Not. Yet.

But he let himself hold them both until exhaustion finally pulled him under.

Chapter 31

The bunker held its silence through the night, wrapped in earth thick enough to smother any sound, any signal, any hint that life pulsed below. Morning, if one could call the gradual brightening of the simulated ceiling "morning", arrived with a soft hum from the ventilation system and the faint clatter of something shifting in the tiny kitchenette.

Callum blinked awake, momentarily disoriented.

Ailín slept between him and Lila, curled tightly into Callum's arm. Her breathing was steady, calm, even. More peaceful than any night they'd spent since the hospital. Lila still slept too, one hand resting protectively over Ailín's shoulder.

For a moment, he simply lay there, a rare feeling settling into his chest.

Warmth. Safety. Normalcy.

It wouldn't last.

It never did.

Careful not to wake them, Callum eased himself out of bed and padded into the main living space. He expected to find the bunker empty. Instead, he found Arthis sitting on the couch.

Callum froze.

"…Arthis?"

The Archivist sat perfectly still, hands folded, expression

unreadable. He wasn't breathing heavily. He didn't even look winded, as if he'd simply materialized there without walking through the reinforced entry.

He nodded once.

"Good morning, Callum MacLeod."

Callum blinked.

"I thought you left."

"I did," Arthis said calmly.

"But I needed to speak with you before my path takes me further from yours."

Callum rubbed his face.

"You walked in through the hatch?"

"No," Arthis said.

Callum frowned.

"Then how, "

Arthis lifted a single hand.

"There are old ways. And old permissions."

Callum didn't like the sound of that.

He sat slowly across from him.

"What's going on?"

Arthis studied him with that unsettling sense of ancient patience.

"Something is shifting. Across the continent. A resonance disturbance unlike anything I have felt in centuries."

Callum stiffened.

"Boroun?"

Arthis shook his head.

"No. This is not his rage."

Callum leaned forward.

"Then what?"

Arthis lowered his gaze slightly, as though reluctant to speak.

"Another Immortal."

Callum's stomach tightened.

"Who?"

Arthis's eyes softened with something like concern.

"One who should not have been able to sense you."

A pulse of cold rippled down Callum's spine.

He in low tone,

"Arkael?"

Arthis shook his head.

"No. But someone from the age after him."

Someone old enough to read resonance the way a scholar reads text. They cast their spark across the night and felt yours in return."

Callum swallowed.

"And they're coming."

"Yes," Arthis said simply.

"They are coming."

The world tilted.

Another ancient Immortal, older than Methos, older than Cadigan, older than Arthis, moving across the world toward them?

Callum's voice was low.

"Why me?"

Arthis answered immediately.

"Because of what is inside you. Because you carry an echo of the First. And because an Immortal who feels such a thing cannot ignore it."

He stood slowly.

"I came to warn you. And to remind you that hiding is only a pause, not an escape."

Callum bristled.

"I know that."

Arthis placed a light hand on his shoulder.

"You have days. Perhaps less."

Callum exhaled shakily.

"And who is this Immortal?"

Arthis's expression darkened.

"An old hunter. Not Renwick. Not Watcher. Not aligned with Boroun."

He paused.

"But someone who has spent far too long looking for a spark to justify their existence."

Callum frowned.

"That doesn't explain anything."

Arthis met his gaze with clear finality.

"You will know him when he finds you."

Callum opened his mouth to ask more,
But the bunker lights flickered once.
Just once.
And Arthis was gone.
No footsteps. No sound. No resonance.
Gone.
As though the earth swallowed him whole.
Callum stood very still.
The warmth of the bunker felt thinner now.
More fragile.
Ailín emerged from the hallway rubbing her eyes.
"Callum...? Who were you talking to...?"
He turned toward her, heart steadying.
"Just someone passing through."
She walked to him, leaning against his leg.
"Are we safe?"
Callum looked at the sealed hatch.
The reinforced walls.
The duffel bag containing THOTH.
Then he looked down at Ailín's small hand gripping his.
"Yes," he said softly.
"Right now, we are."
Whether they would be tomorrow...
that was a different question.

Callum spent several minutes standing in the quiet main room after
Arthis vanished, trying to steady the unnerving sensation in his chest.
It wasn't fear exactly, he'd felt fear in the tunnels, felt it on the island,
felt it when Boroun bellowed his name from beneath collapsing stone.
This was different.

This felt like recognition.

Ailín leaned into him again, thumb pressed tiredly to her lips.
"Callum...? You feel strange."
He knelt, brushing her hair gently.
"Strange how?"
She pressed her small hand against his chest.
"You're humming."
Callum froze.

"My spark?"

She nodded.

"It woke up again."

He forced a slow breath.

"Just tired, little one. That's all."

She studied him with unnervingly perceptive eyes, for all her innocence, the resonance inside her had sharpened her senses in ways he still didn't understand.

"You're pretending."

Callum didn't deny it.

She wrapped both arms around his neck, and he lifted her easily, holding her close.

"You don't have to protect me from everything," she said quietly into his shoulder.

He closed his eyes.

"Yes, I do."

Lila entered the room moments later, rubbing sleep from her eyes.

"Callum...?" She glanced around. "Who were you talking to?"

Callum hesitated.

"Arthis came back."

Lila blinked, startled awake.

"What? When?"

"Just now. He didn't stay long."

She stepped closer, worry sharpening the lines around her eyes.

"What did he say?"

Callum's jaw tightened.

"He said someone else is coming. Not Boroun. Not Renwick."

Lila's breath caught.

"Someone... older?"

"Older," Callum repeated softly. "Older and attuned enough to feel me from across the continent."

Lila ran a hand through her hair.

"Jesus, Callum..."

Ailín tugged on Lila's sleeve.

"He's not the angry one. But he's... watching."

Lila knelt down, cupping Ailín's cheeks.

"Sweetheart, how do you know that?"

Ailín pointed to her heart.

"I can feel sparks if they're close enough. And this one is... curious."

Callum set Ailín gently at the dining table, where she began drawing on a scrap of old notebook paper she found near the control room. The girl doodled a lumpy-looking shape Callum suspected might be the resonance capsule, complete with stone glyphs and crooked waves.

Lila joined Callum in the living space.

"We need to reinforce the bunker."

Callum nodded.

"I know. We're protected from digital surveillance. THOTH is shielded. But physical detection..."

"Well," Lila said, glancing up at the several feet of earth overhead, "that part isn't impossible. Just difficult."

Callum ran a hand over his jaw.

"We need a perimeter. We need fallback rooms. We need escape routes. We need... time."

Lila touched his arm.

"We'll get time."

Callum gave a humorless laugh.

"We're Immortals living in a hole in the ground. Time's the only thing we don't have for once."

As the simulation lights brightened into "afternoon," Callum wandered into the old control center. The room hummed with silence, THOTH's sphere tucked into the bottom safe, dormant, quiet, undetectable.

Callum sat at the old metal desk, staring at the locked duffel bag.

Then at the wall behind it.

He whispered, "Who are you...?"

He felt it again, faint, like static brushing across a radio band. Not Boroun's rage. Not THOTH's hum. Not Ailín's spark.

A ripple of resonance brushing across his own.

Callum stood so fast the chair skidded behind him.

"Callum?" Lila rushed in. "What happened?"

He forced a steady voice.

"Nothing. Just... old ghosts."

She stared at him for a long, unblinking moment.

"You're lying again."

Callum swallowed.

"We need to lay low. We need to reinforce. And we need to be ready."

"For what?"

Callum stared at the safe where THOTH rested.

"For the fact that Boroun wasn't the last nightmare waiting for us."

Ailín appeared in the doorway holding her drawing.

"Callum?"

He knelt.

"Yes?"

She held up the crayon drawing.

"I made this for you."

It was crude, sweet, and unsettling.

Callum recognized the shapes immediately.

One was him, sword in hand.

Another was Ailín, small, smiling.

A third was Lila.

A fourth... was a tall, thin figure shrouded in darkness, spark glowing faintly.

Callum's chest tightened.

"Ailín... who is that?"

"The man who is coming."

Callum swallowed.

"Do you know him?"

She shook her head.

"No. But he knows you."

The bunker felt smaller. The air heavier. The silence louder.

Ailín crawled into his lap.

"Don't let him find us."

Callum wrapped his arms around her.

"I won't."

He didn't say *I promise.*

He couldn't.

But he held her until the tremor in her shoulders stopped.

Callum spent the next hour walking every corridor of the bunker, alone, silent, methodical. The turbine-hum of the ventilation system echoed faintly off the concrete walls. He drifted into each room, checking the seams of the blast doors, the latches on the old storage compartments, the emergency generators embedded beneath steel grates.

Lila watched him from the threshold.

"You're doing that thing again," she said quietly.

"What thing?"

Lila crossed her arms.

"The one where you pretend you're inspecting equipment, but really you're trying not to panic."

Callum exhaled through his nose, continuing to run a hand over an old junction box.

"I'm not panicking."

"Then what would you call it?" she asked.

He paused.

"Preparing."

She stepped closer, lowering her voice.

"We just got here, Callum. You haven't slept more than a few hours since the island. You're exhausted."

"I don't get to be exhausted."

"Yes," she said firmly. "You do."

He turned, meeting her gaze.

"There's someone coming. Someone ancient, someone who can feel my spark across a continent. I don't know who they are. I don't know what they want. And after everything we just survived, after Ailín barely made it out alive, I am not letting anything else near her."

Lila softened, but she didn't back down.

"Then we prepare together. You're not doing this alone."

Callum rubbed his eyes.

"I don't even know where to start."

Lila took his hand.

"Yes, you do. You've been doing it all your life. You adapt. You survive. You protect."

He stared at her, really stared, and the tightness in his chest loosened just a fraction.

Then Ailín's voice echoed from the living room.

"Callum?"

He and Lila turned.

Ailín stood by the couch, one hand clutching the blanket around her shoulders, the other rubbing her eyes.

"Callum... the buzzing came back."

Callum's pulse jumped.

"What kind of buzzing?"

Ailín pointed toward the ceiling, toward the multiple layers of reinforced steel and earth above them.

"Like someone's walking across the sky."

Callum stiffened.

Lila paled.

"Renwick?"

Callum shook his head.

"No. Renwick doesn't have the spark. And his drones couldn't scan through this much earth."

Ailín tugged his sleeve urgently.

"He's looking now. Right now."

Callum knelt in front of her.

"Ailín. Listen to me. You're safe. Nothing can get through these walls."

She pressed her small hand to her heart.

"But he's getting closer."

Lila took a shaky breath.

"Callum... what if this Immortal isn't coming to fight? What if he's coming because he thinks Callum is the First reborn? Or something worse?"

Callum frowned.

"Why would that matter?"

"Because," Lila said softly, "your spark is changing. Arthis said it. Ailín feels it. Even THOTH sensed anomalies before we powered him down. What if the wrong Immortal interprets that as a threat? Or an opportunity?"

Callum didn't answer.

He stood, scooped Ailín gently into his arms, and paced slowly through the bunker.

"We need to create a resonance mask," he said. "Something to hide her spark. And mine."

Lila frowned.

"How? Without THOTH?"

Callum looked toward the storage room.

"...we improvise."

The bunker had been stocked for decades, complete with Faraday mesh sheets, lead-lined thermal blankets, old copper shielding from military-grade electronics, and vibration-dampening panels from the original silo construction.

Callum spread everything across the floor like a man assembling armor from scraps.

Ailín sat cross-legged beside him, watching curiously.

Lila crouched down.

"What exactly are we making?"

"Not a barrier," Callum murmured. "We can't block resonance entirely. But we can disrupt signal patterns. Make our sparks look... dull. Unremarkable. Like background noise."

Lila raised a brow.

"And you know how to do that?"

"No," Callum admitted. "But Cadigan taught me a few things about confusing Watcher drones. And resonance isn't that different. Same idea. Different wavelength."

Lila smirked.

"You're terrifying when you get creative."

Ailín tugged Callum's sleeve.

"Can I help?"

He hesitated.

Then nodded.

"Yes. I'll need your spark for calibration. Just... carefully."

Ailín placed her small palm on the copper sheet.

A faint shimmer rippled across her skin.

Lila gasped.

Callum leaned forward.

"That's it… just like that… good girl…"

He moved the copper panel slightly. The shimmer vibrated, then dispersed.

"We're masking the frequency," Callum said. "Not blocking it. Hiding her spark in the ambient noise."

Ailín tilted her head.

"Like whispering in a storm?"

He smiled.

"Exactly."

Lila let out a relieved breath.

"You're good at this."

Callum didn't look up.

"I don't have a choice."

Just as Callum positioned the final panel,

Ailín froze.

"Callum."

Her voice was thin. Shaken. Afraid.

Callum knelt.

"What is it?"

She pressed both hands to her head.

"He's closer."

Callum stiffened.

"How close?"

Ailín's voice trembled.

"He's…he's in America."

The bunker went silent.

Lila's breath hitched.

"Callum…"

He stood slowly.

"Alright. Then we move faster."

He lifted Ailín into his arms, pressing her tight to his chest.

"Tomorrow, we do a full sweep of the bunker. Reinforce the hatch. Reinforce the ventilation. Build blind spots. Map safe rooms."

Lila nodded.

"And tonight?"

Callum looked toward the sealed hatch above them.

Then toward the control room where THOTH rested in deep-silence.

"Tonight," he said softly, "we stay close. We stay quiet. And we wait."

He felt it then,

A pulse. Subtle. Far away.

But real.

Another Immortal's spark brushing the edges of his own.

Not a threat Not yet.

Just a presence.

Searching.

"Not here. Not tonight."

The resonance faded, But not completely.

Ailín pressed her forehead to his collar.

"He's thinking about you."

Callum swallowed hard.

"Let him think."

He kissed the top of her head.

"That's all he'll get."

Night settled over the Montana plains like a heavy blanket. The wind outside the bunker roared softly against the hatch and the old shed above, but down here, beneath thirty feet of reinforced earth, everything was muted to a low, steady hum.

Callum stood alone in the dim corridor leading toward the old launch control center. His hand rested on the cold steel of the locked door where THOTH lay dormant, deep-silenced behind layers of shielding.

Not yet, he told himself. Not until he could rebuild the AI without giving Renwick the faintest hint of a signal.

Not until they were ready.

He pressed his forehead briefly against the cold metal and closed his eyes.

A spark, faint as a dying ember, brushed across his consciousness.

The same searching presence as before.

The unknown Immortal.

Closer now. More focused.

Like a hunter scenting the air. Not yet within striking distance, but no longer a distant thought drifting across the continent.

Callum clenched his jaw.

"Not here, not tonight."

Lila's footsteps approached from behind.

"Couldn't sleep either?"

Callum straightened slowly.

"No."

She stopped beside him, leaning her shoulder gently against his.

"You felt it again."

He nodded.

"He's moving faster."

Lila frowned, arms crossing over her chest.

"Methos and Cadigan are out there. What if he runs into them first?"

"Then one of two things happens," Callum said softly. "Either he ignores them, because he's focused on me, or he tests them."

Lila swallowed.

"Methos can handle himself."

"That's what worries me," Callum murmured.

Her eyes widened.

"You think this Immortal might be older?"

Callum didn't answer immediately.

He stared at the dark steel door ahead of them.

"He brushed my spark like someone testing the air. Someone who's done it before. That means experience. Power. Age."

Lila's voice lowered to a whisper.

"And intent."

Callum nodded.

"And intent."

They walked back toward the main room.

Ailín slept soundly on the couch wrapped in her blanket, her tiny chest rising and falling in a steady rhythm. She'd insisted on sleeping there tonight, saying she felt "closer" to them in the open space. Callum had agreed without argument.

Lila paused, watching the girl fondly.

"She's the bravest child I've ever met."

Callum brushed a stray curl from Ailín's forehead.

"She shouldn't have to be."

"None of us should, but here we are."

She turned to him, voice barely audible.

"What are you feeling right now?"

Callum slowly sank into the armchair facing the couch.

"I feel like we're standing still while something ancient is walking toward us."

Lila sat across from him.

"And?"

"And I don't know if it's coming to help… or to destroy."

Her eyes softened.

"You're allowed to be afraid."

Callum shook his head.

"No. I don't have that luxury."

Lila reached across the space and placed her hand over his.

"You do. That's what makes you better than the things chasing you."

Callum hesitated… then let her fingers interlace with his.

Ailín shifted, mumbling something inaudible in her sleep.

Lila took a pause, "Look at her. She trusts you more than anything in this world. And I do too."

Callum met her eyes.

Something warm flickered there, fragile, unfamiliar, but real.

"Thank you," he said quietly.

Lila smiled gently.

"For what?"

"For staying."

Her breath caught.

"I made my choice."

Callum rose and checked the hatch one last time. The reinforced steel was cool and silent under his palm. Above it, the shed, weather-beaten and nondescript, was hidden beneath the prairie night.

He turned back toward Lila.

"Tomorrow, we reinforce the perimeter. Strengthen the internal barriers. Build safe zones. I'll start on THOTH's hardware."

Lila nodded.

"And I'll inventory everything we have. Map the structure. Plan our rotation."

He gave a grateful half-smile.

"You're a good partner."

She crossed her arms playfully.

"I know."

Then,

She stepped forward, close enough that their shoulders brushed.

"You're not alone in this, Callum. Not anymore."

He held her gaze.

"And I'm not letting anything take you. Or her."

Lila touched his chest lightly.

"Then rest. We'll need your strength."

He nodded... slowly... reluctantly.

Together, they dimmed the bunker lights until only a soft amber glow remained.

Callum lay down beside Ailín on the couch, one arm protectively draped over the child. Lila curled up in the armchair nearby, blanket pulled to her chin.

Before his eyes closed, Callum whispered, "You won't touch us. You won't find us."

But in the deep quiet of the Montana night, from some unseen point far across the land, the faint spark brushed his again.

Searching.

Growing closer.

Chapter 32

The next morning, the simulated lights warmed slowly to life in the ceiling panels, blooming from amber dusk into soft morning gold. Callum woke to the gentle hum of the bunker's air system and the warmth of Ailín pressed against his side. Lila slept curled on the chair a few feet away, blanket tangled around her legs, hair spilling in dark waves across her shoulders.

For a moment, Callum allowed himself the luxury of stillness.

Only the faint hiss of circulation fans and the soft weight of a child's breath against his arm.

He would remember this moment. Because moments like these do not survive long in the life of an Immortal.

Ailín stirred, murmuring something half-dreamed. Her fingers curled around his shirt.

"Callum...?"

He smoothed her hair.

"I'm here."

Her eyes opened, silver catching the false morning light.

"Is he gone?"

Callum hesitated.

"Who?"

"The man who's coming."

Callum's heart tensed.

"Yes," he said softly. "He's far away."

She studied his face for a long second.

"You didn't say 'gone.'"

He swallowed.

"No. I didn't."

Ailín nodded sleepily, like she understood more than any child her age should. She curled into his side again, small and warm.

Lila stretched in the chair.

"Morning," she said, voice thick with sleep.

Callum looked up.

"Morning."

"You two okay?"

"We're alright," he said.

Ailín looked up and nodded.

"For now."

Lila exhaled.

"We'll take 'for now.'"

She stood, stretching, wincing slightly at the stiffness in her back.

"Alright," she said. "Today, we reinforce this place properly. That's the plan."

Callum nodded slowly.

"Then let's start."

The hours after breakfast were slow, methodical, and necessary.

For the first time since the island collapsed around them, their work was tangible. Practical. Not desperate, not frantic, but purposeful.

Callum felt the shift in his chest. A change from survival to preparation.

He walked Lila through the structure of the old Minuteman control center, the thickest reinforced concrete ever poured in the United States, meant to endure firestorms and shockwaves that could flatten cities.

They reinforced the ventilation grates, the hatch locks, the narrow emergency stairwell, the entry corridor, and the blast doors leading deeper into the bunker.

Ailín helped by handing tools to Callum. She did so with solemn determination, like this was an important mission.

It was.

At one point, she held a copper cable, tilting her head.

"This one feels warm."

Lila glanced at Callum.

"She feels resonance through copper?"

Callum nodded.

"She feels resonance through anything."

Ailín beamed.

"I'm good at it."

Lila kissed the top of her head.

"Yes, you are."

Midday, Lila spread a large sheet of paper on the dining table. It was originally meant for emergency logs; she turned it into a top-down map of the bunker.

"Callum, if we had to block the hatch, how long would it take?"

"Eight minutes," Callum said, tightening a coupling on the new locking brackets.

Lila wrote it down.

"And breaking free if someone breaches the ventilation?"

"Three minutes. Maybe two, with the new panels."

She wrote that down too.

"Fallback safe zones if we can't hold the common area?"

"Your room. No windows. Reinforced interior wall. The old server room is better but tighter."

She circled it.

"Escape routes?"

"Back ventilation tunnel," he said. "But only in extreme emergency, it's narrow, and it runs fifty feet before surfacing in an outcrop."

"Still an option," she said.

"And what about THOTH?" she asked.

Callum glanced toward the reinforced control room door.

"He stays down until I rebuild his core modules," he said. "Right now he's a liability. But once he's rebuilt, he'll be our greatest advantage."

Lila nodded.

"So a week. Two weeks?"

"Three," Callum said.

Lila blinked.

"That long?"

"Carefully," Callum said. "Slowly. Quietly. Any sudden activation might ping Renwick's satellites."

Ailín tugged Lila's sleeve.

"THOTH's scared too."

Lila smiled softly.

"We'll keep him safe."

Later, after sealing the last ventilation grate, Callum paused. A faint sensation rippled across the edges of his spark, like a distant hum underfoot.

He froze.

The unknown Immortal again.

Still far. Still faint.

Callum clenched the metal rAilíng hard enough to dent it.

"Damn it."

Lila saw the tension in his shoulders.

"He's closer?"

Callum nodded.

"Not dangerously close. Not yet. But he's... aiming himself."

"At us?"

"At me."

Ailín looked up from coloring.

"He's making lines," she said softly.

Callum turned.

"What kind of lines?"

She drew in the air with her finger, drifting curves that spiraled gently before straightening.

"Lines like the tunnel. But not a tunnel. A path."

Callum knelt beside her.

"A path from where?"

She pointed toward the west, and whispered, "From the ocean."

Callum's blood froze.

From the Pacific.

Lila's voice broke the silence.

"Callum… what does that mean?"

He stared at Ailín.

Then toward the thick steel walls.

"It means," he said, voice low and controlled, "we don't have as much time as I thought."

They reinforced until evening.

Then they stopped only because exhaustion forced them to.

Callum tucked Ailín into her bed, brushed her hair back, and kissed her forehead.

She pulled him close, whispering:

"When he comes, I'll know."

"I know," Callum whispered back. "Rest now, little one."

Ailín nodded and let her eyes close.

Callum stood in the doorway, watching her breathe.

Lila touched his arm gently.

The unknown Immortal was far.

But not far enough.

For now, the bunker held.

For now, they had peace.

For now, they were a family.

But Callum could feel it in his bones,

The storm was already on its way.

HELIOS DYNAMICS
ADVANCED SYSTEMS DIVISION

CONFIDENTIAL – INTERNAL DISTRIBUTION ONLY

Document HD-ASD-FENRIR-OVERVIEW-V1.4

F.E.N.R.I.R.
Focused Engagement & Neutralization Recon-Integrated Rotorcraft
"Precision in Silence. Power in Shadow."

Program Summary
The F.E.N.R.I.R. Platform represents Helios Dynamics' next-generation vertical-lift system designed for **stealth interdiction, rapid-response extraction, and multi-spectrum reconnaissance**. Developed under the Advanced Systems Division's "Quiet Sky" initiative, FENRIR integrates experimental acoustic suppression, hardened signal obfuscation, and resonance-adaptive composite armor.
The platform strengthens Helios Dynamics' role as the global leader in defense-adjacent aerospace innovation without exposure to conventional procurement channels. FENRIR's systems seamlessly integrate with the THOTH architecture, allowing quantum-precision navigation, encrypted sensor fusion, and autonomous threat prioritization.

Mission Profile
Primary Roles:
Precision interdiction in contested airspace
Extraction of high-value personnel under restricted visibility
Silent insertion for intelligence or reconnaissance operations
Counter-surveillance and signal denial in hostile environments
Secondary Roles:
Overwatch and air dominance support
Multi-vector EM anomaly detection
Deep-terrain penetration without satellite dependence

Key Features
Acoustic Suppression Matrix (ASM-3):
Near-zero audible signature at 300 meters; broad-spectrum dampening across rotor harmonics.

Resonance-Adaptive Armor (RAA-2):
Composite shell capable of absorbing and redistributing kinetic energy while reducing thermal visibility.
THOTH-Linked Sensor Suite:
Includes multispectral lidar, micro-doppler threat tagging, EM substrate scanning, real-time anomaly prediction.
AEGIS-Silent Uplink:
A proprietary Helios Dynamics low-probability-of-intercept communications spine.
Variable Geometry Rotor System (VGR-9):
Adaptive pitch blades capable of urban micro-maneuvering and near-hover silent transitions.

Platform Philosophy
FENRIR is engineered around a simple guiding principle:
"The battlefield belongs to whoever is seen last."
Whether used for reconnaissance, insertion, or surgical neutralization, the FENRIR platform provides operators the tools to act decisively in environments where detection equals defeat.

Operational Integrity
Only personnel cleared under **Helios Protocol SABLE-BLACK** may access cockpit systems or pilot training modules. THOTH-linked navigation requires biometric and emotional-state verification to prevent compromise or unauthorized interface.

Author's Afterword

Stories are strange things. They begin quietly, often long before the first word ever reaches the page. This one began with a spark, an image, a voice, a man who had lived too many centuries but still found himself caught between the past he couldn't bury and the future he feared he wouldn't survive.

Callum MacLeod arrived fully formed, not as a hero, but as a survivor. A man shaped by hundreds of years of loss, discipline, and restraint. Yet the moment he stepped out of the shadows and onto the edge of Vandenberg's cliffs, I knew he was walking toward a collision between ancient myth and the modern world. And I knew he couldn't walk that path alone.

Lila Serrano stepped in as his unexpected anchor, a mortal with more courage than sense, more heart than fear. Ailín followed as the spark of wonder, innocence, and mystery that forced Callum to be something more than a solitary blade in the dark. Methos, Cadigan, Arthis, Renwick, each arrived, not as side figures, but as forces of their own. Fractured loyalties. Ancient grudges. Forgotten histories. Their voices shaped the direction of the story as much as the plot itself.

This book became something larger than a simple clash of Immortals. It became a story about found family, the burden of immortality, the danger of ambition, and the question at the heart of every hero's journey:

What do you protect when the world demands you stand alone?

Callum's answer isn't perfect. It isn't simple. It isn't clean. But it's honest, and it will continue to evolve.

As the Veil begins to tear and the rules of the Game unravel, the world that Callum, Lila, Ailín, and their uneasy allies step into is one where nothing is certain. Not even immortality. Renwick's transformation, the awakening of ancient forces, and the approach of an Immortal whose presence echoes across the ocean, all of these threads will shape what lies ahead.

And if there's one truth I hope lingers after the final page of this book, it's this:

Even immortals fear what they cannot outrun. But love, in any form, is the one thing worth fighting for, even when it hurts.

Thank you for walking through this world with these characters. Thank you for giving them your time, your attention, and your imagination. Book Two is already waiting on the horizon, and the storm is only beginning to gather.

K. A. Beaulieu

Preview of Book 2
The Next Callum MacLeod Adventure

Book 2
Prologue

The waves hammered the cliffs in long, rolling strikes as dawn teetered on the edge of the horizon, a thin band of pale gold struggling to break through the mist. Cape Flattery was a lonely place, the kind of edge-of-the-world isolation Kael MacGregor remembered from a hundred lifetimes before. A place where the land breathed slowly, where the earth still whispered of old things.

He stood still and silent, boots planted on the wet stone, listening to the hum beneath reality itself. The Veil had grown thin. Too thin.

And somewhere across the vast spine of the continent...

Callum MacLeod's spark whispered back.

Clan MacLeod.

Descendants of warriors Kael had known well.

Men who once stood beside his own people, the outlawed and exiled Clan MacGregor, whose blood had written itself across Scottish history through rebellion, loyalty, and relentless ferocity.

Kael inhaled the cold Pacific air.

So much had changed in four thousand years.

But the Game, the endless dance of Immortals, had not.

Another ripple shuddered across the land, faint but undeniable.

Arkael's echo... inside him.

The MacLeod boy carried it.

A dangerous weight for any Immortal, let alone one still learning his true place in the world.

Kael turned from the sea and began walking inland, slow, deliberate, as if the ground itself needed time to remember his tread.

That was when he felt it. A spark. Close.

It was not Callum.

No… this one was young.

Reckless.

Kael exhaled.

"So the game continues," he murmured.

The sensation sharpened, resolving into a direction. A presence. A challenge.

Kael stepped into the tree line, moving between dripping cedars and shadowed trunks. The forest was quiet, unnaturally so. Even the birds had fallen silent.

A figure stepped out from behind a moss-draped boulder fifty feet ahead.

Dark coat.

Sword already drawn.

Eyes flickering with the anxiety of someone who believed the world owed him something.

He couldn't have been more than sixty years into his Immortal life, young by their standards, barely past the arrogant bravado that early Quickening victories tended to breed.

He raised his blade.

"Kael MacGregor," the man said voice steady, hand trembling. "I challenge you."

Kael slowed to a halt.

"Name," he said quietly.

The man swallowed, raising his chin with forced confidence.

"Evander Holt."

Kael nodded once. He'd never heard it.

Most likely a wanderer, hoping his first true trophy would be a legend.

"I dinnae seek a fight," Kael said. "Walk away, lad. Live another century."

Evander's eyes hardened.

"No. If I take your head, they'll speak my name for a thousand years."

Kael sighed.

"You wouldnae last a thousand seconds."

Evander lunged.

Young Immortals always lunged.

Kael slipped aside, movement fluid as water, coat brushing across the forest floor. Evander struck again, wild, untested strength thrown behind each blow. His sword carved fresh bark from a cedar trunk as Kael stepped backward, examining him with the faint annoyance of a man inspecting a cracked blade.

"Your stance is too high," Kael said. "Your footwork's sloppy."

Evander snarled and swung low.

Kael caught the strike on the steel of a hidden short-sword drawn with faster-than-human precision. Sparks flared. Evander stumbled at the impact.

Kael didn't.

"Stop this," Kael warned, voice quiet but sharp as the blade in his hand. "You're not ready."

Evander screamed and rushed forward in a flurry of blind rage.

Kael pivoted, sidestepped, and in a single, effortless motion, swept his sword across Evander's midline, knocking him off balance. Before the younger Immortal recovered, Kael's hand gripped his coat, dragging him forward.

Their foreheads almost touched.

"You should've listened," Kael whispered.

One clean motion.

One downward stroke.

Evander Holt never felt the ground.

His body hit the moss with a muted thump.

His head rolled in the opposite direction.

Silence.

Then the storm came.

The Quickening tore through the trees, lightning bursting from the canopy, branches rattling as wind surged in all directions. Energy spiraled through Kael's body, raw and desperate, clawing its way into his veins.

Kael stood motionless, jaw locked against the surge, until the last crackle of power sank into the earth… leaving only the smell of rain-soaked ozone.

He knelt for a moment beside the fallen Immortal.

"I warned ye, lad," Kael murmured.

He rose, wiping rain from his brow.

More crackles danced across the sky, too distant for mortals to see, too faint for any normal Immortal to sense.

But Kael felt them.

Callum MacLeod's spark…

changing.

Growing.

Becoming something the world wasn't ready for.

Kael sheathed his blade beneath his coat and turned deeper into the forest.

"Hold fast, MacLeod," he whispered.

"Yer clan has stood with mine since before the crowns outlawed our names."

He stepped into the mist.

"I'm coming."

K. A. Beaulieu is an established nonfiction author whose previous work has focused on leadership, complex systems, and the operational realities of modern institutions. His writing is known for its clarity, precision, and ability to translate intricate processes into compelling, accessible narratives. With this novel, he steps into the world of fiction for the first time, blending decades of analytical experience with a lifelong passion for epic storytelling. A United States Air Force veteran and longtime strategist in academic and technical environments, he brings a grounded sense of realism to high-concept adventure, crafting characters and worlds shaped by discipline, resilience, and mystery. This debut marks the beginning of a new creative chapter - one that merges his talent for detail with a deep love of mythology, history, and cinematic storytelling.